THE
PELICAN
TIDE

THE PELICAN TIDE

A Novel

SHARON J. WISHNOW

LAKE UNION
PUBLISHING

Text copyright © 2024 by Sharon J. Ritchey
All rights reserved.

No part of this book may be reproduced, or stored in a retrieval system, or transmitted in any form or by any means, electronic, mechanical, photocopying, recording, or otherwise, without express written permission of the publisher.

Published by Lake Union Publishing, Seattle

www.apub.com

Amazon, the Amazon logo, and Lake Union Publishing are trademarks of Amazon.com, Inc., or its affiliates.

ISBN-13: 9781662518492 (paperback)
ISBN-13: 9781662518485 (digital)

Cover design by Eileen Carey
Cover images: © Stephen Saks Photography / Alamy; © PANG WRP / Shutterstock; © VladimirCeresnak / Shutterstock; © Caroline Ryan / Shutterstock; © Suzanne Tucker / Shutterstock

Printed in the United States of America

To my mother, Doris Wishnow, my first and best cheerleader
In memory of Josephine Francois

The world, we are told, was made especially for man—a presumption not supported by all the facts.
—John Muir

At a time when so many species of wildlife are threatened, we once in a while have an opportunity to celebrate an amazing success story. Today is such a day. The brown pelican is back!
—Secretary of the Interior Ken Salazar,
November 11, 2009

Chapter 1

Chef Josie Babineaux shook a bowl of flour over hot oil in her grandmother's cast-iron roux pot. The flour sizzled as it made contact, and tiny bubbles danced around the edges, releasing its nutty toasted-bread essence. With a practiced hand, she mixed the flour with her roux paddle like she was on a mission, and she was.

In two hours, a food critic and a photographer from *Vacation Ventures* were interviewing her, the spice queen of the bayou, for the magazine's cover story. At least that's what the editor had crowned her last month, when she told Josie they'd selected Odeal's as the 2010 Island Restaurant of the Year. This wasn't the first accolade that her family's restaurant had earned over the past decade. Josie proudly displayed the small write-ups in Zagat, *Southern Living*, and *Gourmet* as if she had won a Michelin Star.

Vacation Ventures' glossy pages, prestige, and dedicated readers were the miracle Josie needed. The international publicity, combined with the full calendar of fishing rodeos and events planned for Grand Isle, would fill the restaurant, making this tourist season the turning point to pull her out of the financial death spiral her husband, Brian, had plunged the family into. But she had no time today to worry about Brian. He was six months in her rearview mirror.

Today, her passion for feeding people mattered most. She'd cook off-menu anytime someone in their tiny Grand Isle community needed a special dish to brighten their day. Food was Josie's love language.

She smashed a lump of stubborn flour, splashing the thickening roux onto her forearm. "Ouch." She shook her arm from the sting. Roux was weaponized wheat.

A firm, warm hand landed on her shoulder and gently pulled her back. "Hey, hon. We have a gallon of roux in the refrigerator. More than enough for today and tomorrow," Maisy Phillips said.

As Josie's sous-chef, Maisy was a force in and out of the kitchen, towering over her at five foot ten. The long butcher's aprons the kitchen staff wore stopped at her knees. She styled her hair in waist-length braids with gold-tone braid rings, pulled back while she cooked.

"You're right. But . . . it's almost done." Josie switched the paddle between hands and scraped the edges of the pot. No one remembered where the cast-iron pot came from. It'd been there as long as they could remember. The heavy metal was coal black from use and looked like a cross between a witch's cauldron and something you'd hang from a campfire spit.

She surveyed her busy kitchen. Linh Nguyen stood on a stool to reach her prep counter. Her white-haired head bent over a tray of baby vegetables as her nimble fingers turned each one into an edible masterpiece. Josie had asked her now-retired friend to come help prepare for today.

Josie's son, Toby, hefted a blue bucket of ice, with a mound of lumpy oysters threatening to spill over. The kitchen aprons, too short on Maisy, used to sweep the floor on his eleven-year-old body. But not anymore. He had shot up like a stalk of okra since winter. The only sweep left was his dark hair hovering over his brown eyes. He needed a haircut. A chore for Brian this weekend. He should at least be able to manage that.

Without looking away from the roux, she said, "Hey, *cher*, where's your mesh glove?"

"I'm not a baby." Toby crossed his arms over his puffed-out chest, contradicting his words.

Josie flicked off the gas under her roux, held her left hand an inch from his nose, and lowered her voice. "I was twelve when I got this scar from an oyster knife." *I damn near lost the use of my hand.*

He rolled his eyes. "You've told me like a million times."

She rested her hand on his head. "Be grateful I don't roll your whole body in stainless steel mesh."

"Haul that bucket to the prep sink. I'll supervise," Maisy said.

"I can shuck oysters," Toby grumbled.

"All new chefs are supervised in the kitchen. You're fast with that blade, even *with* the glove, but I'm not ready to leave you alone either."

Toby softened under Maisy's words. "I guess."

Linh chuckled. She had rocked Josie's kids to sleep when they were babies.

Maisy stood over Josie with her fists resting on her hips.

"What?" Josie asked.

She put her hands on Josie's shoulders and spun her toward the door. "Take a minute, out there." She pointed. Then, in a stage whisper, added, "Before someone gets ugly." That was Maisy's not-too-subtle reminder that she needed to pull herself together.

"Right." Josie wiped her hands on a kitchen towel. She had skipped her morning beach run, and now her body was overcharged like a lightning bolt seeking a path to ground. "The kitchen's yours."

Josie removed her apron and smoothed the chef's jacket she had bleached within an inch of its existence for today. It was the newest of the old chef whites. She patted her light-brown hair, tightly twisted into a bun. In a nod to glam, she wore her best friend Louise's diamond studs. She rubbed her finger along the scar at the edge of her mouth. She'd have to remember to tilt her head away from the camera to hide it.

Josie walked into the dining room. The waitstaff had cleaned the tables after the lunch service. Maisy suggested they close for the rest of the day for the magazine interview. Closing was the logical decision, but Josie couldn't afford an empty restaurant on a Sunday night.

Odeal's Sunday Suppers had been an island mainstay since the 1930s. People brought their fresh catch, and the restaurant would prepare it with all the sides. Sunday Suppers carried the restaurant through the Depression, the Second World War, and years of bad storms. Josie was in a financial storm. Without Sunday's receipts, she couldn't pay for the extra supplies she had ordered for the photo shoot.

The bigger problem now was that the dining room wasn't at its best. The tables were balanced with matchbooks, the linen was showing its age, and long ago she had stopped being able to afford fresh flowers or tea lights for the tables.

She went to her small desk, wedged between the walk-in refrigerator and the dry storage, and grabbed a handful of black Sharpie markers. She next found her daughter, Minnow, along with her friend Bonnie and the rest of the waitstaff, outside on the marina deck, eating a late lunch.

"Who's ready for a fun job?"

Four faces exchanged knowing glances.

"Whatcha need, Chef?" Bonnie said.

Josie handed out the Sharpies. "I need you to color in all the scuff marks on the chairs and tables."

"For real?" Bonnie said.

"For real." She was doing her best to wrap the restaurant in her version of hospital corners.

A steady breeze wobbled the red café umbrellas, casting dancing shadows. Josie breathed in the ocean. The Gulf water soothed her. She tasted it with each breath and felt it on her skin. The best part of living on an island was that the ocean hugged her from all directions. When

4

she'd left for culinary school in California, she went often to the Pacific, but the cooler water just jangled her. It wasn't like home.

The staff cleared the tables and headed inside. Josie caught Minnow's arm, stopping her before she disappeared too. "You didn't eat lunch?"

At seventeen, her daughter, Minnow, was five foot six, a whisper taller than Josie, but that was where the similarity ended. She was Brian's mini-me with doe-brown eyes, sandy-brown hair highlighted from her days at the beach, and a lean body that bounced with nervous energy. Josie ignored the fact that the Odeal's T-shirt Minnow wore was one size too small. Today, though, she couldn't ignore the hollow in Minnow's collarbone and how it had deepened in the past few months, or the belt cinched tight around her waist.

"I ate some." Minnow shrugged. "Guess I'm anxious about all this working out?" She waved her hand over her head.

You're not the only one.

"I've never been in a magazine before. I'm nervous about this big family photo you said they wanted. The 'generations' of Odeal's." Minnow made air quotes around the word *generations*.

The magazine had asked for a photo with Josie's father, her brother, and the kids. It was lucky Brian was still on the rig. She could avoid the uncomfortable choice of whether to have him in the photo for the sake of the kids.

Josie leaned in to hug her, and Minnow pulled away, a scowl on her face. Josie needed to table her hurt feelings. The hardest reality of her split from Brian was keeping the truth about why she left. Minnow blamed her, and it wasn't fair. Yet Minnow always accepted affection only on her own terms. Lately, those terms were like a prison sentence.

Josie forced a smile, wanting a way to redirect both their moods.

As if she had made a wish, their brown pelican, Gumbo, circled the restaurant and skidded to a lumbering stop on the rear deck, almost tripping over his massive webbed feet. The bird swaggered when he landed, like a dancer with a signature move. He dipped his head side to side at Josie and Minnow and fluffed the crown of golden feathers on

5

his head. The family had rescued him two years ago, after Hurricane Gustav left him, then a fledgling, injured and stranded on the beach. And now, Minnow was his favorite person. She squatted, meeting him face to bill, and scratched behind his long neck.

"Hello, handsome," Minnow said to the pelican.

"If you'd all stop messing with that bird, we wouldn't need this sign," Hughdean said.

He clomped up the deck stairs in his work boots, tattered jeans, and a blue ball cap that covered his reddish-brown hair. He dropped his tool kit and a metal sign he was carrying heavily onto the deck.

"Dumbest thing I've ever been asked to do."

"Hi, Uncle Hughdean."

"Well, hey there, Princess Minnow of the High Seas."

Hughdean was Josie's younger brother and a third owner of the restaurant, along with Josie and their dad.

"Such is the glamorous life of a restaurateur," Josie said.

"Mom, I'm heading in to help." Minnow waved the Sharpie.

"Brian shoulda done this last month," Hughdean mumbled.

Brian should have done a lot of things. Last month and all the months before.

"At least help me."

Josie stood next to Hughdean. "He'll be home tomorrow. You can give him your bill."

Hughdean knew Josie could barely make the restaurant mortgage, buy her supplies, and pay her staff. She hadn't taken a salary for two years, once she discovered Brian's gambling had grown from the occasional pastime to a financial hellfire. Hughdean had, surprisingly, held his tongue on that.

"Hold the sign where you want it," he said, dropping to his knees.

Josie smiled at it. **Do Not Feed the Pelican.** They attached it to the post Gumbo liked the most. He'd perch on top for hours, his long neck tucked into his body with his swordlike bill pointing toward the water, waiting for . . . whatever pelicans waited for.

The deck door banged open. "Mom," Minnow said. "Maisy says you can come back inside. Everything's ready, just the way you want." The sass in her voice was not lost on Josie. "I forgot to tell you, Daddy called. He's staying an extra day on the rig for an award-presentation thing. He's coming home late Tuesday, and he'll pick us up Wednesday, okay?"

"Tuesday, Wednesday." She forced another smile. "I'll take another day with my kiddos."

"Yeah, but that means we have to stay longer at Grandpa's house. No offense, Uncle Hughdean. I love you. I just hate living with you."

"And I hate living with you too." He winked.

"You need to get a move on. You've got to change for the photo and pick up Dad," Josie reminded him.

They walked into the restaurant, and Josie stopped in her tracks.

Where was the hum? The air conditioner made an annoying wheezy hum. It was so loud they had to play a continuous swamp pop music loop to mask it. But it wasn't there now.

Josie pulled a chair over to one of the air returns and placed her hand over it.

Nothing. Just what she needed.

Chapter 2

Deepwater Horizon oil platform, Macondo Prospect, Gulf of Mexico

Monday, April 19, 2010

"Babineaux, what the hell are you doing?"

Brian leaned backward over the yellow safety railing of the Deepwater Horizon to scan the communication tower, where a peregrine falcon perched. The three-level oil platform stood a football field's length above the swirling Gulf of Mexico. He wobbled, dizzy from staring straight up into the blue sky. He adjusted the telephoto lens on his camera, tracking the bird patrolling its hunting ground. It was a rush to try to capture the image from this height. His wits against the falcon. And these days, the falcons were safer than the rush from his old obsession, cards.

The railing was slippery with a fine mist from the pulverized Gulf waters smashing against the rig. He planted his feet and licked his salty ocean-sprayed lips as he pressed the shutter. An ear-piercing peregrine *kack, kack, kack* cry cut through the noise of the ocean. He ducked, the bird's razor-sharp beak barely missing his head.

Brian peered over the railing. Miguel Penman stared up, shading his eyes. At six foot three, Penman was an imposing figure, having to hunch through narrow doorframes and hallways as he and Brian did their maintenance rounds. He kept his hair military short on the sides, but with a length hanging over dark eyes. He joked he could shave twice a day and have a five o'clock shadow by 4:00 p.m.

Penman and Brian had been chasing each other up the oil-industry corporate ladder for a decade. Penman was in the lead, now Brian's supervisor, but only because Brian had left the Deepwater Horizon for another rig and was only recently hired back.

Penman was just off his shift, still dressed in his blue coveralls and yellow hard hat. Next to him stood a lanky man, in his uniform of khaki coveralls with a day's worth of grease in the creases of his dark skin. A roughneck just off work.

"Taking pictures." Brian pointed the camera at the two men. "Smile, assholes."

They laughed, and the camera clicked in rapid succession.

He slung it across his body and climbed down.

"If you kill yourself hanging off railings, you'll ruin our safety record," Penman joked.

He shrugged. "Company life insurance. I'm worth more to my family dead than alive. Hey, I'm Brian." He held out his hand to the other man.

"Tripp," the man said and shook his hand.

Something about Tripp reminded him of the kids he grew up with in Baton Rouge. The ones who'd underestimated him, the scrawny kid they called the "little professor" because his mother taught history. Back then the kids teased everyone out of boredom or to establish their pecking order. He befriended them with his ever-ready deck of cards. That's when he took their money and their power.

"Are you planning on a calendar, *Buff Birds of the Macondo?*" Penman laughed again.

"The only calendar I want is with big tits." Tripp pumped his hand in a squeezing motion.

Brian winced. He'd put money on Tripp not having a teenage daughter.

After today, Brian wouldn't have to deal with him until his next rotation. Soon, he'd be back on the island. He'd called Minnow yesterday to tell her he was coming home a day later than planned. Two BP executives were coming to the rig to celebrate seven years without a significant accident. A grip-and-grin event with cake and photos.

"I understand, Daddy," she had said.

Her calling him *Daddy* gutted him. He was *Dad* when he was home, *Father Dear* as a joke, but *Daddy* when she was sad. He'd been so pressed for time, all he said was he loved her and to tell her brother the same.

This had been a hard twenty-one-day rotation. He'd waited a week for Penman to start his tour and then another forever waiting for equipment that never arrived. But the time he spent with Penman was good. Penman was no stranger to relationship trouble and patiently listened to Brian grouse about Josie and there being no money to fix the restaurant because of him. That the Odeal's sign needed painting. The back door needed a new lock, and the air conditioner was part of an appliance prayer circle.

Despite that, Brian wanted to make it right with her. The first chore on his list when he returned was to coax a little more life out of the restaurant's ancient gas range. A new one would cost as much as her car. It was a small act of contrition compared to what he had done.

"You two off shift?" Brian asked.

"I am," Penman said. "Heading to the mess hall for dinner. Walk with me."

Brian removed his hard hat, letting the air cool the sweat spilling down his neck.

"Josie okay with you staying an extra day?"

"Probably not, but I only had time to tell Minnow."

Penman made a sound.

"What?" Brian asked.

"You're avoiding her."

"Damn straight. I don't have anything to tell her that doesn't cause a fight."

Penman shook his head as they opened the dining room door. The promising smell of baked sugar and chocolate pulled him inside. The sweet scent slammed Brian with thoughts of Josie. Three years ago, he and Josie's brother, Hughdean, had just returned from a Texas Hold'em poker game in Houston. An exclusive invite-only event at a private club. First class all the way. The $200 bets were a rush, but nothing compared to the two grand he won. He kept the winnings from Josie. It was money to play with, like always. When it was gone, the game was over. He came home that quiet off-season January afternoon high from his payout and found Josie singing in the kitchen, flour on her nose. Her happiness, combined with his electric mood, was like a sexy spell. He snuck behind her and untied her apron, and she swatted his hand away. She had distracted him by popping morsels of raw tea cake dough into his mouth, tracing his lips with her sugared fingers.

No sugared fingers here.

Penman stopped at a table of men eating dinner. "Can I see your camera?"

"Sure?" Brian said. "Your hands better be clean." He swapped out the lenses, lifted the strap from around his neck, and handed the camera to him.

Penman whistled. "This is some fine piece of equipment." He held the viewfinder up to his eye.

The marriage counselor he and Josie stopped seeing last year had suggested Brian find a hobby to fill his time: "Boredom is a path to relapse."

"I'm done gambling. I don't need a hobby," he had said.

He'd had an old SLR camera in high school, one of the many things he lost when he left home. He found this camera at a pawnshop. It was an expensive splurge, and the source of the last major fight he had with Josie before she moved out six months ago.

"Maybe I'll buy myself one of these beauties," Penman said. "Let's see if I've got the magic touch. Gentlemen," Penman said, aiming the camera at Brian, "this afternoon I received word that this man has been promoted to offshore facility engineer, starting on his next rotation. Now he's the guy overseeing the guys who fix everything."

The camera clicked, and Penman laughed as the men at the table stood and patted Brian on the back and shook his hand.

Brian needed a moment to register that Penman was talking about him. He had put in for that promotion over a year ago. A burst of excitement warmed his chest. He wasn't a complete fuckup. People trusted him. The next rotation meant a pay raise. Good news to share with Josie. The raise would help repay the loan he'd taken on his retirement account—the short-term bridge, now three years old. He had promised he'd pay the whole amount back when she found out. Then he'd emptied the kids' college funds, practically looking under seat cushions for any spare coins. She'd called him a no-good liar. And she was right. The betting made him into a liar and a thief. He hadn't intended on either. Stealing from his family was his greatest shame. With this raise, a solid tourist season, and the side work he planned, maybe by summer's end Josie wouldn't take her profits to the divorce lawyer.

The men he worked with on the rig were his second family, but how could he have a second family when he had lost his first? Josie was the missing ingredient in his life. He *would* find his way back. Guilt tugged at him again for spending an extra day on the rig to eat cake and applaud with the crew.

Penman waved his hand in front of Brian's face. "I lost you there. Where'd you go, daydreaming?"

"Nowhere." Brian shrugged.

"You're already spending that pay raise?"

Brian laughed. "I've got two kids. They spend every penny I earn." *And I spent every penny that was theirs.*

"You're still a good daddy." Penman clapped him on the back. *Daddy.*

Chapter 3

Wednesday, April 21, 2010

6:00 a.m.

Josie left a covered plate of ham-and-egg breakfast sandwiches on the kitchen table to encourage Minnow to eat. Yesterday she'd baked Minnow's favorite blueberry muffins. She was thinking of other sweets too. Maisy had flats of strawberries arriving today. Josie could turn them into shortcake or strawberry ice cream. Who could resist that?

Josie remembered family reunions with cousins, hand cranking a six-quart ice cream bucket by the picnic table, music playing, and her mother in a rare happy mood.

She eased her body through the squeaking back porch door of her dad Daniel Dean's house. Below, the picnic table had turned gray and was starting to split, signs of the island's corrosive sea air. The salt pummeled everything—wood, metal, even stone. Dad's house stood on low pilings with a switchback ramp leading to the front door. The family had moved in after Dad's last stroke when Josie was eleven and Hughdean ten. And now, at thirty-six, eighteen years after her mother's death, she was living here again.

Josie had left Brian six months ago and moved back into her childhood home, where she didn't have to pay rent and she could help Hughdean take better care of their ailing father. Though it was easier for Josie, the move was hard for Minnow and Toby. Until they came up with a better solution, they had to shuffle back and forth between two homes. It was only three miles and didn't change their school schedule or social life, but those three miles were as bad as three hundred miles. Josie knew they were happier in their family home, in their own beds, but she didn't live there anymore.

"It's not forever, only for now." *Smile.* The marriage therapist had told her smiling made you feel happy even if you weren't. *Bullshit.*

She breathed in the magic of the early-morning sky, the blue hour, nautical twilight when the sun and the moon shared their secret handshake. The sky glowed a dim cerulean, and Mercury victoriously held its eastern position as the morning star.

The island felt wild and rudderless. The air held a stillness, the sky and ocean without helicopters, oil platforms in the horizon, the whir of boats, or the rumble of cars on the potholed roads.

The clear air filled her lungs as she walked down the steps and through last season's garden.

She sat on the bench Brian and Hughdean had built with the idea Dad could sit and pull weeds. The thought was nice, but it was an unmitigated disaster. He was unable to handle the uneven ground with his walker—or the exhausting hot sun.

Can I coax the garden back to health? A forgotten sense of hope came over her. Dale and Marcos from *Vacation Ventures* had stayed until 11:00 p.m. Sunday night. Dale, the food critic, had gone to the same culinary school as Maisy in North Carolina, and they traded funny stories all night. They had all sat on the deck, drinking beer and eating fresh shrimp. The conversation turned to hot sauce after Maisy noticed Marcos, the photographer, had used almost an entire bottle of Josie's house sauce—a vinegar-based recipe she'd inherited from her mother but had tweaked over the years.

"We bottle the hot sauce locally and sell it," Maisy said. "But if you like that, wait here, there's something you should try." Then Maisy fetched Josie's personal stash of reaper sauce.

"Are you trying to cause trouble?" Josie leaned over the table, laughing, and pulled the three mason jars toward her. Josie was a hot sauce aficionado. For years, she had grown a variety of hot peppers, habanero, and scotch bonnets. She had moved on to reaper chilies, but only for her amusement—in the wrong hands they could be deadly. The red devils practically pulsed in the jars. Marcos and Dale had left that evening with several bottles of hot sauce and one dangerous jar of reaper sauce. Dale had told her he'd call in two weeks if he had any extra questions. The profile was scheduled to run in the June issue.

A warm breeze tousled her hair over her eyes as plans for the restaurant bubbled in her mind. A way forward. Maybe a way to revive her ideas for the food business she'd abandoned years ago. She was itching to tell Louise—her best friend and Grand Isle's mayor—about the magazine article. For once, Louise had cleared her schedule and would join Josie on the beach for a morning run. Louise's borrowed diamond studs had indeed been good luck.

A voice boomed behind her. "Jesus, Josie, you look like a creepy cemetery gargoyle hiding in the weeds," Hughdean said.

Startled, she fell backward onto the hard ground. "What are you doing scaring me so early in the morning?"

He towered over her like a scarecrow. "You're too easy and too much fun to scare. *'Ow!'*" He mimicked her voice and waved his arm in the air before holding out his hand to haul her to her feet.

Josie snorted a laugh. She could never predict what version of Hughdean would appear on any given day, let alone at any given moment. This morning he was the jokester.

"Why aren't you on the boat?" She brushed dirt off her backside.

He took a long drink from a steaming mug of coffee. "Taking a slow morning."

"Did you bring me one of those?" She nodded at the mug.

"Nope, this was the last of it. And I ate a few of those biscuits."

She huffed. "You're a right prince."

He shrugged. "Not my fault you and Minnow inhale enough coffee to fuel a tank. Dad and I never ran out before you moved in."

Before I moved in, you and Dad ate cereal and frozen dinners.

He snapped a dried bean pod from a pole. "Gosh, I hated picking these." He let the pod fall to the ground.

Tending the vegetables was one of the shared chores their mother, Odeal, had assigned.

"I expect every okra pod from every plant," she had said, dangling kitchen shears and pails from her fingers. Okra was a cut-and-come-again crop. The more you picked, the more it produced. That's when Josie discovered the blue hour. The cool mornings with enough light to work before the summer sun blistered her neck. A time without her mother.

"You used to stand at the corner of the gazebo and hide from her in plain sight. Momma fumed like a kettle."

He turned to where the gazebo had once stood, swept away completely by Hurricane Rita.

She followed his gaze to the now-empty spot. When they were kids, the structure was home base for hide-and-seek. As a teenager, she'd slept in it, preferring the mosquitoes over her mother. And then came Brian. Tears stung the backs of her eyes, and she pressed her cheeks with her palms. *Where's that coming from?* Josie wasn't nostalgic. Thoughts of Brian were often like that, popping up like weeds, some prickly, others that flowered. In another version of her life, Brian would have been with them last night.

"I miss the gazebo." She sat back on the bench and turned away from Hughdean to hide her emotions.

Hughdean sat beside her, his long legs stretched out like ocean pilings.

"Maisy said you want to repaint the restaurant sign. I can send Angelo tomorrow."

She screwed up her face at him. "Is he the one who always wears his shirt inside out or backward?"

Hughdean finished the coffee. "No, that's Hector. Angelo was a housepainter. A talented one too."

"Why's he working for you?"

"Shrimping pays better than painting. You can have him for the day."

Suspicion tapped at her brain. Hughdean usually grumbled like a gator pulled from his winter hole when she asked him to do anything for the restaurant. He liked to remind her that he was a *silent* partner. Though the man never shut up.

"You'll owe me a favor, though, Josephine."

Only a handful of people dared to call her by her full name. He said it the same way Odeal used to, stretching the *feen*, a consonant shy of *fiend*.

His favors could be outsize compared to what she needed from him. She was juggling enough real debt and didn't want to add emotional debt to her balance sheet.

The rising sun warmed the morning sky from kingfisher blue to flamingo orange.

"Pretty day coming." Hughdean leaned back, letting the first rays of light warm his face.

Josie's senses perked. *Here it comes.*

"So, yeah, I was wondering if you'd close the restaurant for a private party to celebrate the Blessing of the Fleet this weekend with my crew and, you know, the usuals."

The Blessing of the Fleet was a Louisiana tradition at the start of the spring shrimping season. The area shrimpers would decorate their boats and parade them while a Catholic priest blessed them for a bountiful and safe harvest. Grand Isle held a community festival.

"You can't spring this on me at the last second. The Blessing is Sunday, one of my busiest nights." Josie squeezed her eyes shut.

"The last second would be me telling you Sunday morning. The idea only came up yesterday. I do own a third of the restaurant. If it weren't for me, you'd have no fresh shrimp."

"I can't afford to close and feed all those people. Let alone the cost of liquor and beer." She shook her head.

Hughdean ran four shrimp boats, and his crew and their families, though good natured, were rowdy.

"How's this. I'll pay for the food, and we'll make it a cash bar. That'll more than cover any losses for the night."

She considered her brother in profile. His short, thick hair and cleft chin. He never could grow a beard. If Hughdean didn't strut like the cock of the walk, she'd say he was good looking in a scruffy outdoorsy way. Different from Brian, who was 100 percent bad boy, dangerously handsome with the longest eyelashes she had ever seen on a man. Like nets. Well, once upon a time.

She nodded. "Fine. But I set the menu." She'd keep it simple and affordable.

Hughdean slapped the top of her leg and laughed.

Josie rubbed her thigh. She had a lot to tell Louise.

"You really drank *all* the coffee?"

"Yup."

Josie hummed and parked her car underneath Louise and Hollis's sea green bungalow. Like most homes on the island, theirs was on stilts to protect against storm surges. She tugged at the diamond earrings still in her ears to remind her to return them to Louise first thing. Her best friends were early risers, and the house blazed like a lighthouse. Josie had grown up with them, and they were as tight as scales on a fish.

When Josie had moved to California for culinary school, three was no longer a crowd. Louise and Hollis both went to LSU and were soon an item, spinning the island gossip mill into a blur. Hollis's grandmother, Rosaline, was the grandam of Grand Isle, and no one was happier to welcome Louise to the family than her. Josie and Louise were still close, the way she imagined siblings who loved and cherished each other should be. Yet to this day she had trouble accepting her two best friends had married, even as they celebrated their tenth anniversary.

She hadn't lost Louise as much as she had lost Hollis's level head. She missed having a man's perspective about, well . . . everything. In the heated, breathless early days of her relationship with Brian, Hollis had pulled her aside, concerned she was making a mistake and that she could do better than Brian Babineaux. She should've listened. But by then, she was pregnant. Hollis, to his credit, hugged her tight and shook Brian's hand. Then Brian became the man she trusted and shared her dreams with. They were a force like a storm, the restaurant a port for the community. They had been amazing together—until he destroyed it. Like one of those named hurricanes that's so bad they retire the name—Hugo, Andrew, Katrina. Brian was on her personal list.

She took the stairs two at a time. She'd have to pace herself to allow her friend to keep up with her on the beach, with the energy she had to run off today.

The door opened, and Hollis filled the space. Eugene Hollis was also Dr. Hollis, an ornithologist. He had overseen Gumbo's recovery and was the pelican's second-favorite person after Minnow. He looked like the birds he studied. He stood tall and leggy like a stork, with a long nose, his dark-brown eyes framed by high-arching eyebrows that always made him appear surprised. This morning, deep wrinkles crossed his forehead.

He exhaled like he'd been holding his breath.

Louise's voice filtered from the kitchen, and Josie followed it inside.

Instead of running shorts, Louise wore tailored navy blue linen pants and a blue pinstripe blouse. Her classic mayor uniform.

"I've been calling you. Where've you been?" Louise's voice cracked.

"Driving, I—"

Louise waved her hands. "Did you hear about the accident?"

"Accident?" Island news before breakfast was never good. Never a surprise lottery ticket or a litter of puppies rescued from a storm.

"The rig." Her fingers pointed to the edge of the television screen flickering in the kitchen.

An armada of boats surrounded a flaming oil platform. Josie peered at the image. A volcanic column of black smoke billowed into the otherwise calm sky. The same sky outside the door.

She counted the fire response boats softly—"Seven, eight"—like toys in a bathtub. The flames leaped from the ocean. The news scrolled at the bottom of the screen and flashed: *Explosion Deepwater Horizon, 11 Missing, Coast Guard Fire Response Active Search and Rescue.*

Josie froze. Air she couldn't exhale caught in her throat, and she swallowed. For years, she'd contained her fear of Brian dying in a helicopter accident, screaming over the Gulf. This was a whole new level of hell. The Deepwater Horizon. Now an inferno.

Louise led her to a chair and took both her hands. Her voice soft. "Have you heard from Brian? He's not answering the house line or his cell phone."

A whoosh of flames filled the screen. The news clock displayed 7:15 a.m. She shook her head. "Minnow said he was staying an extra day—" The words disappeared on her tongue.

Today's Wednesday, right? Her sense of time and space now untethered.

"The rig had a safety ceremony," she whispered as the fireboats pumped useless water onto the rig like toy squirt guns. "When did this happen?" She pointed a shaking finger at the TV.

Louise wrung her hands together. "I got the call at six fifteen this morning. I don't know when the fire actually started. The Coast Guard received the mayday around ten p.m. They probably tried to contain it themselves."

Josie nodded. The crew trained in fire safety. Brian had considered taking a volunteer-firefighter job during his time on shore.

"It's chaos," Hollis said.

Josie fumbled for her keys. "He sleeps when he comes home from the rig. Nothing can wake him. I'll just set eyes on him. He's home. This is . . ." Her voice shook. "He's home."

"*Chère*, he may be on the rig." Louise pointed to the TV.

Josie beelined to the door. "He's *home*." A ringing sounded in her ears. The images on the screen repeated in a hellish loop. Of course he was home. Brian was always punctual about returning home for them. Except he no longer called her with his schedule. He filtered his plans through the kids, and sometimes they got it wrong. Did they get it wrong in the rush to prep the restaurant? *Dammit.* Why couldn't he talk to her like a normal partner? She deserved to know he was safe, needed to know he was safe.

Hollis caught her arm. "I'm coming with you."

She squeezed his hand. "Thank you, but no. Go to my dad's house. He turns the news on first thing in the morning. Toby and Minnow shouldn't hear this alone. Radio Hughdean on the boat."

She raced down the stairs and climbed into her car. *Brian, Brian, Brian* drummed in her mind. But it wasn't just him. They knew people on the rig, families in town. Brian used to call her, laughing and saying "Guess what I just heard?" then dropping a juicy nugget of island gossip he only learned because he was fifty miles safely out to sea.

Her hands fumbled as she tried to stick the keys into the ignition, hitting the steering wheel column and sending the keys jangling to her feet.

She gripped the wheel, breathed deep, and tried again, reversed her car, and stopped. With a shaking hand, she spun the radio dial for the news station.

"The Coast Guard is calling this a massive search and rescue mission as flames roar from the Deepwater Horizon. The first distress call came last night at 10:00 p.m., reporting the explosion."

Explosion. This wasn't a contained fire. The well had raged for eight hours before she woke—over ten hours now. *Brian.*

Adrenaline pushed her and the car the five miles across town to her old house. She momentarily considered running instead. It would be faster.

Chapter 4

Wednesday, April 21, 2010

7:40 a.m.

Josie flew through the yellow light from the main road. *What if Brian is one of the missing?* She rolled through the last stop sign and pulled in front of the house.

The family's four-bedroom home sat on high pilings with a poured concrete pad underneath. She loved this turquoise house with butter yellow trim, situated direct center of the island, near the restaurant, her dad, and Louise and Hollis. When she'd moved out, she'd swayed off center physically and emotionally. It had been a huge triumph to afford their own place after Brian had taken his first position on the Deepwater Horizon. His paycheck had made it all possible.

Brian's silver pickup truck hadn't moved in the three weeks since Minnow had parked it after driving him to the Houma heliport, where he was one of twelve thousand people a month who flew out to the oil rigs and platforms.

The truck being there doesn't mean anything. Brian often shared a ride home to the island or called a car service from the heliport.

She stomped the parking brake, stepped from the car, and slammed the door behind her. The door caught the strap of her bag and yanked her arm back.

Breathe, breathe. She freed her bag and ran her hand over the hood of the truck. The metal was cold and wet from the morning dew. She launched up the long staircase to the front door.

She fumbled for the house key. *Blue, no, the red one.*

She had celebrated the house coming out of foreclosure by having specially colored keys made. Brian had demanded she hand the key over when she moved out to her dad's.

"If your junk is no longer here, you have no need for a key."

She'd brokered an angry agreement to respect Brian's space and not interfere with his relationship with the kids but had insisted it was necessary to have a key. She would call before ever using it.

Screw the rules. This is an emergency.

The dead bolt slid open with a click, and she rushed into the kitchen. The house was dark, the curtains pulled shut. She inhaled the stale air. An empty house was a dead house. Without Brian, this place would be no one's home. She could never return. Leaving had been her decision. And although she had wished many ugly things on him over the last year, never death. He was the keeper of her dreams.

The hairs on the back of her neck tingled like static electricity. She shivered, then heard the faintest noise. The professional, poised chatter of TV news anchors.

"We're waiting for an update on this developing situation."

"Oh" escaped from her throat.

Her bag landed on the kitchen table with an explosive thud in the quiet, and she ran to the family room.

Brian sat on the couch with his head in his hands and his shoulders pulled to his ears. The only daylight in the room came from the flickering image on the television.

She exhaled; her body released like a slipknot. She knelt in front of him. This shaking version of Brian was not the standoffish man she'd been jousting with these past six months. His brick wall posture was cracked.

"Brian?" She rested her palm on his vibrating knee.

He raised his head. His face was gray with red splotches. His eyes stared at her, unfocused and startled.

"Josie," he howled and collapsed, sobbing into her arms. She held his body, her eyes shut tight as his sounds of grief echoed through them both. She stroked his head, as she had done a thousand times before. When his breathing steadied, she pulled away but cupped his face in her hands. Out of the corner of her eye, she saw the rig burn on the screen. It was like watching their house burn. Those people were family too.

"I . . . we—" She rested her forehead against his. *He's safe and alive. Safe and alive.* "Has anyone called?" she asked, her voice like a prayer. "Penman, Daniels?" Close friends, their wives and kids. All like them. Welcoming new babies, saving for college, celebrating weddings, planning for the day when they had enough to end the back-and-forth life.

He shrugged, speechless, a wild fear in his eyes. The room grew stuffy and hot.

Even on the TV the flames were intense.

"We're switching live now to Jason Knight, reporting from BP flight operations in Houma, Louisiana, where helicopter pilots are reporting scenes from the massive Deepwater Horizon explosion," the newscaster said.

"I'm here with Crandell Sullivan, a helicopter pilot stationed in Houma. What can you tell us about the accident site?" Jason asked.

Brian's head snapped toward the screen. He gripped Josie's hand. "I've flown with Crandell to the rig."

The pilot stood, one hand jammed into his thinning hair, the other scrubbing his face. "I had taken off for my first flight of the day about 6:20, when air traffic control called on all channels about an explosion on the Deepwater Horizon with significant safety-of-flight issues, smoke and flames." He shook his head. "The platform was erupting. I've never seen anything like it. Like flying into an erupting volcano. The smoke blackened the sun, and the flames roaring. I wasn't near enough to feel the heat, but the smell . . . the smell."

"Can you tell us about current conditions and the rescue operation?" the reporter asked. "Did you see survivors in the water?"

Brian leaned closer to the TV.

"I counted five fireboats. I'm no expert, but the Coast Guard is underequipped. I didn't see life rafts, but there're a lot of small craft in the area. I hope to God if anyone's in the water, they're rescued."

"Will you be heading back to the site?"

"A hundred percent if the Coast Guard calls for search and rescue air support. Those guys are good people. The best."

The news switched back to the original footage looping in the background.

Josie turned off the flickering TV, extinguishing the rig fire but not the fear. She inhaled, as if testing that the smoke was truly gone, but her mind raced.

Eleven men are missing. Eleven families are waiting. We're not waiting.

She rested her hand on her throat, reassured by the faint thrum of her pulse.

Brian sat in shock. She had no idea when he had heard about the explosion or how long he'd been sitting on the couch. She ran her hands over his face, squeezed his forearms, and slipped her fingers between his, still testing he was real and solid. *He's safe and alive.*

"C'mon." She coaxed him into the kitchen. He needed warm food. Whether that was true or not didn't matter. She only knew how to feed people.

Of course, the refrigerator was empty. She found a box of crackers, a jar of peanut butter, and a half bag of coffee beans. *Carbs, fat, and caffeine. It'll work.*

Brian's voice scratched out a throaty whisper. "I flew into Houma yesterday. Had dinner with friends, home at 7:00 p.m., and crashed. I woke to this twenty minutes ago."

She measured the coffee into the grinder. She'd told Louise he slept hard. He'd learned about the explosion at the time she had.

"When did you hear?" he asked.

The coffee maker clock read 8:05 a.m. "About an hour ago. I was at Louise and Hollis's."

They were expecting her call, and the kids by now had seen the news. She grabbed the phone on the wall and dialed. The phone picked up on the first ring.

"Hello," Minnow said.

"Hi, *chère*. I'm with Dad. He's home, and he's safe."

She heard her sob. "Can I talk to him?"

"Of course. I love you."

She handed the phone to Brian. "Where's your cell?" she asked softly. "We have to tell people you're—"

He nodded. "Bathroom or beside the bed."

Then Brian said into the phone, "Hey, *chère*."

She walked to the back of the house while he spoke to the kids. The family photographs on the walls stared at her—Minnow and Toby with Gumbo between them like three siblings; Josie and Brian with their feet intertwined and perched on the edge of the bay boat, fishing rods dangling in the water. She hadn't thought to take any family photos with her when she'd left. She was too angry and wanted to erase Brian from her memories. But how could she? Those photos were from another version of herself. A better version of her family.

She went into the bathroom first. The idea of going through her former bedroom felt like rummaging in a dead person's house. A dead marriage at least. They hadn't been intimate in over a year.

She switched on the light. A Dopp kit lay on the vanity, and Brian's duffel bag sat on the closed toilet seat. But no phone. She unzipped the bag and pawed through his clothes. He had a detailed packing system. Clean clothes on the left, dirty clothes on the right, both sets folded. She yanked a charging cord like a fishing line until she found his phone, dead as an anchor. That explained why he hadn't heard it ring.

She returned to the kitchen, plugged in the phone, and handed it to him, tethered to the cord. "Give it a few minutes to charge, and then call your mother."

He smiled faintly. Josie had never warmed to Brian's mother. Critical mothers once united them, making them promise to love their children unconditionally.

After the calls, Brian rubbed his face. "Minnow said they are heading to Louise and Hollis's house. We should head over. Though I don't know what Louise will know that they don't." Brian pointed at the dark TV screen in the other room.

She tilted her head. "It's Louise, she'll know something."

Brian plucked his T-shirt. "I need a shower. Will you wait?"

"Of course." She poured a cup of coffee and sat in the family room. The house was tidy, untouched like no one lived here. She could never keep it uncluttered of homework, toys, shoes, sneakers, work boots, and empty plates and glasses. Was she the problem, the mess magnet? Remove her aura, and voilà—order restored.

Exhaustion pooled in her, and she paced the living room to wake up. Brian rarely showed emotion. They'd argued about it during therapy. Where Josie popped off like a firecracker, Brian closed like a bar at last call. Kick out the patrons, quietly deal with sticky messes, and move on. This time was different. The rig explosion unspooled on his face.

No one would be able to survive that inferno, the water, the choking smoke.

Josie walked to the window and opened the shade. The morning light stung her eyes. She had stopped by only a handful of times in the past six months, to pick up the kids or something they'd forgotten. A financial catastrophe had been the reason she left her home. It was only fitting that another catastrophe was the trigger to bring her back.

Chapter 5

Josie and Brian drove silently to Louise's house, with the windows open. The rushing air was better than the silence between them. Though the panic unleashed in Josie's head was like a foghorn. What if Brian had died? What would she have told the kids? How would she move on? The last thought surprised her with its rawness. Hadn't she already moved on? Besides, the question was moot. He was here, without a scratch.

Brian stared out the window at the ocean. Oil platforms were as much a part of the coastal skyline as tall buildings were to New York City. Each gangly, leggy rig rose from the Gulf floor like Godzilla. They multiplied every year as Big Oil drilled deeper into the Earth's crust.

Oil cursed Louisiana like a witch in a fairy tale. *You will be blessed with boundless riches but must suffer horrible monsters in your midst.* Brian had worked on the Deepwater Horizon for a decade. They cashed his checks and counted on the company benefits. Oil and gas were their own sport in Louisiana, a monied sport. And today, a deadly one.

She climbed the stairs for the second time that day, and before Josie could knock on the door, it flew open. Minnow and Toby launched themselves at Brian. He huddled with them and heaved a sob.

"Hey, gang." He kissed the top of Minnow's head and lifted Toby off his feet like a toddler and buried his face into his neck.

The kids wouldn't stop crying, so he stood with his arms out to the side. "I'm okay, see?"

Josie wanted to join their circle but searched for Louise instead.

"Here, Brian, have a seat." Hollis spun a chair away from the TV and turned off the set.

"I appreciate the news," Louise said into the phone. "We'll do anything we can to help. Call with updates."

Louise wrote down a number and a list of names on a sheet of paper next to a mug of coffee and a half piece of forgotten toast. She pulled on her ponytail to tighten the floppy knot.

"Hey, *cher.*" She offered a weak smile and opened her arms as an offering to Brian. A peace offering. For the past six months, she'd been critical of both Brian and Josie for not working harder to find a way to become friends. "Y'all raising two kids together," she'd kept saying.

"You can't manage my marriage like the town's budget," Josie had scolded back.

Brian accepted her hug and exhaled. He wiped his eyes with the heel of his hand.

"Coast Guard." Louise waved the phone. "Seeing you safe is the only good news today. Well . . . and the weather for the rescue."

"Where're the people who made it off the rig?" Brian asked.

Louise read her note. "On the *Bankston.*"

Brian nodded and explained to Josie, "That's the supply ship tethered to us, waiting to accept the pumped-out drilling mud."

"Is there a list of survivors, I mean . . . people?" Josie stumbled over the words.

"Don't know yet. The Coast Guard flew the most injured out first." Louise scrolled through her Blackberry, pursed her lips, and shook her head. "Sam Kress was on the rig. Teri hasn't heard from him."

Brian's head fell into his hands, and he moaned.

"Dammit," Josie said quietly. Toby played baseball with their son, Connor. The boys had a sleepover at the start of spring break, their giggles lingering late into the night. She'd found them in the morning asleep on the floor underneath a sagging blanket fort with an empty bag of potato chips between them. Was Teri now a widow and a single mom? Was there a body to bury? Josie swallowed, her throat dry.

Here, her family was whole. Minnow sat at the kitchen table, paging through a *Glamour* magazine. Toby had gone exploring in Hollis's office, where Hollis had a collection of items from shipwrecks. All the *what-if* plans she and Brian had once made assaulted her as he sat quiet at the table: What if he left the rig and they opened a restaurant in New Orleans or California? What type of life could they build? She used to worry that Grand Isle was too small. A bigger market would mean a better life. Then he would wrap his arms around her like swaddling a baby and say something corny like "Our best memories are here" or "This island is the source of our love." Maybe *his* best memories were here, but this was where she also had her worst.

A fist pounded on the door, and Maisy burst in. "Brian!" She caught her breath. She was wearing her chef whites, and her long braids were piled on her head in a tall topknot.

He stood to meet her, and she stepped forward, patting his chest and arms as if dousing flames.

His face softened. "I'm okay. I came home last night." He embraced her.

"How did you find us?" Josie asked.

"Well, if y'all thought to call me or answer your damned phones, I wouldn't have had to play detective."

"If Mom wasn't so cheap about giving me a phone—"

"You hush up, Minnow. This isn't about you," Maisy said. "I was prepping for lunch, turned on the radio, and heard the news. After I called all y'all"—she waved her hand—"I connected with Daniel Dean. He said you came here and then had me call Hughdean on the restaurant's marine radio."

Hollis handed her a glass of water, and she sat at the kitchen table.

Maisy dropped her voice. "Do we have news about anyone?"

"The Coast Guard hasn't released names yet," Josie said.

Brian held his phone. "It'll be a long day today. Who do I call first?"

"Right," Josie said to fill in the silence. She clapped her hands. "Brian needs a real breakfast. Anyone else?"

"I'm not hungry," Minnow said.

Josie began investigating the pantry. "I can make magic with a mere block of cheese." She joked, but no one acknowledged the humor.

She closed the cabinets. "Change of plans. No sense messing the kitchen. I have a restaurant."

"What plans?" Louise balanced against the table and slipped on a pair of flats.

"Breakfast at the restaurant."

"Sounds yum, but I'm heading to the office. Reporters calling, weather to monitor."

Toby ran into the kitchen from Hollis's study. "The Coast Guard is calling a sécurité alert on channel 16 about the Deepwater Horizon."

They crammed into the small room around the VHF-FM marine radio.

"Be advised, we are continuing to conduct a massive search-and-response effort at the Deepwater Horizon oil platform that began at 21:00 April 20. All vessels not involved in official response activities are to avoid the area 28.736667°N 88.386944°W. Repeat, this is an active fire response with poor visibility from heavy smoke and a column of flames coming from the rig and flying debris. We are actively seeking missing crew, potentially in the water."

"I'm going out there." Brian walked toward the door.

"Where?" Louise said.

"To help search for my friends. I'm useless sitting here."

"How? In the bay boat?" Josie said, her hands on her hips. "Planning to fish while you're at it?" *How like him to think he can fix something raging out of control by simply showing up.*

"Funny with the jokes."

"I'm not joking. The pilot on TV said it's a scene from hell. The Coast Guard's ordered everyone to avoid the area. What do you think *you* can do?"

Brian slumped against the office door. "People are missing. I might've been one of them. Jesus, what if I caused this accident?"

"How?" Josie said.

"So many things were breaking. Maybe I didn't install the correct control panel or left something flammable on the deck. A hundred parts I touched last week or yesterday that—"

"Daddy." Minnow stood beside him. "You count the fishing hooks when we go out and when we come back. You once spent an entire afternoon at the restaurant inspecting the tines on the forks and fixing the bent ones with pliers. You're kinda anal about stuff."

Josie suppressed a smile. The girl spoke the truth.

"I'll radio Hughdean. We'll take the *New Deal*. She's the fastest of the boats and big enough to be out there."

"Brian," Louise said in her oh-so-reasonable mayor voice, placing a hand on his shoulder. "I'm worried too. I'm heading to the office to be available for whatever comes our way. The Coast Guard doesn't need onlookers or crowded shipping lanes. If they need more boats, they'll call. I'll rally everyone. I'll commission Hughdean's entire shrimp fleet into service."

"I'm supposed to just sit and wait?"

"Louise," Josie said. "If reporters are calling, Brian can talk to them, tell 'em about the rig? He can monitor the radio from your office too."

Louise nodded. "It's only our local news so far, but they'll put it out statewide. You'd have more to say than me. How 'bout it?"

Brian shrugged. "Yeah, sure. Maybe I can set up one of those phone-tree lists with the families we know to share news."

"Consider my office your office," Louise said.

"C'mon gang, you can ride to the restaurant with me," Maisy said to Minnow and Toby.

Brian hugged them both, his eyes squeezed shut. He inhaled and gave them a tight-lipped smile.

Outside, at the bottom of the stairs, Josie and Brian watched Maisy leave with the kids. He rested with his back against Josie's car and took a deep breath, a blink away from tears.

"I should be out there, helping, not talking to reporters." He dug his fingers into his hair. "Those missing men didn't survive."

She opened her mouth and shook her head. "You don't—"

"I know the safety protocols. That's no small fire."

Grand Isle Gazette

11 Missing 17 Injured after Deepwater Horizon Oil Rig Explosion

April 21, 2010

Coast Guard search and rescue are conducting an active search for 11 missing crew from last night's explosion on the Deepwater Horizon, an oil platform 50 miles southeast of Venice in the Gulf of Mexico.

An official statement from Transocean Ltd., the Swiss company that owns the Deepwater Horizon and other oil platforms in the Gulf, states 17 workers, including three with life-threatening injuries, were transported by helicopter to area hospitals. The rig had 126 crew onboard at the time of the accident.

"The crew is trained in firefighting, first aid, and drilled for evacuation procedures," said Brian Babineaux, 38, a Deepwater Horizon mechanic and Grand Isle resident off rotation at the time of the explosion.

"This is devastating," said Babineaux. "The rig is a family, and an accident is devastating to the community.

Grand Isle has a lot of off-shore workers."

Clear weather and calm seas are forecast and should aid in the search while fire crews battle the 200-foot-high blaze fed by gushing crude oil. Rear Adm. Mary Landry, commander of the Coast Guard's eighth district, said that the rig is leaking 13,000 gallons of sweet crude oil an hour, but nearly all is burning in the fire. "We do not see a major spill emanating from this incident," Landry said.

Pollution is a serious concern. A spokesperson from the governor's office said, "The Coastal Protection and Restoration Authority team is working with the Louisiana oil spill coordinator's office to monitor any environmental impact."

Chapter 6

Grand Isle, Louisiana

Saturday, April 24, 2010

6:00 a.m.

Josie measured the Community Coffee and poured filtered water into the restaurant's coffee maker. In her experience, coffee drinkers were divided into two groups, team Café du Monde or team Community. For decades, Odeal's had brewed the iconic Café du Monde blended with chicory. The tourists expected it.

When Josie took over as Odeal's executive chef, she had made wholesale changes. Brian only asked for one. He wanted the restaurant to serve Community, because it hailed from his hometown, Baton Rouge. Brian never spoke about Baton Rouge other than to say that he'd left and never planned to return. But he wanted this, so she happily made the change, loving how he loved her and her vision for their future.

She inhaled the nutty, rich beans before resealing the red bag. Since the rig explosion, her hours had melted together. Only the rituals of mealtimes and the changing sky offered any indication of time. Then the rig actually sank, adding another level of crisis. Sure, rigs were damaged by major hurricanes, but they rarely sank. Josie couldn't think of a single one in the United States.

Josie had already been interviewed a dozen times by the media who were now swarming the town. They were waiting for the oil to roll in like it was a sporting event. The reporters, camera people, and slick-talking news anchors had replaced the tourists in the restaurant. But their volume was only a fraction of the number of vacationers they had expected at this time of year. The people she *needed*. The storeroom was filled to bursting with rice and dried kidney beans. She held back her emotions as she handed out bags of wilted vegetables to her staff to keep the produce from being a total loss and help cover for their lack of tips.

I will not brood about any of this. She scolded her negative thoughts. Louise had called last night asking if she was up for a morning beach run. She, too, was stressed, being the face of the island. Together they would pound along the sand, and if Josie left right now, she'd be able to catch the sunrise.

She stepped onto the deck. No sign of Gumbo this morning. No doubt he was off fishing for his breakfast or still tucked underneath the deck in the roost they joked was the restaurant's in-law suite.

Brian had modified a doghouse design with an interior spacious enough for Minnow to crawl inside. Outside, he had laid exterior deck boards in a herringbone pattern—a miniature patio to keep it off the rocks and sand. Most people didn't even realize it was down there, though Gumbo could often be heard shuffling under their feet.

Hope it's a tasty meal this morning. Gumbo fished at first light and would often find Josie at the beach during her runs. His original injury caused him to have one wing slightly longer than the other. Despite this handicap, he would pace her, his lopsided wings no longer an obstacle, merely an adaptation.

Josie wrinkled her nose as a metallic tang settled on her tongue, reminding her of boat fuel.

She tightened her laces and headed for the beach and Louise.

The wind gusted as she ran closer to the water. The tang was stronger now, mixed with the briny air. She sneezed. Seabirds squawked overhead, but no pelicans. She pounded harder, anxiety moving her limbs. She concentrated on her mental checklist. Maisy would arrive at seven and begin baking the day's fresh bread and desserts.

Frothy waves rolled in to the sand. Rabid-dog frothy, not cappuccino-foam frothy. Her feet kicked wet clods of sand behind her. *Thwack.* Sand stuck to the back of her knee. She shook her leg, yet the clod wouldn't release. The sand scuffed, rough and uncomfortable on her skin. She stopped and swiped it but only managed to spread it down her calf.

What the——? She examined the reddish, gooey, caramellike ooze on her fingers. Her stomach heaved as she finally identified the sharp metallic odor. *Holy hell!*

She walked back the way she had come, her eyes scanning the horizon.

Bottle-cap-size blobs dotted the beach. The oil had finally come to shore. It had arrived with no fanfare, no media, no witness. The ocean was empty of fishing boats. Seabirds dove in and out of the water. A regular day for them. They didn't realize their waters had been poisoned.

It's here. It's real.

She spun in a circle and saw a few other early-morning beach walkers crouched on the sand. A dog barked and was pulled away from a pile of sludge. The realization of the oil was plain on their faces.

Everyone needed to be warned. She scooped a handful of the gloppy sand. Her heart raced, and she ran toward Louise's house. She had to tell her. They had to stop it before it got any worse.

Oil on the beach was every coastal community's greatest fear. Sand dunes and walls could be rebuilt, sand redistributed, and piers repaired after storms, but oil smothered life.

She ran with her hands together as if she were in a silly country fair contest using her hands to scoop water from one bucket to fill another.

Her lungs burst as she raced the long stairs to their door. She made it to the top and pressed the doorbell with her elbow.

Louise opened the door and smiled at Josie, then her face dissolved into confusion. Josie gulped air to extinguish the fire in her lungs. Her body shook from the exertion.

"*Chère*, what's wrong?" Louise followed Josie's eyes to her cupped hands.

Josie stared at the sand. "Where's Hollis?" Her voice cracked, high pitched in panic.

Hollis appeared in the kitchen, his eyes alert, and scanned Josie's face. She held her shaking hands to him. He grabbed her wrists and led her into the kitchen.

"Oil," she said.

"Where did you find this?" Louise asked.

"On the beach. All over." The words rushed from her.

Hollis took a plate from the sink and broke Josie's hands apart. He scraped the sticky sand onto the plate before gently rubbing her hands with a towel. He stopped for the briefest of moments and ran the cloth over Josie's scar.

"Sit, and start again," he said, his voice gentle.

Louise rubbed her back. "Take a breath. Is there a lot of oil, or was it just this in one spot?" Louise asked.

She sat back in the chair. Hollis combed through the sand, making tsking and grunting sounds as he shook his head.

"The oil's everywhere. You can smell it too. Nobody's doing anything. Nobody knows yet."

Louise looked at the kitchen clock, the sun climbing in the morning sky, and scrunched her face. She was in high-level organization mode.

"The whole world will know any minute."

Louise was referring to the satellite media trucks and reporters who arrived after their morning coffee and hovered at the beach waiting to pounce on the spill. This was not how Josie wanted Grand Isle to make the news.

Josie threaded her way through a snarl of traffic as she backtracked to Daniel Dean's. Just as Louise predicted, the media and scores of people were rushing to the beach.

What now? Was this the beginning of a new problem or just the same problem ballooning?

"Josephine, is that you in the kitchen?" Daniel Dean called.

"Yeah, Dad."

"Rosaline called. The oil's come to shore." He shuffled into the kitchen with his walker.

She helped him to sit at the table.

"Hi, Mom," Toby said, coming into the kitchen. He had spent the night at the house, a treat for her since he and Minnow had been spending their nights at home with Brian.

"Grandpa, has there ever been an oil spill here on the island?"

He shook his head. "I've seen spills, but not like this. And with the well still open, doesn't look like this will end anytime soon. Josephine"— he turned his head to her—"we should talk about the restaurant and how you're planning to pay your bills."

She opened her mouth to speak, then opened the refrigerator. "I'll make you and Toby lunch before I shower and head to the restaurant. We can talk later." *Or never.* She didn't need Daniel Dean to remind her of her obligations.

Josie showered and ironed her chef's jacket, appreciating how her hands were able to smooth the wrinkles, transforming chaos into order. The feeling increased as she walked into Odeal's. *This is still my restaurant. I control what happens inside, no matter what happens outside.*

She sighed. The dining room was empty, not a single lunch being enjoyed. The marina deck had a few stragglers. One man stood on a chair, a fork in his hand. Another man was pulling at his arm. Maisy, Linh, and Jake, their busboy, stood surrounding . . . *Is that Minnow?*

Josie ran outside.

"Grab that bird," the man shouted.

Gumbo was crouched underneath a café table.

"You hurt my bird and I'll murder you!" Minnow yelled. Jake grabbed her around the waist and hoisted her off her feet as her arms and legs thrashed.

Josie held both hands in front of the man. "Stop this right now. What's going on?"

"That piece-of-shit bird took my keys right off the table. It attacked me. Call animal control and shoot it."

"*You're* the piece of shit," Minnow said. "I told you not to feed him."

"Minnow," Josie said.

Josie dropped to her knees to see Gumbo. Sure enough, a set of keys dangled at the end of the hook on his long bill. If the situation weren't so tense, she'd laugh. Gumbo liked shiny objects. The man was lucky Gumbo hadn't taken off and dropped them into the water.

"And that waitress"—the man pointed to Minnow—"with the rude mouth. Fire her."

"That waitress is your best and only chance of retrieving your keys. And if our pelican swallows them, you can be charged with harming a protected species," Josie said. It was a white lie. The brown pelican had been removed from the endangered list six months earlier. They had celebrated with a party.

"Why did the pelican take your keys?" Josie asked.

The man stepped off the chair, his fist bunched by his side. "It lunged for our lunch. I shooed it away, and then it attacked."

The man's friend moved between him and Josie.

"He's lying," Minnow said. "Gumbo was on his perch, and he started tossing shrimp at him. I told him to stop."

"You mean that perch with the sign that says, Do Not Feed the Pelican?" a new voice said. Brian walked up the deck stairs. He wore sunglasses, but Josie knew he would be sizing up the situation and his blue eyes would be blazing. He had years of experience throwing drunks out of the restaurant.

"Dad, he—"

Brian held a hand up to Minnow. "I got the strangest call from Maisy and just had to see this."

"Is someone gonna do something?" the man said.

"We are," Brian said. "First, you should know, pelicans don't eat shrimp and especially not"—he nodded at the table where he was sitting—"shrimp étouffée. Maisy makes one of the best in the state, but he won't eat it."

"Is this funny to you?" the man said.

"Not in the least. If that pelican swallows those keys." Brian shook his head.

"Brewster," the other man said, "admit it, you were teasing the bird. She did tell you to stop."

"Let's everyone back away from the table. Our poor Gumbo is shaking in his feathers from the commotion," Maisy said.

"Please," Josie said.

"Jake, you can put Minnow down," Brian said.

Minnow stood, her fists by her side.

"Now, *chère*," he said to Minnow. "If you would, you know . . ." Brian nodded his head.

"Not until he apologizes," Minnow said.

"I will not!" Brewster said.

"*Minnow*," Josie said.

"Fine." She put two fingers in her mouth and whistled, one long and two short notes.

Gumbo scuffed his big webbed feet out from beneath the table and waddled over to her. She dropped to her knees and spoke softly.

"Hey there, handsome. You're scared, but I won't let this big bad man hurt you."

The other man picked up a camera, and the click of a rapid shutter caused Gumbo to swing his head, jangling the keys like a bell.

"Shh," Minnow cooed. She backed farther away from the crowd and sat with her legs crisscrossed. Gumbo followed. She grabbed the keys and pulled the bird into her lap, burying her head in his body and stroking his feathers.

"I've never in my life," the man with the camera said.

Brian snatched the keys and placed them on the table. "I suggest you put those away. Now would be the right time to settle your bill and be on your way."

"I'm not paying for this."

Brian stepped closer. "It would be the polite option, considering you almost choked our pelican and insulted my daughter. Who is a fine waitress."

The man opened his wallet and threw some bills onto the table.

"What's the story with the pelican?" the cameraman asked.

"We rescued him two years ago, after Hurricane Gustav," Minnow said, looking up. She was still upset, red splotches coloring her cheeks.

"He was a toddler bird then, all alone, flapping one wing on the beach." She stroked his body. "He had a fishhook stuck in his blood feather. That's the new feathers baby birds have. They're important."

"You know a lot about birds," the man said.

Minnow shrugged. "I didn't before Gumbo came along. You should visit the bird sanctuaries and breeding grounds here." Her voice dropped. "The oil though—"

"Can I come closer and take a picture with you both?"

Minnow looked to Brian.

He nodded.

The man dropped to his knees and snapped a series of shots.

"That's some impressive gear you have," Brian said.

"Yeah, just got it. Canon's new digital, twelve megapixels."

"Jake, would you clear this table?" Josie said. *It's time for these people to leave.*

"Can I ask your name? And what did you call the pelican?"

"Minnow Babineaux. This is Gumbo."

"Gumbo the pelican."

At the sound of his name, Gumbo tilted his head side to side.

"He just said hello—or what we think is hello," Minnow said. "I don't have magic bird-reading mind powers."

"It's a clever name, especially here at the restaurant," the man said.

"My mom"—Minnow looked over at Josie—"came up with a fish goop for him when he was hurt. I was the only one who could feed him—Mom says I'm his person. He loved it. My brother called it pelican gumbo, and the name stuck."

Gumbo hunkered into his loafing position, with his head and long neck tucked close to his body.

"Has he healed from the fishing hook?" the man asked.

"One wing is longer than the other. But everyone has a challenge. He's the best-cared-for bird on the island," Josie said.

"How does he fly with a bad wing?"

"It took a long time, but he learned," Josie said. Adaptation and stubbornness, two traits Josie knew well.

"Mom cried the day he flew," Minnow said.

Josie covered her face with both hands. TMI.

"Here's my card," the man said. "I'm sorry about my friend. He's all city. The only pets he understands are dogs and cats."

"He's not a pet," Josie snapped. "I mean, we don't treat him like a pet. If anything, he owns us, flying in and out as he pleases." She walked over to the other table and helped Jake stack the plates on the tray. "He's a wild animal, a creature of nature. You can't own or control nature," Josie said.

Maisy took the silverware out of her hand and quickly finished for her while signaling to Jake and Linh to follow her inside.

Brian took the card and shook the man's hand. "You're welcome anytime."

The man took out a twenty-dollar bill. "My friend forgot to leave a tip."

When the deck was empty of people, Minnow stood. Brian wrapped his arms around her, and she sobbed. He looked at Josie, concern on his face. She longed to comfort Minnow. This wasn't about Josie's needs, though. Brian had diffused the situation. Josie had been moments from grabbing the fork the man was brandishing and stabbing him in the neck. No one spoke to her kids that way, and everyone on the island knew that she protected Gumbo as one of her own.

Minnow pushed away from Brian and ran to the side of the deck, then threw up into the swirling oily water below.

Chapter 7

Grand Isle, Louisiana

Monday, April 26, 2010

Josie turned off the television hanging over the restaurant bar. She didn't need the constant blather of news documenting the oil spill outside her window. She also had no interest in watching strangers gossip. Gossip was the reality of living on an island eight miles long. Everyone was connected one way or another. Sooner or later, you were part of it. It hadn't taken long for Saturday's pelican showdown to make the island rounds. She did appreciate the support from those who came in for last night's Sunday Supper. All night she heard "Minnow should have decked him. How is our dear Gumbo today? I heard Brian took that bastard down in a half nelson."

Josie sighed. Now it was Monday. *A week of new challenges is about to begin.*

She poured herself a glass of water and walked over to Minnow, sitting at a four-top table. Sunlight splashed across her face, making her look like an arty black-and-white photograph.

"Whatcha up to, *chère?*" Josie asked.

She looked up from a road map spread before her. "Don't worry. I finished the napkins, silverware, and serviced the empty salt and pepper shakers."

"I was asking, not scolding. I appreciate the extra hours on your day off."

The oil spill disrupted everything on the island, including school.

"Are you hungry?" Josie pointed toward the kitchen.

Minnow shook her head. "Maisy made scrambled eggs and brioche toast."

"Did it bother your stomach?"

"No."

"She ate two bites," Maisy said, walking into the dining room.

Minnow threw Maisy a sour look.

"I earned an A plus in eggs in culinary school, and you turned up your nose at them. I won't stand here pretending everything is fine with you," Maisy said.

"I'm calling Dr. Tynsdale about your stomach," Josie said.

Minnow was gaunt, like a stick figure, her complexion blotchy, her hair dull. "You're both overreacting."

Maisy placed a hand on her shoulder. "I'll go with you."

Minnow laughed. "You just want a reason to visit him."

Maisy struck a vamp pose, sucked in her cheeks, and twisted a braid. "I could listen to his Jamaican lilt all day. Makes me want to mix up a rum punch and drink in the sunset."

Josie smiled, grateful how Maisy always lightened the mood when it came to her kids.

Maisy tapped her temple. "I've been tweaking my chocolate-chili-chip brownies. I'll swing by and deliver a plate. See what heat I can stir up."

She left the dining room, humming Bob Marley's "One Love."

"Now that we solved Maisy's love life, what're you working on?" Josie asked.

Minnow traced a road on the map with a yellow highlighter. "My summer-break college road trip for me and Dad. Thought he'd like to leave the island, the oil, and, you know." She shrugged with one shoulder.

Josie nodded. Since the explosion, Brian had been untethered. She didn't know what was worse, the memorial services he attended or the ones he missed. He wouldn't talk to her about them. She'd ask after certain friends, and he'd change the subject, and he'd end any conversation about his work with "I'm waiting like everyone to be reassigned."

His last paycheck had arrived, but that was all they could count on. At least they still had his company benefits.

Minnow tapped the highlighter on the table. "We can drive to LSU and then to Texas. Dad wants to see his friend." She ran her finger along the highway line. "Or drive this way to Tulane and Florida. What do you think?"

Josie hunched over the map and tilted her head. She had to maintain her charade. Brian still hadn't told Minnow and Toby the truth— that they no longer had money for college. She didn't even know if they could afford gas money for this imagined trip. As angry as she was, she refused to assume that blame too. She swiped her hand over her face to calm the tears threatening to turn this conversation into a confessional. That would at best make her into a liar for not telling her. At worst, Minnow would worry about problems Josie wanted to protect her from. The oil provided enough worry for everyone.

She deserves this chance. I'll work harder, leave the island.

"Texas first, or Florida?" Minnow asked, breaking into her thoughts.

Josie coaxed a smile into her voice. "LSU and Tulane both have business programs. You could drive up and back in a day, spread the trip out. And then stop and speak to the admissions counselor at the community college in Houma. That's where I went."

Minnow capped the highlighter and walked to the bar and took a can of ginger ale from the refrigerator. "The truth is, I'm not interested in business. Uncle Hollis wants me to work with him at the wildlife sanctuary. We discussed a research topic about how the oil spill is affecting the number of birds coming to the breeding areas. He wants me to write it with him and see if we can publish it. It's a big accomplishment for a high school student and could be the key to a competitive college acceptance, maybe even a scholarship."

She stood with her back straight, and she spoke with confidence and pride.

"When did this all happen?"

"The day the oil hit the beach. He's worried this spill will wipe out the entire breeding season, but we could do something positive to help the birds."

"I think that's commendable." Louise and Hollis had always been close to Minnow and Toby. She loved how close they were, but it was hard not to feel that Hollis knew the most important parts of Minnow's heart. That was *her* job. She was Minnow's mother. Since she moved out of the house, that gap had only grown wider.

"*Commendable*? That's all you have to say? The oil's already at the breeding grounds. Someone needs to care about the animals. I explained this to Dad. But, since you two don't talk." She sighed in frustration.

Josie took a deep breath. *Man plans, and God laughs.* "A business degree would still be useful. You could minor in wild animals."

"You don't *minor* in wild animals." Minnow rolled her eyes and snapped the tab on the soda can, the escaping hiss amplifying the annoyance on her face. "Mom, I appreciate how hard you work, but I don't want the restaurant or to work in the food business like you do." She took a long swallow of the soda.

Josie rocked slowly in her seat. She *did* want this. Well, not the problems and the awful hours. She had enough kitchen experience before she went to culinary school to understand there was nothing romantic about it.

She'd bloomed away from the island. A freed spirit interning in San Francisco at a trendy fine-dining restaurant. She'd had friends, a career, and independence.

In her mother's world, college was a waste, especially for girls. Josie would work in the restaurant, care for her brother, and complete her chores. Odeal had done the same her whole life. The work would be enough for Josie.

Minnow had Josie's stubborn streak, and it set Josie sideways to see it radiate from Brian's features.

Josie smoothed the map, pressing the creases flat. Maybe she expected too much from Minnow. Lord, stop her if she was becoming Odeal. She rubbed her arms.

"I could take you to Baton Rouge and LSU." She hated the lie. Like telling that awful man the other day pelicans were still endangered.

"As if you could." Minnow shook her head. "You're either here or taking care of Grandpa. We never spend time with you anymore. And . . ."

"And what? That's how it works when you run a restaurant that relies on tourists."

Minnow grabbed a stack of folded bar towels and refolded them. "We used to do stuff together as a family."

Josie pursed her lips. *She's blaming me again.*

"I can take time off. We're not busy." She held her arms out to the empty restaurant. "Maisy can handle the kitchen."

"You'll never stop working. You work at everything except what's important."

Josie inhaled deeply. "What's important I'm not working on?"

Minnow stood behind the bar. The barrier bolstered her bravado. She was almost a legal adult yet in so many ways just a child who only understands her immediate needs.

"Forget it." Minnow shrugged.

"No, tell me." Josie wasn't backing away.

"Mom, you always do this."

"What?"

Minnow shuffled paper coasters into piles. "You never let anything go. Fine. Do you want to know what I think?"

Josie nodded. She really did.

"If you worked harder to be home when Dad was onshore, we'd still be a family. He's really hurting now with the accident. And you don't care. Toby asked you to stay and have dinner with us last night. You couldn't even manage that."

Minnow stacked the coasters like a deck of cards.

Ouch! Not fair. The rig accident didn't cancel Brian's past actions—actions he was too stubborn to tell the kids about. Why was *she* dubbed the opportunistic workaholic more concerned about the restaurant than her kids? She was killing herself to keep their home.

Josie gripped the table edge and swallowed the hurt. Her mother used to bait her, and she had years of evasive maneuvers to call on.

Minnow crushed the empty soda can in her hand.

"*Chère,* I understand this is hard for you." *I will not throw the restaurant at her the way Odeal did.* "Sunday Supper is our busiest night. I need that right now to pay our bills. Grandpa put in for an emergency assistance payment. Once that comes in, I'll work less. I promise. And I respect your decision not to go to college for business."

Josie had always longed for her family's respect. Minnow deserved the same.

"I want to leave this pile of sand and do something important with my life."

Minnow's words stung. Josie had stayed on the island when she was pregnant because Brian loved it. He wanted them to raise their family here. It was safe to him. And over time, it was safe to her in a way that it never was when she was growing up. She once had dreams, and they took her across the country. Then she saw she could have all she wanted here on the island, until Brian shattered it all.

Josie flexed her fingers, pumping them to release the tension she held in her fists. She didn't need to defend herself. *I'm the parent here.* Yet Minnow was honest, probably the only person who ever was.

"This is all I know." Josie waved her hand. "Feeding people and running the restaurant. I hope you'll find your passion and share it with me."

Josie ached for Minnow's love. The little girl with the flashing brown eyes who stood on a stool in the kitchen, nibbling cookie dough when she thought no one was looking. The smile like a sunrise when she held Toby and counted his fingers and toes, mimicking Josie. The squeal when Brian let her drive the bay boat and she bumped it hard and fast over the waves. This island was part of her. Maybe she was rejecting Josie.

"Minnow, the truth is—" But she stopped herself. She couldn't do it. The kids loved Brian. She wouldn't destroy their trust in him the way he did to her. She wouldn't add father-slayer to Minnow's list of her faults.

"What?"

"The truth is, I'm just as rattled by the explosion and the oil. What that man did to Gumbo and the way he spoke to you. I've been sideways since. I about stabbed that jerk in the neck with a fork."

Minnow laughed.

"And you're right about your dad. He needs us all."

Chapter 8

Grand Isle, Louisiana

Saturday, May 1, 2010

In the two weeks since the explosion, Brian had driven to a string of memorial services. He went to the restaurant before the first one to ask Josie for his surrendered credit card.

What he really wanted was to ask her to go with him. The idea of facing those widows, those men's children, alone, scared him. It could have been Josie planning *his* memorial, leaving Toby and Minnow to grow up without a father. Nightmare fuel. But asking for the credit card opened a wound, and he didn't dare deepen it.

To his surprise, she handed him one of the few cards that he hadn't maxed out. He pocketed it, guilt burning in his chest.

Today, he was back on the island, grateful to be working with Hughdean to fix his shrimp boat. He needed projects to keep his hands and mind engaged. He was worried about money, his job, and the oil shutting down the restaurant, and he was bombarded by sadness with the string of memorial ceremonies.

"Damn, it's hot today," Hughdean said. "I hate being docked. At least on the water there's a breeze to cool you." He sat on an overturned bucket and wiped a towel over the back of his neck.

Brian stuck a gloved hand into a cooler full of ice and retrieved two bottles of beer. "One Abita, one Bud."

Hughdean lowered his head and winked at Brian. They immediately held their fists by their ears.

"Rock, paper, scissors, shoot," they said in unison and made their moves.

"Paper covers rock." Brian tossed the Bud to Hughdean, and together they sat, each with their own thoughts.

Brian shaded his eyes with his hand. Most of Grand Isle's fishing fleet was out for the day. The wind carried voices from a neighboring slip. Brian couldn't make it all out, but he didn't have to. Oil. Shoreline. Disaster.

He wiped his forehead with the bottom of his shirt. Hughdean was right about the heat. The boat didn't offer much shade, and the wooden deck reflected the sun at their faces. Pungent diesel fuel mixed with a rank low tide rot of drying nets, making his stomach turn.

The *New Deal*'s outrigger was busted. Brian called Hughdean's boat "the lemon of the sea." It was the least reliable of his brother-in-law's shrimping fleet. But he welcomed the challenge. Solve a problem, move to the next, and the next, and the next. Like cards flipping on a blackjack table.

Hughdean popped the beer cap with a hiss and swiped the cool bottle across his forehead. They had spent the sun-drenched morning coaxing the starboard outrigger motor to rise and lower. The boat needed both sides to extend for stability and shrimp harvesting.

"Damn motor's gonna cost me a month's catch to replace." Hughdean kicked a coil of rope, unspooling it like a snake on the deck.

Brian rewound the rope and tossed it out of Hughdean's reach. "I can rebuild it."

"I may sell her," Hughdean said.

"Sorry, who?"

"The boat, you moron. The other three can cover my contracts, and with orders down." He took a long swallow.

"This won't last long, and your orders will be better than ever," Brian said.

Hughdean tapped the bottle against the bucket seat and sighed. "Are you paying attention to what's happening out there?" He waved his arm, indicating the open water.

The tentacles of a seven-mile-long oil slick had landed on the island and were growing larger by the hour. BP estimated five thousand barrels of oil were escaping from the well each day. Aerial and ocean observations put it at twenty-five thousand barrels a day. The state was demanding the US Army Corps of Engineers build sand berms on the smaller barrier islands.

Brian wasn't paying attention. His focus was to connect with his friends from the rig. Man-eating rabbits could have been discovered in the Himalayas, and he would have shrugged, saying "That's nice."

"My New Orleans restaurants say customers are scared of contaminated seafood. Josie's had a bunch of cancellations too."

"She hasn't said."

"The Blessing of the Fleet party will probably be the last for a while, and that only happened because of me. A bachelor party fishing trip pulled the plug yesterday. She should sweet-talk up the menu. Entice 'em. She doesn't have a sales bone in her body. Guess they didn't teach her any of that at that fancy school of hers. Like talking to a stump some days."

Brian's jaw tensed. Despite the fact he and Josie weren't getting along these past months, he wouldn't stand for the way Hughdean talked about her. Though, he needed to take some blame. Hughdean and Brian had met when Hughdean was still playing stickball and fishing off the pier. He had looked up to Brian back then and still took his cues from him. Brian had overshared the problems and fights he and Josie had about his gambling and expenses. Yet Hughdean didn't need much encouragement to pick on Josie. That phrase, "like talking to a stump," was one Brian had heard Odeal say more than once to Josie. It wasn't a leap for Hughdean to pick up Odeal's mantle.

"Don't be a prick. And don't talk about your sister and my wife that way."

"Lighten up, Brian." Hughdean finished his beer.

Brian collected the disassembled motor parts into a crate. "Tomorrow, I'll head to the marine salvage yard in Morgan City and source the boat parts. The *New Deal* won't be shrimping for another week."

"Lots of oil folks in Morgan City. Did you ever find your friend Penman?" Hughdean asked, interrupting Brian's easily straying mind.

Brian nodded. It had taken him a week to locate Penman through his daughter in Nevada, and she had told him about his burns. He'd had a bag packed, ready to see him, but Elena said he didn't want to see anyone.

"He lays in bed and stares at the ceiling. The bruises and chemical burns in his lungs are the worst. He can't speak, and his breathing is labored. But Dad's made of tough stuff." Elena sobbed; a sound Brian had heard repeatedly these past few days as he connected with friends.

"Josie and I are praying for him. We're here for you both," Brian told Elena. He meant it, too, deep in the blood that pumped through his veins. He was whole and unharmed and had space to hold their emotions.

"Thank you. I'll tell him."

When they'd hung up, Brian punched the kitchen wall in frustration. Another hole to fix. Then he told Josie.

She'd rubbed the scar on the palm of her hand as if she were trying to connect to his pain. She did that when she was upset or lost in thought. Of all the scars on Josie's body, the oyster scar was like an extra appendage.

"He'll recover, right?" Hughdean said, breaking into his thoughts.

Brian nodded. "The physical wounds. The rest?"

He'd heard his friends' stories so many times now that he could imagine everything that had happened on the rig. He pictured the crew scrambling through the narrow smoke-choked halls and dodging burning debris. He couldn't imagine how strong the explosion was to have sunk the rig. An oil platform was like a mountain, engineered to stand in the ocean. The days since the accident were a blur.

At night, he dreamed about the rig, the people, the lights, the way the ocean charged the air in high winds, even the falcons. A gloom crushed him. Minnow and Toby were his bright spot. They had moved back to the house when he came home. Minnow carried on like she'd been away for a year and like privacy was the only thing that mattered in her life. Brian now hated being alone. It allowed his thoughts to roam. He was plagued with the twin torments of nightmares and insomnia. Only the kids rustling through the house pulled him from bed in the morning.

The sounds of a crew bantering in rapid Vietnamese made them turn their heads. Tommy Nguyen's fishing boat, the *Công Chúa*, glided into its slip.

Tommy's family had been in Grand Isle since 1995. He was a third-generation fisherman, but the first born in Louisiana. His family had settled in New Orleans in the 1970s—part of the emerging Vietnamese community. They went back to their roots, fishing. The Gulf's rich waters and the Louisiana swamps felt familiar. The community spread to Plaquemines and Jefferson Parishes. Brian and Tommy met one day when Tommy needed an engine rebuilt. They became fast friends. Soon Tommy's mom, Linh, was working at the restaurant. She taught Josie how to hand roll rice wrappers for spring rolls and pickle daikon radishes for bánh mì sandwiches. Josie still rotated those for lunch, grinning at the thought that Odeal would have hated it.

Tommy stood at the helm and waved as he guided the seventy-eight-foot boat next to Hughdean's equal-size shrimper. Two of his cousins jumped on the dock and tied up. He stepped onto the dock and called over to Brian and Hughdean.

"Got any more?" He pantomimed drinking a beer.

Brian saluted with two fingers, then clawed through the cooler of ice and tossed Tommy one.

"How's the catch today?" Hughdean asked.

Tommy flicked off the beer cap, slid it into the front pocket of his jeans, and downed half the bottle in one swallow. He walked from the dock and stepped onto the *New Deal*.

"Fishing's great. Can't say the same for the market." He shook his head. "Why aren't you out today?"

"Outrigger's toast," Hughdean said. "My orders are canceling. What're you hearing?"

"It's not what I hear. It's what I know." Tommy removed a frayed New Orleans Saints ball cap that revealed a head of receding thick black hair. He leaned against the boat's railing. His forearms were tan and strong, with taut muscles.

"Oil's real bad. You can see it and smell it on the water. Marina smells like a candle shop in comparison. My cousin tossed a cigarette into the water, and it flared."

"Is the catch still clean?" Brian asked. The oil was flowing from a mile under the seabed. The Deepwater Horizon engineers estimated the deposit held fifty million barrels. Enough oil and natural gas that it was worth the hunt. But not the lives of his friends or their livelihoods.

Tommy finished the beer and stuck the empty bottle into the cooler of ice. "We found some clear water, and everything looks fine, but I don't know for how much longer. It's not like the shrimp can move out of the way."

His eyewitness news was more accurate than what Transocean or BP were providing. A Coast Guard investigation was underway over the cause of the explosion. Now the oil was spreading. BP's containment booms were useless. The news channels were calling it an "oilpocalypse."

Brian hated how the community was being portrayed, the poor down-and-out citizens of the oil spill. That wasn't his community. They were resilient storm after storm and through bad economies, when the price of oil plunged. This was another bad time. They would rise above it.

The high-pitched purr of a bay boat grew louder, and the shadow of a pelican circled over the deck.

"Got ourselves a bird visitor." Hughdean pointed to Gumbo with his bottle.

Brian faced the water as Minnow, Hollis, and Josie drew closer. Hollis cut the motor and glided the nineteen-foot bay boat into the slip between the bigger fishing vessels.

Why's Josie here with Hollis? She should be serving lunch.

Minnow jumped off the boat, balancing between the deck and the dock. Gumbo landed next to the cooler and Hughdean. He waddled over to a white bucket and stuck his head inside, where there were often fish. He tapped his long bill against the side.

"'Sup, bird. Didn't shrimp today. No leftovers for you," Hughdean said.

About a year ago, Gumbo began visiting Hughdean as he came in from shrimping. He would land on the deck and ride with him back into the marina. Hughdean would shove a bucket of bycatch fish over to him. Gumbo ignored him anywhere else on the island or at the restaurant, as if they were sharing a secret.

"What're you three"—Brian looked at Gumbo—"four doing here?"

Brian caught the line Hollis tossed to him.

"Hi, Dad." Minnow smiled. She wore a purple LSU T-shirt and hat and cutoff jean shorts. Hollis had a matching shirt and hat, his pockets stuffed with junk like Mary Poppins's handbag.

Josie was dressed for work, her hair tight in a bun. She wore sunglasses hiding her expression. She carried a large Odeal's to-go bag and balanced it on her hip as she stepped onto the dock. He caught the bag from her, grabbing her forearm. She smiled.

"We're checking on pelicans on Queen Bess Island," Hollis said.

"What's happening there?" Tommy asked.

Hollis frowned, the lines on his forehead pulled together in a V, like an arrow pointing to his long nose. "Reports of wildlife covered in oil."

"No shit," Tommy said. "Sorry, language." He nodded to Minnow.

She pretended to be offended. "Oh, my delicate ears." She blew Hughdean a kiss.

"Taught you well," Hughdean said.

"Gumbo, hey. Gumbo, over here," one of Tommy's crew called and dangled a small fish in the air.

Gumbo flapped and hop tripped over a length of rope as he made his way across to the other boat. The man tossed the fish into the air, and Gumbo caught it and took off over the water before circling back to stand by Minnow.

Hollis sighed. "Don't feed him."

"Lighten up, Birdman. It's fish, not Maisy's étouffée," Hughdean said. "What a jackoff that guy was. Good thing Minnow understands the score when it comes to city folks."

Minnow rolled her eyes. The island network had already inflated the story of Minnow fighting for Gumbo's honor.

"I brought lunch for the humans." Josie pawed through the bag Brian held. He felt the heat of her head. She smelled like the kitchen—a mixture of the industrial soap they used, fry oil, and lemon.

"I packed po'boys, tomato salad, ham-and-biscuit sandwiches, and tea cakes. I've got plenty here for you and your crew, Tommy. My box lunches are double what a normal person can eat."

"Who says your brother's normal?" Tommy said.

Hughdean raised his beer.

Tea cakes. Brian opened the white bakery box to reveal a dozen pillowy gold circles. Since the accident, Josie had flipped the switch to comfort food mode.

He really wanted her strong chef's thumbs to work on the knots in his shoulders. Someone who didn't call him out as working on "that" rig like he was responsible for the accident. He wanted to feel safe with her, sitting quiet together like the day of the explosion. He hadn't earned that trust back from her. For now, he was happy with their unspoken truce. She handed him sandwiches, full meals, oysters in bags of ice. It was her way of saying she cared.

She wouldn't bring food for Hughdean. Brian smiled, a rare expression since the explosion. He had no words to describe the dark clawing at him. Josie knew to feed him.

"Maisy's outdone herself with these tea cakes," Brian said.

"I made those," Josie said, pride in her voice.

"You?" Brian inspected a cookie.

"What's a tea cake?" Tommy asked.

"You were born here, right?" Minnow said.

Tommy shrugged. "I grew up with pig-ear cookies."

Minnow made a disgusted face.

Tommy laughed. "Not real pigs."

Brian passed the box, and Hollis took a bite. "Yup, Josie made these." He gestured to Tommy to try it.

Ten years ago, Louise had a miscarriage. She had been so excited that her baby and Toby would play together, as she and Josie had. It wasn't her first miscarriage, but after this she knew she'd never be able to have children. She grieved hard, locking herself inside her house, refusing to see anyone. She quit her job in the DA's office. She lost all her fire and purpose now that "mother" could no longer be her title.

Josie baked tea cakes every day for her, using the excuse of entering a baking competition. After a month, and over a thousand cookies, Josie fixed a batch with orange zest and amaretto, mimicking Louise's favorite drink, the amaretto sunrise. That day, Louise dressed and left the house. She had only made it to the beach, and Josie had sat with her for hours.

"Minnow and I need to make it to the island before the tide comes in," Hollis said.

"You ditching my sister?" Hughdean said.

"Actually, I came to see you." Josie pointed at Hughdean. "Louise heard some news this morning."

Hollis nodded.

Brian was always the last to know anything when it came to Josie, Hollis, and Louise. He was the round peg unable to fit into their triangular relationship hole.

"Tommy, you'll want to hear this too," Josie said.

"What's her majesty the mayor declaring today?" Hughdean spread his legs wide and snapped the cap off another beer.

Hollis stuffed his hands into his front pockets.

Josie took a breath. "The federal government is banning our fishing tomorrow. Governor Jindal has a press conference scheduled later, if you want to hear it from him."

Tommy smacked his hat against his thigh and Hughdean stood, angling for a fight, but he had no one to hit. He grabbed the coiled rope and threw it across the deck, then hoisted the plastic bucket he had been sitting on and screamed.

Gumbo took flight. Brian and Tommy wrestled his arms and pushed the bucket to the side. It was one thing to blow off some steam, another to break something new.

"Hey, it'll be okay," Brian said.

"Will it? Your goddamned rig has completely screwed my business."

"The ban's ten days." Hollis held up his hands as if approaching a wounded animal.

Brian cut a look at Tommy. His one boat supported his entire family. Hughdean had four with crews on each with families to feed. A fishing ban hurt everyone, along with the recreational fishing on the island.

Hughdean sat with a huff and clawed through the food. He tossed wrapped sandwiches to Tommy and Brian. "Eat up, gentlemen. These are the last oysters we're gonna taste for a while."

Brian left his sandwich and followed Josie to check on Minnow. Gumbo had returned, now perched beside her. He crouched his head and lifted a leg as Brian approached.

"It's okay, boy. I won't hurt anyone." *I've already done enough.*

Minnow stroked Gumbo's long neck. He wagged his tail feathers once and tucked his head and neck into his body.

"Everyone's acting upset." Minnow twisted the end of her ponytail. "What's gonna happen to the island and all of us?"

Brian sat next to her and rested his hand on her back. His fingers counted the bumpy vertebrae in her spine. *When did she get so thin?*

"This isn't the first leak. And you're not responsible for the rig. You just work there," Josie said.

Worked. The rig's sitting on the bottom of the ocean. "A lot of people are coming to help," Brian said.

"Uncle Hollis is worried about the birds. It's mating season on all the islands. What if Gumbo gets hurt? We can't stop the oil."

"Gumbo doesn't usually mix with the other pelicans in the outer islands. He stays near the restaurant, and we can keep an eye on him," Josie said.

Brian ran his hand over Minnow's head and pulled her into a hug.

"Everything will settle in a few days. You'll see." He looked over her head at Josie. In truth he had no idea. Last Sunday was the annual blessing of the shrimp fleet. Brian had missed the festival, but Hughdean had been in high spirits about the forecast for the shrimp harvest this year. And now he and Tommy—the entire community—were docked. If they didn't fish, they didn't eat. As for his job, during the memorial services, he'd heard rumors about reassignments to other Transocean rigs. Both the *Discoverer Clear Leader* and the Marianas were options. Brian knew guys on the Marianas who complained of maintenance issues. Oil work offered the best-paying jobs in the state, but he wasn't ready to die for a paycheck, leaving his children fatherless.

Josie nodded and added her hand to Minnow's back. Minnow shrugged her away, and Josie took a step to the side.

Hollis stood on Hughdean's boat and scanned the water toward Queen Bess Island with a pair of binoculars. The oil was surrounding all the barrier islands now.

"I think Uncle Hollis is ready to leave. You're doing important work. I'm proud of you," Brian said.

"Thanks for the heads-up, Josie. I need to sell today's catch before the news spreads," Tommy said.

Hughdean stared at the outrigging motor.

"You okay?" Brian asked.

"Just ducky, queen for a day. No rush repairing this. I can't afford it."

Brian exhaled. "I'm still fixin' to head to Morgan City for parts. We want to be ready."

Hughdean waved him off. "Go. Thanks for the help today."

"You want a ride back to the restaurant?" Brian asked Josie.

They watched as Minnow, Hollis, and Gumbo became specks in the distance. "Sure."

Brian grabbed a sandwich and stuffed a cookie into his mouth. Josie smiled, and they walked to his truck. He reached the passenger side, opening the door for her before she could. It felt like he was picking her up for a date and wanting to impress her with his manners.

He gripped the steering wheel and waited for the click of her seat belt.

"How'd you get to be the lucky one to tell Hughdean about the fishing ban?"

Josie shook her head. "Louise didn't feel it was right for the mayor to be showing special favors to anyone. She's not allowed to say anything until the governor makes it official. And, well, she and Hollis are married, so *he* couldn't say anything."

"Tommy said the oil is bad out there," Brian said.

She rubbed her hands together and stared at her feet. "Hollis said the spill is like nothing to ever hit the Gulf. BP is spraying stuff to break up the oil on the water. He suspects they're trying to hide it. It's toxic, too, and could be worse for the water quality."

"Dispersant, core-something. I don't remember the name. They used dispersants on the *Exxon Valdez* spill," Brian said.

"Gosh, that was what, twenty years ago? You'd think they'd invent a better solution by now."

They sat quietly as the truck crunched over the gravel in the parking lot, and he turned onto the main road.

"Louise is pretty certain that the fishing ban will last longer than ten days," she said. "It'll kill the sport fishing season and the tourist traffic." She shook her head.

"Maybe not." He forced a bright note into his voice. "That magazine is coming out in a few weeks. By then BP will have plugged the well. Once the oil stops, things will settle. I'll be reassigned soon. While I wait, I have that chore list you made for the restaurant."

He didn't believe it. The pressure pent up under the Earth's crust was a power to behold.

"Josie, I didn't mean for this to happen." His voice was soft, his eyes focused on the road.

She tugged on the seat belt and turned her body toward him. "You didn't cause this accident."

Not the accident.

"When're you heading to Morgan City?" Josie asked.

"Tomorrow or Monday." Brian braked at a stop sign and stole a look at her. She fiddled with her sunglasses in her hands. Her eyes looked tired, and every worry line on her face had deepened. *Josie, let me in.* He didn't know how to ask, and he was fearful she'd say to leave her alone.

"Would you mind driving out today instead and doing me a favor?"

"What do you need?"

"A delivery. Hot sauce."

At his questioning look, she explained, beaming. "I had an idea." She turned toward him. "Since the tourists aren't coming to me, I'm going to them."

"Like setting up a booth at a fair? We talked about that once."

"I sat with the yellow pages and searched tour companies. I found a Cajun coast swamp tour in Morgan City that also does a Cajun food

69

tour. They agreed to buy my sauce as part of their tour package. I'm putting in discount coupons, too, for a free appetizer for anyone who comes to the restaurant."

"How many bottles did they buy?" Brian asked.

"A hundred, just to see how it goes. They have about twenty people per tour."

"And how much are you selling them for?"

"We sell the sauce for three dollars a bottle at the restaurant. I offered him a volume discount of two fifty a bottle."

"But that's only two hundred fifty dollars, not counting the free food offer and the gas to drive to Morgan City. You'll lose more than you make."

When they first married, Josie had ambitious plans for the restaurant, but they had no money. That's when he went out to the rig. They delayed buying a house, instead saving his new salary to take the restaurant down to the studs for a complete remodel. His paycheck and the physical work he put into the building were the most satisfying work he had ever done. Daniel Dean and Hughdean had fought them, predicting the change would make it all fancy and destroy what people loved about Odeal's. They wanted nothing to do with it, and Josie and Brian had to pay for it themselves. If they had failed, it would be their lost money.

Josie crossed her arms. Her mouth went from pleased to a hard line. *Crap. Now I sound like her father.* Before he had his strokes, Daniel Dean had a successful CPA practice. He still kept the restaurant's books and wasn't shy about telling Josie how to spend her money.

"Never mind. I'll have one of the busboys do it." She stared out the window.

"Now, hold on. I'm warming to where this can go. No one comes to have just an appetizer. They're gonna have a drink on a hot day on our deck. Unless they're only drinking sweet tea, we'll more than break even. Then, of course, they're hooked and stay for a full meal, maybe buy another bottle of hot sauce. The two hundred fifty dollars you make is like someone paying *you* to advertise."

Her smile returned, and he exhaled. They used to talk like this all the time. She'd test out ideas, and he'd swat them back or run with them. He was out of practice, popping off before taking the time to consider her goals.

"It's not a lot of money. But I won't sit in a half-empty restaurant and do nothing. If this works, I'll find other tourist places in New Orleans, riverboats and such. I can price the sauce higher in the city. Before"—she exhaled with a huff—"the new business plans were canceled, I wanted to rename the sauce. Something catchy and sexy. Outside the island, the name *Odeal's Cajun Pepper Sauce* doesn't mean much. I changed the name and had new labels put on the bottles."

"Did you tell your dad and Hughdean?"

"No." She crossed her arms. "Hughdean would yell that I was messing with tradition and disparaging Momma's name. And Daddy would cluck his tongue over the money."

"You're real worried about money now," he said. It was a statement, not a question. He needed to understand how bad. Was it keeping her awake at night like him?

"I'm always worried. I put in for a relief payment. Louise said people are already seeing checks. The mortgages are due in two weeks and . . ." She stared at him.

"I've got some engine repairs scheduled that'll cover what I spent to travel to the memorial services." That only got them treading water. It didn't bring any balances down or provide any cushion if the spill continued.

Josie sat rubbing the scar on her hand. He wanted to hold her hand and take away the worry.

"If you do go today, Toby would love to go with you."

Brian parked beside the restaurant. The Odeal's sign loomed, a dark eyebrow over the restaurant's roof, like the dead woman herself. *Glad I didn't have to paint it.*

71

"Thanks for lunch." He held the sandwich. "I'm sure Hughdean appreciated it too."

"No, he doesn't." Josie released the seat belt and opened the truck door.

Brian laughed. She knew her brother. "Well, Tommy appreciated it."

"Hey, before we go inside—" Josie said. She closed the door and turned to him. "I'm worried about Minnow. It's time I called Dr. Tynsdale. She scared me the other day. She's turning into a pile of bones. How is she with you? Is she eating and sleeping?"

"She's fine with me, but I won't lie." He rubbed the back of his neck. "I've been so turned around with these memorial services and the rig going down. They don't eat the same with me like they do with you. You were skinny at her age too. And you used to prowl around like a jungle cat at night. Maybe it's a growth spurt? Growing pains?"

Josie shook her head. "Is she following a fad diet? Girls are so body conscious at her age. I make her favorite foods, and she turns up her nose."

"Is she turning her nose up at the food or at you?"

Josie pursed her lips. "If you told her and Toby the truth, she wouldn't treat me like the enemy."

He crossed his arms. Wasn't she listening? *His head was about to explode, alongside the rig. He had side work lined up. He was dancing as fast as he could.*

"You're not anyone's enemy," Brian said. "I don't want us to fight. I was wrong to let you leave. We both said mean things. Breaking all those rules the counselor taught us about how to talk to each other. We're different people, in a different place. Come home." He reached for her hand. "I'll be beached here for who knows how long. We can't work us out if we're apart."

She pulled her hand away. "You didn't *let* me do anything. It's not what you said. It's what you did and haven't done. You promised to tell them the truth."

"The only truth is that oil's covering our island. Come home for the kids."

"I left *because* of the kids."

Come home for me. He opened his mouth to speak, but she turned her back to him and headed to the restaurant. There was nothing he could say, so he followed her inside.

"The hot sauce is in the storage room. I'll call Toby."

"Afternoon, Brian," Maisy said as they passed her in the kitchen. "What brings you by?"

"He's making the delivery for me in Morgan City," Josie said.

"That's right helpful of you."

Maisy was on his side. A month into their split, she had come to him, worried about Josie crying as she stacked cases of produce. Maisy believed in love and their relationship. She kept telling them, "If y'all spend some time together as a family again, y'all be a family again."

He had just tried, and that earned him a tongue-lashing. Josie ran hot and cold like a busted thermostat.

"How'd Hughdean take the news about the fishing ban?" Maisy asked.

"As good as you'd predicted," Josie said.

"He isn't the only one suffering. Reservations are canceling like bubbles popping in a bath."

Josie picked up a pile of unopened mail and tossed junk letters into the trash with more force than necessary. "I don't want to hear about that now."

"We'll make it through this," Brian said. He wanted to reassure her. "Like when a bad storm hits the island on Memorial Day or the Fourth. Tourists cancel, but they come back. The seafood will be tested a million times, and everything will be normal again." *Except my rig is sinking into the Gulf of Mexico.*

"Now I've heard everything. Brian Babineaux, the voice of positivity and reason," Maisy said. "You taking lessons from Louise?"

Brian laughed. Josie glared.

"Right, I'll fetch the box and the address." He marched into the storeroom, grabbed the boxes, and left.

Why is she so difficult? Maybe they *had* run their course.

Brian set the boxes in the back of the truck. The flap was open on the top box, and he pulled out a bottle, curious about the new name. The new label had an exaggerated pair of red lips floating on a yellow background. The new name: CAJUN SMACK.

He spun the bottle and confirmed it was the right sauce. The restaurant address was on the back.

Hot tears surprised him in the corners of his eyes.

Josie had always said the original sauce tasted more of vinegar than of peppers. She had started tinkering with the base years ago to complement a new recipe she had developed for two-bite shrimp cakes. Brian tasted dozens of batches and suffered days of upset stomachs. The improved sauce was *good.* Customers started asking her to bottle it. She found a local company to make it and sold it as *Odeal's Cajun Pepper Sauce.* Locals and tourists bought it. Sauce sales grew into a profitable side business, and Josie began talking about selling both the sauce and the shrimp bites under a new business called Pelican Point Provisions. It was what the restaurant was originally called in the 1930s, when her grandparents ran it as a grocery store. But like the rest of their dreams, it had gone by the wayside.

But the new label made him smile. It came from a different time. Josie had climbed into bed one night after making hot sauce for a Sunday supper. She had kissed him and run her hands down his thighs. He laughed as his lips burned from her snacking on the raw chilies and tasting the sauce. He joked for her to keep her hot Cajun smack off his privates. She laughed, but didn't listen, moving her pepper-stained lips and fingers across the length of his body. Nine months later, Toby was born.

She renamed it Cajun Smack. *After us.* He cracked the cap open and sniffed the top, igniting his nose with the heat. He shook the bottle into his mouth, and the fiery pepper sauce coated his tongue and throat, making him cough. His stomach would complain later, a penance he deserved. He painted his lips with the sauce. The hot burn kissed his mouth as hot tears slid down his face.

Chapter 9

Josie balanced a heavy picnic basket on her hip and walked inside the over-air-conditioned government building. When she told Maisy she wanted to bring lunch to Louise, she had been enthusiastic about helping. The slow trickle of customers had soured Josie's mood. She didn't mean to season everyone's anxiety with her prickly attitude. A restaurant where its employees were unhappy had awful-tasting food. An angry chef made broken sauces, desserts that lacked buttery sweetness, and the most bitter coffee to ever come out of a grinder. Josie remembered some days when her mother ran the restaurant and nothing came out right. It was damned near impossible to ruin biscuits and gravy, but it happened all the time. Odeal's tirades prompted the waitstaff to steer diners away from certain dishes. Everyone on the island knew when Odeal was feeling especially ugly, the biscuits ending up as fish bait. Feeding people should nourish the body and the spirit.

She paused at the double glass door with the name **MAYOR LOUISE E. MARTIL** stenciled in gold letters. The assistant's desk was empty. No matter. Josie pushed her way in.

The door to Louise's office was partially open. Josie paused. A murmur of midday talking heads looped the latest oil spill news on the TV as Louise finished a phone call.

"C'mon in." Louise waved her in from the hall.

Louise was the daughter of an honest-to-goodness beauty queen. As girls, Louise used to wear the rhinestone-studded crown and parade around her mother's bedroom and pose while Josie pretended to take her picture. Josie tried the crown on only once.

Today, Louise didn't sparkle like the crown.

She's worn out.

Louise had been working nonstop since the accident. She had projected a calm appearance and a positive outlook when Governor Jindal declared a state of emergency.

"Yes, the oil on our beaches and in our water is scary," Louise had said. "Grand Isle will be given help to handle the mess."

Now with viscous red-and-dark-brown slicks of oil fouling their pristine beach, Louise's pep-club personality was flaking. But not tender like a buttery pie crust.

Josie's only comfort to offer was food. Louise's idea of a balanced meal was a meatball pizza and a glass of wine, which she claimed was a fruit serving.

The office mirrored Louise's house, orderly as an operating theater, until you hit her desk. The area overflowed with stacks of files and phone books, with sticky notes on her computer like ruffled feathers.

Louise's hand hovered over the phone receiver as if she were about to make another call. She lifted her head and brushed her hair out of her face.

"You brought an actual picnic basket for our picnic lunch," Louise said.

She stood, her sleeveless white blouse revealing her toned arms and a cluster of beaded bangles on her wrist. On closer inspection, the blouse was missing a button, and her boutique black skirt was wrinkled beyond Louise's crisp allowance.

"Thought we'd make it special. I left the ants outside," Josie said.

Louise helped Josie with the basket and her shoulder bag. She reached to hug Josie hello, then covered her face with shaking hands.

Instinctively, Josie wrapped her arms tighter around her. Their relationship meant no questions needed to be asked or answered. They were each other's safe space, porous like dry sand when it came to absorbing gooey, messy emotions. Louise had absorbed Josie's sadness these past six months when she and Brian split. Whatever support Louise needed, Josie would provide. Louise's cheek rested on Josie's shoulder, and when her body slowed its shaking sobs, she pulled away.

"Hey, *chère*, what's wrong?"

Louise stood, her hands over her face.

Josie poked her head into the hall and closed the door.

"Sit, talk to me." Josie guided her to the royal blue chenille office couch.

"Sorry," Louise said, pulling a tissue from a box and mashing it into a ball.

"Hey, none of that," Josie said.

"I'm frustrated is all. That was a tour operator upset that people are canceling. The best I've been able to manage is to convince a BP person to come to the island next month and explain how to fill out all the relief support forms. I can't even help Hollis secure access to the restricted beaches and the barrier islands."

I won't dare tell her about the restaurant cancellations. Josie opened the picnic basket and set the small conference table in Louise's office. She plated thick slices of local creole tomatoes in green goddess dressing, fresh herbed biscuits, a baby vegetable salad with grilled chicken thighs, and tall glasses of strawberry lemonade from a thermos.

"That's great news about BP coming. Everyone will appreciate that you made that happen. The relief checks will come, and they will plug the well. There's a lot of summer left, with good events still planned. People just need to keep busy while we wait. I baked more tea cakes and biscuits this morning," Josie babbled and dropped a biscuit onto the plate. "The *Vacation Ventures* article will publish in June. That helps the whole island. I have an idea to talk to some of the fishing tour operators and the hotel folks and offer a weekend package that includes dinner at Odeal's. We're in this together, the island and everyone." Josie folded two cloth napkins into elaborate rosettes. "That silly class I took in table setting is one of the most used skills."

"Josie, stop. Listen to me."

"Are you using your mayor voice with me?"

"I'm using my shut-up-for-a-minute best friend voice."

Josie repositioned the forks and glasses and stepped away from the table. "I'm listening." *But I'm not liking it.*

"Even if the oil stopped this second, we'll lose half the summer."

"This isn't the Gulf's first oil spill." Josie offered Louise a seat. "Don't you see, *chère*, you're fighting for the town. The town will be all right." Josie placed a hand on Louise's shoulder.

Louise threw her hands up. "Since when are you Miss Happy News and Sunshine? That's my role. We've locked our entire economy to tourists."

Louise sat at the table and buttered a biscuit.

Josie poured glasses of lemonade.

"I'm not blind," Josie said. "It's just this magazine feature has me dreaming again. We all need dreams. Even you. Maybe I can bring Pelican Point Provisions back from the dead. I could start a whole new industry for the island. Imagine my hot sauce in stores across the world. I need to dream something for myself, a time beyond today when I won't worry about the bills." She sighed. "I expected to have enough money this summer to move out of my dad's. Eventually Brian will be reassigned to another rig, and the kids will stay with me again. I'd like to rent my own place where Minnow and Toby would like to stay, instead of sharing my old bedroom. Odeal haunts the house with bad memories. It's not healthy for anyone."

"I have no idea how you're living with those two men. Daniel Dean, maybe, but Hughdean? Are you punishing yourself?"

Maybe I am.

"This lunch is delicious," Louise said. She put down her fork. "You could solve the unhappy-kid problem if you move back to your house with Brian. It won't cost you any more money either."

"Have you forgotten why I left?"

"You've both cooled down since then. I've seen you with Brian. I even heard you laughing. Maybe it's time to try again."

"He said the ugliest things to me when I learned he had pawned my jewelry. Then he bought that expensive camera." Josie touched the scar on her mouth.

"You hated that ring," Louise said.

Odeal had backhanded Josie one afternoon after she came into the kitchen with a returned plate of food. One of the ring's sharp corners had caught the side of Josie's mouth, opening a gash. It had been one of the only times Odeal apologized.

"I hated it because she loved it. Locking it away for safekeeping was like locking her away. Now it's out in the world like a cursed charm. The only thing I have left from my grandparents is the restaurant, and Minnow certainly doesn't want it, and it's years before Toby will think about what he wants to do with his life."

"I have something to tell you," Louise said softly.

Josie looked up.

"I'm guessing since you haven't said anything, Minnow didn't tell you."

"Tell me what?" Josie's throat went dry. Her morning talk with Minnow was the first time they'd connected in months.

Josie cut into the tomatoes as if she were slicing through a tangled fishing net.

"Last Friday, Minnow called me to pick her and Bonnie Trahan up in Cut Off."

Josie's fork dropped with a *clank* onto the plate. "Why were they in Cut Off, and how late was it?"

"Bonnie's car broke down around 11:00 p.m. They were coming home from New Orleans."

"New Orleans? And why didn't she call me or Brian? Wait, she was staying with him last Friday . . ." Josie stood, anger boiling in her belly. "Where the hell was Brian?"

"Minnow said he was spending the night in Morgan City. He didn't know she was out, and she didn't want to call you."

"Where was Toby?" Josie's voice rose as she considered she had no idea what her family was doing.

"A sleepover at Connor's."

"I grounded her last month for sneaking out, and she's doing it again. Or was this Bonnie's doing?" *Was Brian out playing cards somewhere?*

"They went to see the Givers, a band from Lafayette."

"Did she expect you wouldn't tell me?"

"I'm not Aunt Louise for nothing."

Josie glared at her.

"She promised she would. I wanted to give her the chance."

"She's snuck out of the house three times, four now since I moved out. Maybe more since I'm the last to know. She's turning into a bag of bones and doesn't eat, always with a stomachache. Do you think it's drugs? Is she running to see a boy?" Josie collapsed on the office couch and rubbed her palm. "I should have never hired Bonnie."

"You just don't like her mother. She's always had the hots for Brian. And your split isn't a state secret. The minute Hattie rings his bell, you'll hear the buzz."

Josie crossed her arms. "Hattie Trahan has an ice cube's chance in hell with Brian. Besides, this isn't about him or my marriage. This is about Minnow. She disobeyed me again and then called *you* when she needed help, not me. She hates me. We used to be close."

Louise scooted closer to her and rubbed her back.

"You're upset. I don't think she's doing drugs. She doesn't fit the pattern. The sneaking out isn't good, but she was stone-cold sober when I picked them up."

"She must have said *something* to you."

Louise nodded. "She suspected you'd say no to the concert, and she really wanted to go. She huffed she was seventeen and you treat her like Toby. She wants you to trust her more."

Josie was short on trust these days with her family.

"By sneaking out and lying? I can't trust people when they lie to me."

"She isn't Brian. Don't transfer your feelings to her."

"I'm not. How could you even think that?" Josie refilled their glasses.

"She's rebelling, looking for freedom. You remember being seventeen with an overbearing mother," Louise said.

"If I lied to my momma, she'd make me regret whatever small thing I wanted."

Louise chuckled. "But you did occasionally fail to tell her everything you did. I remember the summer you dated that boy vacationing with his aunt and uncle and you two were stranded on Elmer's Island."

"So, it's a boy?"

"She didn't say. I think she's not telling you because, like with Odeal, she doesn't want whatever punishment you'll impose."

Josie spun around. "I am *not* my mother!"

"We're all our mothers at some level. I see you with the kids. You're afraid to let them out of your sight, worried they'll get hurt. Odeal may have had the mothering instincts of a snake, but she kept you within grabbing distance. You keep Minnow and Toby too close."

"You don't have kids. You don't understand."

The moment the words left her mouth, her face paled in shame.

"Louise," she whispered. "I shouldn't have . . . that was ugly of me."

Odeal would say hurtful things too. *Was* she like her mother?

"It's okay." Louise shrugged, her voice soft. She smoothed her skirt and stared outside. A beach-cleaning crew sat under a shade tree taking a break from the heat. "We both have oversize worries these days."

"Where's Hollis again?" Josie asked.

"Raccoon Island. It's one of the few places he hasn't been chased away. BP has hired a load of private-security goons to keep people off the islands. He's still got plenty of work to keep Minnow busy and out of trouble."

"Minnow told me that he wants to work on a bird project with her. She says it would be helpful for college. I wish he had discussed this with me before filling her head with ideas. Unless a project could lead to a full scholarship, all she will have are dashed dreams. You know money is well . . . tight, and I don't have a plan yet to get her there."

"I'm sorry, *chère*, you're right. Hollis is really worried about this spill. Right after the accident, he went to LSU looking for oil spill research. He told me there have been forty-three major spills in the US. That started him thinking about a new research project to track breeding pelican pairs during the spill. He thinks the world of Minnow. She's as bird nutty as he is." Louise dug through the picnic basket. "Where's all this baking you keep talking about?"

Josie bumped her aside and retrieved a container of tea cakes. "I made them with orange zest and amaretto the way you like."

Louise sat on the couch with the entire container on her lap and handed Josie one. "Are you planning to talk to Minnow?"

Josie took Louise's hand, adding another silent apology, and nodded. "Thank you for helping her when she called. I didn't have an Aunt Louise at her age. I need to talk to her and Brian. But first I'm making her a doctor's appointment. Her stomach pain is getting worse."

Chapter 10

Monday, May 10, 2010

Brian knocked his feet against the curb to make sure he wasn't tracking any of the island's relentless sand with him when he stepped inside the minimart gas station. Sweeping sand was a constant chore. He didn't want to add to Rosaline Rivard's list. He was here to bring her to tonight's community meeting at the mayor's office.

Brian was one of Rosaline's many adopted grandkids—her favorite, if you asked him, even over and above Hollis, her actual grandson.

The store was a time portal to Grand Isle in the 1950s. First tourists and now cleanup crews were directed to the twenty-foot-high fake palm tree with a lime-green neon sign that glowed **ISLAND GRAND**.

He inhaled the odd sweetness of the store, a combination of preservative-filled wrapped baked goods, cleaning fluids, and gardenia old-lady perfume. The scent comforted him, like walking into a kitchen filled with the scent of Josie sautéing onions, bell peppers, and celery, the Cajun holy trinity.

He noticed now that the aisle once devoted to T-shirts and Grand Isle souvenirs was now filled with green plastic hard hats and black rubber boots.

He nodded to two cleanup workers grabbing sodas and chips. Eighteen hundred workers were coming to the island each day for the cleanup. Many of the locals felt under siege. They were urged to be patient and thankful for the help. Unfortunately, that was not the mood on the island.

Her back hunched, Rosaline sat on a high stool behind the worn Formica counter. Her head of white curly hair was turned to face a TV that blared a soap opera. At seventy-five, she still ran the convenience store. Her son, John, had been the first person to give Brian a real job, when he was seventeen and alone on the island. That job was a lifeline, thanks to Josie.

Brian had wandered into Odeal's, looking for restaurant work, and met Josie. She had been fourteen and new to her curves, with a full smile, oblivious to the bloom of her beauty.

"You don't want to work for my momma," Josie had said. "Here." She wrote a number on her order pad. "My cousin John is looking for help at the marina where my brother works. John'll do right by you."

"I didn't catch your name," he said, his heart pounding both at the job lead and the pretty girl.

"Josie Austin, but John calls me Josephine." She held out her hand.

"It's a pleasure, Josie Austin. I'm Brian Babineaux."

She had smiled, and the tips of her ears had turned red. They still did that when she was embarrassed or feeling shy.

Brian grabbed a can of soda and put it and a dollar on the counter. He cleared his throat so as not to startle Rosaline.

"I see you standing there, *cher*." She motioned for him to wait, her chunky costume jewelry rings flashing in the air.

The show broke to a commercial, and Rosaline finally turned. "That's it until next week. I'm leaving, Manny. The store's yours," she yelled to her clerk stocking shelves.

"Give 'em hell for me," Manny said.

"Before I forget," she said to Brian, "my ice cream cooler isn't working right."

"I'll come by first thing tomorrow," he said.

Brian helped Rosaline step up into the truck and buckle the seat belt.

She ran her hands over the dashboard. "You keep this nice. It still has that new truck smell."

Brian laughed. He never knew if Rosaline meant to be funny, but something about the way she spoke always lightened his mood.

He started the truck. "What's the island gossip these days?"

"You'd think people thought they were about to win the lottery," Rosaline said.

"How so?"

"All this BP money just announced. Folks don't realize it's a storm of paperwork. Thank goodness for Daniel Dean. Helped me fill out what I needed when BP took those first claims. I was at the top of the line and got a five-thousand-dollar check. I didn't tell anyone though. Now there's some new fund, and we can submit again."

Brian nodded. His last paycheck was already spent. If he wasn't reassigned soon, he'd have to find work, and that would surely mean leaving the island. Josie was filing lost wages for him as a restaurant worker, along with Minnow.

They arrived at the mayor's office and followed a slow-moving crowd into an auditorium. A sign on an easel read: GULF COAST CLAIMS FACILITY. TOWN HALL MEETING TONIGHT 7:00 P.M.

Brian found two seats. It would reach standing room only tonight. He couldn't remember there ever being a meeting like this on the island.

Louise stood next to a lectern, talking to her assistant, her hands flying like she was swatting flies. Hollis stood behind her off to the side. All around, people sat, their arms folded, some hunched over, an anxious soundtrack filling the space. Brian sat next to Rosaline, and uneasy energy flowed through him too.

"Welcome, everyone," Louise said into a microphone. "Mr. Ralston is running late."

"Like our checks," someone shouted.

"I know all y'all have questions, and that's why we're here tonight. I've had several meetings with Mr. Ralston. I feel he truly wants to help us."

"Does Hollis know about those meetings?" The man made a loud kissing sound.

The crowd snickered.

"And what do you mean by that, Mr. LeBlanc?" Louise's voice was friendly, but she wouldn't put up with heckling. Before she was Grand Isle's mayor, she was a prosecutor in the DA's office.

"You know exactly what I mean, Mayor Martil. Everyone knows how money works in government. You gotta put out to get any in."

Hollis stood, his full six-foot height and lanky frame not filling up nearly the space he thought.

"Chief Tibbs, would you kindly escort Mr. LeBlanc from the meeting? I will not allow any disrespect of my office or my character. We're at standing capacity, and someone would appreciate his seat."

"I have every right to stay here."

Chief Frank Tibbs was a former navy commander and now Grand Isle's chief of police. Josie said he reminded her of the street fighter version of Blair Underwood and that his crooked nose must come with a story. He approached the row where LeBlanc sat. The man stood and left on his own.

"Before our guest arrives, and as people are still squeezing in, I've got some announcements. We are aware of complaints of workers cutting through yards and haphazardly parking vehicles, and we are addressing the community's concerns over safety. Please also follow the public health warning against swimming in the ocean and not eating any locally caught seafood. Don't think we don't know about you stealth fishers. Also, Dr. Tynsdale is seeing people with breathing trouble. He suspects as the oil emergency continues, the air quality will worsen. Stay inside more if you're sensitive."

Brian scanned the room, catching Hughdean's eye. He was jammed next to the glowing-red fire-exit sign. Soon the fire marshal wouldn't let any more people in.

"Scoot your chairs closer. These are your neighbors. Don't be shy," Louise said.

Josie walked in with Daniel Dean moving steadily with his walker. Brian stood to meet her.

"What the hell are you doing here, Babineaux?" an angry voice called.

Brian saw Josie's head turn to the crowd.

"If you'd done your job better, none of us would be crammed in here like pages in a Bible."

Suddenly, Rosaline stood. "Who said that?"

People began shushing each other.

"I will not have anyone disrespecting Louise, Hollis, Brian, or the Bible. That is enough. Brian works harder than most of you here." She pointed her finger and waved it across the crowd like a heat-seeking missile. "He's hurting more than you from his lost friends."

Brian's ears rang, and his heart pounded, like when he woke from a nightmare. He pushed his way through the row toward the door. Josie caught his arm.

"Where're you going?"

"I don't need to be defended by a little old lady. This is humiliating."

Josie lowered her voice the way she did when she scolded the kids. "That little old lady is the most powerful person on this island and commands more respect from this community than anyone. You are blessed that she loves you enough to stand for you. Hollis didn't march out of here."

"I'm not Hollis."

"No, you're Brian Babineaux and I expect better. Now take Daniel Dean's arm and help him to your seat, *like you were planning* when you stood up." She nodded. "Then you'll hand Rosaline this here cool drink of water I just poured from the fountain outside, *like you were planning*, and you will stand by your wife, and we will behave better than the shit sitting in this room."

"Dammit, Josie," he said through gritted teeth. He could feel the faces of those nearby straining for a juicy morsel. Their separation was no secret in their small community. She was offering him a way to save face. He guided Daniel Dean to his abandoned seat and handed Rosaline the water. She kissed his cheek.

Louise tapped the microphone. "I hope you're using this time to read through the packet of material you were given when you walked in." She raised her own papers. "Mr. Ralston will answer your specific questions, but here's the speedrun. BP has committed twenty billion dollars to help folks like us."

The crowd began to talk loudly, discussing the unworldly amount.

Louise spoke over the noise. "If you've submitted a claim to BP, it's still in the system. You can file your first or an additional claim for short-term assistance. That's for anyone who lost money for any reason. There's emergency money for medical expenses, coastal real estate loss, and seafood compensation for all our fisherfolk and shrimpers. Good news is you can double and triple file depending on what you need. Bad news is, it's paperwork."

People started to shout questions.

"Hold your comments." Louise read a note her assistant handed her. "Mr. Ralston is here. One more thing before I introduce him. For the next few weeks, my office will be offering paperwork assistance. Josie and Brian Babineaux have been gracious to offer Odeal's three mornings a week for people to meet. Daniel Dean Austin will be there to help answer questions. He's a retired CPA. I'll pop in to answer any legal questions I can. Tommy Nguyen, a local shrimper many of you know, has volunteered with Vietnamese language services, and we will have a Spanish-language translator as well."

"We are?" Brian leaned over to Josie. He had gone from town pariah to community patron in fifteen minutes.

"Smile. Yes, we are, and the mayor's office is providing emergency funding for free beverages."

"I could use a drink right about now," Brian said.

"That makes two of us."

Chapter 11

Grand Isle, Louisiana

Tuesday, May 11, 2010

Josie stood in the walk-in refrigerator, surveying the bare shelves where normally she'd find redfish fillets or bright-red snapper waiting for a simple seasoning, then to be grilled and served with her house-made Cajun tartar sauce. They should have been in the thick of shrimping season, with Hughdean providing legendary large shrimp—one of the reasons Odeal's was on the culinary map. He would set aside each crustacean specially for the restaurant.

During a normal summer season, fresh produce and seafood arrived daily. She could source frozen seafood, but she couldn't handle the expense or the heresy. In the three weeks since the rig explosion, she had been ordering only what they guesstimated they could sell each week. She had modified the regular menu to account for no local seafood and called it the "dry bayou" menu.

The regular flow of reporters was winding down and being replaced by beach-cleanup crews. Josie smiled, welcoming them, and grimaced behind their backs as they tracked in grime from the beach. She opened an outside hostess stand to direct them to the deck. But that only worked on days with a strong ocean breeze. Oil saturated the air. She heard reports the odor lingered as far as New Orleans. Josie had found Maisy in the restroom last week puffing on a rescue inhaler.

Josie finished the refrigerated inventory and was ready to leave when Maisy slipped in, quickly closing the door. "This is the coolest spot in the building."

The two barely fit. Then they giggled. The idea of them hiding out for a moment of cool, quiet air not lost on either of them.

"Are we ready to do this?" Josie asked.

"Not really, but like yanking a bandage—"

They slipped out, and Josie stopped at her desk and picked up a whiteboard marker. She wrote, *The most painful decisions only hurt for a minute.*

"Did Confucius say that?" Maisy asked.

Josie shook her head. The marriage counselor suggested she and Brian write what they were thankful for or the most pressing thought on their minds each day. "Remove it from your head and give it air."

Lately, Josie had been thinking about those painful fifty-minute meetings. They were actually longer when she factored in two hours of travel time to and from the therapist's office in Cut Off. She and Brian had argued about that, too, but company health insurance covered it, and they had no money for anyone closer. The ride up was always tense, and the ride back often worse. It grew so bad that toward the end, before Josie called it quits, they drove in separate cars.

However, Josie learned that she avoided conflict as a survival tactic from growing up with a mother who had few kind words for her. She chose to either agree with Odeal or hide when her mood darkened. But a child's coping strategy was not useful as a spouse. She had no model for a healthy marriage, or any marriage. Her father's stroke recovery had dominated their family life. Odeal had taken care of him. She assumed they loved one another, or had at some point. Did love fuel the obligation, or was the obligation a burden of the marriage?

Josie and Maisy settled in a booth with the restaurant's reservation book, the latest inventory, and Josie's estimated expenses. Today they would decide how many days each week to shutter the restaurant. They were well beyond the *if they would*, and deep into the *how*.

How did all my plans come to this? "I wish we could lock up and take a vacation," Josie said.

"Okay, where're we going? France is beautiful this time of year. I'm up for a wine-buying trip."

Josie reached for Maisy's hand. They shared a calling to cook, to nourish people, and to delight them. There was no delight these days. Josie hadn't felt that in years, since her focus had shifted to financial survival. Where could she cut corners on ingredients and portions? Could she operate with fewer staff? If she raised prices too much, would she lose her regular customers, become the pricey tourist spot with weak online ratings for value and service?

Running the restaurant made her want to run away.

"You don't have to stay here," Josie said. "We've had a good show of it. I would understand. New Orleans—"

"Don't finish that thought. My home is here. This is where I work. Besides, what would I do with my house? The only upside to this mess is my new deck is finished. I already paid for it, so I can sit and enjoy the sunset."

And sit hungry. Josie inhaled, holding back tears. She didn't deserve Maisy's loyalty. Josie had plucked her from a soulless white-tablecloth restaurant in New Orleans and coaxed her to Grand Isle, to where the good people of Louisiana lived. Maisy promised to give it a try even though the town was the whitest in the state. That was a dozen years ago.

Maisy was the beat to Josie's culinary heart. They shared a vision for Odeal's. Where her family said hold back, go slow, Maisy was loading the van, beeping the horn, and yelling at her to jump in. Maisy had already contacted other tour companies about selling hot sauce and was well on board before Brian came around.

"We will move through this." Maisy squeezed her hand in response. "Now, I say we keep lunch service Tuesday through Thursday. You'll be open then anyways for the community paperwork project. The little extra we'll get from the town budget will help."

Josie nodded. "We need to keep on with Sunday Suppers."

Maisy agreed. "That leaves Friday and Saturday?"

"Hey, Mom," Toby said, walking in.

"Whatcha need, buddy?" Josie smiled. He was helping at the restaurant after school, with small jobs like folding napkins, setting tables, and doing simple food-prep tasks.

He held the receiver of the portable phone in his hand. "It's the food man from *Vacation Ventures*."

"The photographer or the writer?"

Toby shrugged. "I don't know, he talked so fast and so funny, I couldn't understand him."

Josie smiled. "Must be last-minute details. Give it here."

Toby placed the phone between them. Josie drummed her fingers against the edge of the table, released the mute, and hit the speaker button.

"Hello," Josie said.

"Josie, hi, it's Dale."

"I thought you said magazine types closed up shop after lunch."

A laugh came through the line. "I wanted to catch you before dinner service started."

Josie and Maisy exchanged glances. *Dinner service such as it wasn't, these days.*

"You're on speaker. Chef Maisy is here with me."

"Oh." He paused. "How's everyone holding up with the oil? We're watching the news here in New York City. But the news is always oversensational."

"Our beaches have looked better, but BP is on top of the cleanup. It's like a regular season, but with people in coveralls instead of bathing suits." She forced a laugh.

Josie needed this call. Now that BP had committed billions, it wouldn't be long before they had the financial crutch they needed. Last night, Mr. Ralston said BP was preparing a junk shot to stop the well.

After the meeting, Brian had explained, "They'll take real junk like golf balls, plastic cubes, shredded tires, and knotted rope and stuff it into the blowout preventer. The idea is to block the oil."

"Grand Isle is a special place," Dale said. "We want to see you bounce back."

"Oh, we will. We've lived with the oil a long time, and we've the best fishing in the Gulf."

Dale was quiet. "Josie . . . we had an editorial meeting last night. With the accident and all the bad news coming not just from Louisiana, but all the Gulf states, we can't in clear conscience recommend our readers travel to the Gulf."

Maisy's hand flew to her mouth. Josie stood and turned her back, with her hands on her head. She breathed deeply and patted her chest. Toby ran to the bar and rushed over a glass of water.

"Odeal's is your cover story," Maisy said. "You surely can't find a replacement that fast."

"I'm sorry, Chef Maisy. We're expanding a feature on a restaurant in Cannon Beach, Oregon."

"You couldn't run further from oil there if you tried," Maisy said and shook her head.

Josie sat and rested her head on her arms on the table. *This can't be happening.* She had pinned all her hopes on the magazine fueling the family's recovery. She already had a frame picked out for the magazine cover and a place to hang it where it would greet diners, confirming they had made the perfect dinner choice.

"I'm sorry. This is unusual. We've never had a situation like this before in the history of the magazine."

We've never a had a situation like this before either.

"Dale," Josie said. "Any chance you'll circle back to us when this is over?" She swallowed, fighting the quiver in her voice.

"Oh, sure. In December, we print a roundup with a listing of our favorite stops of the year. I promise you'll be on it."

But not a cover story. Josie pursed her lips and nodded. *December. The dead of winter.* No one came to Grand Isle in winter. By the time spring rolled around, the magazine would be rotting in a landfill.

"Josie, I need to tell you Marcos finished that jar of reaper sauce, and our staff fought over the bottles of your house sauce."

Josie smiled. Hot peppers didn't pay the bills, but she appreciated the compliment.

"Have you considered entering your sauce in the Ragin' Cajun? It's in New Orleans this July."

"I—"

"This one's not your typical amateur competition. It has a professional-chef category. The *Kitchen Network* is covering it like a sporting event. I worked there for about a minute and called a friend this morning because you have to enter. You would be denying the world your sauce if you don't. You missed the early bird deadline, but if you can make the June first deadline, you'll be in. They pick a few teams and film a profile on them. It would be bigger publicity than the magazine would ever provide. If you want, I can put in a strong word they should profile you. With the oil spill and that amazing pelican, you've got a story, even without your sauce."

Josie stared at Maisy, who raised an eyebrow and drew a series of dollar signs on Josie's inventory sheet.

"Is there a fee to enter?" Josie asked.

"Yes, it's a thousand dollars."

"Wow," Toby said.

"*Wow*'s right." Maisy nodded.

Josie shook her head. She didn't have a spare grand for *anything*.

"I know it sounds like a lot, but it comes with a booth. It's also a vendor fair. You can sell food and your sauces. You'll more than cover the cost. It's a twenty-five-thousand-dollar first prize and then ten thousand each for second, third, and the people's choice. There's talk the winners may star on a *Kitchen Network* show. It's also a networking event to meet food scouts looking for chefs and personality products to market."

"Are you earning a commission on sales here?" Josie asked.

Dale laughed. "No, we just loved your restaurant and our time with you. And your sauce could win. Think about it. I'll make the call to the *Kitchen Network* and fast-track your story to the producers. Your house vinegar sauce is solid, but you'll be up against teams from across the world. Play with that reaper sauce. Brighten it and add some sweetness. Call me with your decision."

Josie hung up and stood from the booth. "I'm gonna take a minute." *Before someone gets ugly.* She walked out to the deck. The oil haze stung the back of her throat.

I wouldn't tell people to come here either.

Gumbo circled the deck and landed on his perch. "I wish you could talk." She leaned on the railing next to him. "No, it's better you can't talk. I'm tired of everyone telling me what to do. I'm so tired. My bones hurt."

Josie wept. Every emotion she'd packed away for the past seven months spilled out, heaving her body. She could handle the fear and uncertainty. She could fight for her family. But the loneliness clawing her insides had left her so empty, she had no reserves.

"Josie." Brian walked up the deck. "Rosaline gave me a mess of roses from her garden for you." He stopped, a stricken look on his face, a bouquet of red and pink blooms in his hand.

She wiped her eyes with the back of her hand.

"Josie?" Brian said, concern etched on his face.

"Hey, I'm—" Her voice choked. She started to say *okay*, but she wasn't. A flood of new tears flowed down her cheeks, and she fell into his arms.

Chapter 12

"Mom?" Toby stood with a glass of water in his hand, his eyes wide and scared from Josie's reaction to the phone call. "You left this inside."

Josie took a stuttering breath and stepped away from Brian. She wiped her eyes with the heel of her hand.

"Toby, could you find some water for these flowers for your mom?"

Josie took the glass and kissed the top of his head. "Thank you for the drink. Some days even grown-ups feel frustrated."

"Hey, *chère*, talk to me," Brian said quietly. He touched her elbow and led her to a café table. He'd seen his share of tears from her. Frustration tears. Angry tears. Genuine sadness. He was the cause of most of it. Her tears today were different. His only solace was he wasn't the source.

She looked at him, her eyes rimmed with red.

"Did someone die?" Death surrounded him these past weeks. A man had fainted at a memorial service. The horror of the rig explosion and the absence of a body to bury had rendered the goodbye unfinished.

"Odeal's," she said.

"Huh?" Odeal had died close to eighteen years ago.

"The restaurant. It's over." She stared out over the water.

"Relief money's coming from BP. I'll be on a different rig soon. With my promotion, I'll make up for this lost pay quicker than you can shuck an oyster. BP is setting up a fund for rig workers to cover pay from this downtime. Here, I have this for you." He dug into his pocket and pulled out a wad of cash. "From my last boat repair, a hundred fifty dollars."

She fingered the folded bills. "You deserve the promotion." She sighed. "It's too late. By the time this magic money arrives, we'll be too far behind on our bills. I can't count on cleanup crews to fill in for tourists."

"The tourists will be back. What's this about?"

"The magazine canceled the story. They can't recommend people come to the Gulf with the oil here."

"Oh, hell." Brian slapped his thigh. Gumbo startled and took off over the water. Even he didn't want to witness this setback.

"This just happen?"

Josie nodded. "The story wouldn't have mattered anyways. Maisy and I were deciding what days to close and eliminate service."

"They loved your food. That matters. And remember, you said if the tourists didn't come to you, you'd go to them."

She nodded. "Dale offered one idea, to enter my reaper sauce in the Ragin' Cajun hot sauce competition."

"Where's that?"

"New Orleans in July."

"Then let's do it! Tell me about the competition."

Josie needed something to focus her energy on. Money was tight, but they just had to hang on until he was reassigned. He'd given the oil industry ten years. Loyalty mattered. Transocean needed him now more than ever. Safety and repairs were under investigation. He was ready to stand shoulder to shoulder with his crewmates.

"We'd have to enter by June first. You get a booth, and you can sell hot sauce and food. The whole event will be televised on the *Kitchen Network*. Dale says it's great publicity." Josie's voice was flat, like she was reading the directions on how to screw in a light bulb.

Brian rubbed his hands together. "We can sell the sauce you had bottled for the summer. You said we can price it higher in the city."

"It's a thousand dollars to enter. I'm barely able to order enough food for the week." She picked up the folded bills and let them fall onto the table.

"Louise said once we send in our paperwork, BP cuts emergency checks within two weeks. Most folks get at least a grand. You're putting in for Minnow's lost wages. That'll cover it."

"You'd have me steal from my daughter? Once wasn't enough? That's her money for her future."

"Josie—"

"Y'all okay?" Maisy said from the back door. "The paperwork team is here. Josie, d'you mind if I put out your last batch of tea cakes and my chili brownies with the coffee and soda?"

"Sure, better to not waste it."

"Is she telling you about us entering the Ragin' Cajun?" Maisy asked Brian.

"We're not. It's too much money and not enough time," Josie said.

Maisy stepped outside. "Why the hell not? It's not like anything else is happening. With the kitchen closed half the week, you can mix up as many batches of that chili death as you want until you nail it."

"I can't even pay for the reaper chilies." Josie began to rebutton her chef's coat. She was heading back to work, then all conversations would be over like closing a freezer door.

"Lunder's Farm." Maisy took a challenging step toward Josie.

"We can't afford his produce now, and you want me to buy specialty peppers from him?"

"No. He'll give them to us for free."

Brian stood back. Josie and Maisy moved like dance partners on most restaurant decisions. This was a change in tempo.

Josie shook her head. "Ridiculous."

"Jimmy Lunder called last week. We're not the only restaurant cutting back on orders. He has produce rotting in the greenhouses."

Josie's face fell. Wasted food and hungry people always upset her.

"I can make a deal for all the reaper peppers you want in exchange for you promoting his peppers at the Ragin' Cajun. Think of all those local hot sauce chefs who need peppers. It'll be like printing money for him. *Odeal's Cajun reaper sauce. Ingredients: Lunder's Farm organic reapers.*"

"That's a terrible name," Josie said and smiled.

"The worst ever. Come inside, let's figure this out."

Josie blinked, her eyes adjusting to the dimmer light in the restaurant's dining room. It was just as well. She didn't want anyone to notice she'd been crying. Exhaustion had turned her limbs into noodles, and her workday was yet to begin.

Daniel Dean had settled at a four top next to a poster-size black-and-white image of Odeal. Pictured in profile, she was working in the old kitchen, a kerchief in her hair and a rare smile on her face. He didn't come to the restaurant often, but when he did, this was his table. It had the best view, and diners would stop and say hello.

"Hi, Dad." Josie picked up the glass of sweet tea in front of him and tasted it. "Who gave you bourbon?" She turned to Maisy, who returned her question with a *Who, me?* expression.

"Now, Josephine. Coffee upsets my stomach. Everyone needs a pick-me-up."

"It's just after lunch."

"Ooh, are we day drinking?" Louise said, walking across the dining room. Her hair was in a bouncing high ponytail, and she wore long pants and hiking boots. She dropped her purse onto the table and took a sip from the glass. "I agree with Daniel Dean. This is refreshing."

"Always knew you were the smart one," Daniel Dean said.

"Nice outfit, but is this how you dress to help people with their paperwork?" Josie asked.

"I'm only here until Hollis comes by with Rosaline. Then we're heading to the beach with Minnow for a shore walk with some visitors all the way from Alaska."

"Why am I only hearing about this now?"

Brian grimaced. "Sorry, Josie. Minnow asked the other day. I said yes."

"The oil's dangerous to be near. And what about those security guards fighting with people wanting to go to the beach? I don't want her messed up in any of that."

"It'll be fine, mama shark," Louise said. "We're not collecting anything. Hollis has a science permit, and I'm the mayor of Grand Isle. If they mess with me, Chief Tibbs will visit them."

"Can I come, too, Aunt Louise?" Toby said, his mouth full of corn bread.

"Don't talk while you're eating," Josie scolded.

"Not wearing shorts and a T-shirt, but we can stop by your house, and you can change. That's if it's okay with your mom and dad." Louise looked at Josie and took another swig of Daniel Dean's tea. He grabbed the glass from her.

"Please?" Toby pleaded. "Minnow gets to do everything. I'll be safe, I promise."

Josie looked at Brian, and he nodded.

"Fine, but you mind everyone and wear your fishing shoes. They're already wrecked, and I can't afford to buy you a new pair."

Hughdean walked into the dining room from the kitchen with his own handful of corn bread. "Tasty batch, Maisy." He raised it in a salute.

Josie huffed. "Y'all fixing to eat your way through my lunch service?"

"Uncle Hollis is here!" Toby ran to the door and pushed it open. Hollis held Rosaline's purse as she stepped over the threshold. "Uncle Hollis, I'm coming with you to the beach."

Hollis wore his usual birding outfit of stuffed cargo pants and a floppy hat. Today the outfit included rubber boots.

"Are you, now?" he said. "I can use another assistant. I was thinking, maybe your dad would let you borrow his camera." Hollis looked at Brian.

Brian held a tight-lipped smile.

"Can I, Dad? I know how to use it. I won't take the big lenses. I'll be real careful."

"Mmm . . . it would be a shame if something happened to it," Josie said, not hiding her irritation.

"What type of pictures are you planning?" Brian asked.

"*SciOlogy* magazine is interviewing me about the spill. They've asked for pictures. BP security isn't taking too kindly to photos, but with Louise here"—he put his arm around her waist—"along with our guests and two kids, I think we can sneak them. You up for it, Toby?"

"That's just the kind of trouble I don't want them around," Josie said.

"Duh, dum, duh dum," Louise sang in the tune of the *Jaws* theme song.

Toby laughed.

"I'm not being a mama shark." Josie stood with her hands on her hips.

"You're being something," Hughdean said.

"Speaking of magazines." Josie sighed. "Since all y'all are here, *Vacation Ventures* canceled on us. They're not running Odeal's in the next issue."

"Why the hell not?" Hughdean said. "I got gussied up for that photo."

Josie sat at Daniel Dean's table.

"The oil spill."

"That's not right," Louise said.

"Josie and Maisy have a new idea," Brian said.

They stared at Josie, waiting. She twisted a paper napkin. This idea was half-baked, and she hadn't turned on the oven yet. "Well, Maisy and I are exploring"—she held up her hand—"entering the Ragin' Cajun hot sauce competition. It's in New Orleans this year with a professional-team category." Her voice spouted certainty she didn't feel.

Daniel Dean's head hunched into his neck like a turtle. She could feel questions popping in his mind. He had mortgaged the restaurant property to stop the foreclosure on her house and put an end to the bill collectors. Josie was responsible for the payments. But the additional caveat was Daniel Dean needed to approve any expense over $500.

"The entry fee includes a booth where we can sell our sauces and food. The *Kitchen Network* is planning to televise it. Imagine, us on TV. That'll advertise Odeal's way better than some limited magazine write-up," Maisy said.

Josie's heart swelled with Maisy's support. Louise and Hollis had always been her cheerleaders growing up, but Maisy understood her passion was the restaurant.

"The *Kitchen Network* is one of my favorite channels," Rosaline said. "I don't make any of that fancy food those chefs make, but I sure like watching them. Especially that couple cooking all that spicy food up in Canada. And the show with the beekeeper with those honey recipes."

"That's exciting," Louise said. "I love the idea of Odeal's on TV. That means Grand Isle will be on TV. We need something good here."

"What's this about an entry fee?" Daniel Dean asked.

Josie's mood collapsed like a failed soufflé. "It's a thousand dollars, but that includes the booth."

"No, it don't. It doesn't cover building the booth, buying the food, gas to the city, parking. Y'all don't factor in the costly bits in your dreaming. Besides, you don't have the money. I say no."

"I agree with Daddy," Hughdean said.

Josie stood and made a show of patting her body. "Yup, I'm a grown woman, and I don't need either of your permission to do this. Brian gave me a hundred fifty dollars today. I have two hundred fifty dollars from selling sauce to a tour company. That's almost halfway to the entry fee. Maisy can source free peppers for the sauce." She might as well lie, as both amounts were committed three times over.

"We'll pitch in, right, Hollis?" Louise said.

"Absolutely," he said.

Josie shook her head no. She had already borrowed money from them. Last September, Louise took Minnow to New Orleans for a back-to-school birthday shopping trip. Louise had shrugged as Minnow unpacked bag after bag of new clothes for the school year. Louise then handed Josie a check to buy Toby new clothes and baseball gear.

Rosaline tapped her ring-covered hand against the table to get everyone's attention. "Daniel Dean, you groused back when Josie dared to remodel the building and change the menu. You and Hughdean were all worried about . . . what was it? Authenticity," she said. "Then she started winning awards as one of the best Cajun chefs in the state. You all did fine by Josie's ideas. I believe in you, *chère*. You can add five hundred dollars toward your fee from me."

Josie hugged her. This woman who was as close to a grandmother to her as any person could be. Fresh tears fell again, but this time they were in gratitude.

"I'll figure out how to build you a booth to make you proud," Brian said. "There's enough construction material lying around the island. I'll make it happen."

"I've got a box of leftover screws from my deck," Maisy said.

"See, on our way," Brian said.

"I'll work on a menu of what to sell that makes us a tidy profit. I'll get those reapers, but you've got to make a killer sauce," Maisy said.

Toby sat at the table with Rosaline, holding the phone. His lips were pinched so tight they were white. Josie pulled up a chair beside him. "What do you think, *cher*?" she said quietly as if his and only his opinion mattered, and in a way it was true. His and Minnow's future were also at stake, though neither understood the extent. "Dad's gonna need someone to help build the booth." She looked toward Brian. Then she scooted close so only Toby could hear. "And you know he can't stomach spicy food, so I need a taste tester I can trust."

Toby nodded and smiled. "I'm in."

I'm in too.

SciOlogy

The Science Magazine for Curious Humans

Gemma Runson, Senior Science Reporter
May 2010

Field Notes: Gulf of Mexico, Macondo Prospect, 41 miles offshore of the United States

Developing story: April 20, 2010, Deepwater Horizon oil platform explodes and leaks crude oil

Impact: Loss of life, 11 crew; evolving environmental crisis

Fact: 1 barrel of oil = 42 gallons / 159 liters

It's been three weeks since the Deepwater Horizon oil platform sank a mile below the Gulf of Mexico. Estimates of the uncontained oil spill vary from 5,000 barrels a day from BP, the well's owner, to 25,000 barrels a day from scientists.

We asked six questions of Dr. Eugene Hollis, an ornithologist from Louisiana State University, for this edition of "Field Notes."

SciOlogy: This ecological disaster has no end in sight. What's worrying the scientific community?

Dr. Hollis: The oil leak hit during the spring migration and mating season. The Gulf of Mexico supports 102 species. The brown pelican, Louisiana's state bird, came off the federal endangered species list in November. I recently returned from Raccoon Island, a barrier island in the Gulf with one of the nation's largest concentrations of nesting birds. What we saw was heartbreaking: pelicans and other species stained with oil, attempting to preen their feathers and flexing their wings to dry out the oil and dispersant. They risk starvation and hypothermia.

SciOlogy: You mentioned dispersant. Is it more dangerous than the oil?

Dr. Hollis: The dispersant, Corexit, causes kidney and liver damage and, like DDT, can affect bird embryos. We can't predict yet how future generations of wildlife will be impacted.

SciOlogy: Could this harm humans too?

Dr. Hollis: Yes, mammals are at risk.

SciOlogy: How many birds are we talking about?

Dr. Hollis: I've seen over 900 pelicans. We're worried about black skimmers, clapper rails, loons, laughing gulls, northern gannets, and terns. Over a million sea-birds are at risk. We also must consider sea turtles, ocean mammals, fish, the coral reefs, and plant life. The entire ocean ecosystem.

SciOlogy: What can be done, and what are you doing?

Dr. Hollis: First is to stop the oil and stop using the dispersants. BP has finally admitted the leak is bigger than estimated. The oiled wildlife we can rescue are treated, but it's not a simple "clean and release." Sea animals and birds need significant recovery time to allow their feathers, pelts, and skins to develop a new protective layer of fat and waterproofing. Then where do we release the animals? It doesn't make sense to put them back in the path of the oil.

SciOlogy: How big is the path?

Dr. Hollis: We've rescued birds west of Galveston, Texas to Fort Myers, Florida. In my hometown of Grand Isle, we've rescued more than 200 animals. Currently 88,500 square miles of fishing grounds are closed. This is the biggest oil spill in US history.

Chapter 13

Grand Isle, Louisiana

Friday, May 14, 2010

Brian maneuvered his truck under the shade of the battered hackberry tree that guarded Daniel Dean's driveway. Like his father-in-law, this tree took whatever nature hurled at it—hurricanes, drought, insects, and pollution.

Brian had been storing building materials, salvaged from construction sites on the island, in the backyard. Today, he and Toby were working on Josie's booth.

The porch door squeaked open, and Josie walked down the stairs. The bright sun reflected off the buttons of her chef's coat. A yellow tank peeked out today. Her hair bounced long and loose. Car keys jingled in her hands, and she stopped on the last step and waved. She looked toward the truck.

"Are you building a booth or a village?"

He walked over. "I hit the mother lode on building supplies. I'll be able to build you anything you can imagine."

The salvaged supplies included roofing shingles, lattice, screws, nails, electrical boxes, and two cans of green paint. As a surprise, he also was rebuilding the gazebo that had once stood in the backyard. It was a Hail Mary romantic gesture he hoped would make her change her mind about coming home.

She squeezed the handrail and sat on the last step. He took it as an invitation to join her. He longed to twirl a lock of her hair between his fingers. They once spent a lazy morning with him spinning her hair into ringlets, both laughing at how the humidity was stronger than hair spray.

"I can't believe I'm actually considering this competition. I still need to fix the reaper sauce, and now Lunder's Farm is counting on us. Is it a jinx to start the booth before we can pay for the entry?"

"We'll be ready. A few of the construction sites told me to take whatever I wanted. I sold a load of discarded copper tubing, rebar, and aluminum ducting to the marine salvage in Morgan City. That money and a job I have repairing a gear case will get us to the finish line." He smiled.

She rubbed her chin, considering her words. "You've been spending a lot of time in Morgan City. Is there something more there I should know about?"

"No."

"Did you know Louise rescued Minnow and Bonnie in Cut Off?"

He nodded. He'd been holding that bombshell. "When did Minnow tell you?"

"She didn't. Louise did. So, you knew?"

Brian closed his eyes. *Dammit, Minnow.*

A hot breeze gusted and carried the metallic tang of oil. His throat grew gummy and dry.

"She promised me she'd tell you."

"And yet she didn't. You also didn't tell me you were spending the night in Morgan City and dumping Toby at his friend's." Her voice turned icy.

This was an ambush.

"I didn't dump Toby. They'd planned a sleepover."

"Were you at a card game?"

He stood and kicked the tread of the stair she was sitting on.

She flinched.

He had seen Josie do that before, once after a verbal assault from Odeal when Josie was eighteen and again from Hughdean after Odeal's funeral. He had defused Odeal's anger with a joke and threatened to beat the crap out of Hughdean if he ever said anything again to his sister.

Who would stop *him*?

She smacked her hand on the step and met him face to face.

"It's an oil town, people without much going on. Maybe some you played with before," she said.

A mixture of sadness and resolve turned down the corners of her mouth and drained the life from her eyes.

What would she say if she knew she wasn't far from the truth? After the last memorial service in Lake Charles, instead of heading home, or even to Baton Rouge to visit his mother, he had driven to the L'Auberge du Lac casino. He sat in his truck watching people go in and out. He battled the urge to join a card game and put down a twenty-dollar bill, money he needed for gas.

I'll just see what happens. Blow off some steam.

As his hand went to open the truck door, a memory of Josie in one of her red tank tops under her chef's coat slapped him in the face. He took three deep breaths but didn't leave. He stared at the entrance, waiting for some sort of sign, an invitation. He invented his own, a distraction bet. If two people walked out wearing red shirts and boots, he'd go inside. After an hour, he saw a man in a red T-shirt and boots. Then another hour passed. He tried to change the rules to just boots or just the shirt.

He sat in his truck for two hours until a rap on the window made him jump. He rolled it down, and a casino security guard stepped back.

"Sir, are you okay?"

"I, um, I'm fine. Waiting for my friend."

"Can we check on that friend? Sometimes people lose track of time."

And all their money. His back ached from sitting, and his hands were sweaty on the wheel.

"No, I'll call." He lifted the cell phone next to him. How many messages had he once missed from Josie while he played cards? How pathetic to sit alone in a row of parked cars.

"Are you sure you're good?" the man had asked.

Shame took over, and he drove home. That night he had sat on the edge of his bed and opened a notebook from his nightstand. He'd found the list of Gamblers Anonymous meetings the marriage therapist had given him. There were regular meetings in Morgan City at the Holy Cross Catholic Church. He'd been going ever since.

"Jesus, Josie." He threw his hands in the air and stepped away, sensing she was about to bolt. "No." He worked to control his voice, softened his posture, and pulled her to sit again with him. "No." He shook his head. "I wasn't at a card game."

"Are you seeing someone?" she whispered.

"What? No. Why would you think that?"

Would she understand about the GA meetings? Facing what he had done wasn't a release. He was angry and frustrated about his life and his bruised marriage. The group leader told him the problems caused by gambling didn't happen overnight and the solutions didn't come fast either. Sometimes it took years.

"I can't handle another lie when you and I are . . . I don't know what we are."

"What do you want to do?" he asked.

She dropped her head and stared at her scarred hand. "I don't know. I've got the kids and my dad and everyone at the restaurant who depend on me for work. Now this competition. It could happen if we can figure it out, the money. Always the damn money." She slapped her hand against the stair again. "I want to cook and feed people. Feel that satisfaction when the people you're with are as good as the food. But I can't." She gripped her chest. "The worry is consuming me."

Her smile was so sad and slight it ripped his heart.

"I want us to move forward, together. Be a family again," he said. *I want you to come home.*

"Being together doesn't solve for everything that dropped us in the middle of this mess. And I'm not talking about the oil spill. You didn't listen to me when we went to counseling, and you're not hearing me now."

"I'll be working again soon and—"

"Stop. Just stop. We have no tomorrows when you won't yet deal with yesterday."

"But I am, I'm . . ." The weekly meetings, the missing money, the broken promises, it was too much for him to handle, yet alone explain, when he didn't understand how he landed here himself.

She stared, waiting for him to continue, three long beats of silence, then her fingers moved to fasten the open buttons of her coat.

"I made Minnow an appointment with Dr. Tynsdale. She isn't happy about it, but I want to know why she has stomach pains and isn't eating." She stepped off the stair. "I'd appreciate it if you'd find time in your schedule to come to the appointment."

She wound her hair into a bun, transforming herself into Josie the restaurateur, the spice queen of the bayou, the strongest person he knew.

She stepped away, and he caught her hand. "Whatever's wrong with Minnow, we'll figure it out, together."

She squeezed his hand and smiled, but it didn't travel to her eyes. He had lost her full smile. He needed to earn it back. Tomorrow he would have the rest of the money.

Toby's fast feet thudded down the stairs. He jumped from the third-to-last porch step and stood, knees bent and arms wide.

"Stuck the landing. Hey Mom, thought you left?"

"Heading out now."

He playfully pushed her toward her car. "Dad and I have work to do."

"Did you finish your homework?"

"Yes."

"Okay. Have fun with Dad."

This time her smile was full as it shone on Toby. She turned to Brian. "Thanks."

"Uncle Hughdean's on the phone," Toby said. "He'll be out in a few minutes to help unload the truck."

Josie drove off, and shortly thereafter Hughdean announced himself by slamming the porch door behind him.

Brian's head jerked to see him pacing the back porch, his long, lanky limbs agitated. Toby stepped behind Brian and fidgeted with a hammer.

Hughdean smacked the portable phone against his hand.

"What's up?" Brian asked.

Hughdean stared, his cheeks with red blotches, his jaw tight. He collapsed into a wicker rocking chair. "Goddammit." He shook the phone. "Tommy Nguyen and his crew are heading to Florida to fish."

Brian climbed the stairs to the porch, with Toby on his heels.

"We're gonna dry up waiting for BP to reimburse us and make this right. It'll never be right."

Brian raised an eyebrow. "You leaving too?"

Hughdean rubbed a hand across his head. "My crews are asking what to do. I can't make 'em stay when I can't pay 'em. I'm not the bank of Hughdean. What happens if I've got no crew?"

"The BP money's coming," Brian said.

Hughdean waved his middle finger in the air. "To BP and their promises. The only thing they're paying on is the Vessels of Opportunity program."

"What's that?" Brian asked.

"I can contract my boats to BP to lay containment booms and stuff. My size boats could be three grand per day and two hundred bucks for each crew member. Got four boats. Even the one with the busted outrigger would be useful. Do the math," Hughdean said.

"Why isn't Tommy joining?" Brian asked.

"He has a single boat, and you need a particular type of insurance. His wife is worried the oil will make him sick."

Brian nodded. "Hollis says the oil and the chemicals they're dumping are toxic."

"Yeah, well, Birdman knows that type of stuff. But easy for him to make pronouncements. He and the honorable Mayor Martil have paychecks. Hell, my taxes pay her salary. This is bullshit. BP better plug that hole." He stared at Brian accusingly.

Hughdean squeezed his temple, where a vein throbbed. "The whole freakin' shrimping season is shot.

"And, get this," Hughdean added. "Now that the junk shot failed, BP has a week left before the town cancels the entire fishing season, including the Tarpon Rodeo. Junk shot. Stupid plan. Sounds like a bunch of kids came up with it. No offense, Toby."

Brian rubbed the back of his neck. How much more could they take?

"I'm heading to sign up," Hughdean said. "If you need help with this playhouse of a booth later, let me know. You and Josie are wasting your time and money. A hot sauce competition? That's for people who don't work for a living." He dug his keys out of his pocket and climbed into his truck, grumbling as he went.

"Uncle Hughdean's real upset," Toby said.

"C'mere, sit for a minute," Brian said.

Toby sat in the rocker that Hughdean had just left, his legs pushing him back and forth in a nervous bounce.

"This is a strange summer," Brian said. "Everyone's home, not working. Oil cleanup crews are walking around town. We can't fish or go to the beach. People are used to working hard on this island, and it's tough when they can't. They don't know what to do with their free time."

"I know. You and Mom are weird all the time now too. Why can't everyone just look at the spill like summer vacation and have some fun or something?"

Brian smiled, but it was sad. He didn't want Toby to feel his family was weird. He shook his finger at Toby and stood up. "You, my friend, are right. Summers are for projects and for fun. Let's have some fun and build a hot sauce booth."

They walked down to where Brian had parked the truck.

"Up you go," Brian said.

Toby climbed up into the truck bed and mimicked Brian by tugging on a pair of leather gloves.

"The way you climb, why don't you just unload for me."

Toby laughed. "What d'ya want first?" Toby asked.

Brian saw a foreshadow of the man Toby would soon grow into. His own father had never had that chance. And it was dumb luck Brian himself wasn't on the rig when it exploded. Karma was doing him a solid and gifting him time to be a real father, to teach his son the value of building and repairing structures in his life and the importance of not destroying them.

"Dad?" Toby waited for directions.

"Paint cans and the box of screws."

"Oof." Toby pushed a long piece of lumber out of the way. He coughed, a gravelly sound in his throat, and sniffed hard.

"Careful, buddy. Don't overdo it." Toby had had respiratory issues as a baby, and the oil pollution threatened to bring it all back.

"I'm not a kid."

"No, you're not. So, pick up the pace, hotshot. Summer vacation is only a few weeks."

Toby laughed.

"What color do you think Mom will want the booth?" Brian asked.

Toby handed Brian a box. "Red and yellow. That'll attract lots of people. Like how hummingbirds fly to red flowers?" Toby said, grabbing the paint.

"An interesting way to consider it, a lure." He took the cans from Toby.

"Uncle Hollis told me about it."

"You and your sister become bigger fanatics every year."

Toby shrugged. "Birds are cool. Especially Gumbo. Kids at school are jealous I have a pet pelican."

"He's not a pet."

Toby rolled his eyes and pushed another piece of lumber. "You sound like Mom."

"Well, he is *kinda* like a pet." Brian winked.

Toby lifted the wooden crisscrossing lattice board over his head. The piece was taller than him but light.

"What's this for?" Toby asked.

"I'm rebuilding the gazebo that used to be here in the yard." Brian pointed to a spot next to the garden. "You were six when Hurricane Katrina tore it in half, and then Hurricane Rita finished the job the following month."

"What did everyone use it for?" Toby asked.

"Lots of things. You kids played out here. Mom liked to sleep out here in a hammock."

Josie had told him the gazebo had been a refuge for her as a teenager. She'd rather bed down with the mosquitoes than deal with Odeal's sharp criticisms and constant chore list. Odeal preferred the air-conditioned house.

The structure held memories for him too. Josie had been in California for two years while Odeal fought breast cancer. She returned for the funeral, a wholly different woman. Chef Josie stood taller, her smile glowed confidently, and without Odeal's shadow darkening her steps, she had bloomed in the light.

He had spied her walking along the pier, stopping to talk to people. She was saying goodbye, making plans to take a big restaurant job in Houston. Then he heard her laugh, a wild, throaty sound, genuine and free and sexy. He longed to trail his lips down her throat as she laughed with her freedom. The desire overwhelmed him. His nerves taunted him. What if she turned him away as Hughdean's creepy friend? He had found her in the gazebo, listening to old tapes on a boom box. That night was his last best shot, his first gamble to hit a jackpot.

How different his life would be now if his shyness had determined his fate. If he hadn't kissed her, or if she had turned him away. He wouldn't be standing here with Toby.

Chapter 14

Grand Isle, Louisiana

Monday, May 17, 2010

"Minnow, are you awake, *chère*?" Josie knocked on the bedroom door. "Dad'll be here soon."

They had a doctor's appointment scheduled. She rapped a second time, then turned the doorknob.

"Don't come in. I'm up," Minnow called from the other side. "Why's Dad coming?" she whined. "He's never come to my appointments before."

The dresser drawer scraped open and slammed shut. Josie winced at the beating the old furniture was taking.

"Not true, he came when you were a baby." Josie rested against the closed door. She understood. Minnow was seventeen and sensitive about her changing body.

She remembered how Daniel Dean had swallowed his thoughts about her own health and parade of stitches growing up. She only ever caught a hint of concern the day she came home with her hand wrapped in a turban of gauze to cover the zipper of sutures on her palm from an oyster blade. He sat with her and did his post-stroke hand therapy exercises as she did her exercises to regain the use of her hand.

This doctor's appointment was different. Josie couldn't explain it, but something wasn't healthy with Minnow. Louise chided her for being overprotective, but something was driving Minnow to sneak off the island, break curfew, and wither before her eyes.

Last week, she had caught Minnow shaking Toby's baseball-glove bank and sorting a stack of coins.

"What're you doing?" she had asked.

Minnow swept the coins into her hand and jumped to her feet.

"Toby owes me money."

"For what?"

Minnow rolled her eyes. "Why do you have to know everything?"

"For what?" Josie repeated, her arms across her chest.

"Baseball cards, okay?"

Toby had stopped collecting cards the summer before.

Minnow headed for the door, but Josie caught her arm.

"Ow!"

Josie jerked away as if she had been hit. *What have I done?* She vowed to never lay a finger on the kids, no matter how angry or frustrated they made her.

Minnow smashed the coins onto Toby's dresser and marched out, slamming the door in Josie's face.

Josie had retrieved the coins and, with shaking hands, deposited them one by one into the bank. All this emotion over four dollars in quarters?

Minnow's moods scared her in a place she didn't want to face. They mirrored Odeal's dark moods and the havoc that always followed.

Louise didn't think she was using drugs, but her behavior and lies suggested otherwise. She had made excuses for Brian's lies and personality changes until it was too late. She was suffering the consequences of her inaction, but those were her personal burdens. Minnow's life was more precious to Josie than her own.

"I'm not a child," Minnow said with another whine through the door.

"No, darling, you're not." Josie sighed. "I'll be in the kitchen with Grandpa if you want breakfast. Cinnamon-and-brown-sugar oatmeal with blueberries."

Josie spun toward the kitchen and cocked her head, listening to her father laugh at an unmistakable drawl. Hollis was here.

She smiled at the unexpected visit. Hollis sat at the kitchen table with her father and a steaming cup of coffee. "What brings you by so early?"

He stood and kissed her cheek. "Hope you don't mind. I wanted to share this with Minnow before you head off to her appointment."

"You're not supposed to know about that." Josie lowered her voice. "Minnow will think I'm reporting on her to the whole island."

"She travels with a pelican, it's not like her whereabouts are a secret. But I won't say a word. Thought this would cheer her up. She's been so down lately." He held a folded newspaper and swatted the table with it.

"She has? I mean, yes, she has." *I thought she was just angry at me.*

Minnow spent more time with Hollis than anyone, except Gumbo. Why didn't she think to talk to him sooner?

"Uncle Hollis?" Minnow walked into the kitchen. She wore a navy blue T-shirt that accentuated the dark circles under her eyes.

He kissed the top of her head. "Brought you this." He unfolded the newspaper. "The *Port Valdez Sentinel*."

Minnow stood over the paper. "Is this from the shore walk we did with Sanna and David?"

Hollis nodded.

Minnow tucked a lock of hair behind her ear, a smile on her face. The first Josie had seen in days.

"What's all this?" Daniel Dean asked.

"Last week, these cool environmentalists came here from Alaska. Toby and I went with Uncle Hollis and Aunt Louise to tour the beach cleanup. They interviewed me. They're working with Aunt Louise to talk to Congress about the spill."

"Read it out loud," Daniel Dean said.

Josie slid a bowl of oatmeal in front of Minnow and handed her a spoon.

Minnow swallowed a bite and began to read.

Ruin, Rinse and Repeat. Big Oil Attacks Again!

Port Valdez, Alaska. It's been two decades since the oil tanker *Exxon Valdez* struck Bligh Reef, spilling 11 million gallons of crude oil into our pristine Prince William Sound and forever changing the lives of our 3,500 residents.

"I thought this was about us?" Daniel Dean said.

"This is context, they lived through the worst oil spill in history, the *Exxon Valdez* spill."

"Keep reading, *chère*," Josie said.

Alaska environmental activists traveled to the small community of Grand Isle, Louisiana, to speak with officials and offer support while oil is still washing to shore from the April 20 explosion of the Deepwater Horizon oil platform.

Here We Go Again

"It stinks," Grand Isle Mayor Louise Martil said. "The active spill and the air. People are getting sick. I never expected I needed to become a chemical engineer to be mayor of a tourist and fishing community. These chemicals cause cancer and severe respiratory problems."

Prince William Sound activists Sanna and David Yazzie walked the beach with Mayor Martil, ornithologist Dr. Eugene Hollis, and research assistant Minnow Babineaux with her brother Toby Babineaux to survey the cleanup efforts.

Minnow beamed and took another bite of cereal.

"We're relieved crews aren't using hot water spray to clean the beaches, as they did in Prince William Sound," Sanna Yazzie said. "Today, thousands of former cleanup workers suffer respiratory and central nervous system problems from breathing in crude oil splashed off the rocks and into the air."

"A new concern in the Gulf is BP has set the sea on fire by burning oil on the water surface. This releases particles in the air that enter the jet stream and harm the planet," Hollis said.

Minnow Babineaux, a Grand Isle student working with Hollis, shared her outrage and frustration. "Big Oil doesn't care about my community. Children are coughing, and our wildlife is dying. All people hear is money is coming to cover cleanup costs. We won't feel the real costs for years, and by then it'll be too late to make a difference."

The Yazzies and Martil have promised not to let Big Oil control their communities' fates.

"We'll knock on every door in Congress," Martil said as she embraced Sanna and David.

As if signaling a wildlife approval, a brown pelican, the

symbol of Louisiana, flew directly overhead and landed on the beach.

"We will continue to watch the cleanup effort and hope
Grand Isle has a better outcome than Prince William
Sound," Martil said.

"I'm proud of you," Josie said. She had heard Minnow's passioned outrage before. However, seeing it in print made it stronger.

"Louise and I are too," Hollis said. "She's a natural spokesperson."

A knock on the door made them turn, and Brian walked in.

"Hi, Dad," Minnow said.

"Hey, everyone. Birdman, what brings you by so early?"

"Our Minnow made the news." He held up the paper.

"Minnow?" Brian showed a quizzical smile. He accepted the newspaper from Hollis's outstretched hand and read the article.

"We've a budding activist in our family. I'm real proud of you, Minnow, but remember, oil has kept a roof over your head and food in your belly since the day you were born."

Minnow crossed her arms. "Your choice, not mine. Have you been to the beach lately?"

"We have to learn to work with the oil industry. We're tied to it."

"And that makes it okay for them to do this to us? Are you too brainwashed to see what is happening out there?" she asked, pointing. "Uncle Hollis and I are finding dead birds, and turtles. Last week in Pensacola a dolphin washed up on shore."

Hollis nodded.

Minnow ran to the bathroom, and their faces pulled in concern as they heard retching noises.

Josie followed her down the hall. "Minnow, are you okay? May I come in?" She opened the door and sat beside her next to the toilet. "It's time. We need to go to the doctor."

Dr. Garrett Tynsdale's office stood in the shadow of the mayor's office, where oil cleanup crews parked during their breaks.

Josie examined the doctor's medical degrees displayed with family photos and a snapshot of a trophy-size sailfish. He was born in Jamaica, grew up in Florida, and had joined the island practice two years earlier.

Minnow sat in front of the doctor's massive oak desk with her legs curled in a fetal position and chewed on a fingernail. Brian sat on her other side. The shark tattoo on his arm bounced as if alive as he tapped his fingers against the armrest.

Dr. Tynsdale's deep voice filtered from the hall. A quick knock sounded on the door. Brian stood as the doctor entered.

"Sit, relax." Dr. Tynsdale offered Brian his hand and patted Josie on the shoulder. He was dressed in a white lab coat over a starched blue-and-white-striped shirt. Maisy had described him as divine, dark, and datable. Josie suppressed a smile remembering her assessment.

"Sorry to keep you waiting. We've a lot of patients today suffering from the oil in the air." The frameless glasses perched on his nose bounced up and down on his freckled cheeks when he spoke.

Dr. Tynsdale sat on the other side of the desk and opened a file folder. He gave Minnow a patient smile. "Do you feel better than this morning?"

She shrugged.

"You've lost seven pounds since last year. Not a shocking amount of weight."

"Told you," Minnow said to Josie. She uncurled her legs from the chair and twisted a lock of hair between her fingers.

The doctor held up his hand. "I don't want you to lose more. Your vitals are normal. We'll have your blood results in a few days."

Josie rested her hand on Minnow's shoulder. Her take-on-the-world teen shuffled through her day withdrawn and quiet. Josie often found her underneath the restaurant deck in Gumbo's pelican shelter, even if Gumbo wasn't there.

"What about her stomachaches and the vomiting?" Josie asked.

"We discussed this during my exam." He nodded. "I suspect she has an ulcer."

"She's seventeen." Brian broke his silence. "Kids don't get ulcers."

Minnow threaded her fingers through Josie's. Her hand was cold. Josie squeezed it once to reassure her.

"Most ulcers in young adults are caused by the *H. pylori* bacteria. We have to assume she's positive. That means she's contagious and not allowed to work in the restaurant. The family should be vigilant with handwashing and not sharing glasses or eating utensils. Especially your father, Josie."

"Am I some Typhoid Mary monster?" Minnow asked.

"You are not a monster. And I haven't seen anyone else come in with your problems. But until we know for certain, let's be safe."

"How would she have picked it up?" Brian asked.

"A few ways—contaminated food or water, kissing."

Minnow rolled her eyes. "I haven't been kissing anyone."

The doctor tilted his head sideways. "I want to conduct a test that I can't do here."

"You just took like a gallon of blood," Minnow said.

"The ulcer diagnosis comes from a simple urea breath test that measures carbon dioxide. We'll make an appointment at the medical center in New Orleans."

"How soon?" Josie asked. *An ulcer at seventeen and a public health issue?*

"She's been taking over-the-counter medication. We need to let it cycle through her for a clean reading."

"You have?" Josie said to Minnow.

"What? Rosaline sells it at the minimart."

Dr. Tynsdale steepled his fingers and waited for their banter to subside.

"I have a diet for her, and we need to discuss stress management."

"What about it?" Brian leaned forward, his hands clasped between his knees. He had tried to apologize to Minnow in the car for snapping at her about the oil industry. Josie had told him to let it rest. Minnow sat silently with her head pressed against the window.

Brian was conditioned to fight for the oil industry. But Minnow saw a different world, a fragile one where her home was fouled by noxious oil. Her reality was the oil industry threatened marine life, including the dolphins she dreamed she could ride as a child. She was standing up for her community, and that included the island's nonhuman residents. Josie was proud of her passion. She couldn't even stand up for herself at Minnow's age, let alone the whole ocean.

"The bacteria causes the ulcer, but the way the body handles it can make an existing problem worse," Dr. Tynsdale said. "I suspect stress is contributing to Minnow's nausea and loss of appetite. I'll get a copy of the diet and a referral form. Minnow, maybe you want to share what you told me with your parents."

Dr. Tynsdale nodded as he left the room. The door closed with a click, and Minnow took a sharp inhale. She pulled her hand away from Josie.

Brian turned to her. "About this morning? I didn't mean what I said to . . ."

Minnow burst into tears and shook her head.

He sat on the edge of the doctor's desk to face her, with Josie standing behind Minnow and rubbing her back.

"Whatever the problem, you can tell us. We love you," Josie said.

"Sure do, *chère*," Brian said. "Team Minnow, one hundred percent."

She wiped her eyes with the back of her hand. "I don't want Team Minnow. I want to be a family again." She spoke into her hunched knees.

She was round and small. Josie wanted to pull her into her lap and make whatever hurt she felt disappear.

"What?" Josie asked, not hearing her.

"I want things to be the way they were."

"Before the oil spill?" Josie asked.

She shook her head. "You guys used to be so extra, all over each other. I was embarrassed to bring friends by the restaurant after it closed and find you making out on the deck. Now you can barely be in the same room together."

Josie's face flushed hot. Brian shifted on the desk and rubbed his neck.

They had never hidden their affection, laughing when the kids called them gross. Brian would tell them, "It's healthy to see your parents like this." It was also harmful to watch them fight.

Minnow pushed her chin out at Josie. "You're mad at everyone."

"Who am I mad at?"

"Me, because I don't want to go to business school. And Dad because he sold your grandmother's ring and bought the camera."

"Wha . . . what?" Josie said.

"I heard you and Dad arguing about college after I told you I wanted to visit schools with biology programs. Then you started in on him about your grandmother's ring and his buying the camera. The next day you left and ruined our family."

Josie's heart pounded in her throat. She had no idea Minnow had heard that fight. Minnow had misinterpreted it all, blaming herself. Her version made Josie sound selfish and petty. How could Josie explain? Odeal had voiced every emotion she had about her father, how she felt obligated to care for him and was trapped with two needy kids. Josie swore she'd never pull the kids into her marriage. She'd left Brian when she was no longer able to hide her broken heart in plain sight. While he was offshore, she could pretend he'd return a different man. But then she was alone with the harassing phone calls from debt collectors, the house in foreclosure, Daniel Dean's lectures when he covered her bills. And Brian would come home and break more promises. She had run to her father's and made them all refugees of her marriage.

Their final argument had come after Josie had spent a frustrating afternoon reviewing their finances with Daniel Dean.

"We can't recoup enough money to fund any of Minnow's college savings before she needs it," Daniel Dean said. "She's smart. She can apply for a scholarship and student loans."

Loans meant more debt, and that spiked a headache.

"How is she supposed to qualify for a loan with our credit?"

Daniel Dean patted her arm. "Keep making your bills on time. We have a year to improve your credit score."

Then Brian came home hyped from a ridiculous helicopter joyride where he'd taken pictures of the Deepwater Horizon. He had been out playing with his new expensive toy, leaving her home to figure out their future.

"Why are you so upset with me?" Brian said.

"Minnow's making plans for college. Something you and I have wanted since the day she was born. You're acting like you don't have a care in the world."

"That's not true. Taking pictures helps me."

"If you lost your camera, you'd be upset. Why aren't you upset over Minnow losing her chance to go to college?"

He sighed, deeply. "My camera is not the same as college."

"My jewelry isn't the same then either. Nice to see how you took what was *mine* and spent it for yourself but can't do the same for your daughter."

That night she had felt unhinged. Everything they had lost jumbled in her brain. The idea she had to take the fall and not tell the kids the truth about his gambling was too much. He had taken what she valued the most, her trust and the kids' future.

"Mom and I want you to go to college," Brian said. "We weren't arguing about you."

"So, then it was that stupid ring you never wore," she said to Josie. "Can't you just forgive him?" Minnow hugged her knees. "You always said you wanted me to have it. But what if I don't want it anymore? If you had asked, I would have told you so, and then you wouldn't have left. I hate living between two places and staying at Grandpa's when Daddy's on tour."

Josie stood. "It's not about . . ."

Dr. Tynsdale's knock interrupted them. "I'm guessing the chef gets the diet?" He handed it to Josie. "No hot peppers or spicy food. That's a reason she hasn't been eating. She didn't want you to change how you cook."

Minnow sniffed and wiped her eyes again.

"Oh," Josie said. Guilt gripped her. All Minnow had had to do was tell her the food was too spicy. Why hadn't she picked up on that?

As they left, Josie tried to put her arm around Minnow, but she leaned against Brian instead.

Minnow was punishing her for her leaving, for her cooking, for her failed relationship with Brian. She deserved all of it. She had allowed her hurt heart to make her decisions.

"I was wrong about what I said about the oil industry." Brian hugged her. "I'm angry about what's happening because of the spill, but you're out there helping. I need to do more."

He doesn't get to be the kind and caring parent while I'm left holding his lit fuse.

"Can we talk?" Josie pointed to a picnic table under a shade tree. She smoothed out the paper Dr. Tynsdale had given her. The new diet prescribed fruits and vegetables and said to avoid chocolate, caffeine, spicy food, and acidic food like tomatoes.

That's the start of most of my recipes. I've been seasoning Minnow's stomach problem with too much heat.

"According to this"—she tapped the paper—"you won't be tasting my new hot sauce." She offered a weak smile.

Minnow picked at the bark of a stick on the table.

Josie sat across from her. "You and Toby don't have to come back and stay with me at Grandpa's if you don't want."

Minnow looked up. "What happens when Dad's away? I'm old enough to stay alone."

"You haven't been responsible. We need to discuss you sneaking out to New Orleans again. We need to trust each other." Josie glanced at Brian.

He looked away and crossed his arms.

"Did Aunt Louise tell you?"

"*I* told her," Brian said. "You promised me you'd tell Mom, and you didn't."

At least he's protecting Louise.

"It was just a concert." She shrugged.

"We don't see it that way. The city has a lot of crime since Katrina. I don't want you there alone," Brian said.

"I can take care of myself."

Josie considered Minnow in profile, her thin arms and legs. Her hair had lost its luster. She still had her spunk. Josie could work with that.

"We know you're not a child. But Dad and I need to look after you until the doctor can tell us how to make you feel better."

"That's treating me like a child." She flicked the food plan. "Now you'll choose my food."

"No," Josie said. "You can choose your food, and we can cook together at home. Whatever home you choose. You heard Dr. Tynsdale: we need to keep you away from the restaurant."

"Are we done here? The air's awful today. I want to check on Gumbo," Minnow said.

Josie looked at Brian. *We are far from done.* Josie wouldn't push Minnow. Their job as parents was to support her. Josie would not add to her stress, but Brian was adding to hers.

Chapter 15

Thursday, May 20, 2010

Brian leaned against the open truck door, a safe distance from a group of protestors demanding access to the beach but close enough to hear the yelling.

"You can't keep me out. I'm a reporter, it's a public beach!" a woman holding a microphone shouted at a security guard. Behind her, a cameraman aimed his lens into the guard's face.

The guard covered the lens and pushed the man's shoulder. "Sir, you need to leave."

"What're you hiding?" a protester asked.

The guard was joined by two uniformed sheriff's deputies.

"Ma'am, you need permission from the central command and an escort to enter the beach premises. This is an active hazard site."

Four-wheeled ATVs rumbled up and down the island streets, adding to the din of heavy machinery. The long arm of a red conveyor belt punched the sky as it moved sand through a Rube Goldberg washing machine. Brian had seen a photo of it on the news. Over twenty tons of sand an hour were passing through, but the oil just kept coming.

Security had increased since Hollis and Louise had walked the beach with Minnow and Toby. He pictured Minnow here, screaming and holding a sign. This is what she had meant when she asked if he had seen the beach.

He hadn't, until today. *What are they hiding?*

Fine grains of debris swirled in the air.

God help us if someone lights a cigarette.

He couldn't remember the beach ever being closed. Even during hurricanes, only red flag warnings were posted to keep swimmers out of the surf.

Minnow's illness had forced him to step out of his head and back into what was happening here. He could opine her ulcer was bad luck or a freak illness. Yet he couldn't sweep away her stress and how it made her problem worse. He needed to take the punch and call it what it was: bad parenting. His.

He wanted to blame that on a lack of role models growing up. His stepfather's idea of attention had been to send him to the store for cigarettes, where he could buy himself a candy bar.

He and Josie had promised each other to be better parents. He hadn't held up his end of the pinkie swear. He would come home from rotation and would check out, either fishing with Hughdean or puttering with someone's boat project, then gambling. As the money began to slip away, working and scrambling for cash consumed him. Make enough—place a bet—win and celebrate. Lose and chase the loss. He was still caught in that infinite loop, scrounging worksites and begging for repair work. How did he let it spiral to this? Who had he become?

How did your personality change when you were gambling? The question had come up for discussion at the last Gamblers Anonymous meeting. "Think hard and sit with it," the group leader had said.

Brian turned away from the protestors and climbed into the truck. He only wanted to move forward. Hashing out the past was a waste of energy. It served no purpose. He'd use his time before his reassignment to be present for the kids. He and Toby would build the hot sauce booth and the gazebo in Daniel Dean's backyard. He would show an interest in Minnow's causes. And today, he'd hand Josie all the entry money he had earned.

Brian parked across the street from the restaurant. A flutter of excitement thrummed in his chest. He wanted Josie back.

Seven months ago, he had been raw from her anger. Their passion-charged exchanges no longer ended in bed. They ended with slammed doors and lumpy couches.

I've been a fool.

He knew for certain after they saw the doctor. Josie kept her promise to Minnow that they would cook whatever foods Minnow wanted, where she wanted. Minnow chose their house. After dinner he had set up the Scrabble board while Josie hummed and washed dishes in the kitchen, a scene from a family he barely remembered. Josie wore sexy cutoff jean shorts and a T-shirt from the 2008 Zydeco festival in Opelousas. That summer and the music held a lot of memories. They'd had a wild hair of an idea to sell hot sauce and shrimp cakes at festivals and use the money for a family vacation.

They had camped at a nearby park. Josie's eyes had glowed as she made plans for a trip and possibly finding other festivals. The excitement had been arousing. They had pulled the tent down in their haste to shed their clothes and make love.

They never took that family trip. He had gambled the $600 they'd earned, convinced he'd double it and they'd travel in style. That was when Josie stopped believing in his "magic," as she once called it. She ran to Hollis and Louise, relied on Maisy for support.

He sat tall in the driver's seat and took a calming, confident breath. He picked up his gas receipt from the minimart and found a pen in the glove box and wrote, *Happy wife, happy life.* He didn't remember when he first heard that old expression, but now he understood what it meant.

"Josie, I want you to come home." He practiced his request. His voice even and strong. *Too direct.*

"Josie, can we talk later today?" Too weak. She'd say no.

"Josie, we've been apart seven months. Do you have a decision about us?" He laughed. That was an invitation to hell.

"*Chère*, can we go out tonight? A walk along the pier, like the old days. The two of us?" Earnest and honest. It could work.

He'd hand her the money; show her he wasn't moving through the motions. He'd stand by her, and just like that first festival in Opelousas, plan for the future.

The restaurant was graveyard quiet at 2:00 p.m. Josie said business was down 60 percent. He headed for the kitchen, where he expected Josie to be prepping for the evening.

He pushed open the door. Josie stood, heaving sobs, her arms wrapped around Linh Nguyen's tiny frame. The two women talking and crying and making no sense to anyone but each other.

Josie looked up, her face broken in grief. "Linh's leaving the island."

Hughdean had said Tommy was bugging out to Florida. He hadn't considered this meant the entire Nguyen family was leaving too.

"Aw, shoot."

"I come say goodbye," Linh said. Her Vietnamese-accented English thicker with her sadness. She held Josie's face in both of her tiny hands. "You do good. I see you at chili show."

Josie nodded as silent tears flowed. "Thank you." Josie sniffed. "That's only a few weeks. Maybe this oil will be over, and you'll come back."

Linh sighed. "Tommy stubborn, make decision." She tapped her temple.

Brian laughed. "He sure is. We'll miss all of you."

She opened her arms, and he accepted her hug. Her body was birdlike, and he could feel her heartbeat.

Josie walked Linh to the door and embraced her a final time. "Okay, go on before I don't let you leave."

Josie turned to Brian and accepted his hug. He understood. Linh had been a lifeline in the kitchen. A confidante and a teacher. She was a model of what it meant to start over when life hurt so hard you didn't know if it was worth fighting for.

He grabbed a napkin from a table and wiped Josie's tears. "I'm sorry for this. I knew Tommy planned to go, just not this soon."

She nodded and exhaled. "I'm okay."

"I've got something for you." He grinned, pulled an envelope from his back pocket, and placed it into her hand. "Open it."

She pulled out a stack of bills.

"You can count it, but it's four hundred fifty dollars, more than enough to cover the rest of the entry fee to the competition."

"How did you get this?"

"Morgan City. I've been buying junked boat parts and restoring them for a tidy profit. Then when I started scrounging leftover building supplies for the booth, I found heaps of scrap metal that I sold. This gets us through the door. Now you make that call to your writer friend and finish that reaper sauce."

"I don't know what to say." Josie stared at the money, shaking her head.

"Say you're planning to win twenty-five grand and put Odeal's on the map. I predict before the summer's over, the beach will be open and we can catch the tail end of the season."

"What's Hollis doing here?" Josie walked toward the back picture window looking over the deck. Hollis was crouch walking after Gumbo, trying and failing to catch him. Gumbo leaped onto his perch and took off over the water. She saw Hollis whistle, but Gumbo wasn't playing. She tapped on the glass, and he motioned for them to come outside.

"I just came back from Racoon Island. Oil's come in hard. I wanted to check on Gumbo. He's more than up to his usual tricks." He whistled again.

"That only works for Minnow," Brian said.

"Gumbo," Josie called and clapped her hands three times.

He circled the deck and landed on Hollis's head.

"All right now, you. Very funny." Hollis lifted him off and ducked to dodge a javelin beak to his face.

"Calm down, boy," Hollis cooed. "I'm not gonna hurt you."

Hollis gently probed Gumbo's belly and inspected his wings.

"Is he okay?" Josie asked.

"Appears to be, but he's jumpy. Usually, he doesn't mind when I pick him up. How's he been?"

"Flying in and out as usual," Josie said. "He's not leaving as much of a mess though. A win on my list," Josie said.

"He's either finally learning your tolerance or he's not eating. He's plump, a bright sheen to his feathers."

"It reeks like a gas station out here." Josie wrinkled her nose.

"Seabirds have an acute sense of smell. My guess: the oil's making him uneasy. Not sure of the quality of the fish he's eating either. That's what I want to talk to you about."

"Let's talk inside," Josie said.

The restaurant's cool air was a welcome relief from the hot deck. Josie poured them lemonade, and they sat on three stools at the bar.

"What's the news?" Brian asked. So much crap came at them lately, he didn't have tolerance for people easing them into anything.

Hollis drained his glass. "I told Minnow earlier. We should feed Gumbo."

"*What?*" Brian said. That went against everything Hollis had told them before. The worry it would make Gumbo lazy or he'd let tourists feed him.

Hollis nodded.

Josie massaged her palm and shifted on the stool. "I don't understand. You always say not to feed him." She voiced Brian's concern.

"I've thought this through. We have bird populations collapsing now. We've sent hundreds of animals to the rehab center in Buras. Most of them won't make it either." He closed his eyes. "I can't remember a time with so many animals in distress from one event."

"Gumbo doesn't mingle much with the wild population," Brian said.

"It's not the other birds; it's the way he fishes, headfirst into the water." Hollis made a diving motion with his arm. "Seabirds have keen eyesight, but they can't detect oil on the surface."

"If we feed him, he won't fish and get oiled?" Brian said.

"He fishes on instinct. We can't completely stop him . . . unless we cage him."

"Oh, no. We agreed as a family"—Josie pointed to them—"to never pen him. He's wild, and he's here on his terms, not ours."

While they nursed him to health as a toddler, Hollis had justified feeding Gumbo because in a zoo or a wildlife center, the zookeepers would feed him. They were his keepers.

"I didn't say cage him, though he would stay safe. We'll feed him and monitor how he does. If he sticks around, we've controlled the problem until conditions clear," Hollis said.

"How do we fish with the ban?"

Hollis said, "I have a permit for scientific collection. We may be able to fish right off the deck here, where we can inspect the fish. It's the best we can do aside from sourcing fish outside the spill zone."

"How much do we need?" Brian asked.

"Four pounds a day should do it. Pelicans mostly eat menhaden, but I doubt he's picky."

The front door opened, splashing daylight across the floor and a whiff of strong air. The sound echoed through the empty dining room. Mr. Mackley, the mail carrier, stood with his bag over his shoulder. He was a fixture on the island in his signature postal uniform of a light-blue shirt, blue Bermuda shorts, and black ankle boots. He delivered the mail and the local gossip as he went through town.

"How're you holding up, Mr. Mackley?" Josie accepted a pile of mail, sandwiched inside the local newspaper.

"It's unhinged driving today. I haven't seen so many work vehicles and men in gear since I was stationed at Fort Polk. A National

Guard officer told me there are three hundred people digging sand on the beach. Lord knows how many more are standing around watching them."

Josie frowned. "Wish they'd drive over for dinner."

"You hang on. It can't last forever. Do you want your home mail and your dad's?"

"Thanks." Josie accepted the bundles.

"Oh, got another letter addressed to Brian to sign for." He produced a large white envelope.

Josie waved an envelope. "My emergency assistance check. She unfolded the letter. Five thousand dollars. You're my lucky charm today, Mr. Mackley."

"Lots of folks getting checks these days. See ya next week."

"I can enter the competition. My first delivery of reapers is coming, and now this. If Linh walked back through the door, the day would be the best we've had in weeks."

Josie's happy mood was like turning on the sun. Her eyes sparkled.

"I think it may just get better," Brian said. "This is from Transocean. Must be my reassignment notice." He waved the thick white packet. He'd be offshore soon, sending home his big paychecks.

He slid his finger under the lip of the envelope. "Ouch." A paper cut reddened with blood. He dabbed at it with a cocktail napkin. *Death by a thousand paper cuts.*

He tore away the envelope, forgoing the niceties.

May 12, 2010

Dear Brian Babineaux,

Due to the United States federal government moratorium on all deepwater offshore exploration and drilling on the Outer Continental Shelf, we regret to inform you your position as Sr. Chief Mechanic has been suspended.

"Holy hell! Those corporate assholes laid me off!" He slammed the packet of paper onto the bar and pounded his fist.

"What?" Josie's hand shook as she read the discarded letter. Brian fanned through the paperwork, taking in every other word. He could be recalled, depending on changes in federal policy. Benefits would continue until the end of June. He was eligible for unemployment. An 800 number was available for questions.

He stood, crumpled the letter, and smashed it onto the bar. A cold gloom bled through him. How could they do this? He was part of the crew. He needed to go back, like a soldier who returned to the front. His breath turned rapid and shallow. He couldn't focus beyond his hands. His pulse echoed in his head, and he swayed on his feet.

"Brian!" Josie reached to steady him. Hollis pulled over a chair, and they sat him down.

"Lean over, breathe deep," Hollis said.

Josie ran behind the bar, soaked a towel, and wiped his face. His breathing steadied, and he sat, his hands resting on his thighs.

Josie and Hollis stood over him as if he were a fragile, fainting little girl. Now he was cast aside like the sticky oil on the beach.

He turned to Josie.

"I'm so sorry. I've let you down, again."

"You didn't do this. You worked on that rig for ten years, putting your life on the line every time you climbed into a helicopter. You did it for the family. You came home to us."

He closed his eyes. *Us.* She was still here. That had to matter in this whole mess.

Chapter 16

Grand Isle, Louisiana

Sunday, May 23, 2010

Josie sat at the restaurant bar and shook her head, reading a special edition island news bulletin.

Geaux Grand Isle

Visit us on the internet at www.geauxgrandisle.com/ events

ALERT—Due to Oil Deposits, Beach Areas Are Closed until Further Notice from the Health Department

Sponsored by the Grand Isle Tourist Commission & the office of the honorable Mayor Louise Martil

Fishing conditions and beach-opening hotline: 985-GO2FISH

This weekend should have been the Pelican State Fishing Rodeo, one of the larger all-ages competitions. Tired parents and hyper kids would scamper across the marina deck after a day of fishing, thankful for the kids' menu of fish bites and curly fries.

Louise had been hailed as the island's hero in March when she announced the upcoming events of the season. She had spent the off-season networking with sports clubs and organizations around the state, convincing them to sponsor fishing competitions. Rental properties had filled, fishing charters had been booked, and Josie herself had expected one of the best seasons in recent history.

Josie turned up the TV over the bar to hear the morning news. The Deepwater Horizon well was still spewing oil into the Gulf. Now sea turtle nesting sites were threatened. The bureaucracy grew thornier each day and had pricked them with Brian losing his job. A swirl of nausea moved from her belly to her throat, and her head buzzed with anxiety. She closed her eyes and breathed deeply.

Concentrate on the competition.

She and Maisy had decided to make hot Cajun chicken wings, a riff on buffalo wings, to sell at the Ragin' Cajun. Josie now had crates of hot peppers and could make gallons of hot sauce.

With Josie handling the sauce development, Maisy had turned her attention to her confections.

Josie had caught her staring at a bowl of sugar the other day.

"What's on your mind, Chef?" Josie asked.

"Selena Martin."

"I'll bite, who is she?"

Maisy had turned into a chef detective, following leads and a people-who-knew-people of chefs they'd be up against during the competition. She had scolded Josie for not staying plugged in to the outer culinary world. Josie had countered with "I'm setting the trends, not following them."

"Selena owns the Hatch chili. Her new cookbook has a chocolate-chili cake recipe. I heard she sells cupcakes at these food events."

"Hatch is New Mexico, right?"

"Mm-hmm, popular and trendy. Foodies love single-origin ingredients."

"We're not making cupcakes."

Maisy shook her head. "No, we're not. I made her cake. She's clever how she's balanced the sweet and the hot. But I'll go head to head with my chocolate-chili-chip brownies. They're easier to eat and package. No fussy frosting."

"Wings and brownies are a weird combination," Josie said.

"That's the novelty. We're aiming for memorable. Don't say it. How're we to pay for all of it? I'm looking for a sponsor."

This competition had stirred a win-or-die-trying mentality in Maisy. Josie had the same spirit when she left for culinary school in California. It energized her to have that excitement surrounding her again. This was about the food and how people enjoyed what she made. The competition was a mental rest from her worries.

Now, Josie watched Gumbo through the picture window as he sunned himself on the deck rail. Hollis had dropped off a day's worth of fish first thing in the morning.

"Where d'you get fish so fast?" she asked.

"Sun goes down, and the fishing rods come out on the pier. I took up a collection from the stealth fishers."

Seeing Gumbo in his usual spot calmed her this morning. He was right where she expected him, posed like a postcard image with his salmon-blush-colored long bill. She fussed at him like one of the kids.

He calmed Minnow, too, especially now with the medical test and news about Brian losing his job. Josie was grateful Gumbo was in their lives. Minnow's voice would float from his shelter under the deck, peppered with laughter, or music from a portable radio. She even read to him.

Everyone knew Josie's wish now was to win the Ragin' Cajun. But what people thought and what Josie kept inside her heart weren't the same.

Josie would abandon all her hot sauce chances to have Minnow healthy. She bongo drummed the bar top, anxious to start on the fresh crate of reapers in the kitchen. The recipe she was working was close to perfect. The newest variation was a sweet hot. A mix of a Carolina Reaper and Tabasco peppers sweetened with a locally sourced molasses from Raceland.

"Reapers are the hottest pepper on Earth. Are we foolish to try this?" Josie had asked Maisy.

Maisy shot her a wicked grin. "Of course we are."

The peppers were face-melting, fleshy pockets of fire, but Josie would coax their fruity flavor to shine. Flavor was the secret to winning. They had discussed pepper options—habanero and ghost peppers. But as a nod to Maisy's roots, the Carolina Reaper was the sentimental winner.

Today, she'd march into the kitchen and create a winner. She never imagined that her private stash of sauce would have landed her here or keep her business hopes alive.

Gumbo's shadow cast a curtain of shade across the deck. Josie held her breath. *Please don't fish.* She jogged outside to distract him. He circled overhead, catching a morning thermal. She wrinkled her nose. As the day's heat rose, the chemical tang fogged the humid air and tasted like pennies.

Gumbo swooped and landed at her feet and waddled the last few steps, clicking his bill.

"Are you Pavlov's pelican?" she said. "Is it possible to overfeed you?"

She fetched him a speckled trout.

"One, two, three." She flung the fish into Gumbo's open throat in a live action game of cornhole. He gulped it down, then hopped back to his favorite perch above the DO NOT FEED THE PELICAN sign.

Josie went back inside and turned off the TV and listened. *Damn.* The air conditioner was silent, no hum to cause the barware to vibrate. She stood on a chair and held her hand over a vent. No air, *again.* She was alone in the restaurant, and this wouldn't be the first time she cooked in a hot kitchen. *Still, better call Brian. If I win this competition, I'll end up using the prize money for a new AC unit.* The unit should have been replaced three years ago. They had nursed it along when the money started to disappear. Then the kitchen range needed an overhaul. They opened the doors and ran fans, a throwback to the old days on Grand Isle. But they needed a range to cook. It was one more problem he'd created and needed to make right. Selling scrap metal and boat parts wasn't enough. He did come through with the entry money. But he acted as if these small gestures were supposed to make her anger go away.

Stop. Time to move on. She could use some of the emergency money for AC parts if she had to. She left Brian a message and headed into the kitchen.

Time to hot sauce.

She considered propping open the back door to the deck, but the morning oil fumes were already bothering her. She'd rather be hot, and she wrapped a cool wet towel around her neck. She set a large pot of water to boil. Her plan was to prep and scald the peppers to mellow the raw flavor. She tugged on a pair of latex gloves and weighed a handful of danger-red, wrinkly, scorpion-tailed Carolina Reapers. Next, she sliced onions and began the slow caramelization process. Never rush the onions. She tapped her knife to the local swamp pop radio station as she diced. The reapers were hot, and she coughed, her body protecting her throat with a choking, gummy sensation brought on by the peppers.

She stirred the onions, pleased by how they caramelized and perfumed the space. Sweat dripped down her throat and back. The cut-pepper juice mixed with steam and filled the kitchen. She coughed harder into her elbow to clear the tickle at the back of her throat. She wiped her sweating face with the wet towel from around her neck, and it slipped. Her gloved finger poked her eye, filling it with reaper juice.

"Ah!" She stumbled away from the cooking onions and wiped her face again. The wet towel spread the burn from her right eye to her nose.

Stupid, stupid, stupid.

The heat exploded, a blinding sting. Her eye flooded in tears. Boiling water propelled the pepper fumes into a chili fog, prickling her clear eye and causing it also to tear. The vapor settled on her face, and it radiated like a sunburn.

She snapped off the pepper-stained gloves. The onions were cooking too fast. She lunged to turn off the burners, scalding her hand in a cloud of chili steam. She shook it in pain.

"UGH!" she shouted again and leaned against the wall. Her heart thudded in her ears as a cold sweat tackled her body. Her nose ran, and her throat burned and constricted.

Stop. Think. Kitchen first aid.

She was trained in food allergies, anaphylactic shock, but not idiotic pepper eye shock. She squinted and felt her way to the sink and pumped a handful of soap into her burned hand. Did she really want to slather this onto her face? A dry heave exploded from her mouth, and she hung her head in the sink.

"Josie?" a voice called from the dining room.

Brian! "Brian. Help," she called and coughed.

The kitchen door banged open. "What's wrong? Are you bleeding?"

She swayed and heaved again.

He held the towel close to her face and examined her hand covered in soap. "Did you get soap in your eye?"

She shook her head and coughed. "Reaper chili juice." Spots floated in front of her eyes.

"I can't see," she shrieked, fear now shaking her body. Her eyes were gushing useless tears, but she couldn't stand to open them from the pain. She swayed on her feet as her head rolled back and her skin pulsed.

"Oh, hell!"

Brian grabbed a gallon of milk and poured it into a bin in the sink.

"I've got you." He ladled the milk over her face, flushing out the chili. She gagged. He stopped and held her tight until she calmed her breathing.

"Show me your hands."

They shook as she held them out. *I'm okay. I'm okay.* With her clearer eye, she examined her hand. The skin glowed tender and red, but not a blister burn.

He sat her on a stool, resting her hands over the sink, and rinsed the soap, then massaged olive oil into her skin.

She winced from the burn and coughed.

"You're okay, *chère.*" His voice was calming as he filled the sink with ice water and dunked her hand.

Blessed relief soothed her skin, and her muscles relaxed.

"Wow." He coughed from the pepper vapor and propped open the back door to exhaust the fumes.

He held a glass of milk to her lips. She drank the cold liquid, dousing the tickle fire constricting her throat.

"Too much." She shook her head, fearing the milk would come up.

He stood behind her, his hands steadying her shoulders.

I can't believe I did this. She collapsed her head against his body, and he massaged her shoulders.

"It's over, breathe."

Ha! Her breath blew as hot as lava. She suspected she could ignite the gas stove if she exhaled on it. The pain in her eye calmed to a sharp throb, but her vision cleared.

"Thank you." Her voice was hoarse.

"Cajun Smack revenge?" he said.

She shook her head. "New sauce, Cajun Reaper."

"More like the Revenge of the Cajun Reaper," Brian said.

She accepted a towel and dried her face.

"What happened?"

"A dumb accident. The dumbest thing I've ever done in the kitchen," Josie said.

Brian took in the disheveled workspace. "I think your onions are ready."

Chapter 17

Monday, May 24, 2010

The waiting room at the New Orleans medical center resembled every other medical facility Brian had ever seen, with clusters of pastel-colored chairs and side tables covered in creased magazines. Brian sat between Josie and Minnow. Worry lines pulled around Josie's tired eyes. They were waiting for Minnow to be called back for her *H. pylori* test.

"What if they can't find what's wrong with me? What if I'm dying?" Minnow sat folded over. Her gray hoodie swallowed her body.

"Are you in pain now, *chère*?" Josie stood behind her and rubbed her back.

"Mom, don't touch me. I feel like crap. I hurt when I eat. I hurt when I don't eat. I'm tired. When I lay down, it's like fire is crawling through me."

Josie stepped back and folded her arms. Even here in the waiting room, Minnow rejected her comfort. Josie wore her pain on her face and in the way she hugged her body and wrung her hands.

Brian put his arm around Minnow. This was the first time he'd heard her complain. *Why has she been hiding this from me?* This explained her bad moods, the weight loss, and why she prowled around the house at night. He had written off her behavior as part of being a teenage girl. And teenage girls had scared him ever since he was a teenage boy.

"You'll be fine. Today's the day everything gets better." Brian forced a bright note into his voice.

"You don't know that. I'm the one with a hole in my gut."

I have a hole inside, too, that I'm trying to fill, but I don't know how.

"The medical intake form we filled in asked you to list all the conditions you have. You don't have any."

"Except for an ulcer."

He needed to believe that his Minnow would be okay. She was his little girl at the cusp of being all grown, and knotted with stress and big-world problems. For months, Josie had told him she was worried, and he had snapped at her. Anything Josie said landed as judgmental, from the way he took care of the kids when they were with him to how he lived his life. Remorse squeezed his chest. He had the chance to show Josie he was responsible. His anger had blinded him to what his daughter needed. What kind of man did that to his family?

A woman in blue hospital scrubs walked over. "Minnow Babineaux," she read from a clipboard.

Minnow hugged herself. "That's me."

The woman smiled. "Are you ready for the test?"

Minnow shrugged.

"Can we go back with her?" Josie asked.

"I'm sorry, it's a patient-only area. But we'll bring her out as soon as she's done."

"How long?" Brian asked. He wanted to be on the other side of this day.

The nurse checked her watch. "About two hours."

Josie hugged Minnow. "See you soon. I love you."

Brian cupped her chin. "Remember, you're Princess Minnow of the High Seas."

Minnow rolled her eyes at the name Hughdean always called her, but smiled.

"I love you," he said.

Minnow disappeared through the door.

"You look tired," Brian said to Josie.

She nodded. "I couldn't sleep last night. Would you mind if we move to the corner? I want to close my eyes and nap."

"Anywhere you want is fine. Would you be okay if I went for a walk? I can't sit here for two hours. I'll be back before she's through."

"Wake me if I'm asleep."

Brian left the medical center and headed for the river. The sky was gray, like someone had pulled a sheet across the heavens. The air was different here than on the island without the brine of the sea and this summer's petroleum. People walked around tending to their business. They lacked the wild, lost ambling his Grand Isle neighbors had adopted. With the clearer air and no visible signs of oil, he could pretend the spill was a world away. But it wasn't.

The Mississippi River flowed as green gray as he remembered as a boy. And it still stank, a rotten egg, decaying-life odor. All manner of debris and pollution hitched a ride as the river flushed through ten states on its way to the Gulf. The Gulf now swirling with oil.

His first job at fifteen was as a busboy on a riverboat casino docked in the Mississippi. He wasn't old enough to gamble or even allowed on the gaming floor. But he learned to play poker with the cooks and waitstaff—five-card draw, seven-card stud, and what would become his preference, Texas Hold'em. He was first invited into the games when the line cooks needed an extra body. He lost more wages than he earned in those early days but soon became a master of the bluff and reading other players. No one expected a kid to play poker. They underestimated him, and he used it to his advantage. He had been working and playing cards more than half his life.

Where would I be if I had concentrated on work, found a way to go to college?

"You'd make a fine mechanical engineer," Penman had once said as they were pulling wire through a ceiling duct.

"What do they do?"

"Design machines. We wouldn't be on this rig without mechanical engineers. The pay is good too."

"By the time I finished paying for school, I'd only break even, and I'd probably still be here on the rig."

No one had ever mentored him about college or a career. He nodded along to Josie's insistence that both Minnow and Toby would go to school. Maybe it was because he didn't understand the reason that he so easily robbed it from them.

The walk along the river led to the Bon Chance Casino. A faux castle with a garish drawbridge door that belonged in an amusement park yet attracted dedicated players. Other casinos in the city were more popular for slots, tourists, and cheap booze. He liked this casino's energy, with its worn and comfortable green-felt card tables, almost a taste in his mouth like a passionate kiss. His brain itched, needing a release from thoughts of Minnow's fear and Josie's exhaustion. Like a casino, bad feelings were open twenty-four hours. *I can't be here.*

He walked deeper into the city, away from the ghosts. The day's heat was rising, and the river's tang was met with the odor of garbage waiting to be collected in the streets. How many times had he been met with that smell and empty pockets? The stench of gambling lingered on him. Could others sense it?

He retraced old steps, with no destination in mind. Today, he had both a devil and an angel sitting on his shoulders. One fed air into his gambling furnace, and the other blew him down a street he never wanted to see again—to Crescent City Pawn. A neon open sign glowed behind the barred window. The storefront reeked of urine and moldy newspapers. He hadn't noticed seven months ago when he craved quick cash. Then, he had focused only on the blue velvet bag hastily filled with Josie's jewelry. He had spun his wedding ring once, then twice. How much was the gold worth?

He stepped inside. A blast of air-conditioning slapped him in the face, and he squinted from the white fluorescent lights humming with an artificial cheerfulness. The place was empty of customers but not merchandise. A rack of guns lined one side of the store in a locked case. Musical instruments hung on the other. Locked display cases of DVDs, tools, and electronics stood in an island. The back of the store held watches and jewelry. He had cared so little for Josie's most personal possessions, he had left them here like a baby on a doorstep. Josie had kept her mother's ring hidden in a dresser to lock away her mother. He caught her once talking to it.

"*Southern Ways* magazine praised me for creating new tastes with Cajun standards. I am more than a pathetic dishwasher. Imagine what we could have done if you had loved me the way I needed you to."

Imagine what she could have done if he had loved her the way she deserved. She had been planning a new side business, starting with the restaurant's most popular appetizer, her two-bite shrimp cakes. "This could be something bigger for the kids."

Hughdean had been interested, too, and for the first time, he had taken Josie's side against their dad, willing to invest his own money.

The store's overhead lights hummed too loud. *I killed their dreams.* The air was cold on his skin, and his pulse throbbed a manic drumbeat. He pushed out the door and ran, pumping his arms and legs away from the buzz, the itch, and the shame. He ran, fueled by something new, the truth. He ran, avoiding the casino, needing Josie. Needing to be grounded.

He stopped outside the medical center and rested with his hands on his knees. His breath came fast, hot, and raspy in his throat. His little girl was inside, his wife twisted in worry, and he had almost thrown down the few dollars he had for one moment to forget these feelings.

I walked away. It wasn't much, but it was enough for today. So much had happened these past months. He had sleepwalked through it and was now awake.

He walked into the waiting room. A woman nursed an infant, and a little girl lay on the floor with a coloring book, swinging her legs and humming. Josie paced a tight circuit in the back.

He nearly cried. A whole life had passed while he walked, yet she was here, a buoy anchored in his mad ocean. She met his gaze, and he must have looked wild based on the questioning expression she showed. He opened his arms for a hug, and she accepted. Her body was warm and solid.

"Josie—"

The restricted-procedure area swung open, and Minnow walked out with a technician. Josie crossed the room faster than a shooting star.

Minnow's shoulders hunched in like crumbling walls. He blinked back a rush of tears. She was safe. He folded her into his arms, and Josie kissed the top of her head.

"She did great," the technician said. "Let's sit." She pointed to a bank of seats in a quiet corner.

"We've sent the tests to the lab, and we'll call you today as soon as the doctor has had a chance to review them."

A moan of worry escaped from Josie.

"It's okay," the technician said. "If she's positive, she'll start a double course of antibiotics and a prescription-strength antacid. Monitor her diet, and within a few weeks, she'll feel like her old self."

"You okay, *chère*?" Brian asked.

Minnow nodded.

"Thank you," Josie said. She cupped Minnow's face between her hands and kissed her forehead. "Café du Monde for beignets?"

Minnow smiled, a genuine light of happiness in her eyes. The iconic restaurant was always part of their family trips to New Orleans.

As kids, Minnow and Toby would transform their faces into sugar clowns, drawing lines of powdered sugar across their lips, laughing until Josie and Brian laughed too.

He needed to have their laughter back in his life.

With the test behind her, Minnow's mood lightened, and she chatted nonstop on the ride over to the restaurant, not allowing Josie or Brian more than space to nod their heads.

"The test was kinda cool. I breathed into a collection bag. Then I swallowed a radioactive pill. A half hour later, I breathed into the bag again. Science is wild."

"Radioactive?" Josie said. Dispersant and oil poison were already in the air; she didn't want anything else hitting Minnow.

"They said it's not enough to hurt me," Minnow said.

They found a table under Café du Monde's green-and-white-striped awning.

"Why is no one here?" Minnow said. She craned her neck around. A few people sat near the street, where a band was playing. "We usually have to wait for a table?"

"The whole city is quiet. It's the oil spill, keeping the tourists away," Brian said.

"Doesn't look like anyone is working here either." Josie began bussing a table, as they were all full of abandoned plates. A path of powdered sugar littered the ground, and pigeons pecked at a plate of half-eaten beignets.

"Sit here, nice and clean." Josie patted her purse. "You should take an antacid before you eat."

"Yummy, beignets and horse pills," Minnow said.

"The sugar will make 'em go down easy," Brian said. He stood, jumpy. "I'll put in our order."

"Can I have coffee?"

"No!" Brian and Josie said together.

Minnow held her hands in surrender. "Not on my diet."

He squeezed Minnow's shoulder and went to the take-out window.

Josie sat. She was overtired, her body wanting to lie down and sleep while her brain performed Olympic-level worrying. *What has gotten into Brian this morning?*

He had come in from his walk like he had seen a ghost. He was worried too. She hated that it took Minnow needing this test for him to take her fears seriously, but he was now, and she needed him to run interference with Minnow.

Brian returned, and his hands shook as he set the coffee and beignets on the table.

"Dad, are you okay?"

He stood and brushed powdered sugar from his hands.

"I'm fine. Anxious waiting on the doctor with your results. Actually"—he sat and reached across the table and took Minnow's hands—"I'm sorry we waited so long. Your momma was right about the doctor." He looked over at Josie. "I shouldn't have fought you."

Josie held her coffee. An apology from Brian was like a rainbow after a storm. Never a guarantee and didn't make up for the damage the storm caused in the first place.

"You should have told me," he said to Minnow. "You may be almost grown, but you'll never be too old to ask me for help."

Minnow pulled her hands away and picked at a beignet. "I didn't want you to worry."

"And here we are, the three of us, not to mention everyone at home who loves you."

Minnow began to cry.

"Oh, *chère*, I didn't—"

"We're not angry with you," Josie said.

Minnow shook her head. "It's not that. I lied to both of you."

Josie caught Brian's eye, and he gave her the slightest shake of his head.

"I wanted to tell you when we were at Dr. Tynsdale's office, but I was scared."

"Of what?" Josie said.

Minnow threw her head back and closed her eyes. "Will you promise not to ground me again if I tell you?"

"Sure," Josie said. *But I may regret that.*

"I was trying to make things better, like before. After you left"—she looked at Josie—"I found the ticket from the place in New Orleans where Daddy pawned your jewelry."

"You did *what*?" Brian said.

"Let her finish," Josie said.

Minnow took a shuddery breath. "I used my tips to make the loan payments until the oil spill happened and I didn't have enough money. I'm sorry, Momma. I was planning on giving Daddy your jewelry and asking him to apologize. And I lost all that money I was paying, too, when I couldn't stay up on the loan."

Brian's head hung, and he pressed his hands on both sides of his neck.

"Minnow." Josie hugged her. "I don't care about any of that. I only care about you. What you did was dangerous."

Josie glared at Brian, her anger at full tilt. Minnow losing her money to solve for his gambling was worse than any money he had lost. Yet that paled in comparison to the danger she had put herself in. For all its promised fun times, New Orleans was no place for a young woman to be walking alone, and not with money stuffed in her purse. She could have been mugged, or worse.

Brian dropped to his knees in front of Minnow and took her hands. He looked up at Josie. "I am so sorry. What I did was wrong, and I'm trying hard to make up for it. I have to be honest with you and myself. Momma left because I have a gambling problem."

"I don't understand," Minnow said. "What about her ring and you buying the camera?"

Brian shook his head. "Uncle Hughdean and I used to play cards for fun. Then we started playing for money. At first, I was winning. I had big plans for what we could do with the cash. We'd take trips. I'd buy your mom fancy things, cars for you and Toby. You know how people dream when there's a huge lottery jackpot? I was like that all the time. It was my excuse to keep betting. But it didn't excuse what I did."

He paused and released one of Minnow's hands and took one of Josie's.

Her stomach roiled at his touch, his hand sweaty, cold, and trembling. The enormity of all he had done hit her again, but she didn't pull away. She had waited seven months for his admission.

"Something deep inside me changed, or maybe I was always this way. If I didn't play, my chest would squeeze tight like it would explode, and my brain thought ridiculous ideas. If I lost, the feeling was worse. I needed to bet again to win back the money so no one would know. I kept losing, but couldn't stop betting. I have an addiction."

"Like you're an alcoholic?" Minnow asked.

Brian nodded. "You can be addicted to lots of things that make you feel a certain way."

He released their hands and covered his face, shaking his head. He took a short breath. "I lost our family's money. Our savings, my retirement money. I borrowed money. I lost that, and . . . I gambled the college money Momma saved for you and Toby. It's gone. And when I didn't have money or any more credit, I stole your mother's jewelry and pawned it. The camera was something I bought not thinking about what I already lost or cost the family."

He turned to Josie, his face ashen, and tears streamed uncontrolled. "I'm so ashamed. I'm sorry."

"We don't have any money?" Minnow's eyes flashed in anger, and a sharp *V* pulled between her brows. "All this talk about a college road trip. Just a lie to, what, trick me?"

"No, *chère*." Josie patted her hand. "We've had a setback now with the oil. We'll find a way for you to go to college. I'm working on it with Grandpa."

Minnow pulled her hand away, and the plate clanged against the table, and she sobbed.

"Why did you leave?" she asked Josie. "Daddy needed you. We needed to be together."

"I—"

"No," Brian said. "None of this is Momma's fault. Living with me was toxic for you and Toby. I wasn't worth having anymore. Momma needed to protect you, and she needed to be away from me to do that. Her leaving wasn't about the ring or the camera. Well, maybe a little about the camera." He shrugged. "I did this, not Momma. You and Toby are her heart. She loves you more than anyone in the world."

He looked at Josie, and she felt his fear. His overdue confession could cause her not to trust him again. You didn't crush someone's dreams and earn a do-over.

"I promised to tell you and Toby the truth, and I didn't. I wasn't paying attention to how I hurt Momma, and that also hurt you and Toby. I was thinking only of myself and not the mess I made."

Josie's limbs grew heavy, like the morning of the well explosion when she feared Brian was dead. Her emotions connected memories and moments in a mad sequence. The day she realized loving Brian was more important than hating Odeal. And the day she couldn't even hold on to that, when he broke her trust for what she declared was the last time. She was glad Odeal's ring was gone. She needed to let everything go.

Brian's truth wasn't the release she expected. What did she expect? A tinge of revenge? She was wrapped in regret. How did she let everything spin out of control?

"My leaving was never about the ring." Josie flung her arms around Minnow. A cloud of sugar dusted their clothes. Whether her daughter accepted her touch or not, Josie needed to hold her.

Minnow met her hug and cried. "I'm sorry, Mom. I've been awful to you."

Powdered sugar mixed with Minnow's tears, like a sad mime. "We're a mess." Josie swiped at Minnow's cheeks.

Brian sat, his face flat and emotionless. Did he worry the kids would stop loving him the way she feared they would stop loving her?

"There's more," Brian said.

"More?" *No more surprises.*

165

"My trips to Morgan City."

Josie closed her eyes. Had he found a card game? Had his shame been a ruse?

"I'm going to a Gamblers Anonymous meeting. It's the closest one I've found to the island. I have a long way to go. But I've started."

Josie's phone rang before she could respond.

"It's the hospital." She set the phone on the table and hit the speaker button.

"Hello?"

"Hi, this is Dr. McKennen, calling with Minnow Babineaux's results. Is this Mr. or Mrs. Babineaux?"

"Yes, we're all here."

"Mrs. Babineaux, Minnow tested positive for *H. pylori*. This is the cause of her ulcer. We're calling in her prescriptions to your local pharmacy, and we'll send the results to your doctor. Is it Tynsdale in Grand Isle?"

"Yes," Josie said, nodding and wiping her eyes. "That's all correct."

"You'll want to follow up with that office. They may order a repeat test in a few weeks."

"Thank you, Doctor."

"Good luck, Minnow. You'll be feeling better soon."

Good luck, Josie.

Geaux Grand Isle

Visit us on the internet at www.geauxgrandisle.com/
events

June 1, 2010

ALERT—Due to Oil Deposits, Beach Areas Are Closed until Further Notice from the Health Department

Sponsored by the Grand Isle Tourist Commission & the office of the honorable Mayor Louise Martil

Fishing Conditions and beach-opening hotline: 985-GO2FISH

Summer 2010 Activities: Fun for Everyone!

Canceled: June 4–5: *Crescent City Post* Fishing Rodeo, Sand Dollar Marina

Canceled: June 12–13: Pelican State Fishing Rodeo, Grand Isle Marina, Ages 6–12 / Adults 13+

Canceled: June 15–17: Bayou Gold Fishing Rodeo, Bridge Side Marina

Canceled: June 25–27: Sisters Who Fish Rodeo, Sand Dollar Marina

Pending: July 4: Fourth of July Fireworks

Canceled: July 9–10: Beach Volleyball Tournament

Canceled: July 17–18: Gris-Gris Brewery Fishing Rodeo

Canceled: July 22–25: 82nd Annual Tarpon Rodeo

Canceled: July 31: NOLA Kayak Club Race

Canceled: August 7–8: Petroleum Association Fishing Rodeo

Canceled: August 13–14: Houma Heliport Fishing Rodeo

Canceled: August 20–21: PACE Union Workers Fishing Rodeo

Urgent August 24: Blood Drive, Blood Mobile, Grand Isle Library **Urgent**

Canceled: August 28–29: 49th Redfish Rodeo

Pending: September 4–8: Labor Day Weekend Carnival, Tarpon Rodeo Pavilion

Chapter 18

Tuesday, June 1, 2010

Josie set bowls of her new Revenge of the Cajun Reaper hot sauce with corn bread on the restaurant bar for people to sample today. It took her two more tries after the chili pepper accident to balance the sweet and the hot. The recipe's solution was garden-variety sweet red peppers, zero on the Scoville unit pepper heat scale.

She was delighted by the variety of hot peppers Jimmy Lunder delivered. After the competition, she'd see what else she could mix up. She was curious about Hatch chilies, but Jimmy didn't grow them. Maisy was still fussing that her brownies were better than any chocolate-chili cake. Josie would have to wait for the competition to try them.

Last week, she had submitted her competition entry and the fee and called Dale from *Vacation Ventures* to update him. He promised to call the *Kitchen Network* about selecting her as a featured contestant. It was a stretch this late, and she thanked him for making the call for her.

"If they don't pick me up front, I'll have to win the whole show. Then they'll have to interview me."

Josie hated asking people for favors. "We take care of ourselves, or we'll do without," Odeal had always said. Odeal would flush red in embarrassment when anyone offered to help with Daniel Dean. Only Rosaline stood up to her, stopping by with treats from the store for Josie and Hughdean.

Louise walked into the restaurant, dropped her bag, and slunk into a booth.

"I know that face. What's wrong?" Josie asked.

"Can I have a sweet tea, Daniel Dean–style?"

Josie sat across from her. "Nine in the morning is early for bourbon."

Louise fished through her bag and produced the latest *Geaux Grand Isle* newsletter. "We're sending this out today."

Josie scanned the newsletter. Every event was canceled or pending except for the blood drive at the library. It was like thousands of dollars being stripped from her bank account. All those tourists with their egos spreading fish stories and opening their wallets, gone.

"Oh, Louise, this is—"

"The worst news ever. The government is extending the drilling ban another six months. The oil's everywhere. No sense in keeping anyone guessing." Louise rested her forehead on the table. "And today, I'm to be sunshine and light, helping pissed-off shrimpers file claims and calming the nerves of people upset about all the outsiders who are only here to help clean our beach. They're yelling at me for money and to lift the fishing ban. Like I can change either."

"Let me fetch you that tea, but sorry, no bourbon."

"I want to run away from this."

Me too. "You should." Josie set her drink down.

"Imagine the gossip if the mayor left the island on vacation? Besides, Hollis won't go. I already floated the idea."

"I'd leave if I could." She sat back down.

"You sound like Minnow, itching to go anywhere." Louise took a sip of her drink. "I saw her this morning, before they took off on their bird checks. Her energy is better. Hollis's research is giving her something important to do."

It had been a week since Minnow started her antibiotics. Dr. Tynsdale reminded them that even with the infection cleared, it would be several more weeks before her body healed and the pain truly stopped.

"I overheard her talking to Hollis about school," Louise said.

"I wish she'd talk to me."

"Give her time. She's working through the truth. Brian's gambling is scary, and she's angry you didn't tell her."

"But—"

"No *buts*." Louise held up her hand. "That was your choice. You made it; now you have to live with it. She's still a moody teenager. Let her have her mood. Soon Toby will be beside her."

Josie nodded. "I'm glad she's talking, collecting facts, considering different options."

"That's what you wanted, for her to make her own choices. Now, you tell me, how are things"—she waved her hand—"with Brian?"

Josie walked over to the hot sauce. "Try this new batch." She handed Louise a sample.

"Killing me with chili peppers won't stop me from asking. It's been over a week since he apologized."

"I haven't talked to him. I'm not ready."

"Are you waiting for a sign from God? Because I can tell you, prayer isn't working this summer."

"I'm waiting until this"—she held her hand in a fist—"choking sadness disappears. I tried to talk to him, but all I can do is cry. And I've cried enough over Brian Babineaux. Do you know what I found?"

Louise shook her head.

Josie left the dining room and returned with a creased folder. "Look familiar?"

Louise scanned through the pages. "This is the paperwork I drafted for you to open Pelican Point Provisions. February sixth, 2007. It's been a while, hasn't it?"

"March was when he overdrew the bank account. April was when I learned about the loan on the 401(k). June was when I used all the money I had set aside for this to cover our bills. And on and on. I've spent every waking moment keeping the family together, scraping money, holding on to staff I couldn't afford. I protected him and lost my dreams. I'm tired of putting my feelings last. I'm not angry anymore. I'm sad because there's nothing left for me. I've waited three years for any type of apology, seven months for him to tell the kids. He can wait until I can figure it out. And maybe, just maybe, this oil spill will stop, and I'll earn some solid publicity from this competition in enough time to save the tail end of the season. 'Cause if I don't find something that's just for me that helps keep the restaurant open, we'll be burning dining room furniture this winter to keep warm."

Chapter 19

Grand Isle, Louisiana

Thursday, June 3, 2010

Josie rested against the railing of Maisy's new porch, a glass of wine dangling from her fingers. This new addition was all Maisy had talked about over the winter. "An outside space to watch the sunset." Then she'd add, "With a certain island doctor."

The wraparound porch had a full view of the water. Today was the first time in forever that the ocean currents had pushed the oil smell out to sea. She closed her eyes, feeling the late-afternoon sun. It would be another hour before it set.

Now with the restaurant closed half the week, a burden had been lifted. Like Louise canceling May and June activities on the island, canceling was painful, and then it was over.

As they closed the kitchen for the afternoon, Maisy had said, "Come over tonight. We'll cook for ourselves, anything we want. The way we want."

"I can't remember the last time I did that," Josie said. She was juggling medical diets between Daniel Dean and Minnow. "I've got Toby tonight, and I haven't been alone with him in ages."

"Then we'll have a cooking lesson. What should we make?" Maisy said.

"Pizza, and I want mine with andouille."

Maisy smiled. "I'll start the dough and see you at five. Now go. I'll lock up."

Here with nothing more important to decide than what else to add to her pizza, she flirted with relaxation.

Toby ran up the porch steps, a grocery bag scrunched in his hand. "Hi, Mom."

He had grown again and was almost as tall as her. The only thing bigger was his appetite.

Brian followed behind. He was relaxed, too, in a T-shirt and shorts. His eyes were bright, a sign he had slept well. Like Minnow, he had lost weight. Stress ate him alive. But they weren't alone. The whole island was edgy. Her once-cordial community reduced to husks. As the spill continued, more people like the Nguyens, who made their livelihoods off the land, were leaving.

Maybe we should leave too. I can sweet-talk my way into an exclusive kitchen. A restaurant with a six-month waiting list. Declare bankruptcy and start over.

"The porch came out nice," Brian said, breaking into her thoughts. He stood next to Josie and peered over the edge. His body was warm next to hers. The sun-and-moon tattoo on his bicep had faded. That predated their relationship. Josie stroked her palm and the oyster scar. It, too, had faded in color but would always be raised like a speed bump. The scar near her mouth was like a mood ring, pink or red. She had other scars, mainly from working in the restaurant as a child without proper training or supervision. *Now I'm just feeling sorry for myself.* Another flaw Odeal never tolerated. *Go scrub away your bad attitude.*

"What's in the bag?" she asked Toby.

"A surprise for dinner." He hid the bag behind his back.

"C'mon, let me see." Josie reached around, but he backed into Brian, who held him firm by the shoulders, a conspiratorial smirk on his face.

"It's for Maisy."

"What's for me?" Maisy came to her front door screen, wiping her hands on a dish towel.

She had just returned from delivering chocolate-chili-chip brownies to Dr. Tynsdale. It had been no quick trip either. On her return, she had floated up the stairs, her cheeks with a rosy glow, her lips missing the pink gloss she had left the house with earlier.

She had quickly hugged Josie hello, smelling of an unknown citrusy, woodsy spice. Then she had disappeared into the house and returned, humming a tune, with a glass of wine for Josie.

"You said I could bring anything I wanted to put on the pizza." Toby made a flourish and produced a pineapple.

"Where did you find that?" Maisy brought the fruit to her nose and inhaled the sweet ripeness.

"Dad and I went to Houma today to pick up something for the hot sauce booth and stopped at a grocery store."

"What did you get in Houma?" Josie said. She was pleased Brian had started building the booth.

Toby looked at Brian, who shook his head.

"Sorry, Mom. It's a surprise."

"Can we afford surprises?" The worry gnaws returned. It was easy to be swept away in expenses. The restaurant was like a riptide, the way it pulled their finances. But if it wasn't the restaurant, there was always something else. Josie remembered decorating Minnow's nursery. All the baby magazines and the ads pressing what you *had* to buy, or your precious bundle wouldn't thrive. What did either of them know about babies? Rosaline was the voice of reason. "A baby needs a safe place to sleep, a dry bottom, her mother's milk, and lots of love." Not that Minnow lacked anything. She was the first grandbaby of the island and a light for Daniel Dean and Hughdean after Odeal's death. Her brother was positively putty when it came to that girl.

"It was a barter," Brian said. "And we got the better deal."

"Are you staying for pizza?" Maisy asked Brian.

He looked at Josie. "I can for a short while. I want to check on—you know."

They had agreed Minnow should have more independence, and they were letting her host her friends on the restaurant deck, where she could also watch Gumbo in the evening.

"Stay long enough to have a drink on my new porch. The ocean breeze is stronger today than the oil." Maisy spread her arms like wings.

"Nothing's stronger than that cologne all over your shirt," Josie said.

Maisy sniffed her collar. "It's heavenly."

"Brian can try that rum punch I made from all those half-empty bottles we found in the bar."

"Maisy, I've got a problem," Toby said.

"What's that?"

"How do you get inside a pineapple?"

She tousled his hair. "I'll show you."

"Looks like we've some time. Can we talk?" Brian asked Josie. She took a step away from him.

He caught her arm. "How about I talk, and you listen."

Josie sat on the porch swing. Brian sat tentatively beside her and pushed off with his foot.

"Not so fast." She laughed and placed her hand over her wineglass. "You look good, rested."

"Yeah, got a few things off my chest. I don't think it's a coincidence." He pursed his lips and ran a hand through his hair. "I told Toby about . . . everything."

Josie sipped her wine. Her brain screamed, wanting the details. Did he tell him a toned-down version of events? Toby was only eleven and worshipped Brian.

"And?" Josie popped the silence with a nudge of the swing.

"I didn't hold back. I tried to tell him in a way that he'd understand, but also not scare him."

No one is more scared than me. Josie pushed the swing.

"Here you are." Maisy handed him a cocktail glass garnished with a wedge of lime. "It's a Depression cocktail instead of a Depression soup. Make do with what you've got on hand."

Brian shook the glass, and the iced tinkled. He took a sip. "Mm. Perfect on a hot day. This would sell well on the deck."

The empty deck. The oil fumes were so thick in the air most days no one dared to sit out watching the sunset. At least tonight Minnow could enjoy it. Even Gumbo preferred to huddle under the tables rather than loaf on his perch. *No old ugly thoughts tonight.* That went for Brian as well. He had kept his promise and talked to Toby.

Josie raised her glass to him.

"Maisy," Toby called from the door. "The oven's at five hundred degrees."

"The pizza chef is waiting." She hurried into the house.

Brian took another taste, and Josie studied his face. Sensitive topics were hard for them. Brian's gambling was the hardest. But thinking about their failed marriage counseling, Josie was fine avoiding any difficult discussion of money, work schedules, visits to his mother, and how cold to set the thermostat.

"What did Toby say?" she asked, steering the conversation back to dark waters.

Brian held the glass between his knees. "He had questions I couldn't answer. He wanted to know if he would go to college, because he had zero plans to be a shrimper."

Josie laughed. "Maybe he'll go into comedy."

"We did once talk about live entertainment on the deck."

Had he thought through how to pay for Toby and college?

"I promised we'd find a way. But I'm not working offshore again. The industry puts profits before people. The best people I know. I'll work ten jobs on shore if I have to." He stared at her as if he had more to say.

"You practically did when you moved here."

"That reminds me." He dug his hand into his front pocket, then handed her a stack of bills.

"Thanks."

"I earned that. It's not gambling money." He pointed.

"I didn't think it was."

"I've met decent people through the GA meetings."

"GA?"

"Gamblers Anonymous. I'm beginning to understand how the betting changed me." He stood and paced across the deck. "Can you forgive me? It's a big ask. You're—"

He stared out over the water, his head sunk between his shoulders.

"What? You wanted to talk, so talk." She was tired of waiting on him to act.

"I took too long to tell the kids. You asked me months ago, and you haven't asked for much, considering what I've done. But I told them, and I accept I have to earn their forgiveness. I thought that was what you wanted. But you're only madder at me. You've been avoiding me. You won't talk to me. It's like Minnow, holding everything inside."

"No, it's not. Minnow sees the world from her teenage view. It's raw and idealistic and revolves around her." Josie held her hand up. "She acted with an open heart without thinking of the consequences. I've been living with your consequences for close to three years."

He sat next to her. "I want you to talk to me."

"Why, so you can feel some penance?"

"No, so I can understand what you need to trust me again."

He pushed off the deck with his foot, and the swing swayed, moving the shadow of their legs back and forth. It was only an outline of them.

"We have a sandcastle between us," Brian said.

"A sandcastle?"

"Like when Minnow was little and insisted on being Princess Minnow of the High Seas. I'd fill buckets of sand and make towers, and she would decorate it with shells and rocks. Then I'd scrape a moat around it for the sea monster to live. But sand is porous, and the water we'd try so hard to fill in the moat with soaked into the beach."

"Am I the sea monster, or are you?" She couldn't help but smile.

"Clearly, I'm the sea monster." He spun his arm to display his dragon tattoo. "I need the water to swim around the castle, but you're not filling the moat fast enough."

"What happens then to the sea monster?"

"He shrivels up alone and becomes fish food. It's tragic. Have you ever heard a dying sea monster?"

"I've heard you snore."

"It's way worse." He smiled.

"I don't know how to fill the moat."

"You wait for the tide to come in."

Josie shook her head. "Then the castle dissolves."

"Doesn't matter. The sea monster has enough water to rescue the princess, and they're on higher ground eating ice cream."

"Nice story." She nodded. A lump was thick in her throat. This was a former version of Brian. They would stroll along the beach, and he'd spin out ideas, walking backward to face her.

"Josie," Brian said, his voice serious. "I need more water."

She covered her face with her hands. "I don't have any to give you."

He pulled her hands away and swiped at the tears she couldn't contain.

"Let the tide come in. Whatever you're feeling, or questioning, or need from me. Tell me."

"I'm just sad and tired of crying. I found the business plan I created for Pelican Point Provisions. That was for me." She rested her hand over her heart.

"I didn't build the restaurant. I constantly fight with Daddy and Hughdean over it. The new business was all my recipes and the contacts I made. Odeal would have never put herself out like that into the world. You took that away and trapped me here in a different sandcastle, one too far away from the water to dissolve. You left me high and dry. I don't understand why. Or worse, why I let you. People have pushed me around my entire life. You were supposed to be different."

Maisy stepped onto the deck. "Anyone need a refill? Sorry, bad timing. Josie, there's a bundle of mail here for you. It was in the shopping bag with the pineapple. I'll just leave it for you." She placed it on the porch rail.

Brian palmed his forehead. "I should've given you that when we arrived. It came today."

"Our pizza crust is waiting." Maisy returned to the kitchen.

Josie pulled apart the bundle, thankful for the distraction. She found a handwritten envelope with a return address from New York City. She slipped her finger under the flap.

> Dear Josie,
>
> I'm sorry we made the difficult decision to print our dining destination issue without Odeal's. I thought you'd like to see the article. You have a beautiful family.
>
> Kind regards,
> Dale

Josie unfolded the pages. It had been a nice day for a photo shoot. Was that really back in April?

"It's the *Vacation Ventures* article. Rub some salt into that wound."

"Read it," Brian said.

"No." She folded the pages and began to slip them back into the envelope.

Brian snatched them away. "I want to read it."

"Please, don't." She turned her back to him and stared out at the pinkening sky.

"Odeal's, Our Number One Island Restaurant of 2010."

"Brian, truly, I don't want to hear this." Her voice choked up.

He ignored her. *"Chef Josie Babineaux is the spice queen of the bayou and a diplomat of true southern hospitality. Her family restaurant, Odeal's, has stood on the same waterfront spot since the 1930s, when it began servicing the island as its only grocery store with a take-out window. Today, diners are greeted with a modern and comfortable dining room, an enticing, rotating selection of fresh Grand Isle seafood, and a Cajun-fusion menu seasoned with influences from Vietnam, South America, and Chef Babineaux's adventurous palate. Those looking for the most authentic Grand Isle experience should sit on the marina deck, where they will share the space with Gumbo, the restaurant's mascot pelican, who rests on his perch, delighting customers with his antics."*

Josie sobbed, unable to contain the sadness that had been building since they went to New Orleans. "It doesn't matter anymore."

"Of course it matters. The words, the photos. They printed your two-bite shrimp cakes, the Cajun bánh mì sandwich, and Maisy's chocolate-chili-chip brownie sundae recipe. You did this. I had nothing to do here. These photos are gorgeous. You could write a cookbook."

"We don't have anyone to serve."

"Look, here's a section with the bottle of Cajun Smack. And yes, I know you renamed it. And I know where that name came from.

"Odeal's house hot sauce, Cajun Smack, alone is worth the trip to the island. This crave-worthy vinegar-based pepper sauce is anything but ordinary and epitomizes Chef Babineaux's Cajun roots and what she values most, feeding people."

"I don't want to cook anymore," Josie cried.

"I don't believe that. We'll leave if you want. A Cajun chef in any part of the country would be a huge hit. I can find a job. Where do you want to go?"

"How? We can't afford to move or open a new restaurant. I don't know anyone looking to hire a Cajun chef either. Besides, this is the only place you've ever wanted to live."

"I haven't figured that out yet. But I love you and only want to be with you." He folded the article and slipped it safely into the envelope and back with the rest of the mail.

"There's another letter here for you. It's from the *Kitchen Network*. You want it?"

Josie took it. "They just got my entry. This can't be good news."

Toby appeared with two plates. "Dad, before you go, try the pineapple pizza."

Brian made a show of inspecting the toppings, tapping on the crust, and running the slice under his nose before taking a bite.

"What's it say?" He peered over her shoulder.

Josie sat on the porch swing, then jumped. "Maisy," she called.

Maisy stepped outside. "Everything okay. How's the pizza?"

"We need to cancel Sunday Supper on the twentieth."

"That's our one moneymaking night. How much wine have you had?"

Josie waved the letter. "The *Kitchen Network* is coming. We made it into the production."

"Ahh!" Maisy hugged her.

Josie turned to Brian, and he lifted her off the ground and kissed her. "Don't close the restaurant. Let them see how this community loves you."

"Are we gonna be on TV?" Toby asked.

"Yes, we are. The letter says to call." She pulled at her hair, spinning a long strand into a curl. Maybe the tide was finally coming in.

Chapter 20

Sunday, June 20, 2010

"Hold still, Josie, or you'll look like you're ready for Barnum & Bailey, not national TV," Louise said.

Louise had set up her workstation in the restaurant bathroom. A bright desk light blazed on Josie, and she tried to remain still against the tickle of Louise's cosmetic brushes.

"I don't understand why we didn't let the network send someone for makeup," Maisy said.

Louise dropped a lip brush. "Hush your mouth. I would never trust a beauty-school-mill graduate with this."

"Isn't that what they went to school for?" Maisy said.

Louise moved behind Josie with a curling iron, brandishing it like a sword.

"Makeup for TV is particular. Y'all are representing Grand Isle. I have a personal stake in this."

"How'd you learn to do this anyways?" Maisy asked.

"My momma was Miss Louisiana 1970, and I was a Fleur de Lis Princess in 1980."

"What type of princess is that?"

"Toddlers in tiaras," Josie said.

Louise yanked her hair.

"Ow, not so hard." Josie winked at Maisy.

"You're finished. No bun today. When you let me do your hair, it's lovely."

Minnow knocked and walked in. "The TV crew is ready. Mom, you look beautiful. You, too, Maisy."

"They look like winners," Louise said. "I've got one more surprise." Louise produced a garment bag with two gleaming white chef coats on hangers.

"Louise," Maisy said. She fingered the cuff of the coat embroidered with *Chef Maisy* on the left breast.

"Aunt Louise, I think Mom's about to cry."

"No, no, no, *chère*. We don't have time to fix your face if you cry. Try it on."

Josie slipped on the coat and tugged at the hem.

"Here, let me." Louise stood in front of her. She folded down a corner of the coat to reveal Josie's red tank top. "You always said the pop of color made you feel spicy inside. Let's show the world how it's done."

The producers agreed a full restaurant would add to the energy of the taping but suggested they invite people instead of random customers off the street. The island gossip network spun like a washing machine on high. The taping became the hottest ticket around. The dining room was fuller than Josie had seen in months.

She hugged Rosaline hello. She had dressed for the occasion in a flowered caftan and matching jewelry. "Did Louise do your face too?"

"A little color in case the TV catches a view of the room."

"Everyone, pretend you're having the best meal of your life," Louise said. She had taken control of the locals. "Don't talk too loud, and be prepared to shush if you're asked. And smile, be happy."

"Chef Josie, we want to start in the kitchen with footage of you and Chef Maisy cooking," the producer said.

Lunder's Farm had sent crates of fresh peppers that Maisy had staged in the walk-in refrigerator with red Tabasco, yellow and red Carolina Reapers, green jalapeños, tiny orange bird's eye chilies, and purple bell peppers for an eye-catching backdrop.

"Where's your father and Toby?" Josie whispered to Minnow. It wasn't like Brian to be late.

"He called, and they're on their way."

The restaurant door opened, and Daniel Dean pushed in with his walker, with Hughdean a step behind him.

"Dad, what're you doing here?" Josie asked.

Josie had stopped discussing anything related to the competition with him or Hughdean after she had told them she had the entry fee.

"You'd be better using that money on the AC," Hughdean had said.

Daniel Dean made his way to his usual table by Odeal's picture, except the table wasn't there; it had been removed and replaced with high stools and lighting.

"Where's my seat?" He stood in the middle of the room.

"I wasn't expecting either of you," Josie said.

The producer came over. "Is there a problem?"

"This is my father, Daniel Dean Austin, and my brother, Hughdean Austin." She turned to them. "This is Grant Williams from the *Kitchen Network*."

"Odeal's is a family business. Thought you'd like to have the whole family," Daniel Dean said.

"It's a pleasure to meet both of you. Can someone help find them a place?"

"I'll take care of them," Louise said. She smiled at the producer and threw Hughdean the stink eye.

"What makes them think they can show up?" Josie said.

Maisy took her arm and pushed her toward the kitchen. "Pay them no attention. This is your day. If they want to sit on the sidelines, let them."

"And where's Brian and Toby?"

"Chef," Grant said. "We'll start in front of these peppers. It's a beautiful shot."

Josie stood in a power pose, closed her eyes, and breathed deep. *Smile.*

The camera lights blared in the small room, and a trickle of sweat rolled down her back.

"Tell us about your reaper chili hot sauce."

Josie smiled and turned toward the camera. "I originally made this sauce only for myself. The Carolina Reaper is the hottest pepper on the planet at 2.2 million Scoville units. Not everyone is a hothead. But like all dishes chefs make for themselves, the sauce escaped the kitchen and made its way into the dining room. This is a balanced sauce, made with sweet red peppers, onions, tomato paste, and spices."

"Perfect. Give us a minute to set the lights for the next sequence with you and Chef Maisy cooking."

Josie poked her head into the dining room. People were laughing and enjoying drinks. For a moment she could believe it was a regular Sunday Supper.

"Brian," Josie called as he walked into the crowded room. "Where have you been?"

"Mom, you look different," Toby said.

"She looks wow," Brian said. "Sorry we're late."

Josie's face heated at the way he stared at her. She suspected her ears were flaming red. *Good thing my hair is down today.*

Josie grabbed the hem of Toby's shirt. "What is all over you? I don't have time for this. Tuck in your shirt."

After they finished the cooking segment, they moved to the dining room for a short interview. Josie was nervous talking with a crowd behind her. She didn't know if it was better because she knew them or worse.

The camera operator positioned the lights and asked her to turn more toward the wall. Odeal's poster-size image loomed beside her. *What do you think of me now, Momma?* The building had her name on the roof and this photo on the wall, but that was all that remained, except for her ghost.

"Talk to me about your cooking influences," Grant said.

Josie glanced at her mother's photo. She wanted to say she was motivated by spite. *Wouldn't that be provocative?*

"I grew up in the restaurant kitchen learning family recipes. Seafood has always been a favorite, as it's fresher here than anywhere I've been. When I returned to the island after culinary school, I was inspired by this community. That's when I added a Cajun bánh mì sandwich and began experimenting with Caribbean spice combinations. I believe chili pepper heat enhances flavor but that you have to start with flavor."

"That's great," Grant said. "I've only got one more segment in my notes. I'm to film the pelican. Is there a picture or a statue?" He scanned the walls.

Toby laughed. "No, you're looking for Gumbo, our pelican. He's outside with my sister."

"A real pelican?"

"As real as any pelican can be," Josie said. "Follow us."

Brian opened the deck door, and the TV crew filed outside, along with most of the dining room crowd.

"If y'all are watching, you're sitting at the café tables," Louise said.

"This is Minnow, my daughter, and Dr. Eugene Hollis, our resident pelican handlers," Josie said.

Minnow wore an Odeal's T-shirt, and Hollis had upgraded to a polo shirt and pants. Gumbo stood next to Minnow, his head turning side to side, taking in the activity.

"How you folks handling the oil?" Grant asked. "We tried to take footage on the beach, but we weren't allowed. We have news footage of the oil, but I don't think we'll use it."

"Why not?" Hollis asked.

"It doesn't fit with the mood, chefs head to head in a flavor battle. The pelican's cute though," Grant said.

Hollis inhaled, about to launch into a lecture, but Josie beat him to it.

"You'll have a hard time pretending there's no oil spill in New Orleans next month during the competition. You won't see oil on those streets, but they're feeling it too. I'm fighting against it right here. That's grit and heart," Josie said. "The outside world is growing weary with this spill. We are too." She turned to everyone sitting on the deck.

"This isn't the story I wanted to tell about my restaurant and my Cajun culinary roots, but this is Louisiana, and I can't run from it."

Brian stood next to Josie and took her hand.

"This is my husband, Brian. He worked on the Deepwater Horizon, and thankfully he wasn't there when it blew. That's part of my story too. Now, I don't mean to turn what's been a fantastic afternoon into a funeral. Minnow, let's show our guests what our pelican can do."

Minnow tapped Gumbo's perch, and he flew to stand above the Do NOT FEED THE PELICAN sign. She gave him a shove, and he flew off over the water. She whistled and he circled back.

"He responds to her. That's amazing," Grant said.

Gumbo turned and landed on Hollis's head. "Hey, there. You were supposed to land on the deck this time."

"C'mere, handsome." Minnow crouched, and Gumbo pushed off from Hollis and landed at her feet. She tilted her head, and he did the same. She stood and picked him up, and Gumbo tucked his head underneath her chin.

"How long have you had him?" Grant asked. The camera operator moved in a circle around Minnow. She released Gumbo as he was turning his head and his swordlike bill.

"We like to say he has us," Minnow said. "We rescued him two years ago."

"Is he full grown?"

"Yes," Hollis said. "He's a brown pelican, the smallest of the eight species. And he's the Louisiana state bird."

"Where does he live?"

"He has a pelican house underneath the restaurant deck, and he comes and goes as he pleases. He's a wild animal," Josie said.

"Can you get him to land on the deck again?"

"As long as we don't run out of fish."

Josie stood against the wall of pictures: Odeal in the kitchen; one of Hughdean's shrimp boats, the *Big Deal*; an image of the restaurant when it was a grocery; and a picture of Gumbo with Minnow and Toby, the same one on the wall of their house.

"Thank you, everyone, for filling Odeal's today," she yelled, trying to direct the room's attention. A gathering of islanders was hard to quiet. Most of the room turned toward her.

"I've never been on TV before. I'm grateful you came to support me. The producers are packing now, and they've given me this stack of free tickets to the Ragin' Cajun." She held the tickets over her head.

A few people cheered and clapped.

"I'd love for you to come and vote for Revenge of the Cajun Reaper. I can't say if we'll have our regular Fourth of July celebration on the island, but it's always fun in New Orleans. The kitchen's open now for Sunday Supper with a limited menu. I can promise there's plenty of hot sauce."

She waved to the waitstaff to move the tables back into place. "Dad, you can take your table if you'd like and stay for supper."

"I think I have to. I don't know where your brother's hiding."

Josie found Hughdean in the kitchen, a beer in his hand. She hated how he used the restaurant as his personal pantry.

"You paying for that beer?" she said.

"Nope." He bent his arm and coughed, deep and throaty.

"If you're not helping, leave. All that oil on the water is making you sick. I won't have you around the food."

"I'm not sick, and I'm trying to help."

Josie tied a long apron around her waist and twisted her hair into a bun.

"Brian needs to come out on the water with me. He'll make more money in a week than you've made all summer. Then you wouldn't have to make a fool out of yourself at this competition in front of the whole country. Cajun bánh mì sandwiches and Caribbean dishes. Momma wouldn't—"

Josie pointed a knife at him and then began chopping herbs. "I'm not a fool. This competition is national publicity." *And it's fun.*

"You don't expect to win, do you? I was talking to the camera guy. Chefs come in from all over the world. There's a hot sauce circuit. You haven't even entered Odeal's original, and that's a solid sauce."

Josie chopped faster, the parsley turning into a mince. "It has a new name, *Cajun Smack*. It's a fine sauce, but it's not a standout."

"Neither are you."

"Hughdean Austin, for once in your life, can't you be on my side?" She grabbed a handful of parsley and slammed it onto the board. "You live with some memory of that woman that isn't true." Josie pointed the knife toward the dining room where Odeal's picture hung.

"All her yelling, and threats, and shoving, and hair pulling. I took most of it to protect you." She dropped the knife onto the board.

"This scar"—she pointed to her hairline—"I was four, and you were three. I pushed you out of the way when she threw a hairbrush at you. We were still babies.

"Do you remember the first day of school, when you were eight and didn't want to eat your breakfast because you were too excited? Momma didn't care. She stood with that pinched expression on her lips when she was about to ground us for a month. I pushed you out the door, and then she shoved me, and I fell down the stairs onto the gravel."

"Did you ever consider you're just clumsy?" Hughdean said.

"Then explain this," Josie pushed her scarred palm into Hughdean's face. He took a step back, and his mouth twitched.

"Your dear Momma said I was a little too uppity after winning the junior oyster-shucking competition."

"I wasn't there when that happened."

"No, you weren't. I spent the best summer of my life working at the minimart with Rosaline because I couldn't be in the kitchen. I am tired of you calling out her name like she's some heavenly spirit. I no longer care what Momma would say, do, or think, and I wish you wouldn't either."

"If you wanted to protect me so much, why did you leave?"

Josie's voice dropped low and steady. "When someone tells you every week of your life to get out of their breath, you find a way to make it happen. Now, take your drunk ass out of my kitchen, and you better not drive Daddy home like this."

Hughdean banged the empty beer bottle onto the counter and left.

Maisy took the knife out of Josie's hand. "Go home. The entire kitchen staff is here. I can handle this."

"I'm fine. We have a friendly crowd, and as soon as food starts to come out, even more will stay."

"You threatened Hughdean with parsley."

"No, I didn't. Parsley isn't pointy enough."

"Brian," Maisy called out the kitchen door.

"He's pouring drinks, let him be."

"Bonnie, you're on bar. Have Mr. Babineaux come into the kitchen."

Brian walked in. "Everything okay?"

"Hughdean has your wife in a tizzy. I want her out of my kitchen." Maisy put her hands on Josie's shoulders. "You were amazing today. I'm so proud to work alongside you. We may not win this competition, but it'll be fun trying. And it *is* a good idea. Now take a minute before someone gets uglier."

Josie didn't mean to color everything with her prickly attitude. Hughdean dug into her like a chigger.

Josie climbed into Brian's truck. *Where am I supposed to go?*

"You shouldn't let Hughdean rile you up. He's jealous of all this publicity. Probably realizes he made a mistake not supporting you in the competition. Why else would he and your father show up?"

Josie shrugged. "They make every hard thing in my life harder. And where the hell am I supposed to go right now?"

Brian smiled. "I've got that covered."

Josie closed her eyes and leaned back against the headrest.

"Maisy's right. You were amazing today. Even the lies were good," Brian said.

Josie's head snapped up. "What lies?"

Brian laughed. "I watched a playback of you talking about the sauce. It's barely made it out of the kitchen, let alone into the restaurant."

Josie smiled. "That's not true. People have tasted it, and I served it tonight. No one's complained yet. A few people have asked when I'm bottling it. Jimmy Lunder loves it and wants to sell it at the farm store."

"Okay, I take it back. I'm happy to hear you fired up."

They pulled into Daniel Dean's driveway, the gravel crunching under the tires.

"How is this getting away from Hughdean?"

"He won't be home for hours. Probably at the Old Salt Bar telling everyone he's a TV star."

Josie stepped out of the car and leaned heavily against the closed door. Brian pulled her to her feet and covered her eyes with his hand.

"What are you doing?"

"Shh. I have a surprise. Just walk," he said.

The ground gave soft under her feet, but she couldn't tell if they were walking in circles or moving straight. Then the ground dipped, and her feet scuffed in gravel.

The garden?

Brian's hand was sweaty on her skin. *He's nervous.*

"Open your eyes." Brian dropped his arm and took a step away from her.

"Oh, Brian," she whispered.

Standing like a castle in a faraway dream was a gazebo. The structure stood where the old one used to rise out of the garden, but this was wholly different. The late-afternoon light reflected off the sides.

The paint color reminded her of green goddess salad dressing, cool and inviting in the open sun. The gazebo had a gray shingle roof and lattice walls. You couldn't see inside, a luxury the old gazebo lacked. She stepped closer and ran her hand along the side like patting a dog.

"Careful, the paint may be wet."

Paint. That's what was on Toby's shirt.

"When did you build this?" She walked around and stopped at the door.

"I've been working on it for a few weeks. Do you like it?"

She nodded, unable to form words from the thoughts swirling in her head. Hughdean had called Odeal's ghost like in a séance.

After the personal storm of Odeal's death, when Josie was figuring out her life, Brian had come to visit. She had been sitting in the old gazebo, enjoying the chirping crickets and peeping toads, like in an idealized Hollywood southern setting.

The island had stopped its angry vibration. No more shaking, stomping, screaming, insults. Only silence.

He had stood silhouetted in the gazebo doorway and knocked. His body heat released a fresh soapy scent.

"Hughdean said you were here." He held up a six-pack of beer.

"Classy."

He let out a genuine laugh. "Well, we ain't so highbrow like you California girls."

"Is it cold?"

"I'm not a complete bumpkin."

She accepted a bottle. "Abita, local and craft. Points for that. Come in."

Brian sat and tapped his bottle to hers.

"Should we say a toast to your mother?"

"Heck no." Josie covered her mouth. "I didn't mean to say that aloud. She was really fond of you."

"You're honest." He pushed a long strand of hair away from her eyes. "I've lived around these parts long enough."

Josie drained her beer. A memory of Brian kissing her two years earlier sent a flush across her body. She was thankful for the darkening sky hiding her expression.

They sat quietly, listening to the insects.

"This was the castle when we were kids."

"Were you the damsel in distress?"

She laughed. "Not that type of castle. Think *fortress*."

"Sounds fun."

Josie shook her head. "Not really." And laughed. "Odeal ran a tight ship, but she couldn't take away my imagination."

"What're you imagining now?"

She shrugged. "If I'll like living in Houston. My dad doesn't have my mother to care for him. Hughdean's managed while Odeal was sick, but . . ."

Brian took her hand. "I've had a ringside seat."

She nodded. "Thank you. You've done a lot for my parents. Above and beyond the best friend code."

She squeezed his hand, and he held it, talking through the night. They finished the six-pack and found themselves side by side in the hammock.

He understood the push-pull she felt about her family. The intoxicating freedom of running away on purpose and the immense satisfaction of making it alone, despite the taunts of failure.

He knew enough about her family to have seen the players in action, but not enough about her to pass judgment on her decision to leave. He had shown an interest in her stories of working in California. The life she was planning in Texas.

He had kissed her. A planned kiss, he later admitted, if he found the chance or the nerve.

Josie walked around the gazebo, needing movement to sort her feelings, a moment of space. Did Brian remember their first night here as he built this? Did he share any of those memories with Toby? This structure was new but already infused with history. She smiled as she met him again at the door.

"I have more to show you." He opened the door. Inside hung a hammock. "It's not the old string kind we tangled in, but it's comfortable. And here." He handed her a tall object wrapped in newspaper.

She patted it. "A coat hanger?"

She sat on the hammock, and it moved, catching her off guard. "Oh." She planted her feet and tore away the paper to reveal a cast-iron weather vane with a chili pepper on top. "Where did you find this?"

"I had it made at the ironworks near the marina. I'll put it on the roof later."

"I, this is . . . thank you."

A ceiling fan swirled above her head, and twinkle lights blinked on and off in the corners. The old gazebo never had electricity. This must have been weeks of work. She'd been so consumed by Minnow and the hot sauce she hadn't noticed what was happening behind the house.

"The hot sauce booth is almost done too," he said.

They stared, an awkward silence.

"Do you have any cold beer?" She pushed the hammock with her foot.

He laughed. "Sure do, in the house." He took a step toward her. "May I sit?"

She made room for him, then grinned, swinging them both off balance and almost falling to the ground.

They swayed in rhythm.

"Josie, please come home."

What was home? A place, or the people who were there? She unbuttoned her new chef's coat and lay in the hammock in her red tank top. Brian lay next to her. She took his hand and placed it on her chest. Her heart was leaping like a tarpon jumping from the water.

Daniel Dean, Hughdean, Odeal, and now this gazebo. Her ghosts were assembling. If she said yes, would she be repeating her mistakes? Was her future with this sweet man, or was it time to move on? Would opportunities come from the *Kitchen Network* or from finding a way to bring back her food business dreams? She had placed her feelings last for so long, she wasn't ready to commit.

"A lot has happened today," she said. "If I give you an answer now, it may not be the right one. I need some more time. But I would love to sit here with you and just enjoy the night."

Louisiana Boating News

Sunday, June 27, 2010

The National Hurricane Center in Miami, Florida, reports the first storm of the Atlantic hurricane season, Tropical Storm Alex, is expected to strengthen to a hurricane and make landfall later in the week as a potential category-three storm. The storm is swirling through the Gulf of Mexico with winds of 60 mph (97 kmph) projected to make landfall near the Mexico-US border Thursday.

The Bureau of Ocean Energy Management, Regulation, and Enforcement said 28 platforms and three oil rigs in the path of the storm in the western Gulf have been evacuated.

Officials are scrambling to reposition booms to protect the coast from the lingering BP oil spill. They will have to reposition barges currently blocking oil from reaching sensitive wetlands.

Chapter 21

Grand Isle, Louisiana

Wednesday, June 30, 2010

With Hurricane Alex's outer bands churning slowly toward Grand Isle, Brian shifted sheets of plywood in the back of his truck, preparing to head to the minimart to secure the store for Rosaline. The last few days had been busy, helping people with storm prep, and he was almost done. After the minimart, all that would remain would be covering the picture window at the restaurant. If he timed it right, he could also have lunch. It would be his last chance to see Josie before they locked themselves away to ride out the storm.

Depending on how long the weather lasted, he might not see or hear from her for two days. He wanted her to come home, but he wouldn't pressure her. He didn't know how much time she needed, but he suspected being shut inside with Daniel Dean and Hughdean would make each day feel significantly longer than twenty-four hours. He was worried about the storm. June was too early for a hurricane. They were unpredictable already. This one could make landfall in Mexico or closer to them, in Texas. All that was certain was its size, expected to cover two hundred miles. He poured his worry into working with Hughdean to secure Daniel Dean's house and to make sure his generator was in top working order. This was a heck of a time to have built a new gazebo.

He leaned inside the cab of the truck to turn on the radio for the latest forecast. As he backed out, he saw Josie was pulling into the driveway.

He couldn't help but smile as she slid from the car. Her hair was in its usual bun, and she wore her regular pull-on chef pants and a purple tank top without her chef's coat.

"Hi. I had hoped to see you first thing this morning to cover the window. I brought you lunch." She held up a bag.

"Thanks. I kinda like this delivery service." He lowered the tailgate and motioned for her to sit. Josie hopped up next to him and looked up. "It's always freaky how clear the sky is before a hurricane. And the air smells like ocean today and not oil. The heavy rain should come in late in the day. As soon as I'm done at the minimart, I'll take care of the restaurant." He reached into the bag for a wrapped sandwich, still warm from the oven. "What do we have here?"

"Egg, tomato, and cheese biscuits." She smiled. "We're cooking everything up before the storm. We've over a hundred storm dinners to cook and pack."

"It's forecast to be a category two. It's a monster, so anything could change."

Josie nodded. "Yeah, about that?" She rubbed the back of her neck.

Brian bit into the sandwich and closed his eyes. Maisy's biscuits were like a warm hug, and he was hungry.

He felt Josie's hand on his knee and opened his eyes.

"Brian, can I come home, for the storm?" Her voice was soft, but direct.

Brian choked on the sandwich and coughed.

"Oh, gosh. I didn't mean to kill you."

He patted his chest. "I'm fine. You're fine. Of course you can come home." He pulled her into a hug and kissed the top of her head. "Yes, come home."

She pulled out of the hug and handed him a napkin.

"What made you change your mind?" he asked and took another bite, trying to act casual. All the while his heart beat furiously.

"The kids. I've never not been with them during a storm." She shook her head. "I've missed them these past few weeks. I'm missing everything."

Brian wanted to ask her more questions, but now wasn't the time. She could turn tail and run. But once she was home, he'd have her attention, and the storm was predicted to be a slow mover.

At 5:00 p.m. with the rain and wind taking up residence in the sky, Brian and Hollis wrestled a large sheet of plywood over the restaurant's picture window. Brian abandoned his rain hood as the lashing horizontal wind proved stronger than the thin Gore-Tex.

"Hold it firm," Brian yelled. Between the wind and flying oil cleanup debris, it was hard to hear each other. Hollis wasn't handy, but he was tall, and this was a chore where height helped.

Next upgrade, hurricane shutters.

Brian could see through the window that the restaurant hummed like a fair-weather Saturday night. Josie, Maisy, Toby, and two waitstaff moved in urgency to pack meals for people buying storm suppers.

"Where's Hughdean?" Hollis turned his face away from the rain and braced the plywood, which threatened to take off like a sail.

Brian drilled screws in place along the window frame. "He should be on his way back home. Daniel Dean ran out of one of his medications. You can let go now, thanks."

The back door banged open, and Minnow, dressed in a red rain slicker, dragged a tub of fish over the threshold and across the deck.

"How many pelicans are you feeding?" Brian asked.

Minnow blinked. Water dripped from her hood onto her face and rested on her lashes like tears. His attempt at humor had missed its target. She was frantic about leaving Gumbo and had asked to bunk here to keep an eye on him. Josie and Brian had absolutely refused.

Hollis peered into the bucket quickly filling with rainwater. "That's a lot of fish. I'll help you."

He heaved the tub, and the three walked down to the pelican house below the deck. They found Gumbo snug in the corner, his head close to his body.

"He doesn't act bothered by the storm," Brian said.

At the sight of Minnow and Hollis, Gumbo flapped his wings and waddled over to the tub.

"Here you are, boy." Minnow tossed him several fish, and he swallowed them.

Brian shoved the side of the structure to test its strength. It didn't move.

Hollis nodded to Brian. "Minnow, he'll be cozy here. Safer than any pelican in the area."

Minnow shook off the water on her head. "I worry about them all." Her face knotted in concern. She rubbed her hands on her thighs for warmth.

"Aunt Louise and I are camping at her office," Hollis said. "I'm patrolling tonight with Chief Tibbs. I'll check on him during our rounds."

Minnow pleaded with her anxious eyes. "What if the water comes up when the tide comes in?"

"Never a problem before," Hollis said. "The only option is to move him to someone's garage."

"Can't we take him home? Fill the bathtub for him?"

"*Chère*, he's never been inside your house. You remember what happened the last time he came inside the restaurant?"

"He broke every glass at the bar trying to fly through the window. It wasn't his fault. Someone chased him inside."

"He's safer here," Brian said.

Minnow squatted and faced Gumbo. "Please stay here." Her tone soft. At the sound of her voice, he wagged his tail feathers and offered his neck for a scratch. "I'm leaving you this fish. Don't eat it all at once."

Gumbo stuck his long bill into the bucket.

A gust of wind rumbled the deck overhead. It creaked like a haunted house. Brian tapped his toe on the deck. The boards would hold. He hoped.

"Time to go inside. Your mom should be ready for us to head home."

Despite Minnow's worry, Brian's was less. Josie was coming home. All day he had replayed her morning visit, trying to guess what caused her to change her mind so he could make this move permanent.

Since Minnow's diagnosis, Josie had eaten dinner with the family every night. After the *Kitchen Network* taping, he began picking her up at the restaurant and driving her back to Daniel Dean's. They'd sit in the gazebo and talk the way they should have in therapy but hadn't. She didn't yell, though there were angry tears. When the storm forecast came out, he had asked her again.

"Storm's coming. Come home with me. We'll bunker with board games and popcorn like when the kids were little. I'll sleep on the couch, whatever you want."

She exhaled, new tears threatening again. "I can't leave Dad."

Whether it was the kids or something else bringing her home, it didn't matter. They would be a family, and that had to count for something.

The generator had gas for when they lost power. He had put the house in order the way he knew she liked. It was once their habit to buy a new board game for each storm. He had unearthed Clue, Risk, Trivial Pursuit, Boggle, and Jenga.

Josie would cook batches of comfort food—fried chicken and biscuits, jambalaya, red beans and rice, tea cakes and pralines. When the storm ended, they would check on their neighbors and offer meals.

Brian and Hollis finished covering the window and went inside. Brian grabbed two warm rolls and tossed one to Hollis as they walked into the kitchen.

"Go drip in the dining room," Maisy said, barely missing a beat as she scooped servings of red beans and rice. "We don't need a slippery floor."

"Looks like you're done," Brian said to Maisy.

"Amazing how we're having a busy night after all these weeks. Gives me hope we'll see the other side of the spill soon."

"The first BP checks have come in. People have money," Brian said. "Thanks for helping."

"That's what we do here."

"You've done a lot more. Josie hasn't been able to pay everyone their usual—"

Maisy raised a hand. "Stop, I don't want to hear it. Especially on the edge of a storm. Better Mother Nature squeezes these tears out of her eyes this week and shines her blue sky on us at the competition. I'd hate to set up in a hurricane. Josie's silly happy about the booth," Maisy said.

Hope flowed through him. He needed Josie to be happy with him, to want to count on him again.

The front door opened, and last-minute customers slick with rain rushed in. The restaurant lights flickered. They wouldn't have power for long.

"The last order's out," Josie said to the staff. "Take your own food and head home. Remember, next weekend is the Ragin' Cajun."

A burst of rain pounded the roof, and Josie stared up. "I hope it holds."

"I hate it when it's loud," Toby said.

"Me too, *cher*. No matter how many storms I live through here, it never gets easier."

"The storm will help break up the oil. That's good for the island," Hollis said.

Josie handed Hollis a cardboard box. "Here's dinner for you and Louise. I added sandwiches for anyone who didn't plan for a long night."

Hollis kissed her cheek. "Thanks. I wish we could bunker with you, but Louise had to go and become mayor."

"Y'all go home," Maisy said. "I've got one more meal to pack for Dr. T." She winked.

"Dr. Tynsdale lives by Daniel Dean. Josie can drop it off," Brian said.

"Brian, how thick are you?" Josie laughed. She turned to Maisy. "Will you be okay alone? You can stay with us."

Maisy shook her head. "I love a good storm. I'll be fine. I even bought new pajamas."

Josie hugged her. "Be careful on the road. Call if you need anything. Just think: next week, New Orleans. Toby, you go with Dad to drop dinner off for Rosaline. Minnow and I will go to Grandpa's, and we'll meet at home." Josie looked around. "Where's Minnow?"

"With Gumbo," Toby said.

Josie sighed.

"I'll fetch her." Brian squeezed Josie's hand, excited like a nervous teen before a date. "See you soon."

Josie and Minnow arrived first to the house. Josie fumbled with the key.

Minnow juggled the heavy load in her arms. "Hurry, Mom. This bag is heavy."

Josie opened the door and turned on the light. They were both drenched. The short drive from the restaurant had turned into a white-knuckle ride. The car's wiper blades couldn't keep up with the rain and the wind. *I hope Brian and Toby are home soon.* Brian's truck was heavier than her car, but nothing was stronger than a Gulf hurricane.

Minnow shivered as she shed her coat.

"Go take a hot shower. We'll eat as soon as Dad and Toby come home."

Daniel Dean hadn't said much when she said she was packing, other than to remind her he had a doctor's appointment the following week. "I'll get you there, Dad."

Hughdean nodded. "Don't be a stranger."

"I can't be any stranger than you."

Hughdean laughed.

Now home, *her* home, she padded quietly into the master bedroom. The bed was made, with the pillows fluffed the way she liked them.

Josie heard the shower running. For the first time in eight months, she would be here for more than a few hours. This was different from the day of the explosion, when she had found Brian sitting in the dark. That day she had been a stranger in her own house. The past few weeks of family dinners had eased her back. This felt more permanent. Was it?

She walked from room to room. Eight months was a long time to be away. She wasn't sure if she *was* back. If she should be back.

Josie returned to the kitchen, where she was most in control. Rain streaked down the window over the sink. The *plink, plink* against the glass sounded like her knife chopping through a carrot, determined and forceful.

She had never worried about storms when she lived in California, though she had heard enough about earthquakes to know she didn't want to experience those either.

The sun would set at 8:00 p.m., but she wouldn't see it tonight. The sky was murky with steel wool clouds and dark with rain. Hurricane season scared her. This was a rare June hurricane, different from an October storm. It was deceptive with its heat and the promise of a summer day on the other side.

Her parents had offered little comfort during storms. She and Hughdean would make a blanket fort behind the couch and wait out the rumbling.

Josie paced the kitchen, tested the faucet, and opened and closed the utensil drawer. *What now?*

The house was spotless. The kitchen counters gleamed, the floor had no crumbs, and the table was preset for a meal. She had brought enough food to cook for a week if necessary.

Her biggest decision now was what to serve for dinner. The fried chicken she had made earlier was warm, and she could coax it back to crisp in the oven. For dessert, she had a tub of tea cakes and Maisy's chocolate-chili-chip brownies with ice cream.

Josie found the strawberry-shaped cookie jar Minnow and Toby had given her years ago as a Mother's Day present. She slid the jar toward her to fill with the tea cakes. She removed the green ceramic stem and discovered it filled with scraps of paper.

What's this? Receipts? A nag of fear gripped her. Was Brian hiding expenses again? She couldn't handle new lies and broken promises. Loving someone didn't mean you sacrificed your life to suffer with their problems. He had no more chances with her. That was why he was sleeping on the couch. She would protect her heart. Intimacy complicated relationships.

She grabbed a handful of paper and was surprised to see it was covered in Brian's handwriting.

I'm proud of Toby for being a good sport when the umpire made a bad call.

Learning to live alone without love is hard. I'm grateful for my brothers.

Josie stopped at that one. Brian meant the men he worked with on the rig. She often wondered what they talked about out in the ocean, away from home. She dug into the jar for more.

I'm learning to talk to the kids. They need me too. It's a blessing.

A working AC on a hot day is a miracle. Josie smiled.

I miss the curve of Josie's back against my chest. I'm working through my insomnia without her.

Josie closed her eyes. The marriage counselor had suggested they each write what they were thankful for every day. These were Brian's. Her hands held dozens of slips of paper.

The door lock clicked. *Oh, crap.* She stuffed the paper back into the jar before Brian could see her. She had no business snooping. Was he writing them every day?

The counseling hadn't gone well. The therapist did tell him about Gamblers Anonymous, but Brian hadn't been listening. And by then, Josie was no longer interested in trying to work out their problems. He had expected the therapist to take his side and tell Josie she was wrong and overreacting to the gambling debts. The marriage was more like a whirlpool, round, deep, and dark.

She hurried to the refrigerator and grabbed containers, making herself appear busy fitting them inside.

"We're home." Brian's keys made a happy jingle as he placed them on the hook. "And soaked."

Josie backed out of the refrigerator and closed it. Brian and Toby stood dripping on the floor. A scatter of wet leaves followed behind them.

A nervous flutter caught in her throat. This was it. She was committed for the storm. "You should change into dry clothes. I'll have dinner ready soon."

Brian hung their coats and leaned against the wall, a serene expression on his face. He needed a shave, and he was weary from the storm prep.

"What?" Josie craned her head around the kitchen. Did he suspect she got into the cookie jar?

"I'm happy to see you in your kitchen."

"I am too, Mom." Toby wrapped his arms around her waist. "Can we have cinnamon rolls tomorrow? Dad can only make scrambled eggs."

Josie laughed, her chest light. Despite the storm, her family needed her and wanted her.

"You can have anything we have ingredients for."

A gust of wind and a *thunk* hit the roof. Their heads snapped toward the sound.

"Debris is starting to fly."

"We should've insisted Dad stay here." Daniel Dean's house rested on short pilings. It was a trade-off. He didn't have to negotiate as many stairs, but he wasn't protected against flooding.

"I can fetch him." Brian reached for his truck keys.

Josie shook her head and put her hand over his to stop him. "No more driving. Hughdean's there. We'd have to have him here too. They'll call if they have a problem."

Brian caught her hand and squeezed it. The lights flickered. "Sun's not set yet, and power is about to blow. Do you want to shower?"

Josie took a personal inventory. Her hair remained in a bun, but wet dangling strands had escaped and clung to her neck and cheek. She was hot and tired from cooking and the stress of the storm. Fresh clothes would be heaven.

"Let's eat, and then I'll take a hot bath." She released her hair, and it flopped damp behind her.

"I could scrub your back." Brian winked.

Her face heated, and she turned away, busying herself with the food. "Go change. Time to eat."

After dinner, Josie floated in the warm bath. *Four days until the competition.* She fluttered her feet in excitement, bubbles and water skipping out of the tub.

The booth was amazing and being stored at the restaurant. The sauces she had bottled for judging were her best yet. She hoped the restaurant remained dry. She had too many things to worry about. As if she needed reminding, the lights flickered twice, and a *whump* vibrated through the house, plunging them into darkness.

So much for my bath.

Soon, Brian would have the generator on, but she wasn't about to sit around in a dark tub, stirring images of shipwrecked sailors lost to the dark seas.

Wrapped in a towel, she unzipped her suitcase and considered what to wear. A year ago, she would have stayed in her bathrobe and crawled naked into bed. The kids were already in their pajamas. The toasty smell of popcorn and the collapse of Jenga blocks and laughter filled the house. Toby and Minnow always retreated to opposite sides of the house at Daniel Dean's. It wasn't their space. This was home.

Josie dried her hair and pulled on a pair of shorts and a sweatshirt.

"I didn't think you were coming out of the tub," Brian said.

She examined her water-wrinkled fingers and grabbed a handful of popcorn. "I almost didn't. What'd I miss?"

"Uncle Hollis called," Minnow said. "Trees are down, but Gumbo's okay."

Josie nodded. "You did a thoughtful job setting him up with the fish. He'll sleep through the storm, the luckiest pelican on Grand Isle."

Minnow shrugged. "I wish I could patrol with Uncle Hollis."

"Maybe in a few years," Brian said.

Josie pursed her lips to keep from saying no and starting a fight. Minnow was calm and happy, a glimpse of her old self. She was feeling better since starting her ulcer treatment. Toby bounced full of energy, looking out each window and reporting everything he saw. Brian sat relaxed. He liked to run the "hurricane show," as they called it. Provisions, generator, entertainment. He had an emergency checklist for a dozen possible scenarios—flood, fire, broken generator, falling objects, super high tide, roof collapse, even the "Oz option"—the unlikely event a tornado would spin the house away. Josie's job was to feed them, and she'd do that anyway.

She was relieved to off-load a part of the worry. She alone didn't have to calm the family like when she was a child.

A *thwack* sounded beneath them as something substantial banged into the house pilings like a pinball. They all jumped.

"We're okay," Josie said. "I say flowerpot."

"Trash can," Minnow said.

This was a game they played with the kids to distract them from the storm. Josie'd made it up for Hughdean when they were kids.

Brian shook his head. "It's the Heberts' doghouse, the silly plastic thing like a kid's play castle."

They laughed.

"I hope Pepper's not inside," Minnow said.

They laughed harder.

"I'm sure he's inside the Heberts' house," Josie said.

"What about Gumbo?" Minnow said, her voice tinged with worry. "We haven't had a storm like this since we rescued him. I want to sit and hold him in my lap. Make sure he's safe."

Josie understood. When she was ten, she'd asked for a dog. She wanted a warm snuggly body to sleep at her feet and make her feel safe. She convinced Hughdean to help her ask Odeal. "He'll be our dog," she had promised, "but he'll sleep with me. Unless there's a storm, and then he'll sleep with both of us."

Odeal had said no. If they had time for a dog, clearly they didn't have enough chores.

Josie refused to consider Gumbo a pet. He was more like an exchange student from the bird world who had come to live with them. He taught them about the natural world. She didn't know what he learned.

She smiled at Toby nodding to stay awake, his DS game by his side. At 11:30 p.m., Brian turned on the late news.

"Stay safe inside tonight, everyone. Hurricane Alex has made landfall in Mexico and is spinning fast toward Galveston, Texas. This storm is a whopper, stretching two hundred miles, with its outer bands reaching into Louisiana," the weathercaster said.

"It wasn't supposed to be this heavy here," Josie said.

Had they prepared enough? Islanders used to boast about surviving sheared roofs and storm surges that breached their tall, stilted homes. That was before Hurricanes Katrina and Rita, when residents learned no one was coming to help. The government response cruel and mocking, with people living in FEMA trailers for years. The oil spill was the same. The government pointing legislative fingers, holding hearings, looking to assign blame, and allowing the oil company to solve the problem.

A battering wind gust rocked the house. Josie straightened her shoulders. Moms weren't afraid of spiders, gators, or storms at night.

The radar screen displayed massive angry red blotches smothering the Gulf of Mexico, heading northeast.

"Winds are gusting to sixty miles per hour. Power is out in communities in three states. We're not expecting winds as bad as Katrina or Rita, but expect heavy flooding. Stay off the roads. Don't become a problem for emergency personnel."

"I hope Hollis and Chief Tibbs aren't out joyriding," Josie said. She had a measure of comfort knowing they were keeping an eye on the island. Hollis would check on Gumbo and the restaurant at the same time.

The news continued. "Earlier today, BP suspended oil-skimming operations and relief well drilling until the storm passes. We're looking at another twelve hours before the weather is behind us."

Twelve hours, then there's the mess to clean. Josie worried she wouldn't be able to reopen the restaurant because of any number of horrors—water damage, power outage, lack of supplies, or sand covering every inch of the floor, mixed with oil and debris.

Brian gently woke Toby and directed him to bed.

"I'm gonna turn in too," Minnow said.

Panic spiked Josie. She wasn't ready to be alone with Brian. He had kept his polite distance, happy to chase after game-board pieces and keep everyone's drinks filled.

They used to always sit touching, whether watching TV or visiting with people. Josie would swing her legs across his lap, or Brian would wrap an arm around her. When they were alone, he'd pull a blanket over them and unhook her bra, kneading the knots in her back and working his fingers to play with her nipples. A slow seduction she eagerly surrendered to. She didn't want seduction now. She wanted safety.

"Don't go yet, *chère*." Josie patted the couch. To her surprise, Minnow came over. It had been years since she'd cuddled with her. Minnow rested her head in Josie's lap and let Josie finger comb her hair. She had missed this closeness with her girl.

Brian returned from putting Toby to bed and raised an eyebrow. Josie kissed the top of Minnow's head in response. He went into the kitchen and returned with a bottle of wine and two glasses.

"A bit late, don't you think?" Josie said.

"We're on hurricane time." He smacked his forehead. "I should've made hurricanes."

Minnow opened her eyes. "Those are yummy."

"Since when do you drink hurricanes?"

"Good night." She hopped up and skipped out without answering. Brian looked at Josie.

"I'm not challenging that tonight," Josie said.

"Cheers." Brian clinked his glass with hers.

The wind howled, and a shutter banged loose from its hinge. Josie jumped.

"I think that one's a goner," Brian said. "I'm happy you're here. I always worried when weather hit the rig and I didn't know how bad it was here."

"I worried how you were and whether they sent you out to prowl around and plug stuff in."

Brian laughed. "You really have no clue what I did out there."

"Not a one. Do you miss it?"

"I miss the people. This is the longest I've gone without seeing Penman in five years. I'm worried with his recovery, it might be another five years before I see him again."

Brian sat beside her, and she leaned against him. He was solid, a comfort in the storm.

"How would you feel about my working off the island?"

"You said you weren't going back offshore." Josie liked the idea of no longer stressing about helicopters and accidents.

"I'm not. I spoke with an HVAC company. They're looking for people. After three months, they offer benefits. I can work a schedule to allow me to get to GA meetings."

"Do you think you'd like that?"

"I'm good at it. That's satisfying. I'd rather be here. You and I need more time together. I was on the rig for ten years. That adds up to five years away from you and the kids. I've missed a lot. I was too much in my own head. I'm sorry for that too."

"I'm relieved to know the man I married is still in here." She tapped his chest.

He pulled her close and kissed her. In her mind, he was always seventeen to her fourteen, like when she first met him. This older mysterious teen who had landed on the island one day and would pal around with her younger brother. That automatically made him immature. She'd wanted off the island while he hustled for enough work to stay. But they'd both changed.

He was still lean and solid from working on the rig. She was sporting grayer hair and a few unwanted pounds from her recent stress baking.

The house creaked and shuddered from a burst of rain. *The house is older too.* This home they bought because he had gone out to the rig. She'd sacrifice the restaurant before she let the house go.

"I'm sorry about everything," Josie said.

He turned again to her, confusion on his face.

"The explosion, your friends, your job, the oil. I haven't known what to do." She twirled a length of fringe from the blanket in her lap.

He stared at the ceiling. "You're here now. That counts." He switched off the television. "It's after midnight, and we're getting too serious." He smiled. "I'll stretch out here on the couch. You take the bed," Brian said.

"No, it's your bed."

"It's not *my* bed. It's the bed. We both need to sleep. There'll be cleaning up to do when the storm's over."

As if the storm weren't joking, another shutter slammed against the house.

Josie faced the window. With the shutter open, she saw the rain lash against it.

Brian stood.

"No, you don't," Josie said.

He turned to her. "No, what?"

"You're not heading outside to check all the windows."

He laughed and shook his head. "I won't. But if I were on the rig, it would be my job."

His shoulders sagged, and he faced the window. The black reflected his features. He looked older. In November, he'd turn thirty-nine.

Brian was right about being apart for the most part of five years. She had changed and had new goals. She missed sharing her fears with him. She was afraid he wouldn't care enough or would see her dreams as a threat, especially now he was out of work. Worse yet, he would tell her to give up or wait until their life was more secure. That's what Daniel Dean always said. It's why the restaurant never changed, not even the menu, until Odeal died.

She needed to exorcise those thoughts. Lots of people wanted her to succeed—Maisy, Louise and Hollis, and the kids. Rosaline stood up for her with her own money for the competition. Did it matter if her ideas failed? She'd rather be remembered for trying.

She refilled his glass and traced the open mouth of his shark tattoo. "The hot sauce booth and the gazebo are amazing. I'm still—"

Bam!

They raced to the window. The wind had increased. The eye was moving closer. Would it change its course and pass over them or stay over the water? Barrier islands took the brunt of storms. The tiny land-masses protected the mainland coast. In sacrifice, they were chewed up and spit out during storms. The smaller islands—Wine Island, East Island, Whiskey Island, and Raccoon Island—had been disappearing for years. Human attempts to control the Mississippi had disrupted the natural cycle that supported these islands. As they sank, so did vital habitats, leading to declining nesting grounds for birds and turtles. Smaller islands meant a bigger wallop to Grand Isle.

Toby walked into the living room, rubbing his eyes. "I heard a noise."

"I bet you did. Your bedroom window shutter is now out to sea," Brian said.

"Is it bad?" Toby looked from Brian to Josie, seeking assurance.

Josie shrugged. "It's a shutter. We'll be fine." Another easy parent lie.

"Do you think the gazebo is okay?" Toby asked.

"You and your dad built a fortress."

Toby sat on the couch, but Josie directed him back to bed. She pulled the comforter over him and lay next to him.

"I'm glad you're here," he said. "The storm's less scary when everyone's home."

Chapter 22

Thursday, July 1, 2010

A rattle like a prisoner banging a metal cup jolted Josie awake. Out of the storms she had lived through, this one would be recorded as the noisiest. A heavy rain continued to fall. Flooding was a new threat. The storm wasn't over. It would be hours before she could check on anyone, including Gumbo or the restaurant.

She hadn't meant to fall asleep in Toby's bed, only to settle him back to sleep. At least it solved the issue of who would sleep in the bedroom. Too much was on her mind to sort out those feelings.

She flexed her stiff neck and slipped silently from the room.

Toby wants cinnamon rolls. The spicy, warm smell of cinnamon and baking bread would be a comforting wake up for everyone.

She crept past Brian, face-planted spread eagle on the couch. A soft blue blanket lay on the floor. He was shirtless and wearing only boxer shorts. She stepped closer to touch his muscled back, his warm skin, and the contours of his shoulders.

Habit or hunger? She stopped, hating the tattoo curved around his shoulder. A red, blue, and black five-card straight flush, ace through ten of spades. Brian had been on a gambling streak two years ago when he added the tattoo. That's also when he bought the new truck. He joked that now he'd always have a winning hand.

Five a.m. is too early to fixate on past gambling debts. I chose to be here. Deal with it, or forget about it.

She covered the tattoo with the blanket and padded quietly to the kitchen to start a pot of coffee and her baking.

The gurgle of the coffeepot and the whir of the mixer soothed her. She stood on her toes to see outside the window, trying to assess the storm damage. The sky remained dark with thick clouds. The air hung heavy in the kitchen, but no way was she opening a window.

She stuck her head into the back of the pantry closet, hoping to find vanilla to make icing. She doubted anyone had even opened this door in the time she had been gone. She took a step back, and a mug of coffee steamed in her face. She jumped to see Brian smiling, his other hand holding his own mug.

"You scared the bejesus out of me." She swiped the mug from his hand, turned off the mixer, and leaned against the sink. "Did I wake you? I was trying to be quiet."

"Between the galloping rattle outside and the smell of the coffee here, I couldn't stay asleep."

They stood side by side, their hips almost touching. His morning erection pushed at his boxers. *Is he teasing me?*

He was behaving like this was a regular morning and not the first time they'd been this close or this bare in months.

"What's in the mixer?" he asked.

"Toby's cinnamon rolls."

He laughed. "You're spoiling us."

"Why's that funny?"

"You always said you'd only bake if you had free time, and you never did. Now you're tearing it up."

She shrugged. "It takes my mind off everything, and working with dough teaches me patience. I don't have Maisy's touch, but I've perfected the tea cake."

She glanced at the strawberry cookie jar. It hadn't moved since she discovered its secret yesterday. Would he write a new one today?

"Building the booth and the gazebo did the same for me."

He took the mug from her hand and wrapped her in his arms. She tucked her head under his chin and relaxed against his bare chest. His heart beat in a comforting rhythm. He smelled like the fabric softener they used on the blanket and his own body warmth. She breathed deep, tasting the scent. It fed her. His body was strong. The house stood solid. A long-forgotten sense of safety warmed her. To her surprise, tears rolled down her cheeks.

"We're safe, Josiegirl." His nickname for her when they first met. He'd said she was like a cornered filly trying to jump the fence. Grand Isle didn't have horses, and she didn't understand what he meant until she did manage to leave. Was she cornered now? Did she need to kick over this fence and run?

He dried her eyes with a dish towel and kissed her. It was a hungry kiss, not a habit kiss. Her fingers pressed into his back, relearning the contours. She ground her hips against him. His erection returned.

"Mm." He hummed and dug his fingers into her long hair.

Their recipe. It produced a heat like a midnight beach bonfire.

A scrape, *pop* shook the roof. Water exploded from a ceiling can light, turning it into a cold shower.

"Oh, crap!" Brian jumped to the light switch and turned off the power.

Josie ducked as water covered them. She grabbed a kitchen towel. *How useless is this?*

Water rushed against the can light, a mere speed bump before it hit the tile floor. The room was dark, the only light now coming from the window. The light wasn't the only energy turned off.

"Do you have an emergency checklist for indoor rain?"

"Sure do." He pulled the mop from the broom closet.

"The landline *and* the cell are dead. No freaking reception." Minnow paced the kitchen and glared at the bucket filling drop by drop. The wind had calmed, and the rain had turned from torrential to misty.

"How come we have TV?" Toby asked.

"The generator's running, and the TV stations have power," Brian said.

They were edgy from the storm, the constant racket, the wet kitchen, and waiting. Josie pulled cinnamon rolls from the oven. Brian's own anxiety included wanting to make love to his wife. He was eager to straighten his life right, starting with the hole in the roof and continuing with the hole in his relationship.

"Okay, crew," Brian said. "I suspect we're clear to head out in an hour. First stop—"

"Check on Gumbo," Minnow said.

"Check on Grandpa and Uncle Hughdean." Brian nodded to Josie. "As long as their house is secure, Hughdean and I can patch our roof." He stared at the ceiling.

"What about Gumbo?" Minnow asked.

"We'll stop on the way to Grandpa. He's probably asleep, dreaming of fish. This would be easier if we could call Aunt Louise for an update about conditions. She must be busier than a tick at a dog show."

"We should look in on Rosaline and Maisy," Josie said.

"Blue sky." Toby peered through the kitchen window. "Let's go."

Brian shook his head. "Not until the ceiling drip slows. I'm not adding warped floor to the damage."

"I'll take the truck," Minnow said.

"Nope, no telling what wires or trees are down."

Minnow huffed and left the kitchen. "Tell me when the jail opens," she shouted from her room.

"Things are back to normal here," he said to Josie.

She smiled. *As normal as an independent teenage girl and boy who want to play in the storm waters can be.*

At 1:00 p.m. Brian tossed the truck keys in the air and caught them.

"Toby, get the storm kit. We're heading out."

"Finally," Minnow said.

Toby dragged a duffel bag from the front hall closet. It had flashlights, rope, first aid gear, blankets and towels, flares, and tools. They would add water bottles, snacks, shovels, Brian's chain saw, and gas cans.

"Wait." Josie stacked to-go containers of sandwiches into a box.

"What do you think we'll see?" Toby said.

Brian understood his adventurous excitement. As a teen, he remembered scavenging along the Mississippi and through Baton Rouge after storms. All manner of debris, from musical instruments to department store mannequins, had beached along the riverbank. It was exciting until the year a dead man washed up, tangled in the reeds. Since then, he had never traveled without basic supplies.

Brian tossed the duffel into the bed of the truck. The Heberts' dog, Pepper, a retriever-mutt mix, barked a hello and wagged his considerable tail. He was no worse for wear, though his doghouse was, indeed, missing.

Minnow scratched his head. "What a wild storm. Bet you're glad to be out in this fresh breeze."

Josie climbed into the front passenger seat. Another victory. Buying the truck had been a sore spot between them. It was his only free and clear asset. He kept considering selling it and putting the money back into their accounts. For now, he was happy to have it.

"Ready, everyone."

"A boat." Toby leaned as far out the window as the seat belt would allow. A dinghy with a torn white sail draped around a light post.

The truck waded through standing water lapping with the tide over the road. The tires sank in hills of sand and debris. As they drove along Highway 1, dark blobs dotted the shoreline.

What is all that?

After a fifteen-minute slow crawl, Minnow called out, "Dad, stop!"

Brian parked on the side of the road, and they waded to the water's edge. The wind blew with a low frequency. Josie secured the hood of her windbreaker. Minnow high-stepped to the edge and probed a blob with a stick of driftwood. It broke open, releasing a gasoline smell.

She stared at them, her eyes dark with anger. She slapped the stick into the water. "Oil. Dirty, poisonous oil." She kicked at the water, sending a spray toward the road.

Brian placed a hand on her shoulder. She shook him off and took a step away from him. A cold gloom coiled in his stomach.

Josie walked over. "Hollis said the storm would help break up the oil on the water surface so it would evaporate."

"This isn't like the oil coming in with the surf. These are tar bars that have been sinking in the ocean, that we didn't know about," Minnow said.

Brian shoved his hands into the coat of his windbreaker and surveyed the shoreline. Eight, eleven, seventeen blobs of oil were oozing in his sight line.

"Storm surge must've churned the floor of the Gulf," Brian said. He looked at Josie.

"I've never seen this," Josie said.

"When does the oil end?" Minnow said.

"I found a soccer ball." Toby pushed it through the water on the street.

"Be careful," Josie said. "We don't know what's under the water."

"Yes, we do." Minnow marched back to the truck.

"I was thinking lost sharks and alligators," Josie said.

The island was a mess, and the oil added to the problems in a way Brian couldn't control. Usually they helped to free cars, return boats to the water, and move trees. The oil was an invasive alien. It traveled with its own rules, and he didn't have a clue where to start.

Josie touched his arm and closed the space between them. "The storm was long. She's watched the cleanup. This is a setback, but not because of you. You told me not to take her anger personally. That was sound advice, so now I'm giving it back."

Minnow sat tall in the truck, staring straight ahead.

Josie's right. I need to let Minnow be upset and support her. I can't fix everything. "We should go."

The truck crept farther along the road toward the restaurant. "I hope the generator held," Josie said, more under her breath.

Brian huffed. "I checked the restaurant's, your dad's, and ours days before the first raindrop."

"I didn't mean—" Brian cared about the family. She had no need to question him.

Minnow sat silent. Toby stared out the window, counting boats on the road.

"Oh, hell," Josie said as they approached the restaurant.

The Odeal's sign had sheared in half and now read *eal's.* The giant stylized *O* sagged over the roof like a closed eye. What would she find inside?

Before Brian turned off the ignition, Minnow opened her door and dashed to the deck to find Gumbo.

Josie, Brian, and Toby followed.

Deck boards were missing and splintered.

"Dammit." Brian dug his fingers into his hair.

Josie turned in a circle to take in the destruction.

Brian tapped a toe, checking for stability. He held Toby back. "Walk slow."

"Gumbo's not here," Minnow wailed, her breath rough from her sprint. She whistled her three-note call. "Gumbo!" Her voice cracked.

Josie jumped off the deck and ducked into the pelican house. A ceiling board was missing. She climbed back up. "The fish bucket's empty, and the enclosure's intact."

"He's not coming when I whistle. We weren't here. He left to fish or to find us."

She whistled again and again until her lips were too dry to make a sound. She held her shaking hands out like a toddler who hates the sticky scratch of sand.

Brian clasped them between his and spoke softly. "He knows to come home."

Minnow shook her head. "What if he left during the storm?"

She whistled again.

"We'll check with Hollis and find out when was the last time he saw him. The sky's clear. Animals know how to stay safe in storms," Brian said.

"He'll come back, Minnow," Toby said. "Can we call Uncle Hollis yet?"

Brian dug his cell phone from his pocket. "No service."

"Back in the truck, everyone. We're checking on Grandpa and Hughdean, and then we'll go to the mayor's office," Josie said.

"What if he comes back?" Minnow said.

"Then he'll be here and safe."

"I'm staying." Minnow crossed her arms.

"No, it's not safe," Brian said. "Post-storm protocol. We stay together. I'm not chasing after you."

Minnow's head dropped. She put her arm around Toby's shoulders, and they walked to the truck.

"Do you want to check the restaurant?" Brian asked.

Josie shook her head. "It can wait. The deck, the sign . . . we can't fix it now."

Brian waved to other drivers creeping through the streets. The island had begun to investigate the damage.

Daniel Dean's gravel driveway had turned into a shallow lake. Brian waded the high truck through and parked at the end of the stairs into the house.

"Dad and I will go in, and if everything is secure, we'll head straight to Aunt Louise," Josie said.

They stepped out of the car, about to go to the back door, when Brian put his hand up. "Shush for a sec. Do you hear that? Talking?" He stepped down and turned toward the backyard. "It's coming from the back."

They jogged to the backyard and found Daniel Dean sitting in the gazebo, a portable radio by his side, and a glass of sweet tea.

"Dad." Josie burst inside. "What're you doing out here? Are you okay?"

"I'm fine, Josephine. It's too hot in the house with the power out. I told Hughdean not to mess with the generator until he came back. I'm catching a cool cross breeze. You did a fine job, Brian, not a scratch," Daniel Dean said.

"Hughdean left you alone?" Brian asked.

"I told him to go. He's at the marina checking his boats."

Josie hugged him. "If you're good for now, we'll be back later."

"That old man is made of hardy stuff," Brian said on their way across town. He pulled over as a fire engine pushed through the flooded streets. Power was out all over the island, but the government center ran on an emergency generator. They waded through the flooded parking lot to the building.

"Y'all okay?" Officer Guerin asked them and yawned. His lined face and bloodshot eyes told them about his evening.

"We're fine, Walt. Did you have a long night?" Brian asked.

"Sure did, and we're starting on the cleanup."

"I'm looking for Hollis and Louise. Can we go in?" Josie asked. Walt was a year ahead of Josie in school. She couldn't escape people from her past, no matter how hard she tried.

"Not sure where she is. Oh, and thanks for the sandwiches you sent. We appreciated them. Roof is leaking, so be careful, the floor's slippery."

"Let's go, kids," Josie said. The air inside was humid and stale with cigarettes, coffee, and urinals.

"HVAC's out," Brian said.

Giant white buckets collected dripping water, and overhead fluorescent lights flickered.

"Spooky." Josie flinched as a drop of cold water hit her neck. "Ew."

A chair propped open the door to the mayor's suite, and a portable fan buzzed to allow for airflow. They stopped outside the glass door to Louise's office. Condensation dripped on the outside. Inside, Louise held a baby in a pink onesie, draped over her shoulder. She bounced lightly as she listened to staff updates.

"Hey, gang." She hugged everyone with one arm as if the baby were a shoulder brooch.

"Aunt Louise, whose baby is that?" Toby asked, the question they were all thinking.

"Y'all doing okay from this mess? How are the roads at your end?" Her animated voice and bright face masked the fact that she hadn't slept all night. "This is Samantha, isn't she precious?" Louise lowered her voice. She ducked to Toby's height, so he could see the baby's sleeping face. The baby had a fuzz of dark-brown hair. Long lashes lined her closed eyes, and her cheeks were pink from sleep. One small arm clutched around Louise's neck, the other tucked underneath her body.

"Where'd she come from?" Josie asked.

Louise took a long drink from a straw in a cup of water. "The night was one unexpected event after another. She's Don and Chrissie Patin's girl. Chrissie had a gallstone flare, maybe 3:00 a.m. Don's ankle is in a walking boot. They made their way here looking for help. Walt and JJ drove them to the hospital in Cut Off." Louise took another slurp of water. "I took Samantha for them."

"She's out. Why don't you put her down," Brian said. "If you can." He turned around.

"We've her car seat. But every time I try, she cries and cries. Breaks your heart, so I've been holding her."

"Here, let me." Josie reached for the sleeping baby. Louise's T-shirt was damp from sweat and baby drool.

"Phew, she's a hot little biscuit. Thanks." Louise shook out her arms.

"Aunt Louise, where's Uncle Hollis?" Minnow asked. "Gumbo's missing, and oil is everywhere."

She wasn't as charmed about the hurricane baby as the rest of them.

Louise's tired eyes opened at Minnow's report. "Oil?"

"Yeah, the size of apples. I thought they were jellyfish, but it's globs of sticky oil turds." She folded her arms tight across her chest.

Louise turned back to the staff waiting for her instructions. "Start the street-by-street sweep. With God's good grace, we'll have phone service soon. Oil's bad. I hope that's the worst of it. Brian!" Louise grabbed his forearm. "Could you use your magic fixing powers on the HVAC?" Louise waved her hand like she was holding a wand. "Hollis went to the building's maintenance room to stare at it. Isn't that just the thing for it to die? We can't reach Cliff. He took his family to wait out the storm in—"

"I got it. C'mon, Minnow," Brian said. "Let's see why this building is turning into a steam oven, and you can talk to Hollis."

The baby lifted her head and cried. Brian ran a gentle palm over her soft fuzz, and she drifted back to sleep. Brian's gaze reminded Josie of a favorite family photo. Minnow sitting in Brian's lap with a newborn Toby cradled in her chubby six-year-old arms. The expressions on both of their faces a mixture of pride and happiness. She had never felt so complete as she had at that moment.

"Where's building services?" Brian asked.

"Here's a map." Minnow pointed to a directory.

They headed to the stairwell. Emergency lights lit the corners. *Josie's right, it's creepy here.*

"Aunt Louise is a natural with that baby," Minnow said.

"She was the same with you and Toby." He needed to add Louise to his list of people to make amends with. She had supported Josie and loved Minnow and Toby. Long ago they had appointed Louise and Hollis to be the kids' guardians if anything ever happened. They weren't blood relatives; they were better.

He opened the door, and a metallic *bang, bang* came from the end of the hall.

"Head that way." He walked toward the sound.

They arrived at an open door and found Hollis next to another man hammering a wrench, trying to turn a bolt.

"Hey fellas, need a hand?"

Hollis stood. "Brian, Minnow. Y'all okay?"

"We're fine. Louise sent me to help."

"We're not fine. Uncle Hollis, Gumbo's gone. I called and whistled. The restaurant deck is torn apart, the fish bucket is empty, and oil blobs are everywhere. What if he's hurt?" She bobbed from leg to leg like a fighter waiting to duck a punch.

"Slow down, *chère*." Hollis hugged her tight.

Brian bristled. When he tried to comfort Minnow, she shrugged him off.

"He was agitated at midnight, but snug and safe. The storm's over. He's probably looking for lunch."

"But we don't want him fishing, and oil's everywhere," Minnow said.

"What oil are you talking about?"

Minnow blew out a frustrated breath.

"We stopped along Highway One," Brian said. "The shoreline is covered in oil the size of apples."

Hollis scratched his chin. "The storm surge pulled it from the ocean floor. There's more oil than we first thought."

"More lies from BP. It's likely covering the barrier islands and the nesting sites," Minnow said.

Brian turned to the man on the floor. "The compressor coils are frozen. When was this serviced last?"

The man ran his fingers through his sweaty hair. "Cliff said it needed refrigerant, but he didn't order the right part."

"Bunch of morons." Brian tossed a wrench onto the floor, and it ricocheted into the unit with a vibrating *ping*. The sound echoed in the space, and Minnow covered her ears.

"It's an air conditioner. Calm down, Dad."

"You're falling apart about a pelican flying around, but I can't be annoyed about a simple fix. Shit like this doesn't happen on the rig. You do your job because people are counting on you." He shook a finger in her face.

Minnow took a step to the side, away from his direct pointing. "Ah, okay, so this Cliff guy won't ever work on an oil rig. That's good."

"That's a joke to you, right?"

No one understood how important his job was. *I'm the guy who fixes everything.*

"Brian, we're tired from a long, hot night. Everyone in this building would be grateful if you can help here," Hollis said.

"Turn off the power. Let the coils defrost, and then we'll see if it comes back."

"Anyone here?" A voice echoed in the hall.

"Sounds like Chief Tibbs." Hollis stepped outside.

"Josie's upstairs, and Brian's here." Hollis's voice floated into the room.

Brian wiped his greasy hands with a cloth. "Hey, Frank, what's up?"

Chief Tibbs's face was tense, and Brian's danger sense prickled the back of his neck.

"We've a situation at the top of the island. We've a report of a tornado touchdown." Frank's voice was low and measured, though they were the only ones in earshot. "Maisy Phillips's bungalow collapsed. Four of the pilings gave way, and the roof caved in. Any chance she's not home and is with you?"

Brian closed his eyes. How could Daniel Dean be sitting fine and happy in the gazebo while Maisy's house had fallen down? "We said good night around five. She joked she had a date with a new pair of pajamas. Why are we standing here? Let's go."

"Fire department is assessing the situation."

"Yeah, not waiting. I'm trained in search and rescue too."

Minnow's eyes grew wide, hearing the exchange. "Is Maisy okay?"

"We haven't found her yet. We need to get into the house."

"Mom has a key." Minnow looked at each of them.

"I don't think that'll help," Frank said.

"Maisy has to be okay," Minnow said.

Brian hugged her. "Minnow, I'm taking the truck. Run upstairs and tell your mom what's happened."

Chapter 23

Brian raced past Chief Tibbs. The island was an obstacle course of debris. The truck had an easier time than the police cruiser driving through standing water and sand dunes.

Maybe she's not inside. Out for a walk on the beach, lounging with Dr. Tynsdale—anything.

Brian turned onto Island Road. Maisy's house was a pile of sticks. Four of the twelve pilings holding it high away from the storm surge had snapped. The new wraparound porch was a tangle of wood.

The sky was post-storm blue and clear, matching the bungalow's siding. The violent winds thankfully had blown the petroleum stench aside, for a short while. Brian's nerves sizzled, along with the day's rising heat. The first minutes after an accident were critical. A lone fire truck was parked sideways, with three of the department's crew standing around and, as far as Brian saw, twiddling their damned thumbs. A crowd of neighbors stood across the street, wringing their hands and pacing.

Brian jogged toward the firefighters. "Why aren't you inside looking for her?"

"We just turned off the gas," Smiley Whitehead said. He was one of those guys whose nickname was the opposite of his personality. He was a half-glass-spilled-and-empty kind of thinker and the biggest of the burly three-man crew. They wore full incident gear of khaki pants and turnout coats with yellow reflective striping. They resembled human-shaped ready-to-ship packages.

Brian's body tensed. They'd spend hours navel-gazing while Maisy remained trapped. He marched over and performed his own review of the perimeter.

Smiley grabbed his shoulder. "Brian, I know you want to help—"

"Don't." Brian whipped around. "The only difference between you wearing gear and me, is I didn't sign the paperwork when I passed the volunteer firefighting test last year." He pointed in his face.

"Well, you didn't sign, so step back and let us do our jobs."

Smiley's reminder slapped him in the face. He hadn't wanted to be on call. His gambling was more important, and the pittance it paid wasn't worth his time.

"You need me. I know about tight spaces." He had crawled through places on oil rigs where people weren't meant to fit.

"Still," Smiley said.

"Still, shit."

"Brian," Josie called, running from Hollis's truck with Hollis, Louise, and the kids close behind. "Maisy!" Josie ran toward the collapsed house.

Brian grabbed her. "You and the kids need to stay back." He wasn't risking their safety.

The house creaked and popped.

"Maisy!" Josie yelled.

"Come stand with us, *chère*," Louise said softly and pulled her back.

Brian spoke directly to Smiley. "No one is walking through the front door. Best shot is the picture window in her bedroom. I'm thinking she's in there."

The bedroom side of Maisy's house faced the ocean. The jagged stiles of the porch poked the edges of the house like toothpicks. The crowd began to move toward the house.

"Everyone, stay back. We don't want more rescues today." Smiley made a pushing motion.

"For Chrissake, break the window and crawl in. If she's in the bedroom, we can pull her out. If not, you can move inside the house," Brian said.

"I don't need you to tell me how to do my job."

"I'm not. Just *to* do it," Brian said.

The two men squared off, with Smiley looming over Brian and the other firefighters ready to pull them apart.

"Hey, knock it off. Maisy's inside. And if you don't go in, I will." Josie stepped between them.

Brian stepped back. "Sorry, man. I'm worried."

Smiley nodded to the others. "Break the window."

The glass cracked, the sound making Brian wince. He stood behind the men at a respectable distance. They pulled away the porch and peered inside. The collapsed roof left a narrow space.

"Ms. Phillips, can you hear me?" Smiley shouted into the space.

Josie broke from the crowd and ran to the house. "Maisy, Maisy, it's Josie. Please, *chère*." Her voice broke with emotion, her face pinched tight, and she gnawed on her lower lip.

Smiley pushed her back, and Brian caught her, folding his arms around her.

Louise stood beside them. "They'll find her."

Brian didn't like the false hope in Louise's voice.

"I hear scratching. Does she have pets?" Smiley said.

"No," Josie said.

Smiley forced his head and shoulders over the sill. "That's a small space. Only thing keeping the roof up is furniture."

"The weight of the house will take that down," Brian said. *We're running out of time.*

The house shuddered, and Smiley jumped back. He evaluated the other two men nearly the same size as him and then Brian. "Hate to say this, but you're the only one slim enough to fit inside."

"Right. I need a jacket and a hard hat."

Smiley handed him his heavy turnout coat, a respirator mask, and a helmet. Brian slipped on the mask and buckled the helmet under his chin. Another man handed him a pair of gloves.

"Brian," Josie said.

"You can't stop me." His voice was muffled behind the mask.

She smoothed the front of the heavy coat and pulled on the strap under his chin.

"I wasn't. Find her. Don't get hurt. I didn't lose you to the rig. I won't lose you to this."

"I promise." He pulled her hands close to his chest and squeezed them. "I'll be out so fast with her, you won't even miss me."

"Be careful," Louise shouted.

Brian peered over his shoulder. Minnow and Toby stood holding hands—his family. Maisy was family too. He flashed a thumbs-up and hoisted himself over the threshold of the window.

The room was dark, and he inched on his stomach. The house groaned, balancing on the remaining pilings. Smiley said the gas was off, but it still scared him. Gas was unpredictable, invisible, filling spaces, and always the first warning sign of trouble on the rig. By the time gas ignited, the problem was out of control. He set aside the flashlight he carried, not taking chances of a spark. Brian wasn't able to help save anyone the day the rig exploded, but he was here to save Maisy now.

"Maisy," he called. "You here?"

He crawled along the floor. With his hollow-sounding breath and the downward force of the tight space, it felt like swimming through a cave.

"D'you see anything?" Smiley called.

A patch of light filtered through a hole in the ceiling, and dust motes clogged the air.

"Maisy," he called. "It's Brian. Time to go, darling."

The bedroom walls skewed like a fun house, with the door open but above him at an angle. Furniture and debris clogged the opening.

The collapsed roof blanketed the floor. They were only leaving through the window.

"Help," a thin voice responded.

Brian turned toward the sound. A dresser teetered half on the floor and half on what were now pieces of her bed. Was she here? "Hang on, I'm coming for you." *Please hang on.*

He waded through swinging electrical wires and splintered ceiling joists. She lay trapped between the bed and the wall, with the dresser crushing her leg.

The house groaned and shook.

Brian covered his head with his arms. *That ceiling is coming down any minute.* His breathing quickened, and his pulse thrummed in his ear as adrenaline hit his system.

Maisy whimpered.

"I'm not leaving without you," Brian whispered.

Using his back, he shoved the dresser off her body, with his legs braced against the wall. The house shuddered from the force. Her leg jutted at an unnatural angle, a definite break.

Maisy's breath sounded shallow.

I pray that's the worst.

Crack! A ceiling joist fell, raining drywall dust and water. He shielded her body with his own and covered his head with his arms, waiting for the pieces to stop. The heavy coat and helmet took the brunt.

"Brian?" Maisy called.

"Hold on."

Drywall dust floated everywhere, like spilled flour.

Get your head together, and fast. This place could explode.

He didn't dare move her until she was secured. He crawled back to the opening of the house and shouted, "I found her. I need a backboard and a neck collar. Shove it in hard, quick."

Smiley forced in the equipment, and Brian pulled it back to Maisy. The house moved again, his weight changing the center of gravity.

"Hurry up, Babineaux," Smiley called, his voice tight.

What do you think I'm doing? Brian knelt over her crooked body. She mumbled, and her head rolled to the side. Her eyes fluttered and then closed.

"Maisy!" He felt for her breath. It was faint. Tears washed white drywall streaks on her skin. "I'm not losing you now. We're almost out."

He fit the collar around her neck. The house trembled, and more of the ceiling fell, opening a new hole to the sky. He had no time for a medical assessment.

"We're moving."

He logrolled her onto the board and secured her. Cold water dripped onto the back of his neck. The house cracked and popped again. He wasn't thinking or feeling, only moving. The window was within reach.

"Ungh," he screamed, gathering his strength to finish the job.

Arms and hands pulled her out while Brian guided her head through the window. The house rocked from the weight now at the front. Brian dove after her as a fifth piling snapped under the weight.

Smiley pulled him away as the house slid forward, swallowing the space where they had just stood. Brian shook, his body sweating from the exertion. He sat on the curb, breathing deep without the respirator. They had almost been crushed to death.

"Everyone back, y'all, stay across the street," Smiley said.

"Maisy." Josie jogged beside the stretcher as they loaded her into an ambulance. Without asking, she jumped in.

The doors slammed shut, and they drove off, lights and sirens at full blast.

"Dad!" Toby launched himself at Brian, followed by Minnow.

He buried his face into their heads and cried, holding them. A sharp pain seized his back and neck from jumping from the house.

He caught Smiley's eye, followed by a nod.

Chapter 24

Thursday, July 1, 2010

Josie watched headlights drive in and out of the hospital's dark parking lot. No doubt, people tending to injuries from the storm.

The hospital had power and a light built into the bed, which glowed without warmth. Maisy's cast leg lay in an exaggerated *L*, propped on a pile of pillows.

Josie fingered the hole she had worried into the hem of her T-shirt while waiting for Maisy to come out of surgery. The concussion was another worry. The room was dim and quiet in anticipation of her waking.

Did I really start this day making cinnamon rolls? Time evaporated from the moment Brian pulled Maisy out of her house. As she climbed into the ambulance, her last view was Minnow and Toby rushing to Brian. That house fell fast, and he had been within inches of being crushed. He had almost died. She could have lost them both.

I don't even know if he's okay. The island still had no phone service, and she hadn't seen anyone here who could give her any news.

Being with Maisy was the right call. Waking alone in a hospital room with no one to answer questions or offer comfort was frightening.

Hospital rooms with flat, slightly antiseptic air stirred nightmare memories for Josie of Daniel Dean from his big stroke.

She remembered the sweaty heat from a tiny Hughdean plastered beside her, squeezing her hand so hard it hurt.

"Don't let go," he had whispered when Odeal prompted him to give Daddy a kiss. Daddy, who lay in a bed with tubes sprouting from his body, his face a bluish white like the morning sky.

Josie was trapped here, unable to return to the island. Maisy was safe, and Josie wanted to go home, put her hands on her family and tell them she loved them.

The air conditioner wheezed on and off, releasing an internal gasp of cool air. Josie checked the blanket covering Maisy.

Thank God nothing had crushed her head. She was bruised, swollen, and bandaged from flying bric-a-brac. Her lips were dry and cracked, dimming what was usually a full-mouth smile. Maisy's injuries were visible. No clogged arteries like those hiding in her father; no cancer cells blooming like algae in Odeal.

As a kid, Josie had suffered enough of her own *accidents* and trips to the emergency room. The wounds you could watch heal were better than the ones you couldn't.

Maisy stirred; her head rolled to the side of her pillow. "Hey." Her hoarse voice cracked.

Josie held her hand, careful not to poke or pull at the snaking IV tubes. "Water?"

Maisy raised the bed to a sitting position.

Josie positioned a bent straw in a plastic cup to her lips.

"What were we saying before I nodded off?"

Josie brushed a hand across her forehead and smiled, relieved Maisy's spark flickered back to bright.

"Oh, nothing. Just chattering to fill the space. Gonna be a few days before we figure this mess out. You can't go home."

Maisy turned her head away.

"Hey, *chère*. Your house will be better than new, and you'll be two-stepping in a few weeks."

"I don't two-step."

"I called your sisters. Vera's on her way. We'll come up with a plan."

Maisy shook her head. "I can't handle Vera. You should've called Shonda. Vera and I—"

"I called Shonda, too, and told her everything. Next thing, Vera calls and says she's on her way."

"She treats me like a baby."

"You're her baby sister. You need baby love now."

A knock on the door made them look up.

"Brian," Josie said.

He sported a two-day beard, and his intense blue eyes had shadows underneath. He blinked in the dim room. Yet he wore a clean pair of jeans and a button-down shirt. His right hand was wrapped in a thick dressing of white gauze to his wrist.

Josie met him at the door and hugged him. "What happened? It's late, why are you here? Are you okay?"

"I came to take you home. No one was coming this way, and without phone service, I had no way to reach you. I wasn't waiting until morning."

Josie hugged him again. She lifted his bandaged hand, and he flinched. "What's this?" *He's hurt.*

"A few stitches from—" He glanced at Maisy. "Small cut. Figured since I was here, I'd stop at the ER."

"Brian Babineaux," she said softly, "you're either the bravest man or the dumbest man I know." What would've happened today without him? She pushed back swirling thoughts of him dying.

"I'm going with *dumb*. It's my fixing-stuff hand."

"You could fix the most complicated machine with your toes if you had to. Does it hurt?"

Josie instinctively searched his palm for a scar, but it was covered in the dressing. She had endured repeated surgeries to repair her hand. Her scar acted like a closed book; it didn't tell the story inside.

"Three stitches on the side. They almost superglued it. I know what you're thinking. I can still play the guitar."

Josie shook her head at his joke.

"Brian?" Maisy called.

"How're you feeling?" He leaned close to her.

"Like a dresser broke my leg. And I've been pumped full of fun-time drugs."

"Don't go blaming a good piece of furniture. The storm's to blame."

Maisy's lips quivered. "You saved my life."

"Who's telling you tales—Josie?" He smiled at her. "If I didn't go after you, Josie would've. The whole fire department had to hold her back."

Maisy covered her face with her hand. "I remember a crash and the roof coming at me. When I woke, I couldn't move. My room was dark for so long. I thought no one would ever find me. I smelled gas, and the house made the most awful sounds. Like a beast from hell coming for me. I don't remember much after that."

Brian took her hand from her face and held it. "Everything will be okay. Heck, better than okay."

"I need a favor," Maisy said.

"More than saving your life?"

"Please."

Brian stood quietly and fixed his attention on her.

Maisy began to cry. "Everything's a complete mess. It feels like there's nothing left to hold on to. Promise me, you'll get Josie to the competition. We've worked too hard to stop now."

"Hush, *chère*. That's not important now." Josie stood on the other side of the bed and fussed with the bedding. Maisy wasn't heading anywhere and certainly not to the Ragin' Cajun this weekend. The family had planned to drive to New Orleans tomorrow and set up the booth.

The show and public judging opened on Saturday. The official judging took place on Sunday, the Fourth of July.

Josie and Maisy had no business thinking about the competition with Maisy hurt. But seeing her here and knowing how they had worked these past few weeks, it was hard to toss aside like a used tissue. Maisy had even consulted with a Mambo priestess in New Orleans.

"She's a botanist. I went to talk to her about herbs," Maisy had said when Josie teased her.

The Ragin' Cajun was more than a potential purse. The contest had reminded Josie that food was more than fuel. Cooking was art and community. It brought Josie and Maisy together in the kitchen. Food had opened the door to Linh Nguyen, who inspired Josie to test her boundaries and her menu. Food provided jobs and was a reason to travel. Food fed Josie's dreams. Dreams she had stopped chasing when money and survival became her focus.

Without Maisy by her side, a fear selfishly gripped Josie. She would fail.

Maisy held Josie's hand tight. "I need this win too. I was a line cook when I met you. That asshole I worked for in New Orleans said I'd never have what it takes to be an executive chef and run *his* kitchen. Then you filled my head with your ideas. The first time I saw Odeal's, I thought you were smoking weed."

"But you agreed," Brian said. "Josie went wild over your baking, saying you can't have a southern kitchen without passionate baking. You had a confidence she didn't have and more experience in the type of restaurant she wanted to run. She needed a partner who wasn't afraid of what she wanted to try."

Josie nodded, surprised Brian remembered all those early worries. Finding the right sous-chef had changed everything for her.

"I never planned to stay this long. Josie was a stop on the way to my own bakery. Then Odeal's grew bigger, and Josie's over-the-top ideas worked. Now the Ragin' Cajun. Dear God, I'm like the Wicked Witch of the West. My house fell on me. This competition must happen, because not even an oil spill or a storm will stop us. When I began looking into all the competitors, I found out my old jerk boss is a judge. It doesn't matter if we win. This is our way of showing that Odeal's is worth the trip, because we're worth it. Like that magazine article said. We're important."

Josie leaned over Maisy. "We are important. You and I have dozens of ideas. We'll pick another one, like building a hot sauce empire."

Maisy exhaled. "Brian, promise me."

"I promise I will get her to New Orleans, and we will make you proud. I will take so many pictures you'll swear you were there."

"Maisy. I found you," a relieved voice said from the door. Dr. Tynsdale crossed the room in a few short steps. "My truck wouldn't start after the storm. Then I heard about the accident. I'm sorry. It's taken me all day to get here."

Josie almost didn't recognize him, dressed in shorts and a T-shirt. But even without his white coat, he walked in and took charge.

"Garrett." Maisy cried fresh tears as he leaned over her and kissed her forehead.

"I spoke to the surgeon. You'll be fine. We need to be gentle with your head. Are you two all right?" he asked Brian and Josie.

"We will be."

"Go home. I'll stay with her now."

Josie and Brian stood to leave.

As Brian shut the door, they heard him talking to Maisy. "You should have listened to me and stayed during the storm."

Once in the hall, Brian picked up a black sling from a waiting room chair and slipped his arm inside.

"What's this? You're more hurt than a few stitches."

Brian shrugged with his free shoulder.

"I didn't want to upset Maisy. I dislocated my shoulder when I dove through the window."

She rested her head in her hands. As a longtime expert at pretending life was all happy and she was fine, she shouldn't be angry.

The rawness of the day had burrowed into her. The last forty-eight hours had upended her life in unexpected ways. She tugged at his hand. "Sit. I'm sorry you're hurt. How long does a dislocated shoulder need to heal?"

He rubbed his leg. "I meant what I said to Maisy about the competition. I'll find a way to get you there and set up. The kids and me. Then I'll work with Hughdean, and we'll fix the restaurant deck and the roof. His crew needs work and—"

His rambling spun a fear in her like a blur of clothes in the dryer. He was making promises for things she hadn't asked for. Too many parts of her life were broken. Promises only added to the pile.

She tapped his bouncing leg. "How long?"

"Maybe twelve weeks with care and therapy."

"Care and therapy," she repeated. Daniel Dean's lifelong prescription.

A high tide of exhaustion crept over her. She had started the day thinking that her family was whole again. Now both Maisy and Brian were hurt. The restaurant was damaged, and she was too tired to fight.

"I need to see the kids," Josie said.

"Yeah . . . about the kids."

A jolt of panic made her sit up straight.

"Everyone's okay, but Gumbo's missing. No one's seen him in twenty-four hours now."

"Has anyone searched for him? Gumbo always shows up."

"Minnow and Hollis drove around a few places on the island. The roads are almost clear, but moving around isn't fast, and he flies. Hollis isn't worried, yet. Storms upset animals. He may be looking for us."

Josie leaned her back against the wall and closed her eyes. She wanted to scoop her scattered family into one safe place.

"Minnow?"

"She asked to camp at the restaurant."

Josie's lips pinched into a hard line.

"I told her she could. Toby too. Dropped them and their sleeping bags off before I came here."

Not the parenting decision she would have made. She pictured Minnow's pleading eyes and the stubborn set to her chin. Brian, with his throbbing shoulder, made the choice of least resistance.

"Is the restaurant even safe inside?"

"Safe enough," he said.

"Did you happen to include sleeping bags for us as well?"

Brian smiled. "I might have." He rubbed the sling. "Would you mind driving home?"

The dashboard clock blinked 11:57 p.m. when the truck's wheels crunched over Odeal's shell-and-gravel parking lot. Josie set the emergency brake and rested her head on the steering wheel.

She considered Brian in profile as he slept, reclined in the passenger seat. *What to do with you?* Waking him would be cruel. She, too, was so tired she hurt. Her shoulders were tight from gripping the wheel while driving across the Highway 1 bridge. *Keep looking ahead*, she had repeated, worried she'd drive into the ocean.

How did he drive to the hospital all torn up on these bad roads?

He once said he'd follow her to the moon if she asked. Heck, he'd endlessly explore the heavens with no destination if she said so. For a man who shut away his emotions, he had a romantic heart.

They could sleep in the truck. In their younger days, they had camped out for concert tickets in a beat-up pickup.

She smoothed her hands over the leather seat. This truck was the blaring smoke alarm of Brian's smoldering gambling problem. He and Hughdean would head to the casinos in Baton Rouge or New Orleans. They took a small purse of fun money and played until it was lost. That's what they told her.

After one heavy winning weekend, he had bought the truck. She had failed to pay attention. The restaurant had received favorable press from an airline travel magazine touting "two bites of spicy heaven"—her shrimp cakes and hot sauce. She jumped on it and decided that was the time to launch Pelican Point Provisions.

Josie loved the restaurant, but when freed from the day-to-day management, she had discovered her true passion was tinkering with recipes. But she had failed when it came to watching the books. Daniel Dean kept the accounts, and he had alerted her to the first problems.

How was she to coexist with Brian? He had gambled their family's future without thought or feeling. Yet without hesitation about his own life, he had climbed into Maisy's collapsed house. Both selfish and selfless.

Josie had once declared to Hollis she lacked the forgive-and-forget gene. People had hurt her and let her down her entire life. Each scar had healed into an impenetrable scale. He countered she needed practice and patience. The Earth took seasons to heal from storms, droughts, and wildfires. Brian's gambling was like a wildfire, hot and destructive. He was working to control his addiction, and she needed to believe he would continue. Perhaps belief was the same as forgiveness.

Besides, was she any different? Counting on one bet, the Ragin' Cajun, to save the restaurant. She could be a three-Michelin-star chef, and it wouldn't matter as long as oil was chasing customers away from her door. She didn't know if she needed to stay or close the door and leave the mess behind.

The restaurant was quiet inside. Battery-powered security lighting glowed in the corners. Chairs had been stacked on the tables, and her nose twitched from the smell of bleach. Brian told her on the ride over that the kids had begun the cleanup. White buckets sat strategically under drips, and the floor remained dry.

Toby had created a hideaway, stretched out on a bench against the wall. He had wrapped himself in his sleeping bag, with a row of chairs in front of him in case he rolled off.

"I missed you." She had last seen him a few hours ago, but it felt like days, and now it was after midnight. She smoothed his hair and kissed the top of his head.

He sighed in his deep sleep.

Her eyes adjusted to the dim light, and she walked the dining room perimeter. Minnow wasn't here. Josie's heart thumped. Where was she?

From the picture window in the back, a light glowed from under the shattered deck, casting a star pattern across the boards.

Josie hurried down the steps to the pelican house.

Minnow lay asleep in her bag, her arms wrapped around a stuffed penguin. She had balanced a flashlight to shine as a beacon through the holes in the decking. She slept alone, no Gumbo in sight.

Josie searched the night sky, the bright stars a celebration after the storm.

"Where are you, Gumbo?"

She found the extra sleeping bags, returned to the truck, and wrapped Brian, tucking the thick quilting around his shoulder to support him against the truck's seat.

"You saved Maisy's life today." She kissed each of his closed eyes, his long lashes forming feathery half moons.

Brian turned and mumbled. She backed out of the truck to return to Minnow.

Chapter 25

Grand Isle, Louisiana

Friday, July 2, 2010

Brian's eyes fluttered open as a cool breeze washed over his hot face. He discovered his body cocooned in a camo-patterned sleeping bag he didn't remember seeing yesterday. Or was it last night? The last twenty-four hours were stitched together in intensity and exhaustion.

"What the . . . ?" He sat alone in the passenger seat of his truck.

"I could say the same." Hughdean stood in his usual ripped jeans, holey T-shirt, and a frayed ball cap, leaning on the open truck door.

"You fish your clothes out of the bay?" Brian asked.

"You get shit faced and pass out in your truck?" Hughdean snorted. "Remember the weekend you bought it? What was the name of the blonde I met with the legs from here to the sky?"

Brian held up his hand. "Angela, and I'm not in the mood to reminisce about your love life."

He patted the top of his head and spun around to the driver's seat. No note, but the sleeping bag meant Josie was looking after him.

"Last I remember, Josie and I were driving home from the hospital. Must have fallen asleep." He unwrapped the puffy bag and swung his legs out.

Hughdean tugged at the sling hanging from Brian's shoulder. "What's with the arm cradle?"

Brian gently rolled his tender shoulder. The doctor had suggested he sleep in a recliner. He guessed the truck seat counted.

"Dislocated it yesterday."

Hughdean offered him a hand to stand. "Sorry, buddy. Being a hero doesn't come free."

"I'm no hero." He flexed as much as his body would allow and inhaled. The bitter scent of petroleum caught at the back of his throat, and he coughed, sending a throb to his shoulder. *Gonna be a long day.*

"What're you doing here?" Brian said.

"I went looking for you yesterday," Hughdean said. "I found Louise, and she told me you went to fetch Josie and to come by this morning and check on Minnow and Toby. Did you hit your head too?"

Brian rubbed his face. "I'm not sure what I did after we pulled Maisy out."

"The rescue was the talk of the barflies at the Old Salt Bar last night. Smiley gave you your dues. You should consider his offer."

"What offer?"

"Joining the fire department instead of heading back to a rig. You passed the test."

Brian hadn't been looking for fame and honor when he climbed inside Maisy's house. He would have done the same on the Deepwater Horizon when it exploded.

I was at the right place this time. The thought offered him a lift, a feeling he wanted to keep close.

"How's the bar open?" Brian asked.

Hughdean tapped the side of his head. "They dragged a keg into the parking lot and collected picnic tables. Waste not, want not."

Brian squinted toward the brown water, scanning for birds. A milky haze limited the visibility. The sky was empty of seabirds. No gulls, cormorants, skimmers, or pelicans. Minnow knew the seabirds, and by association, he did too. Only one bird mattered now: Gumbo. The area was too quiet. Brian sensed he was still missing.

He patted his shirt and pants pockets. "Got your restaurant keys?"

Hughdean twirled his keys, which hung on a chain attached to his belt loop. "Back door only, but I could break in with a butter knife. When're you changing the lock?"

Brian sighed. "You could help."

Hughdean shrugged. "No one wants anything in the restaurant."

They walked to the back deck. The damage was worse than he'd first thought. The storm surge had washed the lower portion away. What remained reminded Brian of tiger pits covered with debris, waiting for a victim to fall in.

"We can add insurance claims to our BP claims," Hughdean said. "Take a number and stand in line."

"Hugh, it's too early." Brian stomped a plank of decking. His boot splintered it with a *pop*. He yanked the board with his free hand and brandished it like a club. The controlled destruction soothed his annoyance.

He tossed the plank and repositioned his arm, wincing from the activity. He had expected to check on the restaurant, make a few repairs, then return to the house with a bottle of wine and pick up where he and Josie had left off in the kitchen before the house had sprung a leak. Now, his shoulder throbbed like a marching band was holding tryouts in the sling. Nature was extinguishing all his fires.

"What's that light?" Hughdean walked toward the steps to Gumbo's shelter. "C'mere, look down there."

A flashlight leaned against a broken board, its beam weak after running for hours. Josie and Minnow spooned each other in the tiny space. His breath caught in his throat until he saw the steady rise and fall of their chests. They were asleep. This was a welcome change from the weeks of fighting.

Hughdean put his hands on the sides of his mouth to shout down.

Brian knocked them away. "Leave 'em. Can't imagine they're comfortable. Don't shake the Lord out of them. Let's find Toby. He must be inside."

Hughdean's keys jangled as he opened the back door. The light switches clicked, but the island was without power.

"It's dark in here. Better turn the gas on the generator. Fridge is only cold for a day or so."

Brian waved his hand. "Josie used everything perishable, either cooking it into storm meals or sending it home with the staff. The dry goods and canned supplies are fine for weeks."

"Josie's smart about not wasting stuff. Momma used everything but the squeal of the pig."

"Daddy?" Toby stood like a thin shadow on the kitchen threshold and rubbed the side of his face.

"Toby." He held his good arm out to hug him.

Brian forced a relaxed posture, seeing him barefoot in a pair of shorts and a T-shirt, his hair standing straight up. *What was I thinking, leaving them alone?*

"How was the campout?" Hughdean asked.

Toby touched Brian's sling. "What's wrong with your arm?"

"Sore shoulder. I had a doctor examine it yesterday when I got your mom." He moved his arm to demonstrate he was fine and inhaled as a sharp pain shot through his shoulder blade.

Toby frowned. "Where is everyone?"

"Would you believe Mom and Minnow are sleeping in Gumbo's house?"

"Is he home?" His face lit up.

Brian ran a hand over the back of his head. "We didn't see him. Can't tell if he's come back or not."

"What if he doesn't come home? What if he *can't* come home?"

Lying would be easy. Take the positive all-is-well path. Toby was too smart. With the oil fouling the island and the destruction of the storm, raising his hopes was wrong.

"Gumbo's missing. We're here now, and soon everyone will wake up hungry. We need to take care of ourselves so we're focused enough to make a plan." He was out of ideas, but Josie would feed them, and it was always the place to start.

Toby nodded. "Is Maisy hurt?"

"Yes." Concern crawled over his face. "Her leg is broken, and she's worried about where she'll live. She'll be okay. Dr. Tynsdale was with her when we left."

"She can live with Grandpa. Mom's home with us now, and his house is perfect for someone with a bad leg." He turned to Hughdean. "You would look after her, right?"

Is Josie home, or will she leave again?

Hughdean pointed to himself. "Me? Let's not jump ahead of ourselves."

"You look after Grandpa; you could do it."

"You were talking about breakfast." Hughdean headed to the pantry.

"Maisy taught me how to make biscuits." Toby trailed after him.

Brian followed them through the kitchen toward the outside deck door. "Hughdean, start some coffee," he called as he went outside.

Brian tested the first step to the pelican house. The last worry he needed was a broken leg, on top of his shoulder. The steps were secure, and he crouched at the entrance, amazed Minnow and Josie both fit inside.

Brian reached in and rubbed Josie's leg. She kicked, sending him back on his bottom.

"Dammit!"

"Brian? Is that you?" Josie poked her head out. "Oh, gosh. I'm so sorry. Did I hurt you?"

She crawled over to him on the sand. A long braid like a lifeline swung over the front of her shoulder toward him. Her right cheek was red and lined from where she had been sleeping moments ago. He could see down the front of her T-shirt.

"Everything hurts." He pushed himself clumsily with his left hand. She sat next to him and pulled her knees close to her chest.

"Did you sleep? I wrapped you up. I thought it better than waking you."

Brian swiped his hand over his face. "This place's a mess. Please tell me Gumbo is out having an early breakfast."

"I hope he is, but I haven't seen him. I found Minnow asleep when we arrived."

Josie stood and offered Brian a hand. This sore shoulder had already overstayed its welcome.

"Minnow." Josie crawled back inside the pelican house. "Wake up, *chère*."

Minnow crawled out and rushed to Brian. He wrapped his good arm around her.

"Gumbo's missing." She buried her head in his chest. Her body was tight, anxious, like a stretched rubber band. Her breath came in short gulps as she tried not to cry. He looked over her head to the water and sky, willing Gumbo to appear. He'd do anything to keep his baby girl from crying.

A boat motor rumbled to a stop.

"That's Hollis," Josie said.

Hughdean came out the back door. "Coffee's ready. By the ass-dragging looks of all of you, I'll need to make more."

Hollis tied his bay boat to the dock and hopped out.

"Careful, Birdman," Hughdean said. "The deck has holes bigger than your size-thirteen feet."

"Thanks for the warning," Hollis said.

Hollis's face was flat, like someone had unplugged his good humor. He pointed to Brian's arm with a questioning expression. Brian waved him off.

"Uncle Hollis, Gumbo's still gone. No sign of droppings or feathers. I'm worried. Mom and I stayed out here all night," Minnow said.

"In the pelican house? When Brian said you were staying at the restaurant, I expected you to be inside." He shook his head.

"Doesn't matter now. He's not here." Minnow folded her arms.

Hollis pushed out his lower lip and nodded his head. "I was at Queen Bess Island at first light. The nesting grounds are a mess with tar balls and dead wildlife."

"What're you saying?" Josie said.

"I expected Gumbo back by now. Birds don't necessarily roost in the same spot every day, but Gumbo has for two years. And since we've been feeding him, he knows this is where he can eat. All we can do is rely on his past behavior, which would have him here in the morning."

Hollis took a small Moleskine notebook from a pocket of his safari vest.

"Last summer, we had a radio tracker on him." Hollis flipped to a dog-eared page.

"The tracker fell off." Minnow peered over his arm to read his notes.

"Before he lost it, we tracked him to Queen Bess, Beauregard Island, and Elmer's Island. The major pelican colonies." Hollis ran a finger along the entries. "All are close to home, so it makes sense. He was specific about those three spots. My notes say he spent most of the time on Elmer's."

"You think he's there?" Josie asked.

"Maybe. He wasn't on Queen Bess." Hollis scanned the sky, as if Gumbo would reappear. "He's not back. I'm worried."

"We need to search for him." Minnow's chin jutted in a determined angle.

Hollis nodded. "One bird may be hard to find."

"He's not one bird. He's ours," Brian said. A memory of Gumbo as a chick alone and hurt on the beach came to him. He had wrapped him in a towel and removed the fishing hook from his wing as gently as if he were removing it from one of the kids. Gumbo's survival had become a family mission. He wouldn't fail again when it came to his family. The oil spill had hurt so many innocent people, him included.

But now, it was personal. This wasn't about needing a new job or waiting for reparation money. This was life and death. Brian had cheated death by one day, fewer than twelve hours, when the rig blew. Yesterday, he missed being crushed by inches. Gumbo's life was worth whatever effort he could give it.

He turned to Hughdean. "Which boat came through the storm the best?"

"They all did. Who do you think I am?"

Brian shook his head. "We're searching for Gumbo. He responds best to Minnow and Hollis. We'll split up three and three. Can you take Hollis and Toby on the *Big Deal*? She's the fastest. Beauregard Island, right?" He nodded at Hollis for confirmation.

Hollis nodded. "Sure."

"I'll go with Josie and Minnow to Elmer's Island in our bay boat."

"We're seriously hunting for a pelican? You're all nuts. What are the chances we find him?" Hughdean said.

"Maybe none," Brian said.

"We'd hunt for a lost dog," Toby said.

"Doggos don't fly."

"Please, Uncle Hughdean." Minnow sat on his lap and laid her head on his shoulder.

Hughdean kissed the top of her head. He liked to tell the story of how she told him, when she turned seven, that she was a big kid and he shouldn't call her Princess Minnow of the High Seas. She had then leaned in and whispered, "But it's okay when it's the two of us."

"What's the plan?" Hughdean said.

Hollis flipped through his notes. "We'll start with his last locations and then Grand Terre Island, Mendicant, a dozen sand bars along the way, even Raccoon Island. But we're not there yet."

"What do we do if we find him and he's hurt?" Toby asked.

"I've got animal carriers in my truck. And we can radio each other if we find him."

"How will we know Gumbo from the other thousand pelicans?" Hughdean said.

"Minnow and I'll know," Hollis said.

"Where's your truck?" Brian asked Hollis.

"At Louise's office."

Josie tossed Brian's keys to Hollis. "Grab those carriers and meet us back here."

Chapter 26

"How long does it take to drive four miles?" Minnow paced on the restaurant's front porch.

"Hollis will be here in a few minutes. Do we have what we need?" Josie asked.

Minnow threw her an are-you-kidding stare and kicked two packed duffel bags. They had enough provisions to rescue an entire pelican pod if necessary.

"I should've gone for him yesterday," Minnow said. "I'll wait for you out back." She grabbed a bag and left.

They could hear her faint whistling for Gumbo.

Josie held her hands in a prayer pose. "Do you think we'll find him?"

Brian looked over his shoulder. "Honestly, no. But we won't stop trying. And before you ask, it wouldn't have mattered if we searched yesterday, or the moment the storm stopped."

I'm the one who always says he needs to be free. We should've sheltered him. This is my fault.

Josie took his hand and squeezed it. "I agree, but if we had—"

"I see the truck. Louise is here too." Brian went to meet them across the street.

Louise parked and pulled two animal carriers from the back seat of the cab. Hollis carried two more.

Louise marched across the street, her blonde ponytail swinging with purpose and the carriers flanking her sides. They met her on the front porch.

"Hollis told me about your shoulder," she said to Brian. "Does it hurt bad?"

"Like a son of a bitch, but I made out better than Maisy." He hugged his arm close to his side.

"Climbing in was the most selfless act I've ever witnessed."

"The in part was easy. The out was the hard part." He patted the bent arm resting in the sling.

Brian never admitted anything was wrong. *He must really hurt.*

"Don't be frowny when you see me," Louise said to Josie. She wore an oversize faded olive-green shirt rolled to the elbows. A tiny notebook and pen peeked out of the breast pocket. Her version of military readiness.

"What? No, I'm not. I'm happy you're here." She hugged Louise.

"What's this?" Josie pointed to the notebook.

"My emergency numbers. The only comms we can rely on is the marine radio. I thought I'd stay and serve as your personal Coast Guard."

"Louise to the rescue. You won't be alone; Bonnie and Jake are here to help with the cleanup."

"Enough with the chitchat," Hollis said.

Louise stuck her tongue out at him.

"Where's Minnow?"

Her whistle sounded again from the back deck.

Hollis turned to Brian. "If you find him, or any bird in need of help, put them in the carrier and radio me. Don't overhandle him. Even if he's fine, he'll be skittish."

Josie shared a knowing look with Brian. This was a Hail Mary mission. Two boats on a search and rescue mission for oiled birds after a storm. If only they could print lost pelican posters and float them on the water like a lost dog sign. Do not chase, do not feed, handle with extreme caution.

Brian rested his forehead against Josie's. "We'll try."

Holes in the roof, holes in the floor, holes in the ocean. So much to fill, and Josie was running on empty.

Minnow handed Josie and Brian life vests and began to help Brian thread his arm through and buckle it. "I'll drive."

Josie stepped back. Despite the emotions flooding Minnow, she was calm, acting with purpose. She really could take care of herself, maybe not in all aspects of her life, but this young woman was becoming a force.

"Hang on," Josie said quietly. Minnow drove the boat like she owned the ocean. She navigated the surrounding waters as well as any fisherman. They were barely sitting before she gunned the motor toward Elmer's Island.

"Slow down, Minnow," Brian said. "We need to investigate any pelicans out here. Maybe he was ready to return to the wild."

She glared at him as if he had insulted her. "No."

They bumped over the water, Minnow only slightly easing on the throttle.

"I appreciate Louise monitoring the marine radio," Josie said.

"Not much work for her to do. Chief Tibbs is patrolling. Smiley is clearing the streets. The power outage is the main problem. Louise needs to stay busy," Brian said.

In the distance, an oil rig blinked bright red and blue lights. The crew was back, though the drilling moratorium continued.

How strange to be on the rig with oil from BP swirling around your legs. Josie looked over the side of the boat as they skipped over waves. "The water's clear. The storm did some good."

"Minnow, I see a pod. Slow down and whistle. We might get lucky," Brian said. He scanned the area with a pair of binoculars.

Minnow slowed the boat, the roar turning into a purr with a frothy churn of water kicked behind them. The group of seven pelicans bobbed lazily on the Gulf.

Minnow whistled twice, and they didn't move or turn their heads.

"He's not there." She gunned the motor before they could agree.

Of course he's not here. I didn't listen to Minnow. I left him alone in the storm.

The boat motor roared in her ears. The rising humidity made the oil's tang cling inside her nose, and the salt spray hit her face and stung her eyes. The sound rushed louder. The boat skipped hard over the waves. She flung herself to the edge and vomited.

"Minnow, ease up on the throttle. Your mom's seasick," Brian said.

Minnow turned around, a mixture of determination and annoyance flashing in her eyes, but she slowed the boat.

"You okay?" Brian asked.

Josie shook her head, still feeling sick. She turned her back on Minnow. "We're not going to find him, are we?"

"He's territorial. He'll fly to a safe place," Brian said.

"I let this happen. My speeches that he should be free. He needed me. This wasn't another storm. The oil spill changed everything." Josie flexed her scarred palm.

"Hollis checked him twice the night before. We did everything we could."

"I didn't do enough to protect him."

"Josie, what are you talking about?" He put an arm around her to steady her as Minnow urged the boat closer to Elmer's Island.

"Brian, this place just cuts deeper and deeper. I can't stand any more scars. I don't have any fight left."

She bent forward, her head between her knees. The rolling waves shook her resolve. A helplessness had planted inside her.

"You're hurt, Maisy's hurt, Minnow's sick, Gumbo . . . it's all too much. I spent my whole life wanting to leave all the hurt this place heaped on me. I am as dumb as my mother always said. I came back, and it's hitting me again. And now, I'm trying to fight nature? I was never strong enough then, and I'm not strong enough now."

Brian grabbed her hand. "That's a lie. When're you going to forgive the girl who took her mother's tongue-lashings? That girl became a strong woman. I watched you grow up and change the course of your life. You needed to leave the island the way I needed to leave Baton Rouge. I saw it burning in your eyes. You made it happen."

"What good is that now? I'm powerless again, right back where I started." She searched his face.

Brian steadied her shoulder as Minnow gunned the motor. "The last few days have been frantic. Heck, the last few years. You've kept us all together. And not just us, but everyone at the restaurant. The girl you once were wouldn't have been strong enough to do that. The woman who came home from California, now she had something—ideas, and passion, and power."

"I don't feel powerful."

"I've loved you for as long as I can remember. The first time we kissed. That passion was so intense, it scared me. Then I let you go. I didn't want to be your summer fling. It was either all or nothing for me. I wanted you to feel the freedom I felt when I left home."

He traced the scar on her palm. "This doesn't define you. None of it does. And don't think your stitches and bruises went unnoticed. I heard the gossip from the adults who traded stories of your pain but did nothing to stop it." He stared out at the water rushing past them. "Everyone has scars. Don't let these shape who you are and who you can become."

"I'm not defined by my scars." She yanked her hand away and curled it into a protective fist. "I should've never come back from California. Life's too hard here."

"Then you wouldn't have us." He nodded toward Minnow, now slowing and holding the binoculars to her eyes, scanning the water.

He laced his fingers with hers. "Look at our daughter. She's a fighter. You taught her that. Maybe you needed to leave so you could find your way back, on your terms." He placed her palm against his cheek. "Louise told me recently this was the reason she became a lawyer."

"We're here," Minnow shouted over the motor. She cut the engine, and they floated to the island.

The barrier island was a long, skinny stretch of beach a few feet above sea level and shaped like a gnarled hook, with a maze of channels sliced through and around it.

"Minnow, cut through the shallow channel that runs through the marsh. We can see a lot of the island from there," Brian said.

Josie shivered despite the heat. Shredded vegetation and apple-size oil blobs tangled in the standing seagrasses. Would dead birds be scattered in the tide pools and oil-soaked nesting sites? Would one of them be Gumbo?

The boat made a rumbling purr as Minnow guided it, like a stalking cat, through the marsh. She whistled. The notes evaporated in the wind.

High cirrus clouds skipped across the sky. The island was desolate.

Minnow turned in a circle and scanned the sky. Her sunglasses and hat shielded her expression but didn't hide the hunch of her shoulders or the quiver of her mouth that prevented her from whistling again.

"This is stupid. He can fly. He won't be standing on a rock waving an SOS sign." She sat on the boat bench and cried.

"You're right," Josie said. It was the only truth she had. She couldn't let Minnow feel helpless. She had felt it her whole life. It wouldn't be her legacy. "If we don't try, we'll never forgive ourselves. Other birds may need help."

Minnow sniffed hard and stood. "The nesting sites are close. It won't take long to search."

As they gathered their gear, the marine radio squawked to life.

"*Pelican Runner, Pelican Runner, Pelican Runner.* This is Odeal's Restaurant. Over."

Josie scrambled for the radio.

"Odeal's Restaurant, Odeal's Restaurant, Odeal's Restaurant, this is *Pelican Runner.* Over."

"Switch and listen to channel seventy-one. Over."

"Switching to channel seventy-one. Out."

Josie switched the channel. "That's Louise."

They all leaned closer to hear her.

"Thank goodness I found you."

"What's wrong?" Josie said.

"Gumbo's here. He jumped on the deck and scrambled under an umbrella table."

Minnow grabbed the radio. "Is he okay?"

"He's not, *chère*. A fishing line's wrapped around his beak, and he's dirty, spreading his wings like they're laundry he's airing out."

"Is he bleeding? What do his wings look like? Oh God. Oh God." Minnow's eyes pleaded with Josie and Brian.

Brian held his hand for the radio. "Louise, can you cut the fishing line?"

"We tried, but he lunges at us. The line is snagged on his nasty hook bill."

Our poor chick. He must be so scared.

Minnow shook, her body causing the boat to shimmy with her anxiety. Her breathing increased, and her skin paled.

"Minnow!" Josie moved her to the center of the boat. "Focus on me. He's back. That's good. We'll save him." It was a lie at worst, magical thinking at best.

It's not a lie. It's hope, and that's all we have.

Josie took the radio. "Give him space to calm down, and don't let him leave. We're heading back. *Pelican Runner* out."

"*Pelican Runner, Pelican Runner, Pelican Runner.* This is the *Big Deal*, message heard, heading back to the marina. And we found an oiled pelican. Out."

Minnow started the boat. "Hang on."

Josie tossed the boat's line to Toby's outstretched arms on the restaurant deck. He guided the boat in as Minnow ping-ponged in her haste to dock. She jumped from the boat, with Josie and Brian on her heels.

Louise stood behind Hollis, who now crouched near the table, talking softly to Gumbo. Toby and Hughdean crouched around the other side.

"How did you land here before us?" Josie asked.

"Faster boat," Hughdean said.

Minnow scrambled under the table. Brian grabbed her waistband and hauled her back. "Whoa, he's jumpy."

"He's not afraid of me." Minnow struggled free.

"Brian's right." Hollis joined her at eye level. "I'd rather he came to you."

"I've got wire clippers for the fishing line." Hughdean squeezed the tool in his hand.

"Y'all give him space. Minnow, whistle for him," Hollis said.

The crowd moved away from the table, no longer shading the area from the sun, leaving Minnow in a spotlight. Sweat plastered her hair to her face. She crawled back and sat on her heels. Her knees bled from the rough, busted boards. She stuck two fingers in her mouth and whistled.

"Come on, handsome, we're here to help you," she whispered.

Gumbo skirted out from under the table, leaning heavily on his longer wing. His body was a dark-red matted mess, and his yellow crown of feathers stood straight up in an oily Mohawk.

The humid air and blowing wind carried a rank smell like food rotting in a hot dumpster. It was Gumbo. As if he couldn't stand his own stench, he shook his head and sneezed. The fishing line coiled tight around his beak. He flexed and shook again to shake it off. A high-pitched warble erupted from his throat. Was it his equivalent of a death rattle? Would he die a miserable death, bound by a lazy fisherman's cast-off line? This was the hubris of a behemoth multinational company that considered the oil spill within its risk tolerance.

The group moved back, never having heard that sound from Gumbo or any pelican before.

"Oh" escaped from Minnow. "Dad, help him."

Josie stood behind Minnow with a protective hand on her shoulder. She nodded at Brian, just as she had the moment before he climbed in after Maisy.

Would Gumbo strike at them, attempt to fly off? Did he have the strength? Now no longer penned under the table, he waddled to Minnow, then to Hollis, and then to Brian, where he stopped and dipped his head from side to side.

"That's his hello," Josie said. "I think he knows you can untangle him."

Brian slipped the sling off his shoulder and handed it to Josie.

"Hey, big fellow. Got yourself in an oily mess," Brian spoke softly.

He dropped to his knees and took a cautious step forward. Gumbo moved backward and lifted one leg, his head down in a charging stance.

Brian held out the clippers. "See this. Shiny. It won't hurt you."

Gumbo lowered his leg, spread his sticky wings, and toppled, unsteady on one side.

Brian nodded to Hollis to move behind Gumbo.

"Josie's gonna get a towel, and Hollis will catch and hold you while I cut off that nasty string." He kept his voice steady and calm. "Minnow's staying right here where you can see her. Y'all ready? One, two, three."

Hollis grabbed Gumbo, and he beat his sticky wings in the air. Josie wrapped his oil-soaked body in the towel. Hollis caught Gumbo's long bill and held it while Brian cut the fishing line and unwound it, from his hook to the middle of his throat pouch.

"Got it!" Brian held the knotted line and scurried away from the now thrashing bird. Josie released him, and Gumbo clicked his beak open and closed and shook his head, testing that he was free.

Bonnie and Jake applauded. Gumbo spread his wings and waddled to Minnow.

"He's trying to dry out," she said to Hollis, her voice breaking.

Hollis sat beside her. "Yes, but he never will. The oil has matted his feathers. If he starts to preen, he'll swallow it."

Josie stood to the side, an alarm sounding in her head. Gumbo needed help. Minnow's face was a map of pain. Her eyes fixated on him, and her hands shook, unable to comfort him or clean him. Minnow had never lost anyone close to her. They had never had a traditional pet who succumbed to old age and had to be put down. These emotions and thoughts were new to her. They were new to Josie too.

"What about the other pelican in the pet carrier in the shade?" Toby said.

Josie snapped out of her daze and peered inside. This bird had the same strong odor, mixed with a muskiness Josie couldn't describe, but it made her shiver. *Fear.*

"Poor baby. They rescued you and then left you."

Minnow knelt beside Gumbo, her shirt and shorts splotchy with the sticky crude oil and her knees bleeding.

"We can't do any more for them," Josie said. "But we have to find help for them, fast."

Hollis blew out a long breath and scrolled through his phone.

"We have phone service?" Josie said.

Hollis nodded. "Came on as we drove in."

Hollis held his phone to his ear. "I'm looking for Sarah Myers."

Josie leaned against a table, allowing it to support her. She thanked Bonnie and Jake for their help. They were decent people who cared about each other. This was how Brian felt about the crew on the rig. An odd family who worked together. Pelican rescue was not part of their job description.

"Okay, everyone." Hollis slipped his phone into his vest. "That was my friend at the International Bird Rescue. We're bringing the birds to the Fort Jackson rescue facility in Buras."

"What'll happen to Gumbo?" Fear crept into Minnow's voice.

Josie paced a small track around the outside tables. Sending him out of their care felt like letting him down.

"They'll be evaluated by a veterinarian, and usually after resting, they're cleaned."

"They need to be cleaned now," Minnow said.

"Their bodies are in shock, and they need to rest. They have to be strong enough to recover from the cleaning or it could kill them. The vets will take care of them."

"But you're a bird expert," Minnow said.

"I'm not a vet."

"What are we arguing about? Let's go," Brian said.

Josie held both hands up. "Everyone, take a second. We look like we've been oiled. The crude's dangerous to us too. We need to clean up. It'll take us three hours to drive to Buras."

"They could die in three hours." Minnow pulled over the pet carrier and grabbed the remaining clean towels. "Why're y'all standing there? Get what you need, and we're leaving."

"I'm ready," Toby said.

Louise waved her phone in the air. "Wait, everyone. I pulled the mayor card. Mel at Hello Helicopter Tours can fly the birds to the wildlife center."

"Not without me," Minnow said.

"Mel agreed to Hollis and the birds," Louise said.

Minnow wiped her hands on a towel. "I'm not leaving Gumbo again. Uncle Hollis needs help with two birds."

"We'll follow in the car," Josie said.

"You just said that'll take three hours. The roads are a mess. I'm flying with Gumbo," Minnow said.

"You've never even flown on an airplane, and you expect me to let you strap in a helicopter?" Josie said.

"Dad flies all the time." Minnow stood with her hands on her hips.

A familiar coldness coiled around Josie's middle, a reminder of the long nights she waited to hear Brian was safe as he hurtled through the Gulf sky.

"Mom, we need to be Gumbo's wings. If we don't help him now, he may never fly again," Minnow said.

It had been weeks since Josie ran on the beach with Gumbo tracking above her, pushing her to move faster. With the sand beneath her feet and his shadow floating above, she had worked out her sadness and anger and made plans for the future. During the day, she had visited him on the deck and talked to him about hot peppers and problems with the restaurant. He had no answers, but he was always there for her.

Josie shook her head. The oil was taking everything. She wouldn't risk her Minnow.

Gumbo attempted to preen his tail feathers and spread his wings wide to dry the sludge on his body. With his feathers matted, the difference in the wings' lengths was easy to discern. They looked like shaggy sticks. He settled with a clumsy plop onto the ground. His head swiveled, taking in his surroundings. Was he capturing a final memory of his family?

"Mom," Minnow said.

"Is it safe?" Josie asked Brian.

Minnow wasn't scared of the world the way Josie had been at her age. Josie had made sure nothing held the kids back. They could try for anything, become their own people. This was Minnow, fearless and determined.

"Mel's an experienced pilot," Brian said. "This is important to her and for Gumbo. We'll follow behind and meet in a few hours."

Josie rubbed her scar with her thumb, and Brian took her hand. *I can't define her by my fears.*

Josie nodded, afraid if she spoke, she'd lose her nerve.

Minnow and Toby coaxed Gumbo into the carrier, speaking soft words of encouragement.

"I'd never let anything harm her," Hollis said.

"Go, before I change my mind." She couldn't believe this was happening. Minnow was about to climb into a helicopter.

Brian offered Hollis his hand. "Keep my baby girl safe."

Hollis pulled him in for a hug, an unlikely gesture between them. Brian's back stiffened; then he patted Hollis's back.

Twenty years. Guess relationships move slow around here, but they do move.

Josie caught Louise's eye, and she smiled.

"Are you coming to Buras?" Josie asked Louise.

She shook her head. "I can't. But I'll find a place for y'all to stay for the night. I'll drive in tomorrow."

Hughdean and Hollis each carried a bird to Hollis's truck.

Minnow hugged Brian and Josie. "See you soon."

They watched until the truck was a speck on the road. Would Gumbo even survive the day?

Brian turned to Josie. "You can't come with us."

"Of course I'm coming." Josie pointed toward where the truck had been. "You can't drive that distance with your sore shoulder."

Brian dug his fingers in his hair. "You have to head to New Orleans to set up the booth."

"I'll drive with you and Toby and come home early tomorrow. Jake and Bonnie can come with me and—"

Her head throbbed. The logistics of setting up the booth and running a team who were unprepared smacked her again, as before in the boat. She sat on the busted deck. Her jumble of thoughts and the rush of emotions since the storm landed brought fresh doubt. She wrapped her arms around her middle.

Too much, too much.

"Hey." Brian rubbed her back. "I've got this."

She brushed off his hand. "Stop. You don't have *anything*. Nothing works."

Brian was wrong. Part of her would always be the girl who her mother said talking to was like talking to a stump, barely able to stand on her own feet.

"This competition is my stupid gamble. You don't bet against the house." She leaned back on her hands and threw her head to the sky. "Nature's the house."

He stepped back at her scolding. "Okay, miss know-it-all, what do you want to do, since you don't need my help?" Brian's voice was angry.

The restaurant's back door snapped open, and Toby and Hughdean stood quiet. Hughdean opened his mouth to speak.

"Not a word from you," Josie said in a growl. She wouldn't tolerate his mean-spirited jabs and sarcasm at overhearing her argument with Brian. How he loved to kick her when she was down.

"Mom, Dad, are we ready?" Toby asked. Next to Hughdean's long frame, he appeared younger than his eleven years. Her son, her daughter, Gumbo, Brian. Everything was out of proportion.

"Ah, well—" Josie stuttered and pressed her palms over her eyes. "Let's clean up and drive to Buras."

She wrapped her arms around Toby and kissed the top of his head.

"What're you doing?" Brian asked.

Brian may have forgotten the promise they made to be better parents than theirs, but she hadn't. It wasn't a meaningless middle-of-the-night romantic gesture she had made.

Growing up, she had a shortage of grown-ups who plain loved her in the it-doesn't-matter-if-you're-ugly-on-the-outside-or-the-inside way. Josie had plenty of days she felt ugly on the inside. Odeal's last words before Josie left for California were "Don't embarrass yourself." When she returned, Hughdean called her a carpetbagger. And Daniel Dean, well, his silence said everything she needed to know.

She was proud of Minnow, and she would not send her off to face life's hardest challenges alone, and she would not be silent.

"I made damn good hot sauce, but it doesn't come close to the kid I made. I need to see her win. And if we lose Gumbo, she'll know I saw her try."

"Are you sure? I promised Maisy," Brian said.

She swallowed the lump forming in her throat. "Maisy would tell me to go. She's the real reason I put up the **DO NOT FEED THE PELICAN** sign. She's the biggest offender."

Hughdean stood behind Toby. "Do *you* have to be at the booth or the show to win?"

"Technically, not me, but someone representing Odeal's or I'm disqualified."

Josie thought back to the *Vacation Ventures* article and the *Kitchen Network* taping. *National marketing tours are overrated.*

"Can't you call and explain everything?" Toby asked.

"I can, and I'm sure they'll be sympathetic, but seven other professional teams will be there and are ready. They won't wait for me."

"I'll go," Hughdean said. "I'll take Dad. He's a charmer. Heck, Rosaline can come too. We'll spin a story about old family Cajun traditions with our geezer family."

Josie was speechless. Hughdean never offered to help without being begged, bribed, or browbeaten.

"Hughdean, I don't—"

"I know as much about those sauces as anyone, and I'm part of this family too. I own a third of the restaurant. We may not win a fancy food deal, but we'll stand strong and represent Grand Isle."

He looked around.

"The island's an oily stink hole, but we don't quit here. You're a better cook than Momma. You've made this place into a reason to come to the island. Besides, I want twenty percent of what I sell."

"We're not going to the competition?" Toby's eyes widened in concern, and his mouth hung open.

Hughdean was revved for a fight, but for the first time, it wasn't directed at her. It was to protect her.

"Uncle Hughdean can set up the booth for us. Then we can take care of Gumbo. He came home because he's hurt and needs our help. We're his family," Josie said.

Toby nodded.

"This summer isn't following my plan. I'm changing it," Josie said. *Or maybe plans are changing me.*

"Uncle Hughdean, put the sauces in the display before you turn on the light or it's too bright and will blind you. Turn the labels so you can read 'em or it looks messy." Toby screwed his face in thought. "And we had a surprise for Mom, an LED blackboard. Make sure it says 'Vote for the people's choice award.'"

"You got that?" Brian asked Hughdean. "I made a construction plan and packed the tools in the garden shed."

"Yeah, I think I can manage it," Hughdean said.

A steady breeze brought a fresh surge of petrochemicals, reminding Josie their health was at stake here too. "We need clean clothes. Hughdean, I can't—"

"Don't make this weird. Take care of my Princess Minnow of the High Seas and that goofy bird."

Chapter 27

"I see the Fort Jackson sign." Brian pointed to the left.

Five years ago, the eye of Hurricane Katrina made its first landfall in Buras, and its windy legs kicked this community like a can. Close to a million gallons of oil spilled there during that storm, and now this community, like Grand Isle, winced from new oil. No matter where they went, the oil industry smothered them. How shortsighted for the bird rescue to be in the hurricane zone, but Brian didn't make the rules. Common sense, stress, and government decisions often didn't align.

The potholed road taunted his shoulder, despite the painkillers and ice they had found at a gas station along the way.

"What did Maisy say when you told her about the Ragin' Cajun?" Brian asked. Josie had called her when they had stopped.

Josie changed her grip on the steering wheel. "She was really quiet, then she busted out laughing. Said with the way our luck was running, we couldn't do worse with Hughdean representing us. He does have a financial interest in the restaurant."

"Are you okay not being there?"

She shook her head. "No. It's like racing to the airport and missing your flight when you're the pilot. This was a big flight to miss. A lot of people were counting on me. In the mess of this oil, it gave us some control. Toby is so proud to have built the booth with you. People came by the restaurant just to try the new sauce and give me their opinion and cheer on the hometown gals."

The truck stuttered over another pothole, and Brian grimaced and supported his sore arm. They were exhausted.

Josie's hair bounced in a high ponytail like Louise often wore. Maybe she was channeling Louise's never-take-no-for-an-answer attitude.

"I bet we can make it to New Orleans before the competition's over," Brian said.

"Thought you gave up gambling?"

"Right, not my best choice of words." His face heated, and he stared out the passenger window.

He breathed deeply to release his rising anger. Not every word Josie said was an indictment of his behavior.

"What I meant to say is—"

"I appreciate your cheering, but I made this choice. I've learned stuff about myself," Josie said.

"Yeah?"

She nodded. "My heart can only be in one place at a time. When I left Grand Isle for culinary school, that was where my heart needed to be. Even Momma's cancer wasn't enough for me to come back. So, I didn't."

"You did come home."

She nodded deeply. "For the funeral. My heart was with Daniel Dean. Then you knocked on my gazebo—" She glanced at Brian. "I could've asked you to move to Texas or done the long-distance dance for a while. I had choices. I considered bunches of them. I sat with Louise on the beach and talked her ears off for hours. My life, our life, would be way easier had I taken even one of them. Your heart was here, and my heart said stay. Take the restaurant, build a life with you, care for Daddy. One heart in one place. You and Grand Isle."

Me and Grand Isle. And I went and messed it up. I took away her space to keep growing.

She drove silently. "Then Minnow came, changing everything I thought I knew about love."

"You already loved me," he said with a tease.

"I still do." She sighed and reached for his hand.

Brian swallowed a lump in his throat. She hadn't said she loved him in over a year. Though now she frowned. Was she ready to let him go?

"The moment I held her, my heart about burst. I'll never know, but I don't think Momma ever wanted me. I was terrified I wouldn't love Minnow, or worse, want her. Love's real scary when you learn backward and don't know how to handle the feelings. I still don't."

"My mom's no prize either."

"I agree, and she married a skunk. But"—she tapped her finger on the steering wheel—"she does love you."

"Daniel Dean adores you."

"He was really sick when we were kids. He barely spoke above a whisper for two years after his big stroke. I loved him the way you love a grandparent who lives in a nursing home in another state. He didn't make real improvement until I started high school."

"And now?" Where was this conversation headed?

Toby mumbled in his sleep in the back seat.

She wiped her cheek with her sleeve and cleared her throat.

"I can't be grandstanding at the Ragin' Cajun with Minnow and Gumbo hurting. One heart in one place with my family."

He and Josie had lain awake one night watching Josie's pregnant belly shake. He was young and scared witless about becoming a dad. They didn't have a huge extended family to help and had barely enough money to take care of themselves. They had hooked their pinkies and promised to be better parents than their parents. Maybe they overcorrected. Josie practically rolled the kids in foam to keep them safe.

"What's it feel like, inside?" Brian had asked, his voice serious.

She placed his hand on her belly. "Like I swallowed a bucket of squirming minnows."

But for all his fear and her overmothering, she had insisted they learn to swim, drive a boat, learn to cook, and respect the power of the ocean. The way Minnow handled herself today was proof they hadn't completely blown it as parents.

He wanted to see his children grow into the people they wanted to be, not the people the world forced them to be.

"I'm sorry how Minnow's treated you these past months," Brian said.

Josie's eyebrows pulled into a question. "Why are you sorry? She's her own person."

"I let her think our troubles were your fault." He turned to check if Toby was sleeping. "I was mad at you for leaving me. I didn't correct her when she was upset, saying you left them too. Toby had a different attitude. He hated packing his bags for the shift to Daniel Dean's, but he said his bad dreams stopped when he was there."

Josie's hand went to her mouth, and her other hand gripped the wheel tight. "He never told me that." Her voice broke with tears.

"I'm sorry I didn't tell you. He needed you, and I said—" He stared out the window. "I said something awful that my mother once said to me." He shook his head. "I told him bad situations cause bad feelings and that they work out. She never helped me work anything out. And I didn't tell Toby I caused the bad situation."

Brian felt the truck speed up, Josie pushing hard to make it to Minnow. Her eyes, rimmed red, flicked to the rearview mirror to see Toby.

"Being their dad is easy; being their father is hard. I can love on them and spoil them. But I don't always know how to correct them and teach them how to navigate the rough patches."

Josie chewed on her bottom lip but said nothing.

Questions he wanted to ask her zipped through his brain. He didn't know when he'd have her attention like this again.

It's now or suffer. "*Chère*, I need to know if I have to learn to be their father by myself or if I'm going to be their dad with you." His heart pounded in his chest, and he shook. This was a fear wholly different from what he had felt, crawling after Maisy. Josie would be better off without him. He wouldn't be better without her. But he'd try and work hard to be the type of father he'd always wanted.

She drove, silent.

"Well?"

A grin spread across her face. "During a negotiation, the person who speaks first loses."

"I didn't think we were negotiating anything."

"Couples are always dancing. Fighting for space." She sighed. "I don't know what I want from you."

Ouch! Brian's fist bounced on his leg. Maybe he deserved that. Dammit, he knew what he wanted. He had asked her to come home. She'd said yes. Wasn't that enough? But that was while she was moving toward her dream. Now she was moving toward Buras and what they hoped was a living and flying pelican.

"I'd appreciate your decision."

"Gosh, Brian. I'm not your judge and jury."

Feels like you are. Where had he lost his control? He and Josie had been on track until . . . Brian couldn't say, exactly. Until he grew lonely? Impatient? Until his jealousy of her success made him shrink? Poker put him in charge. When he won, when people watched him play a hand and even bet on his play, the high was too much to give up. Until he couldn't stop. The urge to escape into that world, the invincible rush of winning, circled his head like a buzzard.

Every hour of every day.

The truck jostled over a speed bump, and he flinched.

"The building's ahead." Josie pointed.

Toby stirred and opened the window. A burst of warm, briny air flowed inside. Buras smelled like Grand Isle from the oil.

"Welcome back, buddy. Did you have a good nap?" Josie asked, her voice cheerful in a way neither of them felt.

She drove past people dressed in T-shirts and jeans, wearing tall rubber boots. Several carried buckets and clustered by a hose bibb, rinsing equipment.

"Over there, Minnow!" Toby pointed from the back seat.

Josie reversed the truck and opened the window.

"Minnow," she called.

"Mom, Dad, Toby."

Josie parked and ran to her, then held her tight. Minnow was as tall as her. When did that happen? These two women, these two hearts who'd had a wall between them for too long.

Josie looked over Minnow's head to Brian. They registered the same dark thought. Where was Gumbo?

Minnow pulled away and rubbed the tears off her face.

"The little pelican's really sick. The vet says the oil shock can be too much, and they won't recover. It's worse than seeing the dead birds on Elmer's Island."

"Minnow," Toby said, his voice barely audible. "Where's Gumbo?"

"He's, he's . . ." Her voice stuttered. "Not doing well."

A woman with red cheeks streaked in grime and with blonde frizzy hair escaping from a ball cap came over.

"Hi, y'all," she said.

Minnow turned to her. "Sarah, these're my parents, Josie and Brian, and my brother, Toby. Sarah Myers is Uncle Hollis's friend. They've been teaching me to clean the birds."

Sarah gave Minnow a side hug. "She's a natural. The day's been rough. We lost a few today. We celebrate the ones we save."

"Where's Gumbo now?" Brian asked.

"With the vet. If he stabilizes overnight, we'll clean him in the morning," Sarah said.

"Sarah says I can help," Minnow said, a bright note in her voice.

Brian hated idle time, waiting for hours to pass for a body to respond to what? In this case, a pelican body. What would time do for Gumbo? He could tell what Sarah wasn't saying. Gumbo could die as the other birds had. But not tonight or tomorrow. Gumbo had come home for help, and they owed him that.

"*Chère*, where's Uncle Hollis?" Josie asked.

"In the aviary, where the birds recover after they're cleaned. I'll show you." Minnow opened the back door and slid in beside Toby.

"Where will Gumbo sleep tonight?" Toby asked.

"In a warehouse room with a pool inside."

Minnow sighed and clicked her seat belt.

The bigger question was, Would he survive to the morning?

At 11:30 p.m. Josie hugged Toby and pulled the blanket to his chin. "Will you be okay here? I can stay." They were emotionally and physically tapped out, but after learning he was having bad dreams, she didn't want to leave him alone.

His head bobbed, and he mumbled. Then his eyes closed like a baby's who drifts off without control. She kissed him and smoothed his hair.

Thankfully, Buras had electricity, and the hotel air conditioner wheezed on with a rumble, but the noise wouldn't keep them awake.

Josie moved to sit next to Minnow on the other bed. Her hair hung damp from a shower.

"I'm happy to be out of my grimy clothes," Minnow said.

Josie pushed a lock of wet hair away from Minnow's eyes and whispered, "Today, I'm grateful the most amazing woman I've ever met is my daughter."

Minnow draped her arms around Josie's neck with the hug Josie remembered from when Minnow was a girl. The hug she hadn't had from her daughter in a long time. The hug that made staying here and not going to New Orleans the only decision worth making.

"Do you think Gumbo will be okay?" Minnow asked.

Josie learned from Hollis the survival rate for oiled birds was dicey. So many conditions mattered. All out of their control. The little pelican wasn't responding to treatment, but her chances were higher with trained caretakers.

"I hope so. I believe staying here with him helps," Josie said.

Before they'd left the facility for the night, they'd peeked into the holding pen. Gumbo sat resting in a corner, his long neck close to his body. The vet let Minnow feed him, encouraged by how he responded to her. Tomorrow would be the test to see how he recovered after the cleaning.

"You know what?" Josie said.

Minnow shook her head.

"You'd make a great vet."

"I thought you wanted me to major in business and take over your restaurant empire."

Josie shrugged and took her hands in hers.

There may not be an empire after this weekend. "A lot of people can run a company, but the way you handle animals is special. You can become a bird specialist and work at a zoo or a rescue center. You have a gift, and you'll find the right way to use it."

Minnow hugged her again, her eyes filling with tears, but they didn't spill over.

"We all need sleep," Josie said.

Toby mumbled again, and they looked over at him, face down in his pillow.

"Does he always talk in his sleep?"

Minnow chuckled. "Yes. But it never makes any sense."

She grew serious. "Uncle Hollis said they'll evaluate the birds in the morning around eight. If they're okay, they'll clean them."

"Does the cleaning hurt?" Josie asked.

"I helped with two today. They certainly don't like the treatment. Then they need to dry and rest."

Minnow sniffed and wiped her eyes with the sheet. "I heard Uncle Hollis talking to Sarah. Gumbo's really hurt. What if he dies?"

"We won't think like that. We flew him here as fast as we could."

"What if it's not enough?"

What do I tell her? "No matter what happens, we'll be with him."

Minnow snuggled into the pillow.

"Sleep now," Josie said.

Minnow nodded. "Good night."

Josie and Brian shared a room across the hall. She unlocked the door, wanting a space to quiet her mind and her emotions. Brian's latest confession about Toby upset her. Yet she understood. In their early days, they talked about their families and what they missed and wanted. Having Minnow so young made them grow up. But it didn't make them grow wiser.

Brian sat in a chair, watching TV. He turned it off when she walked in. He had said his good night to them early and left to ice his shoulder.

"Kids okay?"

She collapsed in a chair. "Toby immediately fell asleep, and Minnow is probably asleep now too."

"I found us a nightcap in honor of being in Buras, the citrus capital of Louisiana." He held up a carton of orange juice and poured it into two wineglasses. "Sorry about the inappropriate stemware."

Josie laughed. Brian knew she liked her drinks in the right glasses. It tasted better.

"You're the bartender. If you say it's okay, I'm happy. This is nice."

They clinked glasses.

"Louise called earlier. She'll be here around nine tomorrow," Brian said.

"That's near when we were going back to the rescue."

Brian emptied his glass and gestured to the carton for a refill.

"No, thanks, this is perfect."

"With Louise here, we'll have two cars. It's less than two hours to New Orleans and the competition," Brian said.

New Orleans felt like another planet. "Not until I know about Gumbo and if Minnow is okay. What do we do if we lose him?"

"Don't—"

"I'm being honest." She swirled the juice in her glass.

"Let's try for hopeful this time. This is one of those hard situations we will face as a family. If he dies, we will not hide those messy emotions. We will grieve like when people lose a pet. Though he's not a pet."

"No," Josie said. "He's so much more." A fresh sting of tears threatened, but she wouldn't allow them.

Brian's face was half in shadow from the table lamp. He stood. "I'm ready to turn in."

Decision time. The house, with its larger, familiar space, was easier. The intimacy of a hotel was, well, intimate. She used to love hotels with Brian, pretend hideaways far from the problems of the day, even for an evening's escape.

"Do you want more ice for your shoulder?" She stood, ready to dash out the door.

"No. It's feeling good right now. Which bed do you want?"

"Huh?" Josie looked up from her glass.

"Bathroom side or door side?"

"Ah, bathroom?"

Brian pulled back the covers on the other bed and stripped to his boxers. He folded his jeans and T-shirt and placed them on a chair. With his back to her, she saw his bruised neck and upper body from Maisy's rescue. His wounds were more severe than the dislocated shoulder.

She wanted to touch him. Her body screamed at her, begging for comfort and connection. Her head kept her feet rooted on the carpet. They had thawed their relationship during the storm. His arms, his lips, the few times they'd bumped together, were familiar yet exciting in the new-lover way. Though it had been decades since she had a new lover. This confessional, raw, open Brian scared her.

She escaped to the bathroom.

I'm a grown woman. He's my husband. Am I afraid of him, or am I afraid of myself?

She stripped to her underwear and stared in the mirror. Her body was softer. *Baking.* She shook her head.

She stroked her arms, enjoying the clean from her earlier shower. Would Gumbo feel this fresh tomorrow?

She examined her scars, the pink divot at the corner of her mouth that turned red after too much sun. She fingered the inch-long scar hidden by her hairline. She twisted to inspect the ugly, wrinkled patch of skin behind her left shoulder. The bump on the bridge of her nose. Her hands were nicked from her own fumbling with sharp knives. The scar across the palm of her left hand won the most-visible award. Yet there was no accounting of the scars inside she carried. She sighed, hating her own melodrama.

The scars don't define me. That was a lie. They were ugly, the scars and the lies.

Brian had kissed each one.

"This one at the top gives you wisdom."

He'd move to the bridge of her nose. "This one gives you character."

Next, he'd slide his hand over her shoulder. "This one is sexy, like a tattoo you removed when you realized I was your true love, and you needed the other guy's name off your body."

He'd run his finger over her palm. "This is the mark of a warrior. A first-kill ritual, or proof you survived a storm."

Finally, he'd kiss her mouth. "This scar is my favorite. It makes your smile bigger."

The scars do define me. She had pretended they didn't. Pretended not to hear the murmurs of "Odeal's on a tear today. Josephine and Hughdean better take cover from her yelling." No one had thought to offer them shelter.

Then Brian had arrived. An outsider with his own scarred past. He lit a fire to every cell in her body. From teen flirtation to first kiss, she wanted him but not the hurts he was dragging like an anchor. She was trying to free herself and couldn't rescue anyone with her. Not even Hughdean.

That had been before Odeal died. Before her life changed again. And here she stood, alone and afraid of herself, not him. She didn't want to be alone, and if she remained alone, she would remain afraid. Those feelings had pushed Brian to come after her all those years ago. Being alone, for him, was like being scared.

She unhooked her bra and stepped out of her underwear and released her hair from its tie, freeing the waves like a flag over the scars at her scalp and shoulder. She could brood over them or accept they were a part of who she was. She could mourn the competition or find another way.

It's one opportunity. It doesn't define me.

She opened the bathroom door, and a triangle of light spilled into the dark room. The air conditioner blasted high, and the cold air electrified her skin. Brian's back and the playing card tattoo exposed to her. *Another scar.*

She stood in the margin between the two beds.

"Brian?" She held out her left hand to his body.

He rolled over and opened his mouth to speak but didn't or couldn't. He stood, took her hand, and kissed her palm. He dropped to his knees, hugged her at the waist, and inhaled her scent. They fell on the other bed. His body warm over hers and his mouth hungry for her and the places he knew best. Tomorrow, she knew what she'd be thankful for.

Chapter 28

Buras, Louisiana

Saturday, July 3, 2010

At 7:00 a.m., Josie dumped the contents of her backpack onto the hood of the truck, searching for her ringing phone.

"Hello?"

It was Hughdean.

"What the heck am I to do with three hundred pounds of chicken wings? They're sitting here on ice, all pale and puckery."

Josie slumped against the truck, then stood back up as the morning dew soaked into her jeans. *I forgot the Cajun hot wings.*

"When you checked in yesterday, you should have approved a delivery order."

"I don't remember what I did yesterday. Got my guys to help set up the booth. Then we decided to, you know, see the town."

Josie's jaw set hard. *Guess I should be thankful he wasn't too hungover to show up this morning.*

"Right, so the plan is to cook Cajun hot wings, a riff on buffalo-style chicken wings to show how versatile the hot sauces are. You should also have celery sticks, a soft Mexican cheese, butter, and oil for frying."

Josie heard him tearing open boxes and swearing. "Yeah, it's all here with paper-boat serving things."

"Did the portable kitchen come with a fryer?" She paced a track in front of the truck, parked in the hotel lot. Brian, Toby, and Minnow walked toward her, ready to drive to the bird rescue.

"You expect me to cook these damned things?"

"Cook and sell 'em. It's how I plan to pay for the booth. Four wings per order at six bucks an order."

"Six? Are they gold-plated?"

Josie closed her eyes and turned on her chef de cuisine voice, the one to snap the kitchen staff to attention. "People come to this event to eat. They expect to pay more in the city. They're portioned and priced for a profit."

"We're ready," Minnow said.

Josie held her finger up for them to wait. "Talking to Hughdean."

"Hi, Uncle Hughdean," Minnow shouted.

"Is that my Minnow?" Hughdean said. "You tell her I'm real proud of what she did yesterday."

Minnow climbed into the truck to wait. Josie had packed her clothes, and she wore a pair of jeans, white sneakers, and a pale pink T-shirt that read "Grand Isle" with a jumping fish. She had pulled her hair in a tight ponytail. The overall picture was a girl, not the young woman who had strapped into a helicopter yesterday on a rescue mission.

"Buckle in, I'm almost done," Josie said through the open window.

Josie mouthed "Hughdean" to Brian as he approached. He wrapped his arm around her waist and kissed her neck. She leaned against him, distracted by the warmth his kiss set off.

"You there?" Hughdean asked.

"Yes, sorry, Hughdean. You'll find a portable cash register in the box marked 'restaurant operations.' Rosaline can work that blind."

"Hold up, I'm working this out. How many servings you counting on?"

"Five hundred. If we're lucky, we'll run out."

He whistled. "Three thousand bucks, minus my twenty percent. Six hundred for me, just in chicken."

Josie bit her lip at his insistence on taking 20 percent, but she hadn't said no, and she was in no position to negotiate for a crumb.

"So, you'll do it?" Josie's voice had a hopeful note.

"Got nothing else to do."

"Great, I'll walk you through the recipe."

Minnow beeped the horn. Josie jumped, then collected the scattered contents of her backpack.

"I can fix your Cajun wings. I worked in Momma's kitchen too. I know my way around a fryer."

Josie clenched the phone. "Better start your mise en place."

"How's the bird?"

Josie pulled the phone away from her ear. This softer version of Hughdean would take some time to get used to.

"We're heading to the rescue now."

"Call me with updates."

"Of course. You, ah, do the same."

Josie followed signs leading them to a huge building set up for the bird cleaning. She gripped the steering wheel, readying herself for what they might see inside. "Everyone set?"

Minnow opened the truck door. "I can do this," she said softly.

Josie met her at the door. "Oh, *chère*, you're the best medicine for our Gumbo. You're his person. You can do anything."

Minnow nodded deeply and squeezed Josie's hands. "I learned from you. Thanks, Mom." *Good or bad, this day will define her. I hope not with a scar.*

Brian kissed the side of her head. "Meet you inside."

Josie, Brian, and Toby held hands as they walked into the cavernous hangar set up to clean the birds. Several cleaning stations were in use as teams of three worked on the first group of birds. Gumbo and the little pelican would be arriving soon for their lifesaving bath.

"I see Uncle Hollis." Toby pointed.

Hearing his name, Hollis turned and started toward them. He had covered his usual college tee and safari vest with a protective blue gown.

He hugged Josie, holding her tight as if bracing her for bad news. In an odd role reversal, she said, "What's wrong?"

He stepped back, nodded to Brian, and high-fived Toby. "We lost two this morning. A cormorant didn't survive the night, and a pelican I banded before the spill. The energy here is dark this morning."

"You sound like Maisy with her tarot cards and tea leaves," Brian said.

"Hold her," a man from one of the cleaning teams called out as they wrestled with a soapy, flapping gull.

"Some of 'em have fight left," Brian said. They turned to the bird now contained and being doused with water.

"Where's Gumbo?" Toby asked. He walked toward the gull.

"Toby, don't go disturbing anyone, *cher*." Josie pulled him close, her own chick needing protection.

"Everyone." Hollis waved for them to follow him to an empty station. "Minnow is with Gumbo and the other pelicans now. And this is where they'll clean them."

Stacked buckets and hoses, along with plastic squirt bottles and towels, waited for the birds.

"Are they okay?" Josie asked.

"*Okay* is hard to define. Both birds ate. Minnow's with the vet, feeding Gumbo electrolytes, since he's used to her spoon-feeding him. The vet gives them other medicines for their stomach to help them recover from the ingested oil. But they're listless."

"What's *listless*?" Toby asked.

"Not moving around much," Hollis said.

"Is that bad?" Toby rubbed a hand up and down his thigh. Brian did the same when he was anxious.

Hollis draped a long arm over Toby's shoulder. "They ate, and the vet's treating them."

"Are you part of the cleaning team?" Josie asked.

Hollis pinched the sides of his gown and curtsied, making Toby laugh. "I'm learning. It hurts to watch nature die and do nothing to stop it."

"Oh, sweet Lord," Josie said as Sarah Myers and Minnow wheeled Gumbo and the little pelican in a cart to the cleaning stations. Both birds looked like they had been rolled in red clay, matted with oil, and shrunken in on themselves. Where they would usually put up a fight from being handled, neither bird protested, their long necks bowed in defeat.

Minnow stood in front of the birds like a protective paladin. She, too, wore a blue plastic gown, along with long yellow gloves pulled high past her elbows to keep the oil off her skin.

Josie, Brian, and Toby stood to the side. Toby leaned against Josie, and she draped her arms around his shoulders.

"Y'all can come over," Sarah said. "Be calm. Don't make any sudden movements or noises. They're scared enough as is."

The pelicans smelled worse than before, danker. Josie coughed as her gag reflex kicked in.

Toby held his arm across his mouth and nose and squinted, with a look of disgust on his face. The smell didn't stop him.

"Hi, Gumbo," he said softly. "You're gonna be okay. We're here for you." He looked over his shoulder at Josie and Brian.

Brian stepped forward and crouched to the bird's height on the table. "You and your new friend here will be flying in no time."

Gumbo turned his long neck and stared at Brian and Toby.

Josie inhaled and held her breath as she joined them. Gumbo's neck shot up, and he opened and closed his bill and dipped his head left, then right.

"I'm here, too, big guy. We're staying with you the whole way. Minnow and Hollis are fixing you up. Getting clean is the best feeling of your life. We love you."

She turned to Sarah. "How long does this take?"

"About an hour. We're gentle, and we move as fast as we can. Can't say I ever had a family come in for a wild animal before. Oiled pets, but—"

"Gumbo's not a pet," Minnow said. She dipped her head left and right at Gumbo, and he copied her. "We named him, but"—her voice quavered, and she spoke to Hollis—"we respect he's a wild animal. I'm blessed he chose me as his person."

Hearing her words come from Minnow was like a forgiveness for leaving Gumbo during the storm. Odeal had never forgiven Josie for anything. Forgiveness was a dirty quality she'd fought against in herself. Here was proof Josie had done better for her daughter.

Hollis patted Minnow's back and allowed her to take her place by Sarah and another cleaner.

"Ready, Minnow?"

She nodded and picked up a spray bottle and misted Gumbo's body.

"Is that Corexit?" Brian said, with alarm.

Hollis shook his head. "Canola oil. Oil's a gentle cleaning agent, even for other oils, and they rub it into the feathers and beak to loosen the crude."

Gumbo beat his wings in protest as Sarah rubbed in the oil.

"Hey, handsome, you're okay." Minnow moved him to a basin of sudsy water.

"What's happening now?" Toby asked.

"They clean the birds with water and Dawn dishwashing detergent, like we use at home to clean our dishes. The soap is gentle. Watch Minnow, she's giving him a shampoo."

Minnow rubbed soap into his long wings while Sarah grabbed hold of his swordlike bill and opened it wide and began cleaning the inside.

"Oh" escaped from Josie.

The room was noisy with birds squawking in a dozen languages, their wings flapping, water running, and the staff calling to each other over the commotion.

Brian pulled her beside him on one side and Toby on the other.

Josie wanted to help Minnow. She had scrubbed thousands of pots over the years, watched the simple science of soap against oil. Her only jobs now were to be here while Minnow tried to save Gumbo and for Brian and her to offer comfort if she failed. Nothing in life had prepared them for this experience. They would grow wiser together.

Hollis joined the second team, cleaning the smaller pelican.

Sarah reached directly inside Gumbo's gular pouch to clean it. He pulled away.

"You're safe, boy," Minnow said, softly. "You can't have an oily throat. The menhaden will taste awful."

Minnow rinsed Gumbo until the water ran clear and naturally beaded off his feathers.

Gumbo beat his wings like a dog shaking after a bath. The little pelican stood tall and swerved her long neck and then collapsed, exhausted.

The staff opened the enormous hangar doors, encouraging a fresh breeze and sunlight to spread across the facility. The air inside was humid from the day's heat and the water pooling on the floor. The natural light caught Gumbo's clean crown of feathers, now yellow again.

Minnow leaned, spent, with her arms outstretched on the table and her head hanging between them.

Josie walked behind her and rubbed her shoulders. "You were fantastic. I'm proud of you."

Minnow stood, streaks of grease on her robe and her face. "He fought me," she said and smiled. "He's not giving up, so I won't either."

Don't ever give up.

"What happens now?" Toby asked.

Sarah placed a hand on Minnow's shoulder. "The birds stay in a recovery pen for about an hour until they dry. We'll monitor them, feed them, and encourage them to swim in a pool. Then we'll move them to a temporary aviary. It can take two weeks for seabirds to regain their natural waterproofing. Then we'll see how they are and make plans to release them."

"Sarah, can I show my brother where Gumbo will spend the next few days?"

"Sure, just don't get near the birds."

Minnow and Toby left to be with Gumbo. Josie's mom pride had never swelled so strong. Gumbo had taught them compassion, kindness, and respect for nature. Her kids would never let the world beat them without fighting back. Gumbo was a better parent. She had taught herself to fight. The compassion and kindness were a work in progress.

"I'm glad you're here," she said to Brian. "Now we wait."

"I'm here for as long as it takes."

Chapter 29

Buras, Louisiana

Sunday, July 4, 2010

Sunlight cracked through the hotel's blackout curtains, telling Josie a new day with new challenges was here. The Ragin' Cajun. Weeks of preparation and planning. Well, seventeen years, if you started the clock from when she created Odeal's Pepper Sauce, newly renamed as Cajun Smack.

The old plan didn't matter, because being here for Gumbo and for Minnow was where her heart said to park.

I'll make a new plan. Though she hadn't a clue what that would be.

Today, they'd learn when Gumbo could come home. Last night, she had an urge to return to the kitchen. It might not be Odeal's, but she'd find one. Maybe she would write a cookbook like Brian had suggested. She mulled over a new seafood recipe, once the waters cleared: Gumbo's Gumbo. The dish would be a celebration meal with specialty ingredients, a crawfish broth and Spanish sherry vinegar like what she used in the Revenge of the Cajun Reaper sauce.

Brian nuzzled her neck, and his hand traveled the length of her body.

"Happy Fourth of July. Want some fireworks?" His voice was sleepy and warm.

"Mm," she said, almost a purr.

His hands moved with more attention, and she rolled on her side and traced his eyebrows, the tips of his ears, mapping his features with her fingers.

A rap sounded on the door.

"Ignore it." Brian trailed his mouth down her neck.

"Hey, it's Louise. Wakey, wakey. I brought coffee and muffins."

Josie breathed out a deflated sigh, kissed Brian, and swung her legs out of bed. She tossed on a nightshirt and opened the door enough for her head.

"Morning, sunshine," Louise said. She wore white jeans, blue sneakers, and a red-and-blue-striped off-the-shoulder blouse, a walking holiday display.

"What time is it?" Josie yawned and rolled her neck side to side.

"Seven thirty."

"When did you get here?" Surely Louise hadn't left the island at 4:30 a.m.

"I missed Hollis and drove late last night. We've canceled the island activities, so no sense staying." Her voice fell with disappointment.

Memorial Day, Fourth of July, and Labor Day were Louise's favorites. This summer, though, people had cast her as the villain who canceled the fishing season, maligning her as ineffectual in speeding up BP reparation money and wrongfully as the person who allowed their town to become a mini industrial complex of heavy machinery and migrant workers. That was a lot for one person.

"What's happening here?" Louise tried to see over Josie's head. "Minnow said you were here with Brian."

"Nothing's happening anymore," Brian called out.

"Oh, did I—" Louise blushed and took a step backward.

Josie stepped into the hall. "We'll talk later."

"Right. Hollis wants to leave soon for the rescue center. I'll take Minnow and Toby, and you and Brian can meet us . . . when you're ready."

Josie grabbed the take-out bags and blew her a kiss.

The bird recovery center was a huge brick building retrofitted into an aviary, holding dozens of birds with a giant pool for them to swim in.

The odor of fish, feathers, and humidity assaulted Josie first. As her eyes adjusted to the dim light, the cacophony of squawks, flapping wings, and territorial skirmishes drew her attention. Here was the reason she had insisted Gumbo remain free. It was unnatural for a bird to be kept away from the sky and the ocean.

He'll be home soon enough, loafing under the deck, flying with me on my runs, and stealing shiny objects from customers.

The family followed Hollis inside to observe Gumbo and the other pelicans. Volunteers in tall rubber boots hauled buckets of fish and washed the area, adding to the constant fishy-smelling damp.

Minnow raised her hand in a wave, and a tall man shot her a two-finger salute.

"He's hunched in the corner like yesterday," Josie said to Hollis. "What does that mean? Is he okay?"

"The vet said he's responding to treatment and perked up with Minnow."

"I'll see if I can feed him," Minnow said and left.

Brian squatted eye level with Gumbo, held his camera around his neck, and clicked a half dozen shots.

"Can I take pictures of the birds over there?" Toby pointed to a cormorant and a pair of gulls.

Brian bowed his head, and Toby removed the camera.

"I know, don't drop it."

"Don't get too close either," Hollis said.

"Hey, birds, say cheesefish," Toby said.

Josie smiled as Toby took pictures and spoke in gentle tones to the birds.

"Do birds feel depressed?" Brian asked.

"I think so, and other researchers agree." Hollis stood with a serious look.

Despite the stakes of all the birds in the aviary, he was calm, in his element with these gentle creatures.

"Watch the pelican swimming in the far side of the pool." He pointed.

Brian nodded.

"He's missing feathers on his back. Stressed birds will pluck their feathers."

"Like people pull their hair," Josie said.

"Some species who lose mates die soon after or will change behaviors. Any one of these birds could become aggressive."

Josie understood the pang. Her moods had changed, and she had raged when she left Brian. She took a step closer to him and lightly rubbed his sore shoulder. Gumbo's wing, Brian's shoulder. This family had a pattern. They all needed time to recover. And like Gumbo's shorter wing, they would adapt and fly.

"Gumbo's whole world has changed. He's not used to being with other pelicans," Hollis said.

"Good morning," Sarah Myers said. She carried a to-go mug, and today her curly blonde hair was swept back in a black headband.

"Hollis, here's the relocation map, if you want to show the Babineaux family."

"Relocation?" Brian asked.

"The pelican colonies where Fish and Wildlife release the birds. Thought y'all would like to see," Sarah said.

"We're taking him home as soon as he's better." Josie grabbed Brian's hand. "He doesn't roost like other pelicans. We've given him a home since we rescued him as a chick."

Sarah's face softened. "I appreciate this is hard. These animals are special creatures. That's why we need to save them. Y'all have an unusual relationship with that bird. But he's a wild animal. Until BP plugs the well, the spill is active and dangerous. That caused this mess with the birds in the first place."

Brian dropped Josie's hand and crossed his arms over his chest. "It's more than birds. Eleven people died on the rig."

Sarah hugged the map. "It's awful for the families. I've got two cousins working rigs in Texas. D'you have family out there?"

"Brian was off rotation on the Deepwater Horizon when the accident happened. We've had so much loss."

"And not a lot of good news," Brian added.

"I hope we can change that for you folks today," Sarah said.

"Minnow, we're moving to Sarah's office," Hollis said.

Brian took the camera from Toby and snapped pictures of Minnow feeding Gumbo and another pelican before she handed the bucket to a volunteer.

"You're fantastic with them," Sarah said to Minnow.

"I've had a lot of practice," Minnow said.

"You smell like fish," Brian said.

"Occupational hazard," Hollis teased.

"This is what I'm talking about. We can care for Gumbo. Surely, we can do—" Josie said to Hollis.

"Do what?" Minnow looked between the adults.

"*Chère.*" Josie's voice choked up. "Sarah says Gumbo can't come home."

Hollis's expression confirmed what she feared was true.

"The water's too oily." Brian put an arm around Minnow.

Her shoulders slumped, and her eyes shone with threatening tears.

"No!" Toby grabbed Hollis's arm. "Uncle Hollis, Dad, do something. He has a shelter. Dad and I will build a bigger one. Mom's right. We'll watch him." Toby directed his anger toward Sarah. "You can't take him away."

"What about a new tracker?" Josie wasn't giving up on Gumbo.

"Hey, y'all." Brian gestured for everyone to calm down. "We've always agreed every decision we made was in his best interest."

"This can't be the only way. He'll die in the wild. He's not like other pelicans." Minnow whistled her three-note call, and he swung his head toward her.

"See, he responds to me. He knows us. He does tricks for Uncle Hollis," Minnow said.

They followed Sarah to a makeshift administration center. Piles of folders and cleaning supplies spilled across desks and the floor. The human smell of sweat and stale coffee worse than the bird smell in the aviary.

"Sorry for the mess." Sarah pushed aside empty coffee mugs and opened a map displaying the Gulf of Mexico. Large red circles indicated bird colonies.

A few weeks earlier, Minnow had plotted a college tour route with circles around LSU and Tulane and a tentative route to Cornell.

"I can't let him go. He's my best friend." Minnow collapsed into a chair, her body betraying her emotions, and she sobbed.

Hot tears stung Josie's eyes, and Brian turned away to conceal his own emotions. Hollis bent over the map, hiding his face in the science.

Maybe we just take him home in a carrier. A jailbreak.

Sarah didn't know Gumbo.

"He spends most of the day at our family restaurant on the water. We've been feeding him since the spill. If it weren't for the storm, he wouldn't have been oiled," Josie said.

"He's a wild animal, Ms. Babineaux, and storms happen in the Gulf. He's not a pet. You don't own him. Fish and Wildlife is responsible here. I wish I could tell you something different," Sarah said.

He's not a pet. He's family. My special chick.

"This isn't fair," Toby said.

"It's not," Sarah said. "I'm real sorry, folks. Look at this map. Both Texas and Florida have established pelican colonies. We want the birds to stay along the Gulf."

"Gumbo was born in Grand Isle," Toby said. "He doesn't know Florida."

Hollis tapped the map. "Ten years ago, the brown pelican was endangered in Louisiana because of a chemical called DDT. Louisiana decided brown pelicans like Gumbo were too important to lose. Our pelicans came from Florida. Going to Florida would be like meeting his relatives."

"We're his family." Toby stood next to Minnow. She pulled him into a hug.

"We're Babineaux. We don't give up hope," Minnow said to him.

"Fish and Wildlife chooses habitats as close as possible to their original home," Sarah said.

"What prevents them from leaving once you release them?" Minnow asked.

"Nothing. With a reliable source of food and other birds of the same species, they settle in well," Sarah said.

Minnow studied the map like she was planning an invasion. Her hair bobbed loose, and she tucked a lock behind her ear.

"I know I can't pick, but Texas has fewer storms. He'll be safer."

Josie sat under a magnolia tree in a picnic area while Brian took the kids to find lunch. Gumbo wasn't coming home.

How stupid am I? Of course he can't come home. Her plans for a new gumbo recipe were just as dumb. No one knew when the spill would end or when the seafood would be safe for humans to eat. That meant safe for the birds too. How could she plan to reopen the restaurant in these conditions?

Minnow acted brave, asking Sarah about survival and reproduction rates of oiled birds, but Josie knew better. She felt every emotion Minnow ever had. She had made understanding her daughter her mission in a way Odeal never had.

Josie couldn't erase the heartache of losing Gumbo, but she could teach her daughter how to fly. She would talk to her about leaving the island. Whether that was finding a scholarship or all of them leaving and working a year or two. Josie remembered the power of leaving home, how it opened her mind to the outside world. She had sheltered her daughter for too long.

"I found you." Louise sat next to Josie. "Minnow and Toby are taking the news about Gumbo hard. What about you?"

Josie shrugged. "I never considered he wouldn't come home. My restaurant just lost its mascot. How's Hollis?"

"He's hopeful the spill will end and the waters will clear enough before Gumbo is ready for release, but—"

"That's a fantasy," Josie said.

A pair of mourning doves cooed on the far side of the tree, pecking for seeds on the ground. Their sad song matched Josie's mood.

"Hey, I didn't tell you. I spoke to Maisy." She squeezed Josie's arm.

Josie leaned forward. "I've left her a dozen messages. Her voicemail is full. Is she okay?"

"She'll be at a rehab center for a few days until Vera makes arrangements."

Josie's heart raced. *I can't lose Maisy now.* Vera would want her to go back to North Carolina. It made sense, but selfishly Josie needed her to help put her life back in order. Decide if there was enough to salvage for a new plan, help her develop a plan.

"She's going to heal." Louise patted her arm. "Get this, Hughdean called her from the competition needing a chicken-wing recipe."

Josie shook her head. Just like Hughdean to tell her he knew it all when he didn't.

Louise continued. "He said people from the island are coming to the city to vote for you. Canceling the Fourth of July gave folks an excuse to head to the competition."

"That and the chance to be on TV again and free tickets," Josie said.

"Stop that. People really care. You did a kind thing opening the restaurant for all that community paperwork support, and the day of the TV taping, that was the most fun we've had on the island all summer."

Josie squeezed her hand. "How're you? In this mess, I haven't been a supportive friend. I am so proud of you and how you've handled the oil, the cleanup crews, and the pissed-off shrimpers. Now the Fourth is canceled. You had amazing plans for the island."

Louise spun a bracelet on her wrist. "Next year will be better. It can't be worse. And I'll have a prizewinning chef heating up the island for me."

Josie forced a smile. Everyone was doing their best to invent a narrative of how missing the competition wouldn't matter.

"I may take the booth to the Citrus Festival if they have it here in October. Do you remember going when we were kids?"

Louise turned her head sideways. "Duh, how could I forget? You won the junior oyster-shucking title."

"I don't think there'll be oysters this year unless they bring them from outside the state."

Governor Jindal had approved the Department of Natural Resources to release fresh water from the Mississippi River to divert oil away from the marshes. The deluge of fresh water had killed the oyster beds.

Louise stood, her hands on her hips. "Foreign oysters will never happen. Killing the oyster beds should've never happened either. I've been spitting in the wind all summer, and I can't take it any longer." Louise leaned close to Josie. "I haven't told Hollis, but I want to run for Congress."

"You what?"

Louise nodded. "Ever since I started working with those environmentalists from Alaska, I've learned a lot. They've helped me make important contacts, and I'm flying to Washington, DC, in September when Congress goes back to work. Can you believe Congress takes the summer off?"

"Who'll be mayor?"

"Oh pish." Louise waved her hand. "Anyone. Heck, Hughdean could be mayor. What Grand Isle needs, what everyone needs, is a champion. That's why I went to law school."

"Brian started to tell me something the other day."

"Let me guess, he's thinking of running for mayor," she attempted to joke.

"No. He said you told him I was the reason you went to law school."

Louise sat on the top of the picnic table, with her legs resting on the bench seat.

"Sure, there were lots of reasons. You went to culinary school. I needed a profession too. You're a hard act to follow, Josephine."

"You're full of BS, and you know better than to call me that name."

"Are you calling me a liar? I've been called a lot of things—"

"He was talking about my scars."

Louise pulled at her ponytail, and the flag ribbon she'd used to tie it came undone, releasing a cascade of blonde hair.

"For such a stoic man, he has a flair for the dramatic."

Josie moved to sit next to her and waited. Once Louise finished talking herself into a corner, she'd come out.

"We talked about many things the day of the explosion. I don't think I've ever spent time alone with Brian like that. He was a ghost, worried about you and the kids, his friends, what he would do with his life. We talked about how we've all changed since we were teenagers. Don't give me your surprised face. I'm an excellent listener."

"We're talking about those things now too," Josie said. She hugged her knees to her chest.

"You forget. Brian, Hollis, and I were on the island while you were off California dreaming. We watched Odeal get sick. The island did what it always does. People pitched in and helped. Brian was a loyal friend to Hughdean. I think since Brian didn't grow up watching her be so mean, he had more patience for her. She thought the world of him."

Josie hung her head. "You're making me feel bad for not being here."

"Oh, *chère*." Louise took her hand. "I don't mean to. Obligation is a funny way people are connected. If there's no love or a legal and binding contract, I don't think it counts. She gave you life, but that was where it ended. At least, that's how I saw it as a kid. And that means you weren't obligated to help her in death."

"Now I feel even worse," Josie said.

"Don't. Motherhood is a gift, but only if you accept it that way. She didn't or couldn't. And we'll never know. It makes me mad. I tried so hard to be a mom for so long. I hated her. Hollis did too."

They sat next to each other, their arms and legs locked like when they were girls sitting on the pier.

"Odeal didn't like you much either. When she saw your mother, she'd say Nancy Lee the beauty queen was a social climber."

"Well, she was a beauty queen," Louise said with pride. "And she's still beautiful."

"You are, too, and even more so in all the inside places that no one can see," Josie said. "You would have been a great momma."

"I know." Louise smiled. "That's why I became a lawyer. To protect people who needed protecting."

"Maybe you should have gone to the police academy."

"I'm not a uniform kind of girl."

Josie laughed and rested her head on Louise's shoulder. "Can I tell you about me and Brian?" Josie whispered.

"Judging by the way you shooed me out the door this morning, I think I've figured it out."

"I see them," Toby's voice called from a distance. Brian, Hollis, and Minnow were with him. Minnow shuffled her feet, her shoulders sagging. Josie's chest tightened at this beat-up version of her daughter. Where was the defiant chin? The sass in her eyes?

Hollis kissed Louise, taking a seat next to her at the table. Josie held her hand out, and Brian squeezed it in greeting.

"Hey, *chère*," Josie said to Minnow. "What's the news?"

"The birds cleaned this morning are doing good." She sat at Josie's feet and raked the grass with her fingers, releasing a dark, earthy smell.

"Wonderful." Josie forced a brightness into her voice. "Gumbo wasn't exposed long to the oil. Sarah predicts they'll release him in two weeks, once his waterproofing has returned."

"Mom, your bag's ringing," Toby said.

It's Hughdean. Josie's heart thudded.

"Hughdean? You're on speaker. We're all here."

"Hey, everyone." He paused. "I'm at the competition."

"Yes," Josie said. Her stomach did a pancake flip.

"I've spanked these Cajun wings, and it's only twelve thirty. I upped the price. Almost sold out on sauce too. We'll settle the bill when I get home and—"

"You *what?*" Josie swallowed a shriek. She had priced the wings to the nickel, and he was changing it without asking.

"People expect to pay more in the city. I'm just updating you. The real goal is to win votes for the sauces, and that's Dad's job."

She rested her head in her hands. "What's he doing?"

Hughdean chuckled. "It was his idea. He's strategically placed himself at the corner of the booth and periodically sticks his cane out and causes people to stumble. They look up and see the old guy and apologize into the next week. Then Rosaline hits them with a sample and plays on their emotions to vote for the sauce."

"No." Josie covered her mouth.

"It gets better."

Josie covered her eyes and shook her head.

"Tommy Nguyen showed up with his whole family. I was, um . . . falling behind on chicken orders, so Tommy's mom, Linh, is cooking them. The whole Nguyen family is talking up your sauces. Got an undercover island network at your disposal."

Linh was the miracle Josie needed! She could feed an entire convention center. Her list of people to thank was growing longer by the minute.

"Tell Linh thank you." Josie crossed her hands over her chest and felt her heart beating.

"Tell her yourself," Minnow said.

"I will, when we're home."

"No, you need to go *now*. We can't do any more for Gumbo," Minnow said.

"*Chère*, it's good for him to have us together."

Minnow glanced at Hollis. "Uncle Hollis is here. You, me, Dad, and Toby, we need to go to New Orleans before Grandpa hurts anyone. You should come, too, Aunt Louise." Minnow took Louise's hand. "Mom needs you, and someone has to round up the locals."

"Hey, what's going on? I've got a line snaking around the corner," Hughdean's voice came from the phone.

Brian put his hand on Josie's shoulder. "Let's do this. Toby built the booth and can fix anything Hughdean breaks." Brian nodded to Toby, who stood tall at the compliment.

"I'm a mess. What if someone wants to interview me?"

"Now you're showing your nerves. Everything you need is in my makeup kit. We'll make you interview ready in a jiff." Louise snapped her fingers.

Judging started at 5:00 p.m. She still had time.

"Hughdean, I'll be there in two hours. Don't break anything."

Chapter 30

*The Ragin' Cajun Hot Sauce Competition, New Orleans
Convention Center*

Sunday, July 4, 2010

The family raced to the entrance of the convention center. Hughdean
had Josie's exhibitor credentials, and they shuffled through the amusement park–style rope lines. It was 3:00 p.m., and with just two hours
before judging, precious time was disappearing.

"Mom, do you have free passes left?" Toby pointed to the prepaid
line.

Josie said a prayer, pawed through her bag, and produced a thin
stack. They were in, sporting neon wrist bracelets and a map of the
competition floor.

Music boomed through the cavernous space, and thick electrical
cords crisscrossed the floor, lighting the booths to rival Bourbon Street.

The show was an all-ages event. Families roamed with kids, and
thirtysomethings carried cups of beer. The city had a business-as-usual
vibe. This was partly because Grand Isle had done its job as a barrier
island, protecting the coast and New Orleans from taking the brunt
of the storm. The city also had an almost completed 350-mile ring of
protective levees, flood walls, gates, and pumps.

Josie couldn't discern a hot sauce demographic. Her senses were overfiring with the scent of fried food, loud music, and chatter.

"Where's the booth?" Toby turned the floor map and squinted at the signs hanging from the ceiling.

"We're on the other side with the professional teams." Josie ran her finger along a possible route.

"Are y'all waiting for a bus?" Louise grabbed their hands and pulled them through the crowd. They shouldered through the aisles, and Josie caught snatches of conversations.

"That's a hot one!"

"This is all heat and no flavor."

"I'm breathing fire. Bring it on."

Hot sauce aficionados were a daredevil bunch, eating chilies for the thrill and often to prove their toughness. She smiled. She, too, had something to prove.

A flash of impostor syndrome flushed her with panic. Why would her sauces win? Teams had traveled from around the world. This was her first event. Hughdean was right. Had she done enough? They'd had to abandon Maisy's chocolate-chili recipes. Would her Cajun wings win the hearts and taste buds of the crowd over Selena Martin's chocolate-chili cake?

They passed the judging area. A long, skirted table sat high on a platform with a banner printed in a repeating pattern: **2010 KITCHEN NETWORK RAGIN' CAJUN, NEW ORLEANS**.

An enormous digital clock counted the minutes to judging. Her fate would be sealed in ninety-five minutes.

Louise pulled them toward the booth and hit a wall of people blocking their path. It was like people running for snacks during a half-time show. "The booth's up ahead."

"May I have your attention, please?" an announcer boomed over the speakers, and lights flashed. "Voting for the people's choice award closes in fifteen minutes. Watch the judging at five p.m., winners announced at seven p.m."

The crowd made Josie dizzy. "I'll find Hughdean." She pushed through the throng. As she reached the front, she tripped, landing on a mother rocking a baby stroller.

"My goodness, a whole pileup," Daniel Dean said. "Let me help you ladies and offer you some hot sauce and Cajun wings."

"Dad?"

Daniel Dean sat on a high stool and wore a red Odeal's hat and a black T-shirt. He had never worn black in his life or a T-shirt in public.

"Josie, *chère*. You made it. Rosaline, look who's here."

Josie righted herself and apologized to the woman and her baby. Dad's cane poked into the crowded aisle.

"Dad, you can't trip people. It's dangerous," she said quietly to him.

"Oh, you, it's working."

The booth filled the corner spot, making it impossible to miss. The hot sauce display glowed bright with illuminated bottles like red-hot holiday bulbs. *Look at my sauce.* Brian had thought of everything. People leaned against the counter, reaching for napkins and wings.

Linh Nguyen was buried in orders tacked to a post, with chicken wings in various stages from raw to ready to serve. All Josie saw was her salt-and-pepper hair hanging at the bottom of an Odeal's cap. The matching apron was so large on her small frame, she had wrapped the ties twice around her waist. Despite her size, her hands moved quickly between the fryer and the ingredients as she paused to consult a sheet of paper.

Where's Hughdean?

"Josephine!"

She met Rosaline's smile. Sweat trickled down her temple and dampened her gray curls.

Josie hugged her, a pier in this hot sauce ocean.

"This is unreal." Josie rested her hands on her head. "Where's Hughdean?"

"Thank goodness you're here. He's casting our votes for the people's choice winner. The line's been nonstop. Hughdean was doing his best, but . . ." Rosaline rolled her eyes. "Linh jumped in and told him to do something useful. Louise, Toby." Rosaline waved them in like a boat coming to dock.

Brian leaned in and hugged her.

"Why are you in a sling?" Rosaline's eyes filled with concern.

"It's nothing." He kissed her cheek.

"Holy moly. This place is hopping," Louise said.

"What's taking so long?" a man in line asked.

"Right." Josie snapped into chef mode. Brian was hurt, Minnow still couldn't be near food, but Toby was the ultimate helper.

"Minnow, pretend this is a busy night on the marina deck. Take orders up to that lady in the pink shirt." She pointed.

Josie and Louise had switched clothes before leaving Buras. Josie wore Louise's Fourth of July–inspired red-and-blue-striped shirt. Louise had applied a quick touch of makeup to Josie to make her interview ready. Josie bounced like a runner on starting blocks, her hair in a ponytail with Louise's flag tie in a bow. Now she wrapped an apron around her waist, washed her hands, and snapped on a pair of gloves.

"Here, Mom." Toby tossed her a hat.

She gave him a fist bump and turned to the cooking station.

"Linh, you're a godsend."

Linh turned with a pair of tongs in her hand, her face red from the heat and the exertion. "Josie. I just about to—"

Josie hugged her and held her close. "You didn't have to do this. I can never thank you." Josie handed her a bottle of water. "Take a break. You deserve it after all your hard work."

"You need chopsticks," Linh said.

Josie smiled. Each chef had her favorite tools. Now it was her job to feed all these people.

"Louise, you're on tastings. Rosaline, you're on register. Toby, I need you to set up the paper plates with celery and cheese."

Josie inspected the tiny area. Linh had created organized stations for frying, saucing, and plating. *She did this alone? My momma would have never done this for me.*

Josie easily slipped into Linh's flow, and within fifteen minutes, she had fresh orders ready.

She missed sharing this with Maisy but didn't feel alone. People like Linh really cared.

Daniel Dean had offered his seat to Linh and stood by her side, chatting away the afternoon. Josie chuckled, sure that neither understood each other's accent.

"You're blowing up a storm of Cajun wings," Hughdean said.

"Thanks to Linh. Get back here and help me." She hip checked him as he came around. Despite the chaos, Hughdean had made this possible.

"Yes, ma'am." He tied on an apron and portioned wings into servings. "Things were out of hand." He grinned. "TV people came by this morning to interview you, and you missed someone from Sunny Tastes Foods. I've got a card." Hughdean patted his shirt pocket. "I took care of 'em."

Josie shook the fry basket with all her strength. Her chance to shine was over. No opportunity to use her practiced, witty comments or gush about how exciting it was to be at the competition. No dazzling cooking skills on display.

She drained the wings and kissed Hughdean on the cheek. "Thanks, baby brother." She laughed at Daniel Dean dabbing sauce on wooden tasting spoons and talking like the sommelier of sauce.

"How's the bird?" Hughdean's voice turned serious.

"Clean now. We'll know more in a day or so."

She wasn't ready to unpack her feelings about leaving Buras.

Hughdean was another reason she had installed the **Do Not Feed the Pelican** sign. For all his complaining about how they fussed over the bird, he had his own relationship with Gumbo on the boat.

Josie's earlier melancholy returned.

Louise put her hands around her mouth and called, "Time for the judging."

The judging area was standing room only, and Daniel Dean happily cleared a path with his cane.

Giant twin screens descended from the ceiling and played a contestant video loop.

People jostled with their food and drinks to see the stage. Josie wrapped an arm around Toby so as not to lose him. Brian stood behind them, and Minnow leaned against Hughdean.

"The New Mexican Hatch chili sauce is the one to beat," a woman said to her friend. "Did you try the chocolate-chili cake? Amazing."

No doubt, Maisy's chocolate-chili-chip brownies would have won in a head-to-head food battle. Perhaps they could enter a baking competition. Josie looked around the small cooking station and smiled. They had almost sold out of Cajun wings. Hundreds of people who liked her food and her sauce. That mattered, right? Josie strained to hear other comments. *Stop, I'll worry myself into a hole. The voting is done.*

Toby pointed to the video screens. "Gumbo."

Two images of a larger-than-life-size Gumbo with his yellow crown of feathers circled the Odeal's sign and landed on the **Do Not Feed the Pelican** perch on the deck.

Minnow had been able to make him circle and land to allow them to capture the perfect angle.

Josie believed he sensed he was a star. Minnow buried her head into Hughdean's chest, and he patted her on the back.

Thank you, Gumbo. You've made Odeal's my restaurant. Momma would have shooed you away with a broom.

"I'm Chef Josie Babineaux," Josie's voice echoed through the giant speakers, "and this is Gumbo, Odeal's mascot. I'm thrilled to be part of the 2010 Ragin' Cajun with my two sauces, Cajun Smack and Revenge of the Cajun Reaper. Can you handle the heat?" Josie winked at the camera.

The video continued with the next contestant, and Josie covered her face, the blush starting from her toes.

Please, don't let anyone recognize me.

"If they play the video again, I may shrivel up and die. 'Can you handle the heat?' And I winked. I sound so—"

"Confident," Louise said.

"You're a badass, Mom," Toby said.

"A winner in every way." Brian pulled her close and kissed her.

"They're being gross again," Minnow said.

Josie pulled Brian close. "I'm so happy you're here." For all the time she spent alone, working on her recipes and the logistics of the day, she didn't want to be alone now.

"Look at that judge's face," Daniel Dean said. Judge two was bright red from the sauce he'd tasted and was downing a glass of milk while the others laughed at his reaction.

"Which one's ours?" Toby asked.

Josie shrugged. "It's a blind tasting."

"Do they have taste buds left after the first few?" Rosaline asked.

"Good question. See judge four, Chef Walker, he's Maisy's old boss. I want to win to stick it to him."

The judging took an hour, with video footage shown in between each sample to entertain the audience.

Music boomed from the speakers. "Ladies and gentlemen. Our judges will be catching their breath, and we'll announce this year's pro chef winners in thirty minutes."

"Josie," a voice called.

She spun and found Tommy Nguyen.

"Tommy!" She flung her arms around his neck and hugged him. She didn't recognize him without his New Orleans Saints hat. She could tell by his tan he had been working on the boat.

Two small faces with dark hair poked around his back, curious who he was hugging.

Tommy looked down at a girl hanging on to his leg and swung her to his hip. "This is my niece, Tam, and my nephew, Vinh. Say hello to Chef Josie."

Josie held her hand to Tam. "Nice to meet you."

At Josie's voice, Tam buried her head in Tommy's shoulder. He spoke softly to her, and she turned with a shy smile.

"Do you like the hot sauces?" Josie asked Vinh. He gave her a thumbs-up. She high-fived him in return. "I was worried I wouldn't see you. Your mom, I have no way to thank her, and you've been rallying votes all day."

Tommy laughed. "Your brother was a disaster and kept muttering, 'Josie's gonna freak.' My mom took pity on him. We haven't had this much fun in ages. Right?" he wiggled his forehead against Tam's and gently squeezed Vinh's hand.

Josie smiled. Minnow used to demand Brian carry her so she could see everything that was happening. Toby, like now, had wanted to be part of the action.

"We needed this with this summer's fishing as bad as it was after Katrina. Hughdean told me about Gumbo. I'm sorry. How's Minnow?"

"She's . . . upset, but Gumbo's doing well."

"He's not coming home to the island because of the oil." Toby stood beside Josie, and she put her arm around him.

Hearing the resignation in Toby's voice added to the hurt. Her nose stung with threatening tears.

"Where's he going?"

"Texas or Florida," Josie said.

Tommy frowned. "If he comes to Florida, I'll keep an eye out for him. I don't expect we'll be returning to Grand Isle to fish."

Josie squeezed his arm. She understood. Tommy needed to act now to take care of his family.

"Tommy," Brian said and threaded through the crowd.

Tommy hugged him. "Hey, man, what happened?"

Brian looked at his sling. "Got hurt in the storm last week. I'll be fine. And it keeps me from having to work. It's great to see you. Thanks for coming."

"Three minutes, Josie." Hughdean pointed to the countdown clock.

The *Kitchen Network* theme music blared throughout the convention center, followed by a commercial to watch the entire Ragin' Cajun two-hour special next week.

Josie's phone rang, and she dug in her apron pocket.

"Hello," she said, with one hand blocking the surrounding noise.

"Have you won yet?" Maisy asked.

The sound of her voice was a long-distance hug.

"Maisy! How did you know I was here?"

"Louise called, said you were about to hop in the truck and race to the city."

"You should be here. We're cooking, and there's hot sauce everywhere, and music. And Linh saved the day and jumped in to help cook before I arrived. The day's been amazing and loud, and my heart is beating out of my chest."

Maisy laughed. "But have you won?"

Josie smiled at her family. She had. "They haven't announced the winners yet."

"How's our Gumbo?"

She sighed. "He's clean, and now we're waiting. Oh, they're about to call the winners. I'll put you on speaker, and you can listen."

Josie was bone tired, but now her senses were firing again.

"You ready?" Louise asked.

"I'm not sure what I'm ready for."

"To win." Daniel Dean hooked his arm in hers. He had never been an affectionate man. She held him tight, a rare gift after a long day.

"Shush, y'all," Hughdean said.

A new video loop of the chefs flashed on the screens, and the crowd fell quiet as the loudspeakers popped with music. Josie appeared on the screen, holding a bottle of each of her sauces, and it rolled to the next contestant.

"Every time I see my huge face, I want to die."

Louise nudged her. "The price of fame."

Sweat sprouted under Josie's arms. The crowd was thick, and the air scented with greasy food and beer, both making her nauseous.

Trumpet music blared, and the screens flashed 3RD PLACE. Josie closed her eyes. She'd take a third-place win. She only needed to be on the podium to be part of the national promotion, maybe a chance at a TV show. Imagine her as the modern Cajun chef or the spice queen of the bayou?

"In third place, from Brownsville, Texas, is Chef Julio Gonzalez with the Bandit."

Applause erupted from the audience, and Josie squeezed her eyes tighter. Daniel Dean patted her arm.

"Second place is coming," Toby said to Maisy on the phone. "I think Mom's gonna faint."

"In second place, from Santiago, Chile, is Chef Pablo Torres with Ojos del Salado."

The trumpets blared again.

"In first place, from Santa Fe, New Mexico: Chef Selena Martin with Down the Hatch."

And her famous chocolate-chili cake.

That was it. A knot of disappointment tightened in her gut. She applauded, appreciating that each winning recipe had come with hours of work and gallons of failed attempts. They would sell out of sauce and chicken wings, making a respectable profit. They wouldn't go home empty handed. She would return with the most important people in her life.

More trumpets sounded. "Today's people's choice award winner, the sauce earning the most votes over the last two days, is a hottie from Grand Isle, Louisiana—Chef Josie Babineaux, Revenge of the Cajun Reaper."

Josie froze, her hands covering her mouth. Toby held the phone to her ear, where Maisy screamed. The crowd applauded, the rise of voices like staticky confetti.

Josie stared at the twin screens now displaying a duo of Hulk-size images of her holding a bottle of Cajun Smack and the hastily bottled Revenge of the Cajun Reaper. If she didn't catch her breath, she might just turn green. Holy hell, she'd done it.

"All right!" Hughdean punched the air. He grabbed Josie and spun her.

Rosaline and Louise hugged her, and Toby whooped into the phone with Maisy.

Brian wrapped his good arm around her waist, and she kissed him.

"Don't forget me," Minnow said and hugged them both.

Tommy gave her a thumbs-up. Rosaline and Dad clapped, and Hughdean pounded on her back while Louise mouthed, "Hot Chef Summer 2011."

"You did it, Mom," Minnow said.

An unexpected rush of fear flooded her, and she swayed on her legs. Toby's prediction she would faint was about to come true.

"*Chère*, what's wrong?" Louise asked.

Josie squeezed her eyes tight. *Fear and excitement are the same emotion. I'm not afraid.*

"They're calling for the winners." Louise pulled Josie's apron over her head before pushing her toward the riser.

She exhaled, letting the excitement carry her up the first two steps. This was a dream, the type where you can't control your voice or your body. The crowd applauded as the winners took their places and shook hands with the judges. She turned back down the stairs and grabbed Toby and Minnow's hands and grabbed Brian's shirt to stand beside her.

"No, Mom, you go," Toby said.

"No way. I didn't win this alone."

Chapter 31

Sunday, July 11, 2010

Josie sat at the desk tucked between the restaurant's kitchen and the walk-in storage room. A small fan added a high-pitched percussion to the sound of hammers and workers outside on the deck.

She clicked through the flood of email congratulations from around the world for her and Maisy. She was surprised where their fellow culinary school alumni had landed and how far news of something as specific as a hot sauce competition traveled.

"Take it down easy," Brian said, his voice coming from outside. He was directing a work crew to remove the plywood over the restaurant's picture window.

Without Grand Isle's particular natural light, the restaurant had no personality. She could pick the building up and move to any town with the same effect. But not the same heart.

She sighed. Gumbo was the restaurant's heart. Sarah Myers had called earlier with news. Both Gumbo and the little pelican were responding to their care and would be released to a pelican colony in Texas.

He's really gone.

Dr. Tynsdale had called as well. Minnow was now cleared of her infection. She needed to monitor her diet for a few more weeks, but he expected her to make a complete recovery. Her gut maybe, but not her heart.

She and Brian agreed to give her the space and love she needed to grieve for as long as she needed. They all missed Gumbo. Louise said that Hollis was out of sorts and he had suggested a vacation—and for once, nothing bird related.

Josie wanted to use some of the Ragin' Cajun prize money and take the family on a trip. But she wouldn't. That money and the most recent BP relief check were a lifeline, and she needed to spend it wisely. This was the summer of paperwork, and they added insurance claims for the house and restaurant to the list.

She stared out the window, bored. *I don't have anything to do.*

The zip of a tape measure echoed, alerting her attention.

Who's trespassing in my kitchen?

She stood, almost tripping over the chili pepper trophy at her feet—silver, eight inches high. It needed a display, but with the restaurant all torn up, a place would be found later. The storm had done more damage to the outside of the building than they first thought.

She walked into the kitchen and found Brian leaning over the stove, clumsily measuring the back wall with his arm still in a sling. A workman crawled along the floor, laying lines in chalk.

She cleared her throat.

Brian turned. "Hey, I need your opinion. How do you feel about moving the range to the far wall?"

"What?" She covered her mouth with her hands.

Last night, fueled by a bottle of wine, they had lain in bed, discussing changes they wanted to make to their relationship, Brian's career, and the restaurant. They made a new pinkie promise, this time for themselves. They would return to counseling, and no matter how messy it was, they would stay with it. For the first time in more than a year, she had felt a forgotten energy coursing through her like when she first took over the restaurant. She lobbed possible ideas, and Brian volleyed them back with the same energy and excitement.

"Have you thought any more about my idea?" Brian asked. He was eager, like a boy trying to convince his parents to buy him a boat that he'd then use to fish for everyone's benefit.

"You really want to rent a food truck?"

"It's your prize money, and you can do what you want. I'm sure Daniel Dean has ideas."

Ouch. He knew where to stick it to her. Her loss of financial independence.

As they were taking down the booth after the competition, Brian struck up a conversation with a group from Michigan. They had paid their way to New Orleans by running a food truck.

"The profit margins are minimal on food, and we need a place to sleep every night and feed ourselves. Then there's gas, supplies, and we haven't priced rental fees."

"Now you sound like Daniel Dean."

She tipped her head side to side.

"I made a few calls this morning," Brian said.

"To who?"

"I've worked on the rig for ten years. I know people all over the country. People who would love to have me and my family stay with them for a night or two as we're passing through. And you know people from culinary school as well."

"So, we just motor into random towns in a food truck and park in someone's driveway?"

"Yes. For a few weeks. Maisy has a ways to go before she comes back, if—"

"Don't say it." Josie didn't want to face Maisy leaving, though she wanted what was best for her.

"Hughdean can oversee the repairs to the restaurant and the house."

"Do you really trust him?"

"We'll find out. He's done with the Vessels of Opportunity Program. He now needs something productive to do until the spill ends. He won't be shrimping until next season."

It would be exhilarating to leave for a few weeks. She'd design an easy menu—Cajun wings, maybe source some clean shrimp, jambalaya.

"And when we come back, my shoulder will be better, and I'll look for a job. You'd have time to consider how to take advantage of your TV fame. Or we could discover a new place to settle."

She and Brian hadn't talked like this in years. It was like when they first decided he'd take work on a rig. The steady paycheck and having him home every other month were the trade-off.

We could move. She had thought this more than once this summer. First out of necessity, but now because it might be best for the family.

"Toby would love the idea. But you really think Minnow would ride in a food truck the rest of her summer vacation and work?"

Brian laughed. "It's all in how you market it. I'll let them pick the cities we visit, make it more like a working vacation."

A workman stepped into the kitchen. "What should we do with the busted Odeal's sign?"

"It goes with the rest of the construction debris," Josie said.

"Are you sure?" Brian asked.

She nodded. Doing away with the all-seeing eye of Odeal's was one decision she was certain of. The rest of what was ahead was harder. Staying was one of those decisions. *Maybe traveling would help.*

Her plans for the restaurant were ambitious, and if the tourists didn't come back, they would be investing in failure. *If I choose wrong, what happens?*

Brian pulled out the tape measure and wrote a number on the wall. *Shoop*, it went back into its compact shape.

"We have options. And a few days to decide. But we should decide soon on the food truck. Rent it for August, return Labor Day weekend. Fingers crossed we have tourists here then."

Josie nodded and exhaled the breath she hadn't realized she was holding. The same breath she'd been holding all summer.

Chapter 32

Grand Isle, Louisiana

Sunday, July 18, 2010

The gazebo fan spun a butterfly of shadows across the ceiling. Josie set three champagne flutes on a table.

"Stand back, y'all." She released the champagne cork from its cage and twisted the bottle with a happy *pop*. "Should you be drinking?" she asked Maisy.

Maisy shifted in her wheelchair and patted her leg, now in a blue cast.

"My leg's broken, not my spirit."

Louise held a glass for Josie to fill. "I'm celebrating."

They had just finished watching the *Kitchen Network*'s two-hour Ragin' Cajun special, with expert commentary from Toby.

"I should've been there." Maisy shook her head. "Seeing it on TV was a nice consolation prize."

"The way they cut you into the interview footage, I'd swear you were there if I didn't know any better," Louise said.

"To the magic of TV." Maisy raised her glass.

"No, to Maisy and Louise. Maisy, you got me here, and Louise, you pushed me over the finish line." Josie topped off Maisy's glass.

"Well, I'll take that credit," Louise said. They clinked glasses.

"Thanks for wheeling me out here. It's cramped inside with my sister and Hughdean trying to outtalk each other," Maisy said.

"I still can't believe Hughdean invited you to stay here."

"I can't believe she accepted," Louise said.

"Oh, Hughdean's not so bad, and the house is perfect for someone who can't walk. At least until therapy starts."

Josie took her hands. "Maisy, I want to find a way for you to stay."

"Both my sisters want me to come home to Raleigh for physical therapy. It's not like Grand Isle has easy medical care," Maisy said.

"We've always managed with Daniel Dean's care."

Care and therapy once again.

Maisy sighed, her eyes full of uncertainty. "Truth is, I'm stressed. My house is a pile of sticks, and I don't have two nickels to rub together. Josie's on top of the world, and I need help to pee."

Maisy's defeated mood took the bubbles out of the champagne they were drinking. Josie had lived through this negative self-talk for years as Daniel Dean fought for every inch of regained mobility. Time moved slowly when you couldn't move.

"We have FEMA money coming from the storm, and I'm working with bunches of insurance people. I'll help," Louise said.

"Brian's your new general contractor. You tell him what you want. Imagine running a kitchen but with lumber and paint," Josie said. "And once you redesign your house, I want you to help redesign the restaurant to add a bakery."

"You'd bust down a wall so I can play with my flour?"

"I'll help if you put your beignets on the menu. Tourists will line up. Y'all don't serve breakfast, but beignets and coffee to go before they hit the boats—"

"Hang on, little mayor," Maisy said. "I'm not able to do anything now."

"You said I was a stop on your way to your own bakery. I know you have to heal. Think about it." *That's what Brian asked me to do.*

Maisy's mouth twisted in an expression Josie couldn't read.

"The family is counting on me. That includes you," Josie said.

"Josephine Austin, when will you stop thinking you're the only axle on the car?" Louise stood with her hands on her hips. There was no tease to her voice.

When it no longer feels like the car is backing over me.

"You two, stop your bickering." Daniel Dean stood in the gazebo door. "Maisy has a visitor."

"Sorry I missed the Ragin' Cajun show," Garrett Tynsdale said. He presented Josie and Maisy each a bouquet. "You both earned the win."

Maisy inhaled the flowers. Josie nudged Louise.

"Champagne?" Josie picked up the bottle. "And you're welcome to stay for dinner. The men are turning out a feast on the grill tonight."

Maisy pushed up in her wheelchair.

"I came to check on Minnow and see if Maisy would like to go for a stroll—or a push, rather—on the pier, stop by my place for a light bite. I'm no chef, but I know my way around a kitchen," he said to Maisy.

"We were just talking about how to help Maisy stay on the island," Josie said.

"I have some ideas," Garrett said.

Maisy gripped the wheelchair armrests, about to launch herself into the yard.

"It's a rare treat someone wants to cook for me. But the chair and—"

"I can handle a wheelchair." He turned to Josie. "Before I go inside, how is Minnow?"

Hollis had come home three days ago from the wildlife center where he left Gumbo. Minnow had barely left her room. She almost didn't come to watch the Ragin' Cajun with the family tonight.

"Her stomach pain is gone. The bigger problem is she's depressed about losing Gumbo. We all are, but she . . . I've never seen her like this. She won't talk to me. I've tried. She says I crowd her."

Garrett nodded. "Many people will miss him. Knowing he's out on the Gulf somewhere is hard. She's worried. Like losing a pet. You need to let her mourn. You all do."

"Minnow's a fighter. We'll see her through this," Daniel Dean said.

"Your dad's right." Garrett turned to Maisy. "Ready to head out?"

"Have fun, you two," Josie said. She held the gazebo door open while Garrett pushed Maisy out into the warm night.

Daniel Dean eased himself into a chair. "You've the lights and the fan rolling. Not caring a whit about my electric bill."

"Why are you so cranky?" Josie asked.

"Too many people in my house. Got the family and your restaurant folks, shrimpers. Rosaline's talking like she won the contest herself."

"How about a glass of champagne?" Louise offered.

Daniel Dean was jealous and needed attention.

"A fine idea. All they have is beer. To my Josie and to Louise." He raised his glass.

"Don't toast us. Your magic tripping cane deserves the kudos. How many people did you snag in the booth?" Josie asked.

He chuckled. "Enough that we won."

They sat quietly, listening to cicadas, peeping toads, and music filtering from the house. How different this gazebo was from the refuge of her youth. The family never had parties and rarely had visitors. No wonder Daniel Dean felt his space was invaded.

"Are you okay with Maisy in the house?" Josie asked.

"Maisy's like a daughter. I already taught her to play rummy 500."

"No betting," Josie said.

"I'll always bet on you to win. Just like when you left all those years ago. It changed you for the better. And you"—he turned to Louise—"I hear you're running for office."

"Not right away. But, even if I lose, the island wins with publicity," Louise said.

"I don't say this enough, but I'm proud of you. You've both brought a lot of business to this island. I admit Josie making the restaurant fancy-like was hard for me at first."

Josie huffed. *Hard* described a piece of granite. Daniel Dean was a whole different layer of geology.

"You brought the outside world here. The change was worth it and still is. After watching that TV special, I expect the world is about to taste your hot sauces."

"She's just warming up," Louise said.

"I wish your momma was here to see this," Daniel Dean said.

And we're done.

"Dad, I'm heading in to check on dinner."

"Daniel Dean, can I help you inside?" Louise stood and offered him her arm.

"Sit, both of you. I'm not done talking. You two have been joined at the hip as long as I can remember."

Josie and Louise sat, morphing into younger versions of themselves.

Daniel Dean closed his eyes. Josie thought he had fallen asleep. A few moments later, his delicate blond lashes were wet. He took Josie's hand and examined the scar on her palm.

"This"—he squeezed her hand—"was my fault."

Josie pulled her hand away and closed it into a fist.

"You weren't there. It happened."

Now, I'm really done.

"Louise, I think—"

Daniel Dean tapped his cane on the ground and pushed himself to standing. The twinkle lights illuminated the side of his face. He traced the scar on her forehead and the corner of her mouth.

"I'm so sorry, *chère*." His voice choked. "Your momma and I had planned to move to Colorado, to the mountains, where the weather's cool. She hated the hot weather."

The hot nights had been Josie's only refuge when she slept in the gazebo. She didn't want to relive any of that and not today. Not during their celebration.

"Dad, please—"

He ignored her. "She caught the baby blues. After the stroke, the bad one that dumped me on my ass, I was barely able to talk. When I realized how hard she was on you, I was learning to hold a spoon. She took her frustration out on you and Hughdean. I was a ghost watching my family from the other side. I'd shout in my head for her to stop her yelling. And the chores. That was Odeal's way of controlling the world, with work. I was who she was mad at, not my Josie."

Josie scrubbed her hand over her face to push back her own tears. She had never blamed him for Odeal's temper. He had relied on her for everything.

Josie took his hand. "Dad, that's history, swept away with the tide. You helped me move to California. I wouldn't have made it without the money you gave me."

"I wasn't alone."

Josie let out a laugh. "It certainly wasn't Momma."

"No. We kept it quiet."

"We?"

Daniel Dean nodded. "Can't remember everyone, but Rosaline started the collection. Folks on the island who wanted you to find something better. She asked for ten-dollar donations."

That check was for five grand. She blinked, trying to understand. "Five hundred people?"

"Not that many. Three hundred for certain."

"Did you know?" Josie asked Louise.

She nodded. "Half my paycheck from working at the Grocery Mart went into that kitty."

Josie bolted up. "Why didn't you tell me. Hollis too?"

Louise turned away, her eyes filling with tears.

"Who else?" Josie's mind raced through everyone she knew—the families, the tourists who came back every year. She didn't want to be a charity.

"Did she put out a sign, 'Help poor pathetic Josephine Austin'?"

"Don't be disrespectful," he scolded her. "More like a scholarship. People helping one of their own. They pitched in and kept it quiet from you and Odeal." He pointed at her. "That's why the restaurant has succeeded. People made the right investment. They invested in you."

Josie softened. It made no sense to be angry about the one big break she had been given twenty years ago. She still wasn't used to people standing by her side. She hugged Daniel Dean. "I love you, Daddy. Thank you. I wish I had known all those years ago."

This new truth would take time to settle in. She was still working on the old ones.

Chapter 33

Tuesday, August 3, 2010

Josie stood on a ladder and polished the outside door to the restaurant. The morning light glinted off the water, and the bay boat bumped against the mooring with an anxious energy. High, pale, thin white clouds added a surprise face to the horizon. The restaurant's outside repairs were almost complete. Josie was leery about leaving until everything was done. But a food truck was parked in the restaurant lot. Brian and Toby were testing a hanging banner that would advertise the food truck. Minnow asked if they could call the pop-up business "Gumbo's."

"It doesn't seem right to have a restaurant, even a traveling one, without him," Minnow had said.

Today would be a beautiful morning to fish. Louise had held a community meeting to announce the governor had lifted the recreational fishing ban. BP capped the well on July 15, and the air had smelled fresher since the oil had stopped. No one knew when the commercial fishing ban would be lifted, and Hughdean still grumbled. Cleanup crews would be here for the rest of the summer. Maybe, just as Brian predicted, there would be tourists here by Labor Day.

Hughdean and two workmen thunked on the roof overhead, preparing to install the new restaurant sign.

Josie ran her fingers lightly on the glass over a notice taped to the restaurant's front door.

Closed for Renovations

To our guests, thank you for supporting Chef Josie Babineaux and Chef Maisy Phillips for the People's Choice Award during the Ragin' Cajun Hot Sauce Competition.

I am thankful this community supports my desire to show the world that food is love.

Our beloved mascot and friend, Gumbo the pelican, has a new home in the oil-free waters along the Texas Gulf Coast.

We will return Labor Day with a new name and menu.

Keep it spicy, y'all.

XO

Chef Josie

Daniel Dean walked up the porch ramp. His cane made a rhythmic tap. He was using the cane more than the walker since the competition, to everyone's surprise, including his own.

"Dad, what're you doing here?"

"Came to say goodbye one more time and see that fancy new sign Hughdean's been grousing about. And I could use a glass of sweet tea with a splash of bourbon."

Josie kissed his cheek and took a pitcher from behind the bar and poured two glasses.

"I'm not sure about this new restaurant menu you're planning. I was only now happy with the old one." Daniel Dean frowned.

Josie smiled. Change was hard for him. "Don't worry, Dad. We're keeping all your favorites."

They sat quietly, listening to a heated discussion outside. Minnow was fighting with Hughdean. He wanted to store building equipment in the pelican house.

Josie hovered in a half-sit-stand position, hating the tone and the ugly words. Daniel Dean grabbed her arm.

"Let her be. She can handle her uncle better than you ever could."

A thunder of footsteps rumbled across the deck.

"That'd be my grandson and his huge feet. He'll stomp down that new deck," Daniel Dean said.

The back door flew open, and Toby shouted, "Mom, come quick."

Josie helped Daniel Dean stand, and they went outside.

Minnow sat on the deck away from them, a sound like laughter mixed with tears shaking her back. Brian crouched over her.

Is she hurt? Josie ran to her. In her lap sat Gumbo.

"Ah!" Josie hugged Brian. She dropped to her knees in front of them.

"It's really him?"

Brian laughed. "Only one pelican sits in Minnow's lap."

Gumbo flapped his wings and bobbed his head side to side.

"He's saying hello." Tears streaked Minnow's face.

"Hello to you too, handsome." Josie gently stroked his warm body. "I don't understand how you're here."

"He found his way home. Please don't say we have to send him away. I worried he thought I abandoned him."

"Oh, *chère*, I don't think it works that way," Josie said.

"Toby, call Uncle Hollis. Tell him Gumbo's home," Minnow said.

Gumbo flapped his wings, and Minnow released him. He waddled across the deck and launched into the sky toward the water and landed near a piling. Perched on the top was a second pelican.

"Look." Josie pointed. "Another bird."

Minnow stood at the end of the deck and shaded her eyes. "I see a band on its leg. I wonder if he or she is from the wildlife center."

"Is the other pelican okay?" Brian asked.

"I can't tell." Minnow whistled, and Gumbo launched into the air and circled the deck, then landed briefly on the **Do Not Feed the Pelican** sign. The gentle breeze ruffled his crown of feathers. He pushed off and returned to the other bird.

Toby ran back, out of breath. "What'd I miss?"

Josie pointed. "A second pelican."

"He brought a friend home."

"Maybe a girlfriend." Brian swatted Josie on the behind.

Josie laughed. Leave it to Brian to think of goofy bird sex.

Hughdean joined them. "What's the fuss—hey." He waved his hat in the air. "'Sup, bird? Still ignoring me, I see."

A few minutes later, a car door thudded, and footfalls ran up the steps. Hollis and Louise stood at the edge of the deck. Hollis trained a pair of binoculars on the pelican loafing on the piling as Gumbo soared overhead. "I'll be damned."

He hugged Louise and whooped, his fist raised in the air.

Minnow sounded her call, and Gumbo made an immediate turn for the deck and landed on Hollis's head.

Hollis lifted Gumbo and examined his wings and feet and placed him on the deck. Gumbo dipped his head from side to side.

"I missed you, too, my friend. Is that your girlfriend out there?"

"Ha, I told you it was a girl," Brian said.

"Are you sure?" Minnow said.

"Educated guess. I see a band on her leg."

"Uncle Hollis, please tell me we won't send them back to Texas."

Hollis put an arm around her. "Doesn't look like he wants to be there."

"We're his family." Josie sat with them, along with Brian and Toby. "Is he all right?" Josie asked. "He flew a long way."

The idea of how hard Gumbo had fought to come back, to navigate unknown waters to fly home, made Josie tear up.

"We can't leave now," Minnow said. "I won't go. I have to make sure he's okay."

Josie recognized that stubborn tone. Her mom pride swelled, listening to Minnow take charge.

"I need to talk to Mom." Brian offered a hand to Josie, and they went inside.

They both understood this trip was a break from the island. A reset to give them time before their lives changed again.

"Let's stay for a few days and then go," Brian said.

Josie shook her head. "This is the part where we need to work this arrangement out for our family, all our family. That includes Gumbo. Minnow is old enough to stay by herself. She won't be alone, with Hughdean here and my dad and Louise and Hollis. It's only a month. We can take Toby and stick with our plan."

Brian laughed. "Now you're trusting Hughdean?"

"I trust Minnow. That's enough."

Josie and Brian went back outside, arm in arm. Together, they watched their family. The second pelican stood at the edge, investigating them.

Gumbo pecked at the shiny new restaurant sign, waiting to be installed on the roof. Pelican Point Provisions. As if approving, he flew to his **Do Not Feed the Pelican** perch. His crown of yellow feathers glowed in the early-morning sun. He dipped his head. *Hello, family.*

The End

Author's Note

On September 19, 2010, BP announced the Deepwater Horizon oil well was permanently sealed. It was the largest oil spill in US history.

Eleven men were killed, and seventeen others were seriously injured in the initial explosion. The characters in this book are a product of my imagination and in no way represent any of the men, women, or families who suffered the day of the explosion and the subsequent years as the entire Gulf region worked to recover.

As a modern-day disaster, the Deepwater Horizon explosion is highly documented in video, US Government documents and websites, newspaper and magazine accounts, and scientific papers. I spent more than a year researching volumes of material to understand the oil spill, how it affected the communities it touched, and the marine and animal life that was harmed.

Two excellent books used in my research are:

A Sea in Flames: The Deepwater Horizon Oil Blowout, by Carl Safina.

Bird Sense: What It's Like to Be a Bird, by Tim Birkhead.

Additionally, Gumbo the brown pelican is based on Big Bird, a rescued white pelican who became an internet sensation in 2013. You can read about his life here: www.nomad-tanzania.com/hub/goodbye-old-friend.

Estimates on the ecological effects of the spill vary. According to the Center for Biological Diversity, over eighty-seven days, 205.8 million gallons of oil, 225,000 tons of methane, and 1.84 million gallons of chemical dispersants spilled into the Gulf of Mexico. The oil fouled 1,300 miles of shoreline along five states.

The death of species and the destruction of habitats cannot be accurately measured, and government and nonprofit environmental organizations have varied accounts over different periods of time, such as the following:

- 21 species of marine mammals were harmed, and thousands of marine mammals were killed.
- 102 species of birds were harmed, with an estimated death of 800,000 coastal and 200,000 offshore birds.
- 4,900–7,600 large juvenile and adult sea turtles and upward of 166,000 small juvenile sea turtles died. A year after the spill, small turtles were still washing up on beaches.

The recorded numbers fail to account for the entire marine ecosystem, the microscopic organisms at the foundation of the food chain, and the five hundred species of fish in the Gulf of Mexico.

While my primary bird research was focused on the brown pelican, 1,245 birds were rescued, cleaned, and released, including 582 oil-covered pelicans.

In March 2021, a rescued, tagged brown pelican flew seven hundred miles from where it was released in Georgia back to Queen Bess Island, eleven years after the spill.

On August 29, 2021, Hurricane Ida, a monster category-four storm, slammed into Grand Isle, Louisiana. The island suffered 100 percent property damage, with 40 percent of the community a total loss. The good people of Louisiana are rebuilding.

Acknowledgments

Once upon a time, I believed the only way to write a novel was to sit alone and pound out paragraph after paragraph until somewhere on page 350 you wrote *The End*. And while that is true, the lesson of my story is that I cannot write alone.

This book would not exist without the Women's Fiction Writers Association (WFWA). Through this community, I have formed a kinship with authors who have held me when I stumbled and pushed me harder when I needed it most. There are too many people to name, but I would not have any of them in my life without WFWA. All of you are in my heart and infused in these pages.

WFWA opened the door to my agent, Ann Leslie Tuttle, and her belief in my stories and shared love of the natural world. From Ann Leslie blossomed my relationship with my editor, Chantelle Aimée Osman, who made my heart skip a beat when she called me "the pelican lady." Thank you both for loving my pelican and his story. To the entire Lake Union team, Tiffany Yates Martin, Anna Barnes, Stephanie Chou, and Angela Vimuttinan.

Each book has a story midwife, and this story was birthed with the help of the amazing Dr. Bella Ellwood-Clayton, whose editing, honesty, and ideas from the other side of my world made each twist and turn meaningful. To Christina Nguyen and Melany Barrett, who read for me with friendship in their hearts and also with honest feedback.

Thanks to Melissa Lanning for brainstorming, insight, and friendship like no other. To Caleb Ajinomoh and our portal of mutual admiration and love. To Sharon Kurtzman, who is "THE" in my life. To

Christine Gunderson, my debut sister. Scott Herscher, for his always quick reads.

Lifelong thanks to Maria Fara and Tagg Timm for their expert knowledge, friendship, and all the cold drinks. To Denis-Jose Francois, who provided the hot sauce recipe and whose creative energy, friendship, and love have sparked my inspiration for three decades. To Ellen Dawe, the real Louise in my life. To my backbone: Amy Conwell, Katie Philbrick Iantosca, Erin Kramer, Kristen Larson, and Rhonda Miller.

Thanks to Deborah Ginsburg for filling all my buckets. To Brandon Ginsburg, who somehow made me smile. To Trina Kaye, who believed in me even when I didn't.

To my family: Doris Wishnow, who is my first and best reader; Robin, Barry, and Adam Fleischer; Harold, Mita, Noah, and Evan Wishnow; Marjorie Sanders; Tricia Kane; and Russell and Thomas Ritchey. You may never know what I'm throwing at you, but you always catch it.

There are two Josies who are no longer with us. My father, Joseph Wishnow—he would have loved all of this. I write at his desk. He insisted I take it when I left home. It is well worn and impractical for my actual needs, and I will never replace it. Josefa Garcia del a Grana, whom I knew as Josephine Francois. She left us too soon, just as I was struggling to name my main character. In the best of Jewish tradition, you name a baby for the family member who most recently died. The writers of the world understand books are like children. May their memory be a blessing.

To the beats of my heart, Renee and Lydia, who inspire me book after book to write strong women who care about important subjects, though nothing I create will ever top the two of you. To Ron, who took my hand thirty years ago and said, "Come with me." I'm so glad I did. Our love story continues to be a page-turner.

Josie's Favorite Recipes

Revenge of the Cajun Reaper

All measurements are after peeling and deseeding. That's quite important. Please be careful and wear gloves when working with hot peppers!

Ingredients

250 g Carolina Reaper chili peppers
280 g sweet red bell peppers, deseeded, pith removed
200 mL Spanish sherry vinegar
150 g yellow onions
Juice of 1/2 large lemon
20 g fresh Italian parsley, chopped finely
15 g whole garlic cloves
1 Tbsp. tomato paste
10 g smoked paprika powder
3 cloves
1 1/2 tsp. dried basil
1/2 tsp. salt
1 Tbsp. olive oil

Slice the onions thinly, and caramelize them. Fry with a little olive oil over a low heat for 20–40 minutes. The lower and slower, the better.

While the onions are caramelizing . . .

Cut the red peppers into large chunks, deseed them, and remove the pith.

Remove the stalks from the Carolina Reapers (keeping as much of the flesh as possible), and break them open to make sure there are no black seeds inside. Discard any black seeds or soft mushy flesh that you find. Avoid chilies with blackened seeds, as these will be bitter. (If you wouldn't eat it, don't put it in the sauce.)

Place red peppers, reapers, and whole cloves of garlic in an oven tray. Sprinkle lightly with olive oil, and toss to coat. Roast in a convection oven for 20–30 mins at 375°F.

Add the roasted peppers, chilies, and garlic to the pot with the caramelized onions.

Add lemon juice, smoked paprika, salt, and tomato paste, and mix well.

Add the Spanish sherry vinegar, cloves, and dry basil, and bring to a simmer. Simmer on low heat for a further 10 minutes.

Remove from heat, and stir in the parsley.

Cover the pot, and allow it to cool completely (about an hour).

Blend, using a stick blender so that the sauce is relatively fine but not completely smooth. This sauce should have flecks of red (peppers), white (chili seeds), and green (parsley). A completely smooth sauce will lack complexity on the tongue.

Allow the sauce to mature for at least 2 weeks before using.

Keep a small amount separate, and test every couple of days. This will allow you to know when it's ready.

When using the sauce, mix lightly with a clean spoon to avoid getting a spoonful of oil! Oil will eventually rise back to the top.

Sauce is good for 6–9 months at room temperature or indefinitely if kept in the refrigerator.

Josie's Tea Cakes

Ingredients

4 oz. (1 stick) unsalted butter, room temperature
134 g cup granulated sugar
1 egg, room temperature
2 tsp. orange zest, finely grated or chopped
2 tsp. amaretto liquor or almond flavoring or a combination
250 g all-purpose flour
2 tsp. baking powder
½ tsp. salt
1 Tbsp. buttermilk
Optional: sugar for shaping and rolling

In a large bowl, cream together butter and sugar until well combined.
Mix in egg.
Mix in orange zest and amaretto or almond flavoring. Set aside.
In a medium bowl, mix flour, baking powder, and salt.
Mix the dry ingredients into the wet ingredients, alternating with the buttermilk.
Turn dough on a smooth surface, and knead until ingredients are combined. The dough will be very soft.
Shape into a disk and cover with plastic wrap.

Refrigerate for 1 hour or overnight.

Preheat oven to 375°F.

Line a large baking sheet with parchment paper. Set aside.

Remove dough from the refrigerator and unwrap. Allow it to soften.

Knead dough, and roll it out to ¼-inch thickness. If the dough is sticky, spread a layer of sugar on a work surface, and roll out the dough. Optionally, roll it out between two layers of plastic wrap. This will make it easier to work with the dough.

Use a round cookie cutter to cut out shapes, or roll the dough into balls and flatten with your thumb.

Place cookies on prepared pan, about 2 inches apart.

Bake for 7–9 minutes, until bottoms are lightly golden.

Remove from pan, and place on cooling rack to finish cooling.

Once cooled, store in an airtight container.

Note: oven temperatures vary, as will cooking time.

Maisy's Chocolate-Chili Bark and Chocolate-Chili-Chip Cinnamon Brownies

Chocolate-Chili Bark Ingredients

12 oz. good quality chocolate, 54 percent cacao or higher
½ tsp. ground cloves
2 tsp. ground cinnamon
2 tsp. ground cayenne or red pepper
2 tsp. sweet paprika
1 ½ Tbsp. unsweetened cocoa powder
Optional: ¼ c. pepitas or pistachios or a mix

Melt chocolate over a double boiler until creamy.

Stir in ground spices and cocoa powder until blended.

Prepare a baking sheet with either parchment paper or a silicone mat. If using nuts, spread them on the baking sheet, and pour melted chocolate over to cover.

If omitting the nuts, spread the chocolate on the prepared tray.

Refrigerate until hard, 1 hour or longer, or leave at room temperature until solid.

Note: chocolate-chili bark is excellent all on its own and pairs nicely with red wine.

Cinnamon-Chili-Bark Brownies
Ingredients

200 g sugar
200 g brown sugar
65 g flour
125 g cocoa power
½ tsp. salt
1 Tbsp. cinnamon
4 eggs
8 oz. butter, melted (2 sticks)
1 c. chopped chocolate-chili bark
2 tsp. vanilla

Preheat oven to 350°F.
    Butter 11×7 pan, and line with parchment paper.
    Beat eggs until light yellow.
    Mix in sugar, brown sugar, flour, cocoa powder, salt, and cinnamon.
    Slowly pour in vanilla and melted butter.
    Stir in chocolate-chili bark.
    Pour batter into prepared pan, and bake 45–55 minutes.
    Brownies need to rest until cool and will be soft and delicious.

Reader Questions

1. After Josie discovers Brian has pawned her jewelry, she leaves him and moves in with her father and brother. Do you think she was right not to tell Minnow and Toby why she left Brian?

2. Minnow develops an ulcer that is made worse from the stress of her parents' separation. What signs did her parents miss?

3. Throughout the story, we learn about Brian's gambling and that he has confided to his friend Penman and spoken about it during marriage counseling. However, he refuses to apologize and take ownership for the emotional and financial havoc he has caused his family. Why do you think he is so reluctant?

4. Hughdean and Josie have a complicated relationship, where he is often cruel to her yet tender to Minnow and Toby. We learn that Odeal was abusive to him as well, yet he holds Josie responsible for the strain in the family. Why do you think he treats her the way he does?

5. The devastating explosion on the Deepwater Horizon was caused by a lack of company and government oversight and a series of what was determined to be preventable maintenance and leadership problems. Brian defends the oil industry, counting on a reassignment, and like

others in the community, he accepts an oil spill as part of doing business. What do you feel is the responsibility of government and industry to protect people and the environment?

6. Gumbo the pelican is important to the family. How is his relationship different for each member? What does he represent in the story?

7. When Josie learns that *Vacation Ventures* is canceling Odeal's as island restaurant of the year because of the oil spill, she's ready to give up. Do you feel the magazine was right to cancel the feature? Why do you think she agrees to enter the Ragin' Cajun?

8. Josie wants to repair her relationship with Minnow and not have her hate her like she hated Odeal. When Minnow is planning her college road trip, Josie doesn't tell her that her college money is gone. Do you think this is fair to Minnow? Is Josie lying to her?

9. Both Josie and Brian are jealous of Louise and Hollis: Josie because Louise and Hollis are close to her children, Brian because he feels left out of their friendship. Why are Louise and Hollis important to Josie and Brian's relationship and reconciliation?

10. Throughout the story, Josie has several opportunities to press Brian to tell Minnow and Toby the truth, but she doesn't. Why do you think she holds back, and is she right?

11. Despite all Brian has done to hurt Josie and the family, Josie reconciles their relationship. Why do you think she does this?

12. When Gumbo is determined to be missing after the storm, the family takes off in two boats to search for him. Then when he returns oiled to the restaurant, Josie agrees to allow Minnow to travel by helicopter with Hollis to

the animal rescue center in Buras. Do you think these extreme measures were appropriate to save him?

13. While Josie reconciles with Brian and finds a way to reconnect with Hughdean, she never forgives Odeal. She never came to see Odeal when she was sick and only came to the funeral. Louise says, "Obligation is a funny way people are connected. If there's no love or a legal and binding contract, I don't think it counts." Do you agree? Was Josie justified in not seeing her mother?

14. When Gumbo returns to the restaurant, the family is preparing to leave in a food truck for the rest of the summer. Brian and Josie decide to let Minnow stay behind. Do you think this was a good choice for the family and for Brian and Josie's relationship?

About the Author

Photo © 2023 Brandon Ginsburg

Sharon J. Wishnow is a transplanted New Englander who makes her home in Northern Virginia. She writes fiction and nonfiction in the science, technology, and lifestyle categories with a passion for research, seashells, birds, and the ocean. For more information, visit www.sharonwishnow.com.